EXCEPTIONAL MERIT

By George P. Norris
Retired Sergeant
NYPD

George Norris retired as one of the most decorated Police Officers in the history of the New York City Police Department. Published by George Norris

CHAPTER 1

The first uniformed officers on the scene realized it would be fruitless to attempt to help the victim. The bullets had ripped through the skull of the man sitting inside of his 1994 Lincoln, killing him instantly. The officers set up the yellow CRIME SCENE tape around the Lincoln as the bereaving widow looked on. They made all the necessary notifications—including one to the Operations Unit—that a New York State Supreme Court Judge had just been murdered.

The call had come shortly before 2:00 AM, waking Lieutenant James Keegan from his sleep. It had been over four years since Keegan had been transferred from the Commanding Officer of the Brooklyn South Homicide Squad to the Executive Officer of the NYPD, FBI Joint Terrorist Task Force. It had also been over four years since he'd had the middle of the night wake up calls to inform him of a homicide. Keegan thought to himself that of all the assignments or details that there are on the job, this was his favorite for many reasons. For starters, in this detail he was the Executive Officer, not the Commanding Officer, whereas, in almost any other Detective Squad in the city, his rank would carry the job of C.O. As the X.O., he didn't have to worry about any major problems because those would always reflect on the Commanding Officer. He also didn't have to be concerned with robberies, homicides, or the rate of case clearances as other Detective Squads did. The best benefit of this detail, however, was to be working with the Feds. Between the credit cards, the take-home car, and the occasional trip to another country, he felt that this was certainly the best detail in the job today.

It was shortly after 3:00 AM when Keegan exited the Long Island Expressway at Little Neck Parkway. Looking down at his watch, he thought to himself, *Less than a half-hour. Why can't it be this quick when I'm working day tours?* Keegan made a right-hand turn through the red light and followed the directions. Keegan pulled his dark blue Crown Victoria up to the crime scene, which was in a rather posh area of Queens known as Douglas Manor. *The Manor*, as it was affectionately called by its residents, was a small community in the northeastern most section of Queens. It is set on a peninsula that extends into Little Neck Bay. Keegan admired the houses in this hilly community. They were mostly Colonial, Tudor, and Queen Anne style that must have been built close to one hundred years ago, he guessed. He remembered reading somewhere that there was a house in this community built in the mid-1700s.

There were some neighborhoods in the city

that violence was not uncommon. Seeing the police manning crime scenes was a near everyday occurrence. Not this neighborhood, however. Keegan figured this upscale neighborhood had to be one of the safest in the city. In a city where the homicide rate has topped two thousand murders per year, Keegan felt it was a safe bet that this particular area probably hasn't seen a homicide in decades. As he exited his car, he observed many neighbors standing outside of their houses, despite of the frigid temperatures. The look on their faces was clearly of concern as well as shock. He observed an older couple, probably in their mid-sixties, standing in the driveway of their home, two doors away. They held each other tightly, apparently undaunted by the time of night or the sub-freezing temperature. Keegan wondered if they knew the victim or were just taking in the horrific scene which was clearly unfamiliar to them.

The patrol sergeant on the scene stood off to the side and studied the man exiting the Crown Victoria for a clue to his identity. Keegan stood six feet tall and weighed about two hundred pounds. His reddish-brown hair had a hint of gray to it, the only clue that gave away his forty-two years; his polished looks and muscular build were more like that of a man in his early thirties. Keegan put on his suit jacket, covering up the Sig Saur nine-millimeter handgun which was holstered at his waist, and walked toward the Sergeant. As he got closer,

the Sergeant was sure he recognized him from somewhere but couldn't place where it was.

"How are we doing tonight Sergeant, uh, Gentry?" asked Keegan, gazing down at the Sergeant's
nameplate.

"I'm doing a lot better than *that* poor bastard."
Gentry shook his head, looking down at the homicide victim. "You have an advantage. I'm wearing a
nameplate, and you're not. Would you at least mind
telling me if I should salute you?" A tentative smile
came across Gentry's face; obviously, he was hinting
at Keegan to identify himself.

"Lieutenant James Keegan, Joint Terrorist Task
Force," said Keegan, extending his right hand.
Though Keegan wasn't much of a rank-and-file man,
he understood its necessity in a quasi-military organization such as the police department. He was a
cop's cop. No matter what rank he would ultimately
attain, he would never look down on another cop.
He would always treat each one of them as an equal.
"Call me Jimmy." Gentry gave a knowing nod, realizing where he'd recognized Keegan from.

Keegan studied the scene in front of him from
outside the perimeter of the crime scene tape. The
house was a Colonial-style home, white in color that
was easily sixty or more years old. It was set on top
of a hill, which was common for the area. It had a
grey roof and a large porch in the front. In spite of
its age, the house was in immaculate condition. The
house had a generous size front yard and a fairly

large evergreen tree at the end of the driveway. Keegan decided this house probably would sell for close to a million dollars, especially since it was directly across the street from the water.

As Keegan got closer, he studied the 1994 black Lincoln which was backed into the two-car driveway of the home. The driveway was on a moderate incline leading to the house. The driver's side window was reduced to pieces of shattered glass, both inside and outside of the vehicle. Blood and pieces of brain matter were visible on the front windshield and the passenger side window, which remained intact. Keegan fixed his attention back on the evergreen tree; *the perfect place for someone to lay in ambush.* The victim's body was still in a mostly upright position slumped toward the passenger seat.

Keegan looked back at the house. It was curious. There were lamp posts on either side of the walkway leading to the house. Neither of them was on, nor was the porch light, Keegan noted. *Something's not right.* Keegan didn't believe in coincidence. *Even if they had just been off somebody would have turned those lights on by now.* He was willing to bet the light bulbs were removed or loosened if he were to examine them. He decided he was getting a bit ahead of himself and would wait for some more details. The crime scene would tell the story of what happened here.

Light snow had just begun to fall as the Crime Scene Unit Detectives took photographs of the dead man and his surroundings to memorialize the scene. There were half a dozen or so suits from the precinct Detective Squad and the night watch team running around, pads and pens in hand, talking to various neighbors and other potential witnesses. Keegan observed the uniformed officers standing off to the side, talking amongst each other and the ambulance crew. The members of E.M.S. were standing by, awaiting the orders to remove the body from the scene. Once the Medical Examiner gave the okay and the Crime Scene Detectives had concluded their initial investigation, they'd be free to do so. He stared at one of the E.M.S. technicians. She was a petite and rather attractive young lady. She was only about five feet tall and couldn't weigh much more than ninety pounds. *Now, how in the world is she supposed to be able to lift somebody into an ambulance?*

The M.E. peeled off a pair of rubber gloves, discarding them in the street. His initial on-scene investigation was concluded—now the body could be moved so that the Crime Scene team could gather other evidence. Death has a way of humbling someone. In life, this body had been a very important and influential New York State Supreme Court Justice. In death, he was just like anyone else. A lifeless body that was nothing more than a memory to those who loved him. To the NYPD, he became a statistic. Both men ducked under the yellow crime scene tape and entered the perimeter, being careful not to disturb any evidence. "Did the *whip* of your Squad come to the scene for this one?" Keegan hinted, hoping the

Sergeant would introduce him to the Lieutenant in charge of the Precinct Detective Squad.

"Yeah, that's him over there. I'll get him for you." Gentry called out to a short, husky man in his mid-fifties, wearing a trench coat—the type that had become the earmark of a New York City Detective. The husky man approached, staring cautiously at Keegan. The irony of this job, Keegan thought, is that everyone is suspicious of everyone else until they know who they are. Everyone was on the same side, yet there was such division at times between different units within the department. If the unknown person was from a different investigative unit, that was one thing. But if they were from Quality Assurance Division, Inspections, or Internal Affairs, that was another story. They would be unwanted if they showed up on a crime scene. Their jobs were to investigate other cops and were generally looked down upon by the rank-and-file. It was just the healthy paranoia the job instills in you, he reasoned.

"Lieutenant, Vito, this is Lieutenant Keegan of the Joint Terrorist Task Force," Gentry introduced Keegan to the Squad Commander as if he had known him all of his life.

"Jimmy," Keegan quickly stated extending his right hand.

"Sal's the name," the Lieutenant reciprocated as he accepted Keegan's hand. He already knew who Keegan was. He studied Keegan briefly before curiosity got the better of him. "What brings the Joint Terrorist Task Force into a homicide investigation?"

"To be perfectly honest with you, I don't even know the circumstances of the homicide, other than the fact that a judge bought it. But the Chief of Detectives called me at three am and suggested I get right over here." Keegan paused for a moment. "I guess when the Chief of D's calls you at any time to go somewhere it's more than just a suggestion."

The men shared a knowing chuckle. Keegan inched his way closer to the Lincoln, examining the crime scene up close. Keegan had noticed that part of the victim's skull had been blown off, which suggested that a high-powered gun had been used at close range. He immediately ruled out robbery as a motive. A gold watch was clearly visible on the man's wrist and his briefcase lay untouched on the passenger seat. *The poor bastard never knew what hit him.* Keegan shined his flashlight on the ground but didn't see any spent shell casings in the light coating of snow. He wondered if a revolver had been used or if a careful assassin had bothered to pick up the spent shell casings.

It was a funny thing, how the mind of a trained investigator worked. Keegan had studied the scene up close for less than a minute but already he was trying to formulate a motive and had ruled certain things out. Was it a Police Officer's training, his years of experience, or just his suspicious nature that so quickly yet accurately allowed these men to draw their conclusions? He had learned that any first impressions at a homicide scene were usually right on the money. It had been quite some time since he was involved with a simple homicide investigation. His adrenaline was pumping, and he was excited to put the pieces of the puzzle together.

It was also a long time since he had seen what was often so mundane to a Police Officer, yet so devastating to the family involved. That part of the investigation, he certainly did not miss. Keegan glanced up at the house where the car was parked, presumably the judge's home. In a second-floor window of the Colonial home, he saw a middle-aged woman in a pink bathrobe, weeping uncontrollably. It didn't take all of Keegan's vast skills as a Detective to figure out who the woman was. He could remember the countless widows and mothers he had tried to comfort by guaranteeing justice for their dead spouses or children. Such justice could never be achieved. The murderer could spend the rest of his life in prison, but the family of the victim would suffer for the rest of their own lives.

Lieutenant Vito took a cigar out of the case he had in the breast pocket of his shirt. He bit the end, spit a piece out, and lit up. He held the cigar case out to Keegan. Keegan declined. "Are you trying to tell me you don't know any of the details?" Vito looked at him with skepticism.

"Not really," Keegan answered. He forced a cough, hoping to give Vito the hint that the cigar smoke offended him.

Undaunted by Keegan's coughing; Vito continued to draw on his cigar, letting large puffs of smoke escape into the air. He began filling Keegan in on the details of the homicide.

"It was after midnight when the judge parked the car in the driveway of his house," explained Vito. "There were no eyewitnesses that we know of, but some of the neighbors said they heard about five or six gunshots."

Keegan turned his attention back to the crime scene as Vito filled him in on the details. The judge's lifeless body was carefully removed from the Lincoln so the officers could search the body. Keegan watched as the uniformed officer assigned to the job put plastic gloves on to conduct the search. All the glory on this job belonged to the bosses and the Detectives, but when it came down to it, all the dirty work was always done by the average street cop. *They were the real heroes of this job.* Patrol was the backbone of the department. He watched as the officer removed a. 38 caliber revolver from the deceased judge's ankle holster. Keegan became angry.

"Goddamn it!" He sighed. "I never understood why anyone would wear an ankle holster, if you need to get to your gun, you can't reach the fucking thing. It just doesn't make sense."

"I wouldn't get too worked up over it, Jimmy. He never even had a chance to go for his gun, no matter where it was. I'm pretty sure Judge Boden never saw it coming."

Keegan's face went flush. He suddenly felt nauseous.

"Judge Samuel Boden?" He asked the question but honestly didn't want to hear the answer.

"Yeah, that's right. Oh...you knew him, didn't you?" Vito made the connection.

He did. Keegan stared blankly at the dead judge's face, unable to recognize the man he had spent a week testifying in front of. He reflected how he and his men had made the headlines after the arrest of three Middle-Eastern radicals who had planned to bomb the Brooklyn Federal Courthouse in retaliation for the arrests and convictions of their fellow countrymen in connection with the World Trade Center bombing the previous year. He thought of how well the trial had gone and what excellent police work his men had done. They'd seized over three hundred pounds of explosives and won the convictions of the three men. The jury had convicted on all counts after only two days of jury deliberations. Keegan then realized that it was later today that the three men were to be sentenced. Each was presumably to receive life sentences, handed down by Judge Boden himself.

Keegan had admired Judge Boden during the trial. He was a real law and order man whose own morals were not swayed by the death threats he had received during the trial. *Why did he refuse to let me give him round-the-clock protection as I'd offered?* Keegan grew angry. In his mind, he remembered Boden standing behind the bench in his black robe, a sharp contrast to his snowy white hair. He looked down at the slain judge, unable to tell that his hair had once been white, let alone recognize any feature about his now disfigured face.

"Yeah, I knew him. He was a good man," Keegan said, his solemn voice barely audible.

"I'm sorry, Jimmy," Vito said softly. It was the only thing that came to Vito's mind to say before he continued. "Anyway, it was only about five minutes later when one of the guys on patrol grabbed the perp."

"Are you telling me there's been a collar in the case!?"

Keegan greeted this notion with mixed emotions. He was happy an arrest had been made so quickly, but also disappointed he would not be the one to bring this animal to justice. Keegan, like many other Detectives, was proud and confident about the job he did. He enjoyed being a Detective and was quite good at it. He had led the six-seven Detective Squad in arrests and clearance rate for each of his six years assigned there. As the *whip* of the Brooklyn South Homicide Squad, he motivated his men and, in many cases, did the footwork with them, closing out homicides at a rate the department had never seen before. He continued to be a rising star in the department. He had certainly closed out his fair share of high-profile cases. But this one had the potential to be the highest profile case to date, next to the courthouse bombing, of course. *Oh well, at least we got the scumbag*, he thought, trying to convince himself he was happy that he didn't have to work the case.

The two men arrived at the Northern Boulevard

stationhouse shortly after five am. Lieutenant Vito led the way up the stairs to the interrogation room, where a precinct Detective was interviewing the suspect along with a member from the FBI's Eastern District office. Also seated quietly in the squad room, was a young Police Officer, who didn't appear to be much more than twenty years old. *He must be the arresting officer*, decided Keegan.

The interrogation room in this precinct was generally the same as it was in every stationhouse throughout the city. It was a ten by twelve-foot room with large cinderblock-styled bricks painted a dull yellow. The walls were filthy from years of neglect. There was even some dried blood on the wall. A reminder that police work can sometimes be violent. The room was windowless except for the one-way mirror that is used by victims to view police lineups. A large wooden desk was near the wall where an iron bar used to handcuff prisoners to, was fastened into the wall. Opposite the desk were two chairs, used by the Detectives when they interrogated a suspect. Some boxes containing cold cases were piled in the corner.

"How's it going, Bob?" Keegan asked the FBI's Eastern District Supervisor, Robert Wolf. Wolf had been interrogating the suspect for the last hour without much success. Wolf, a medium-sized man with a neatly groomed beard and piercing blue eyes, carried the reputation of a real professional, as well as that of the Bureau's most skilled interrogator.

Wolf had been working counterterrorism for well over a decade.

"Not bad, Jim, and you?" replied Wolf as the two men shook hands.

"It seems we're seeing way too much of each other lately, doesn't it?"

"Let's go, Richie," interjected Vito, dismissing his Detective from the room. "I think the big boys are going to handle this one."

Keegan had detected the sarcasm in Vito's voice but politely responded, "Thanks for all your help, Sal."

In truth, he knew that Vito hadn't actually done anything to be thanked for, other than his obligated hospitality. Keegan watched as they exited the interrogation room and silently thanked God he was getting away from Vito's raunchy cigar. Keegan locked eyes with the animal who had murdered a man Keegan greatly admired. He was seated on a bench against the wall and handcuffed to the bar on the wall. His eyes brushed over the man. He was short, with a very thin build. He couldn't have weighed more than a hundred and fifty pounds. His caramel-colored skin implied he was from somewhere in the Middle-East. The man's dark eyes stared back at Keegan, unimpressed. They showed neither remorse for what he had done, nor intimidation in light of his current situation. If they showed anything at all, it was disdain. The two men walked out of the interrogation room leaving the man handcuffed to the wall. "Did he give anything up, Bob?"

Robert Wolf just shook his head. "Nope, his only statement is that his name is Taroq al-Azir, and that he assassinated Judge Boden as a political statement protesting the United States politics in the Middle-East. He also said it was in protest of the unfair and illegal convictions his brothers in Jihad received for standing up for what they believe in."

"Standing up for what they believe in?" Keegan shook his head in disbelief. "Bombing innocent people in the World Trade Center? Attempting to bomb the Lincoln and Holland Tunnels? Plotting to blow up the Brooklyn Federal Courthouse? These fuckers are crazy! Do we know anything else about him?"

"Unfortunately, not very much. He was born in Syria and has been in the U.S. for about two years. He won't tell us who gave the order, who he works for, or anything other than that one statement. I ran it up the chain of command. They decided not to pursue it on the federal level but instead to prosecute as a state case. They felt the murder itself did not constitute an act of terrorism but instead a retaliatory act."

Wolf looked at his long-time friend and colleague and took a deep breath. "Make no mistakes, Jim, this guy is a professional terrorist. I highly doubt he will say anything useful to the investigation. With that being said, since our office declined, it's your case. Would you like to take a shot at interrogating him?"

"No thanks. If you can't break him, there is no

way I can. I'd just like to interview the arresting officer and take his statement and close this one out."

Joe Esposito was a burly young cop, twenty-two
years old. His clean-shaven face and his olive skin
complemented his handsome looks. He had light
brown eyes. They were soft and forgiving eyes. He
was very quiet and polite, a trait Keegan felt would
disappear after a few more years on the job. Keegan
had seen many young officers like Esposito. After
a few years of dealing with hardened criminals and
witnessing many gruesome and heinous crimes,
they always became a little hard. It wasn't their
choice, Keegan understood. It was a matter of survival and a way to deal with the harsh realities of the
job. "Why don't you tell me how you came upon this
collar?"

Esposito began to explain. "Well, sir, Tony and
I had just turned out for the midnight tour. We
just got a cup of coffee and we were sitting by the
Long Island Rail Road's Douglaston Station drinking
the coffee when we heard a bunch of shots. Honestly, Tony said they were gunshots. I'd never heard
gunshots before except at the pistol range," Esposito
sheepishly admitted.

Keegan understood. Being so young on the job
in what was probably one of the quietest precincts
in the city; one wouldn't hear gunshots too often.
"That's all right. Go on."

"It was only about a minute later when we saw
the Buick come flying away from where we'd heard

18

the shots. The car had its headlights off, and Tony said to me, 'This is the guy that just let those rounds go, kid.' He told me if we wanted to get this guy I'd better step on it, and if I didn't care about it to let..." Esposito then caught himself, remembering he was talking to a supervisor and not wanting to get his partner in trouble he edited his story slightly. "I mean, he said I'd better get moving before this guy got away. We followed the car along Douglaston Parkway until it stopped in a vacant parking lot. We got out of our RMP and began to approach his car. He got out of his car with a gun in his hand. I thought I was going to get killed. I reached for my gun and remember Tony yelling to me to take cover, but before I could, the man put the gun to his own head and yelled, 'In the name of Allah.' Then, I heard the click of a gun's hammer falling on an empty chamber. We tackled him and without any resistance, I placed him in handcuffs. When I looked at the gun, I saw it was a .44 caliber snub nose revolver with all five chambers containing spent shells."

Keegan nodded, showing his approval. "You did one hell of a job, Esposito."

"Thank you, sir."

"Esposito, I tell you what. I'm personally going to write you up for a Commendation. I see you don't have any medals. A Commendation is a pretty high medal. Not bad for your first one. Send me a copy of all of the paperwork and your information (and your partner's, too) in department mail when you get the chance."

Esposito looked satisfied. Cops liked medals. It was a way of bragging to other cops without having to say a word. Cops were always impressed when they spotted another cop with a nice rack of medals. Keegan would probably be considered a highly decorated officer, as he had been cited with over fifty medals in his eighteen-year career, not to mention the medal he and his men would be receiving for the thwarted courthouse bombings. Keegan reflected on the night's events over the forty-minute drive back to his East Northport home. Something Robert Wolf had said kept haunting him as he pondered it. *What exactly was a professional terrorist?* It's a contradiction of terms, he thought. *There is no such thing. Can you imagine if it were a job or something, a professional terrorist?*

CHAPTER 2

"Would you like me to fix you something for lunch?" Kate asked as she brought Keegan his coffee. The couple sat in the kitchen of their suburban home. The kitchen had been recently remodeled. With light oak cabinets and a charcoal grey countertop and backsplash, the kitchen looked pristine. It had cost over six thousand dollars to get redone, including the all-new stainless-steel appliances, but Kate was thrilled with how it turned out and that was all that mattered to Keegan.

"No thanks, sweetheart. I'm not hungry. Just a bit tired. It's been quite some time since I've slept past noon," he replied as he rubbed his bloodshot eyes.

"Well, whose fault is that? Get in before the sun is up and you won't sleep so late." She opened the blinds allowing the sun into the kitchen. She set the coffee down in front of Keegan, on the kitchen side of the island that separated it from the dining room. Kate was slightly annoyed. Not so much at her husband, but more at '*the job*' and how he let it run their lives. Kate had never told him how close she had come to leaving him throughout the years when he had always put the job ahead of his family. The three am wake up calls, the forty hours of overtime every month, and the unpredictable hours had almost ruined their marriage. Kate was so happy when Jim was transferred to the Terrorist Task Force. He had finally begun to live a semi-normal life, working normal hours. Her heart had dropped when she heard the phone ring in the middle of the night. Her worst fear was that one day; the job would once again steal her husband away from her.

"Don't worry, Kate," he assured her. "This was a very isolated incident; the Task Force doesn't involve itself in routine homicides." Keegan could sense the concern in his wife's voice. He had also noticed a bit of fire in her eyes—the very same fire that he hadn't seen in quite some time. Being the wife of a Police Officer was certainly not easy, but Kate just didn't understand the job and the calling that came with it.

He stared at his wife, taking in her beauty. She was as beautiful today as the day they'd met over sixteen years ago. The sun caught her long auburn hair and it seemed to gleam even brighter. It flowed down past her shoulders and nicely complimented her fair complexion. He looked into her hazel eyes which he was sure could hypnotize anyone who gazed long enough. And—looking at her figure— one would never guess she was the mother of three. Keegan realized he was a very lucky man. Nevertheless, he knew right now she was not happy with him. "Do you have any idea who got killed last night?"

She snapped back at him, "How should I know?"

"Judge Boden."

She was confused. "Who?"

"Judge Boden. The judge who sat on the **Fed Courthouse Caper** trial." *The media always came up with such catchy titles for even the most heinous crimes.* "He was scheduled to sentence the mutts this morning to life sentences to deter any further terrorist activity. I guess they wanted to send the government a message of their own."

Kate gasped. "Oh my god!" She shook her head in disbelief and a sudden feeling of anxiety came over her. "You were on the front page of every newspaper in America as the cop who broke up the largest terrorist ring to ever operate in this country. What if they come after you next? What about the kids? Are they in danger?"

"Relax, Kate. Nobody is coming after me," he assured her. Keegan knew the terrorists had already made their point. The possibility of them coming after him was extremely unlikely.

"I just worry about you, hon. I love you." Kate seemed to be soothed by his reassurance.

"I love you too, sweetie."

He opened the morning paper, glancing at the date. He couldn't believe that next month, February 1995, would mark the second anniversary of the bombing of the twin towers in which six people were killed and a thousand injured. After briefly reflecting, he got back to his newspaper. The headlines read of a fire in the Bronx killing a two-year-old. It was obvious that word of the assassination had not gotten out in time for the morning edition. Kate began telling him how much it would cost for the family to take a trip to Ireland this summer to visit her family. Keegan pretended to listen as he thumbed through the paper.

There was a small article on page twenty-five that caught his attention. Martin Devine, a native of County Armagh, Northern Ireland, and now a prominent civil rights lawyer in New York had been named as the Grand Marshall for this year's St. Patrick's Day Parade. The article continued to say that Devine was to be the first Protestant Grand Marshall of the often-political parade. *They name a Protestant as Grand Marshall and then they wonder why there is always so much controversy,* he thought to himself. The parade in the past has dealt with such political hot potatoes as gay and lesbian marchers, the imprisonment of Joe Dogherty in a U.S. prison, the hunger strike, and former members of the I.R.A. marching, but how could they have a Protestant lead the march in celebration of a Catholic saint. It didn't make any sense, he thought. This is a tiny article buried in the middle of the paper during the middle of January, but he guaranteed that the story would be front page news by March. He shook his head in disbelief and anger. Before closing the paper, he noticed another article on the same page about a British soldier in Northern Ireland being assassinated by the I.R.A. It was no coincidence that both articles appeared on the same page.

"You'll be home on time tonight?" There was a touch of concern in her voice.

"Yeah, I'll be home by twelve-thirty."

"You know I hate when you work the four to midnight shift. I get so lonely."

"And that's exactly why I do so few of them."

Keegan arrived at 26 Federal Plaza promptly at three o'clock. He approached a set of double glass doors that bore the insignia of the FBI. He stared at the scales of justice within the shield and the words *fidelity, bravery, integrity* on a ribbon flowing below it. He scanned his identification card through the card reader, allowing him access past the doors which warned, Authorized personnel only. He got off the elevator and walked down the hall to the last office on the left. He stared at the signs on the big wooden door as he approached:

NYPD Joint Terrorist Task Force
Commanding Officer—Captain Ronald Anderson
Executive Officer---Lieutenant James Keegan

The FBI's offices were in sharp contrast to police precincts. It wouldn't be uncommon to have mice or even roaches in precincts. This was not the case with the FBI offices. They were cleaned and well maintained on a regular basis. The office had short gray carpet and off-white walls. It was a fairly large space broken up into smaller cubicles, where each Detective worked. Each of the cubicles had a modern white top desk with its own computer.

This was a luxury that precinct Detectives did not have. Even the chairs were a better quality and more comfortable than one would find in a precinct Detective Squad. On the walls were some wanted posters as well as television sets tuned in to a variety of news stations. There was even a small kitchen in the back of the office with a refrigerator and most importantly a coffee machine. Across the hall from Keegan's office was a large conference room and command center furnished with a large wooden desk, leather chairs all around, and giant screen televisions mounted to the wall. Certainly, no precinct in the city had any of those amenities.

Keegan opened the door and was promptly greeted by one of his Detectives. "Hey Jimmy, did you see Judge Boden got murdered last night?"

Although he was designated the XO, or second-in-command of the unit, his men, as well as the department's top brass knew he ran the show on the police department's end of the task force. He worked very closely with his men and most of them called him by his first name at his own request. He always believed any cop would risk his own life for another cop. The police department was a sort of brotherhood. It didn't make any sense to him to have someone calling him sir or boss when that guy could be the one to save his life.

"Yeah, Mike. I did, as a matter of fact. They called me in from home. I was on the scene."

"That's some scary shit to just take a judge out

like that, huh?" The Detective glanced at the calendar. "By the way, what are you doing here? I thought you took the day off."

"Well, it is payday, isn't it?" Keegan made his excuse as he walked into the office that he shared with Captain Anderson. Their office was quite spacious and more impressive than the Detective's office. Both men were afforded a five foot long, cherry wood finished desk, accompanied by a high back leather chair. Anderson's desk was in front of the six-foot-long window overlooking Worth Street in lower Manhattan. To the right of Anderson's desk was the American flag, to the left, a dark blue flag with the emblem of the FBI. That wasn't the only difference between the desks, Keegan noted. It seemed his desk was always full of case folders and both his in and out baskets generally had three times the amount of papers Anderson's did. That didn't bother him as he didn't mind the workload. On the beige walls behind each of the men were various pictures of family, promotion ceremonies, and awards they had received. Although Anderson outranked Keegan by one rank, there was no comparison regarding the prestige of the personal attributes hung on the walls.

"Good afternoon, Cap." Captain Ronald Anderson was a thirty-year veteran of the police department. He was a stout man in his late fifties with gray hair atop a round face to match his gray mustache. He was very well liked throughout the department, but even he knew the star of this unit was his Lieutenant. Anderson let Keegan run the investigations and the unit the way Keegan saw fit with very little interjection of his own. Anderson was sifting through the arrest reports regarding Judge Boden's homicide when Keegan entered the office.

Anderson looked up at Keegan as he entered the office. "That rookie made one hell of a collar. He probably had no idea what he had stumbled on to."

"You're right about that," Keegan agreed.

"I was just looking through the paperwork. They never sent over a copy of the *forty-nine*. Do you know who prepared it?"

"Yeah, it was a Sergeant named Gentry back in the precinct of occurrence." Keegan wondered why the department always called a form by number rather than name. After all, an unusual occurrence report sounds more official than calling it a *U.F. forty-nine*.

"Jimmy, do me a favor. See if you can reach out to this Gentry and have him fax a copy over. Also, ask the Desk Officer over there to have the gun transported to the lab forthwith. If we could trace where the murder weapon came from, it could be a big help. Maybe we can find some co-conspirators after learning where and when the gun was purchased."

Keegan knew it was a long shot, but nevertheless, it was a lead that needed to be followed up. Keegan walked over to his desk, made a phone call, and had the desk officer at the precinct fax the unusual occurrence form over. He opened up the desk drawer, took out a pad, and pen and wrote himself a reminder to put Esposito and his partner in for departmental recognition. He walked over to the desk separating two sets of file cabinets and waited briefly by the fax machine for the report to come through. Once it did, he perused it before handing it over to Anderson. He collected his paycheck and started towards the door. "Do me a favor, Cap. If Kate calls, just tell her I'm in the field."

"You got it, Jimmy," Anderson said through a devilish smile. "Enjoy your night off."

As Keegan got in the elevator, he thought to himself how easy it was for a cop to cheat on his wife. You just take the day off and tell whoever answers the phone to tell her you're in the field or on a stakeout. You could even call her yourself and tell her that you're at central booking with an arrest. Cops get lost for days at a time down there and nobody can track you down. He never had cheated on Kate and he knew that he never would. It used to bother him that all the guys in the office thought he was having an affair, but he realized it was better they believed that than knew the truth.

CHAPTER 3

Keegan parked unmarked Department Auto Number 8567 on Forty-Third Street, just off Third Avenue, partially blocking the crosswalk. He reached over the sun visor and took down the auto's unrestricted parking permit. He placed the permit, which read *N. Y. C. Police Department Auto 8567 on official business*, in the windshield of the auto. Now, he didn't have to worry about an overzealous meter maid having the car summonsed and towed away. From his jacket, he removed a pair of black leather gloves and put them on. He walked as quickly as he could along Third Avenue, fighting the seventeen-degree temperature and the twenty-mile-per-hour winds. No matter how bundled up you are, when the wind is that strong, you're still going to feel the cold.

Keegan entered McBride's Bar and Grill at twenty minutes past eight. It was a welcome relief to get out of the cold. He walked straight across the bar, nodding hello to a few of the regulars he had come to recognize. He stopped when he reached the last stool at the bar. He took off his coat, draped it over the back of the stool, and sat down. He made sure to face the door. It was something every cop learned in the academy. Whether you were in a bar, a diner, or any other public place, always take the seat facing the door and try not to let anyone stay behind you whenever possible.

This lesson had been learned by a rookie cop years ago, who was sitting in a bar when a perp came in and announced a stick-up. The rookie, trying to implement the best tactics he knew, didn't react until he was sure the perp wasn't paying attention to him. He then drew his off-duty revolver from its holster, ready to take appropriate police action. Before he could even identify himself as a Police Officer, however, he was shot in the back of the head by the perp's accomplice. The second gunman had been planted in the bar earlier to look for possible off-duty cops or anyone else who may get in the way of the robbery.

Most cops will never forget that story. The lesson was extremely costly for the twenty-one-year-old rookie who paid with his life so others like Keegan could learn to keep their backs to the wall and their eyes to the door. There is no shortage of tactics learned at the hands of a previous cop's mistakes.

Keegan had barely sat down when the bartender placed a pint of Guinness stout in front of him. He studied the crowd. There were probably less than two dozen people in the entire bar, he calculated. This was virtually empty for a Thursday night at McBride's. *The weather must be what was keeping the crowd away*, figured Keegan.

McBride's was divided into two parts, the bar area, and the dining room. The two were separated by a wooden partition standing four feet high. A mural of Ireland's flag with the words '**Ireland unfree shall never be at peace**' was painted on the bar side of the partition. Behind the bar, was a glass mirror with a shamrock etched in all four corners, and in the middle, a large leprechaun standing over a pot of gold. In front of the mirror, lined up perfectly in three-tiered rows were the assorted bottles of alcohol readily available for sale. The bar itself was a dark brown, forgiving to the years of spills and scratches it must have endured. There were approximately twenty barstools in front, mostly unoccupied tonight, thought Keegan. There was a space of about eight feet between the bar and the partition to allow for people to stand and talk on nights busier than tonight. Above the door leading to the hallway where the restrooms were, flew both an American and an Irish flag. At each end of the bar was a television broadcasting a sporting event. The one right over Keegan's head was showing the Ranger-Islander game being played at the Garden.

There was only one bartender working tonight. His name was Daniel O'Brien, a native of County Antrim, Northern Ireland. Keegan felt the bartender's salt and pepper hair and mustache added at least five years to his actual age of thirty-eight. He was a portly man despite his six-foot frame. Once anyone heard O'Brien speak, there was no doubt he was from Northern Ireland. Keegan loved his brogue. It was as strong today as the day he came to New York back in the mid-1970s.

The other half of the bar was the dining area. There were two steps at each end of the partition, leading to the twenty or so tables in the adjacent room. The room was carpeted with a dark green and maroon print which was nicely complemented by the cream tablecloths. Each table had a candle in the center, creating a slight glow n the dimly lit room. The light brown walls were decorated much the same as many other Irish pubs Keegan had seen over the years. There were pictures of Ireland, beer advertisements, an Irish Rugby jersey, pictures of many Irish leaders and rebels, and even a copy of the Proclamation of the Irish Republic. In the middle of the room, against the back wall, was the stage where every Thursday, Friday, Saturday, and Sunday night, Tommy McDermott and his band played.

Keegan liked the seat he was in. He could see everything and everybody in the bar. He watched as Tommy McDermott set up the keyboards and the drums, preparing for another night's work. McDermott's long black hair was in a ponytail as he set up, he would undoubtedly set it free once he began to play. Keegan enjoyed listening to McDermott's music. He played a variety of traditional Irish songs as well as many rebel songs. Keegan figured Tommy has been playing here for about five or six years now; a steady gig for someone not yet thirty years old.

As Keegan scooped up a handful of peanuts and threw them in his mouth, he glanced into the kitchen, seeing an Asian cook. He shook his head and smiled as he read, '*Traditional Irish cuisine*,' from the menu. *Imagine that*, thought Keegan, *some Chinaman is going to prepare my Sheppard's pie and they have the nerve to call it traditional Irish cuisine.*

Keegan had finally shaken the chill out of his bones and took his first sip of the Guinness. A man sitting alone at a table in the dining area had caught his eye. At first, he thought the man had been staring at him but then he realized the man was watching the hockey game which was being shown on the television overhead. Still, there was something weird about this guy. *His complexion was too dark for him to be Irish. Spanish, or maybe Italian*, figured Keegan. He was now the one staring. The man was about thirty-five years old, had dark hair, and wore wire-framed glasses. *Why is this guy coming to an Irish bar by himself to eat dinner?* The answer was simple. *He must've been craving the traditional Irish cuisine they serve here,* he thought, amusing himself as he once again glanced at the Asian cook.

After setting up and tuning their instruments, it was time for the Tommy McDermott Band to begin their first set. "Welcome to a quiet Thursday evening here at McBride's Bar and Grill," began McDermott.

Keegan turned towards the band with Guinness in hand. "Tonight, I'd like to begin with a song from my hometown of Dublin. It's called <u>Dublin in the Rare Ould Times</u>."

Keegan applauded as McDermott began singing

the ballad. This had always been one of his favorite Irish songs, so he quietly sang along with McDermott. The bartender brought Keegan another Guinness just as he had finished the first. Keegan swallowed another handful of peanuts and raised his glass to the bartender.

"Thank you, Dan, you're right on top of things as usual."

"I hope you wouldn't expect anything less from me, now would ya?" O'Brien joked. "I'm awfully glad to see ya, Jim."

"Don't act so surprised, Dan. It is the last Thursday of the month isn't it?"

Keegan's palms began to sweat; he knew when O'Brien told him he was glad to see him that something needed to be done. His heart started to beat just a little bit faster now.

O'Brien offered a friendly tap on Keegan's shoulder. "And sure, it is lad, sure it is."

Keegan, not wanting to appear apprehensive, changed the subject momentarily. He motioned with his head at a very attractive young waitress, waiting tables in the dining room. "Hey, Dan, who's the waitress you've got working over there?"

She was about five feet, four inches tall, wearing a black skirt and a white turtleneck sweater which clung to her body in all the right places to accent her flawless figure. She had strawberry blond hair and piercing blue eyes.

"Ahh, you wouldn't be talking about Nora, now would ya? Forget about her lad, a man your age could have a heart attack just thinking about a lass like her."

"Speak for yourself, old man, "Keegan rebutted the bartender's comments. He looked O'Brien dead in the eyes, made a fist, and flexed his muscle. "Go ahead, feel that. I'm still pumping iron three times a week."

O'Brien declined the invitation to feel his muscle but wouldn't pass up the opportunity to further tease Keegan. "Well now, that's all well and good, because that'll be the only thing you'll be pumping around here."

Both men laughed at the lewd joke as they continued to leer at the waitress. O'Brien's smile faded first. "Getting back to business, Jim, I'm glad to see you tonight."

O'Brien reached inside his vest pocket, pulled a white business-size envelope, and slid it across the bar to Keegan. Keegan picked up the envelope and slipped it into the inside pocket of his jacket. O'Brien stepped away momentarily to tend to his customers.

Keegan remained stoic as he accepted the envelope. "Thank you, Daniel."

Keegan turned away from the bar as he once again focused on the music of Tommy McDermott. "...*and I'll never forget the green grass or the rivers as I keep law and order on the streets of New York*," sang McDermott.

The Streets of New York was another one of Keegan's favorites. The song was about an Irishman whose family was fighting poverty, so they sent him to New York to become a Police Officer, following in his uncle's footsteps. He wondered how many past or present cops, aside from his late grandfather, this song could have been written about. Thousands, he guessed. McDermott continued, "that song is, as always, dedicated to any members of the NYPD that we might have with us tonight."

"Yeah, that's me!" yelled out one rather inebriated young man sitting at the far end of the bar, clearly trying to impress the young lady he was with.

What an asshole, thought Keegan. Keegan figured he must have been out sick the day they told the story of the rookie cop. Now everybody in the entire bar knows this guy is a cop. If there was somebody planted in here to do a robbery, this kid would be dead before he would have any idea what had hit him.

He looked down at his watch and decided it was time to leave. He put a twenty-dollar bill on the bar as he said good night to Dan. He put his hat and coat back on and wondered if it had gotten any colder than it was before. It couldn't get too much colder, he rationalized. As he walked towards the door, he put his hand in his pocket, making sure he didn't drop the envelope. Even though he hadn't opened it yet, Keegan had a pretty good idea of what was inside.

Tommy McDermott had ended the music set with <u>The Streets of New York</u>. The sparse crowd had applauded and a few more members of the audience began to leave. McDermott shouted goodbye to Keegan as he left the bar. The bar grew quiet as the band took their break in between sets.

The man with the wire-framed glasses asked Nora O'Donnell to bring him his check along with his final beer of the evening. He closely watched as the stout bartender held a mug in his hand, pouring into it, the draft. It was almost an art form how he deftly tilted the mug and just at the right time, he swooped it up in one motion without spilling a drop.

The sound of Nora's spiked heels against the wooden floor echoed throughout the bar. She stepped down the steps onto the carpeted floor muffling the noise. She walked over to the man, placed the mug of beer down on a cocktail napkin, and then placed the check face down on the table. "Thank you, come again."

She sounded rather insincere, the man thought. He stared at Nora as she walked away, taking in her figure.

The man then focused his attention on Keegan, who was now exiting the bar. He watched as Keegan reached his hand into the pocket where he had put the envelope. He hoped he would take the envelope out and open it before he left the bar. To the man's disappointment, Keegan did not. He just removed his hand from his pocket and walked out of the bar.

Once Keegan had left, the man picked up the check and examined it, making sure his arithmetic matched the waitresses. Five dollars for a beer was a bit much, but then again, this was Manhattan, he reasoned. Picking up the mug by its handle, he chugged half of the beer down in one big gulp.

He then reached down to his side and picked up a book that had concealed a digital camera. He was amazed at how technology had advanced. Disguising a camera as a paperback novel was ingenious. He placed both elbows on the table holding the camera up to eye level. If anyone had bothered to look in his direction, he would appear to be a bookworm, deeply involved in his novel.

He focused the camera closely on Dan O'Brien's face. He hoped the dim lighting would not interfere with the clarity of the photos. Of course, he had been assured it would not, but nevertheless, he was troubled that the picture of James Keegan accepting the envelope might not come out. This entire evening would be a waste of time without that picture. He snapped the picture of O'Brien and placed the book on the table in front of him. He wondered the extent of Keegan's involvement. Was he involved or had the passing of the envelope been an innocent exchange of some sort? In his gut, he thought it was not innocent. He hoped he was wrong.

As soon as the man opened the door exiting McBride's, the wind hit him. It had to be ten below zero with the wind chill. He was aware of the coldness of his wire-framed glasses against the bridge of his nose. The fact that he had left his gloves in the car didn't help matters much. He kept one hand in his pocket, while the other had to suffer and hold his briefcase. As he walked down Forty-Fourth Street, he noticed two men standing off to the side in front of a building. The man, who was concerned by their presence, took his right hand out of his pocket. He then loosened the strap of his trench coat, making the nine-millimeter handgun worn in a shoulder holster under his sports coat more accessible. He continued to keep an eye on the men who had paid no attention to him. After safely passing them, he once again secured the strap to combat the frigid weather. He wondered if he had been paranoid, or if he was just being careful. In today's world, there didn't seem to be much of a difference.

He got into his 1991 Chevrolet Caprice Classic which was parked closer to Second Avenue than to Third. He turned the key and the car slowly rumbled to life. After allowing the car to warm up for about two minutes, he turned the heat up to full blast and began to thaw out. The man looked in the rear-view mirror to see the two males were still in the same location he had last seen them. They obviously had no interest in bothering him, he realized. The man then threw the car into gear and drove away as he reflected on everything that he had witnessed.

CHAPTER 4

Louis Castillo was an eight-year veteran of the New York City Police Department. He was not an imposing figure, standing five feet eight inches tall. He had an average frame, with dark, wavy hair and a thin mustache; he wore black wire-framed glasses. Castillo walked with a slight limp, which served as a reminder of his early days on the job.

Castillo, only two months removed from his training at the Police Academy was assigned to a Field Training Unit in Brooklyn North. That particular area in Brooklyn had one of the highest crime rates in the entire city. It had been a muggy August night and Castillo, like most rookies that night, was assigned to a foot post. He diligently patrolled his beat along Knickerbocker Avenue careful to walk around the puddles which remained behind from the earlier thunderstorms. The smell in the air reminded him of a wet dog. It was an uncomfortable evening to be walking a foot post. He could see the steam rise from underneath his bulletproof vest as he pulled it away from his body at the collar, allowing it to air out.

His post was only six blocks long, although he

was by regulations, allowed to walk one-half block up each side street. It wasn't a large area and became boring most nights, but Castillo didn't mind. He reminded himself that in another month or so cooler weather would be here and in another three months, he would be assigned to his permanent command, where he would not be walking a foot post every night. He'd be in a radio car answering jobs and making a difference. Castillo walked his post, looking for parking infractions so he could issue summonses, as his training Sergeant has instructed him to do. He walked from one end of his post to the other dozens of times a night. Castillo nodded hello to the same group of young men he saw every night. They were in their teens or early twenties and were always respectful of Castillo. He knew they were out there selling crack cocaine, but he wasn't sure how he knew that or how to catch them. Some nights he'd ask them to leave, others he'd ignore them. They would usually leave on their own if Castillo stood on the same corner as them, only to reappear once he left.

At 2000 hours, the adjoining foot post went to meal. Castillo welcomed this every night. He now had to cover the adjoining foot post as well. The additional six blocks were a welcomed change of scenery. He would normally spend most of that hour on the other post and then at 2100, he would go to meal. As he walked the additional six-block post, he stumbled onto an armed robbery in progress; he noticed a man with a gun holding up a liquor store. Castillo's heart began to race. His training Sergeant had instructed them time and time again not to take any police action when they were by themselves unless it was absolutely necessary. They were instructed to call their adjoining foot post over the point-to-point feature of their radio.

Realizing he was alone; he took cover behind a parked car. He had immediately called for backup over his portable radio, but the backup didn't get there soon enough. Castillo had watched the perp complete the robbery, fearing that if he tried to intervene right then it could cost the store clerk his life. As the armed robber exited the store, Castillo, who was still alone, jumped into action. "Police. Don't move!"

He had his .38 caliber revolver trained on the gunman. Instead of complying with the officer's orders, the man fled on foot with Castillo in immediate pursuit. The man had taken only about five steps before whirling on Castillo with his nine-millimeter handgun and opening fire. Castillo had returned fire as a hail of bullets littered the air. Castillo had been struck twice and could barely put the 10-13 radio code over the air. He fell backward into a puddle in the gutter, between two parked cars.

He remembers the first radio cars on the scene frantically yelling, "10-13, COP SHOT!" before lifting him into the radio car and taking him to Jamaica Hospital. Lying on his side in the back seat of the radio car, Castillo could hear the frantic yelling on the radio. It was just noise to him; he couldn't make out what was being said. He explored his chest with his hands, unsure if the round had pierced his vest or if the Kevlar held up. He felt himself drifting into a state of shock.

Castillo will never forget the feeling of the impact when the bullet had struck him in the chest. Although it was stopped by his bullet-proof vest, it had knocked the wind out of him and hurt really badly. But it was the shot that had shattered his right kneecap that would continue to torture him. The pain was excruciating. He had unfortunately learned how painful having your kneecap blown apart was. It wasn't until the next day, after the surgery, that Castillo had learned the perp had died of the gunshot wounds that he'd sustained during the gunfight.

The therapy had been a slow and often painful process. After eight months, Castillo was put back on full duty. Castillo had been offered a three-quarters retirement—something desirable to many Police Officers (as long as they were not too seriously injured to enjoy it, of course). A tax-free pension is often quite lucrative. However, Castillo wanted no part of a disability pension. He worked as hard as anyone, and harder than most at his physical therapy. He was a cop and that is what he wanted to remain. His goal was to continue to be the best cop he could, for as long as he could.

Once back to full duty, Castillo had been assigned to his permanent command in a Brooklyn North stationhouse. The precinct that he had been

assigned was always among the leaders in homicides and shootings, year after year. Castillo was
happy to stay in Brooklyn North; that's where the action was. Many of his friends from his training unit
were hoping to get to a Queens precinct as their permanent command since so many of them lived on
Long Island. Some of them had even told him he was
crazy for wanting to stay in Brooklyn.

"You were shot," they would tell him. "You're
a hero. The job will give you your choice of com-
mands. Why not go somewhere quiet? You've already paid your dues...more than most of us will."

"Brooklyn is what being a cop is all about," he'd
argued. "This is where the people need the most protection. Go ahead guys, be Queens Marines. I'm staying right here."

Over the next three years, Castillo impressed
both other cops and supervisors alike. He made stellar arrest after stellar arrest, ending up with more
arrests than anyone else in the precinct. That included the arrest-oriented, Anti-Crime cops. He had
made numerous gun and robbery arrests—exactly
what any commanding officer would most take note
of. He had even affected a bribery arrest after some
drug dealer offered him two thousand dollars to forget about the seventy-four vials of crack cocaine he
had in his pocket.

Castillo's commanding officer was so impressed
by his integrity and arrest record that he'd ap-
pointed him into the precinct's Anti-Crime team.

This had always been Castillo's ambition. He knew that after about two or three years in Anti-Crime, he could move on to a Precinct Robbery Unit, Detective Squad, or a Narcotics Division. Either way, he knew his appointment to Anti-Crime was the steppingstone to what Police Officers referred to as the *gold shield*...a Detective's shield. What Castillo didn't know at the time was that his appointment to Anti-Crime would get him his gold shield a lot sooner than he expected. It would also crush his ambitions and put his career on a completely different path.

One of Castillo's partners in Anti-Crime was Mark Hutter. Hutter carried the reputation of an aggressive cop, who had made numerous quality arrests of his own. He was a tough street cop, who few of the bad guys on the street were willing to challenge. A reputation goes an awful long way on the streets, good or bad. You didn't actually have to be that tough on people, as long as you had the reputation that you were. Castillo knew, as did the other cops in the precinct, of Hutter's reputation, but it wasn't until they were on patrol together in Anti-Crime that Castillo would find out why he earned that reputation.

A cool October night had netted them a gun collar. In Castillo's opinion, it also ended his career as a Police Officer—at least the type of Police Officer he wanted to be. The call was for a man with a gun on Utica Avenue and Linden Boulevard. He was a black male in his late teens, wearing blue jeans, a St. Louis Cardinals jersey, and a red baseball cap, the radio reported. Castillo and Hutter pulled up to the scene and exited their unmarked auto to stop the male in question. Seeing the officers' approach, the young man began to flee on foot, throwing a Davis Industries .380 caliber handgun to the ground as he ran. Castillo stopped to recover the gun *before it grew legs*, while Hutter continued to chase the male on foot. Hutter had cornered the perp in an alleyway as Castillo arrived on the scene. Hutter barked at the teen, "Who the fuck do you think you are running from, motherfucker!?"

"Yo Gee, word to God, I didn't know it was you, man...I swear, Hutter."

The teen was clearly terrified of his fate and tried to explain away his actions. He continually licked his lips and apologized to the agitated officer.

Castillo observed as Hutter took a blackjack out from his back pocket.

"Let's just cuff him up, Mark, I got the gun."

Castillo also sensed the intensity of the situation and was hoping to diffuse it.

Unmoved by his partner's plea, Hutter stared menacingly at the youth, slowly walking toward him. "Maybe you should pay for making me chase you, asshole. You know what the run-rule is, don't you, boy?"

Hutter was now taunting the teen as he menacingly slapped his own hand with his blackjack. "If you run, you best pray you don't get caught because if you do...," added Hutter as he shook his head slowly.

The teen backed up against the alley's wall and with the look of a cornered animal in his eyes, saw he had no apparent way out. Castillo looked on; unsure what was going to happen or what he should do at this point. He made one final effort to deescalate the situation. He placed the recovered gun in his waistband and reached for his cuffs.

"I'll cuff him up, Mark," Castillo said, but it was too late.

The youth, in obvious self-preservation, clenched his fist as tightly as he could and punched Hutter in the face, just as Hutter had raised his blackjack over his head. The youth tried to run, but his attempt was in vain. He was met with Hutter's blackjack. Hutter rained blows down upon the male's skull with his blackjack until he collapsed to the ground in a fetal position, protecting his head. There was now a decent amount of blood seeping from the open lacerations that would eventually take over a dozen stitches to close.

Castillo raced over not only to handcuff the youth but also to save him from further injury, as he had seen a wild look in Hutter's eyes. There was no mistake about it, Castillo had witnessed firsthand why Hutter had earned the nickname of Hutter the hitman. Hutter then kicked the teen square in the face, splitting his lip wide open, just for good measure.

Castillo looked over at Hutter in disbelief as Hutter boasted, "Another asshole who wanted a shot at the title."

Castillo will always remember how Hutter had bullied this kid that he outweighed by about a hundred pounds into a street fight with him, how the kid had been lying there in a pool of blood and Hutter was saying how if they wrote the reports up correctly, they would get a medal. Castillo was sick to his stomach. He was outraged at Hutter's brutal behavior.

He had read Hutter's arrest report, which told a very different story from the one that Castillo had witnessed. The report detailed how Hutter had chased the armed youth into an alley. Once in the alley, the youth pulled the gun from his waist and started to turn on Hutter, who quickly disarmed him by striking him over the head with his portable department-issued radio. He further explained how once he saw the male turn on him with a gun in his hand; it was too late to go for his own gun. So, fearing for his life, he struck the male with the portable radio and disarmed him. The entire incident had greatly disturbed Castillo, but he was unsure what he could possibly do about it. He didn't want to get one of his partners in trouble, but he had sworn to himself that he would never let Hutter, or anybody else bully and brutalize somebody like that ever again.

It was later on that evening that Castillo made the decision which he would regret for the rest of his career as a New York City Police Officer. Castillo wrote the Commanding Officer an anonymous letter detailing the incident and slipped it under his door. It was at roll call the next day, that the label of a rat was first cast upon Castillo. A cop would refer to another cop as a rat if he had broken the blue wall of silence and snitched on another cop. There was nothing lower than a rat in the police department. If enough people believed the label, it could follow you around your entire career.

Hutter had been called into the Captain's office and confronted with the letter. It had been so detailed that it could have only come from Castillo. Hutter marched straight out of the captain's office and into the muster room where the dozens of uniformed officers were seated in rows of chairs, waiting for roll call to begin. Hutter walked up to the sergeant's podium and asked for everyone's attention. Hutter, who was one of the most popular cops in the command, had no trouble getting complete silence. Castillo silently squirmed in his seat as he felt sudden nausea come over him. Could Hutter have found out about the letter? He prayed he had not.

Much to Castillo's dismay, all the admiration and respect he had earned from his fellow officers over the past few years was about to be impeached in a matter of seconds. There was nothing he could do or say to prevent it. "I would just like everybody standing before me to know that we have a rat among us," Hutter announced. "Louie Castillo is a fucking rat!" Hutter then walked over to Castillo and jabbed his forefinger in Castillo's chest. "You're a piece of shit

Louie."

Castillo found he was unable to say anything. He stood there in stunned silence. The look on his face and his silence were as good as admitting he had ratted Hutter out. His lack of word or action was his indictment among his peers. He felt the eyes of every member of the outgoing platoon fixed on him for what seemed like an eternity.

The next day, Castillo could no longer be the active street cop he once was and wanted to continue to be. The word had spread throughout the precinct that Castillo was a rat. The entire command was constantly talking behind his back. All of the other cops in the precinct, even the bosses, could not look him in the eye without a look of disdain. Later that week, as Castillo went into the locker room to suit up for the street, he saw a dead rat hanging from his locker. The rat's throat was slashed and there was a small pool of blood at the base of Castillo's locker. This was a message from the other cops that they would not work with a rat. It was an outright threat to his safety. Castillo prayed this would soon blow over but deep down he knew it would not.

With few other viable options, Castillo requested an administrative transfer that same night. Castillo's Commanding Officer immediately pushed the transfer through. The transfer was not only in Castillo's best interest but also that of the entire precinct, reasoned Castillo's boss. The telephone message transferring Castillo to another borough came through the very next morning. Castillo looked forward to starting over and putting this nightmare behind him. He could once again go back to being the cop he had until recently been.

The phone calls, however, had preceded Castillo to his new assignment in the Bronx. It didn't take very long before the talking behind his back and the word RAT started appearing on his locker. Castillo had regretted ever writing that letter. He realized that he was right, but he'd never expected how negatively coming forward would affect his career. Maybe he could have talked to Hutter. Maybe he could have done something to stop him or talk to him afterward to make sure at least it would never happen again. He could never undo what was done, however, and had to deal with the consequences. He faced the fact that he would never again be a real cop. It was the low point of his career—the day he realized he needed to go to the one detail on the job that so many before him and after him went once they were labeled rats. He found himself assigned to the Internal Affairs Bureau.

Almost every day of Castillo's life, since the day he wrote that damned letter, he wondered if he had done the right thing. Today was no different. What did it change other than his own situation? Hutter was still in Anti-Crime, and never even received charges over the incident. An internal investigation ruled it unsubstantiated. The only thing that changed in Castillo's mind was that he threw his career away. It was cops like Hutter that gave the department a bad name. He reassured himself that he'd done the right thing after all. Regardless of the outcome, if he had not reported it, he was no better than Hutter, he concluded. The same conclusion he always reached after wrestling with this dilemma hundreds of times.

Castillo parked the department auto on East Twentieth Street in front of the Police Academy. He grabbed his briefcase from the seat next to him and exited the auto. He walked under the overhang towards the Academy's glass doors. He watched as the new recruit class stood in formation under the overhang, despite the twenty-degree temperatures. The instructors were inspecting their companies and he thought back to when he, himself, had stood in their shoes eight and a half years earlier.

It was hard to imagine, but it was true that every member of the New York City Police Department, past or present, had come through this building. Castillo walked through the double doors and identified himself to the Police Officer on desk duty. He entered the elevator, pushing the button for the eighth floor. Castillo got off the elevator and made a right turn walking into the department's laboratory. He entered his name in the sign-in log. The sign-in log was commonly found at almost all department facilities to keep a record of all visitors. The main office of the department lab looked similar to any Detective Squad in the city. It was overcrowded with light green file cabinets, black steel desks with brown laminate tops, and chairs. On each desk were a typewriter and a phone as well as an assortment of paperwork. The only thing separating this office from any Detective Squad in the city was the fact that there were no holding cells.

Castillo called up his command and asked them to sign him in via outside wire. He would be starting his tour of duty at 0700 Hours at the Police Academy. He spoke to the same lab technician who had shown him how to operate the camera. He handed over both the camera and the mug he had lifted from the bar to the lab tech. He explained almost apologetically, how dark it had been in the bar the previous night. The technician once again assured him the photos would come out fine. The lab tech invited Castillo into the lab. From the pocket of his white lab coat, the tech removed a pair of latex gloves, and put them on.

Placing the mug on its side, the lab tech applied a small amount of black fingerprint dust on it. Slowly, the tech dusted the entire side of the mug. Twisting the brush ever so gently, spreading the thinnest of coats of dust over the mug. Castillo could see prints jumping out at him. The tech very carefully lifted the prints with a piece of clear tape and then set the tape down on a glossy white fingerprint card. The print looked perfect to Castillo, but he was not the expert. He hoped the prints that were lifted would be helpful.

Castillo decided to go and have some breakfast since the tech explained that tracing the finger-prints could take a while. He went to the same corner coffee shop he had eaten many meals in dur-ing his academy days. The coffee smelled great. He ordered a toasted bagel with cream cheese and a cup of coffee. He watched as numerous instructors walked in and out of the coffee shop getting their morning coffee. *Most of them are so young. They can't have much time on the job. How much could they really teach the recruits?* He slowly ate his bagel as he read the morning paper. There was nothing in the paper which caught his interest and his mind once again drifted back to Mark Hutter. He wondered if Hutter had changed at all. Had writing that letter at least served as a warning to Hutter to change his ways?

After breakfast, Castillo returned to the lab. The technician relayed to him that the city and state had no record on file concerning the fingerprints, but the FBI file had come up with a match. The fingerprint belonged to a man named Daniel O'Brien. He was a native of Northern Ireland and was granted citizen-ship of the United States in 1982. He had no arrest record in the United States and had only been fin-gerprinted for citizenship purposes. He also handed Castillo a manila envelope which contained eight by ten photos taken the previous night in the bar. Cas-tillo momentarily examined the photos and signed out.

Looking down at his wristwatch, Castillo saw it

was after nine am when he arrived at the Poplar Street headquarters of the Internal Affairs Bureau. Castillo took off his overcoat and hung it on the coat rack in the far corner of the office. After checking the corkboard to see if he had any messages, he sat at his desk. He opened the desk drawer and put his newly attained information inside. Castillo picked up the phone's receiver and held it between his shoulder and head as he punched in the number for his friend who worked over at the FBI's Eastern District office. *I hope he's doing a day tour today.*

"FBI, Balentine, can I help you?"

Castillo would have recognized his friend's voice even if he had not identified himself.

"Frank, it's Louie Castillo! How've you been?"

"Great Louie, and yourself?"

The two high school buddies caught up on recent events. After the small talk, Castillo got to the point of the phone call. "Frank, do you think you can do me a favor?"

"Just name it, Louie, and you got it."

"Thanks, Frank. I appreciate it. I'm working on this case and I need a background check done on this guy," Castillo explained. "His name is Daniel O'Brien. He's a male white, thirty-eight years of age, and an Irish immigrant. I'm looking for any possible connections with the Irish Republican Army."

Balentine was a nine-year veteran of the FBI and a special agent assigned to investigate white collar crimes. Despite his assignment, Balentine still had all of the resources at his fingertips that any agent in any other division had. "I'll look through our files and see what I come up with. If I get anything, I'll fax it over to you. Hey, Louie, what do you say we get together for some drink sometime?"

Castillo politely agreed before the two men said their goodbyes. Castillo sat at his desk studying the photos. As he stared at Keegan's photo, he thought of how it had just been a hunch that Keegan might have ties to the I.R.A. Now, it seemed as though his hunch may be correct. Keegan had become somewhat of a celebrity after he broke the Federal Courthouse Case and everyone on the job would surely recognize him while the case was still front-page news. Once the case died down, so did Keegan's celebrity. But Louie Castillo was a sharp cop that never forgot a face.

It was at a political rally in front of the United Nations, protesting the Queen of England's visit to the United States, that Castillo had first taken an interest in Keegan. Castillo had seen a picture in the newspaper concerning the protest and thought he had recognized the hero cop's image in the background of the photo. After an investigation, Castillo learned that Keegan had in fact been at the rally and was there to help raise money for the Irish Northern Aid Committee.

The committee, better known as NORAID, was a committee dedicated to raising money for the families of Irish-Catholic political prisoners and those who struggle financially living in Northern Ireland. At face value, it seemed to be a noble cause. Many familiar with NORAID, however, also believed this money was used to fund the outlawed Irish Republican Army Soliciting money for any political group was prohibited conduct for a member of the department, and Keegan had clearly been in violation of this statute. Castillo, after getting permission from his commanding officer, opened a case on Keegan and began his investigation.

Castillo jumped from his chair as he heard the fax machine begin to spit out a fax. A warm feeling came over him as he read it. This could be the break he had needed. Castillo walked over to the commanding officer's office and knocked on the door.

"Come in."

Castillo entered the office of Deputy Inspector John Marsh. Marsh was seated at his desk, drinking a cup of coffee. Marsh has been assigned to Group One of the Internal Affairs Bureau for the last three years of his thirty-one on the job. Group One handles allegations against high-ranking members of the department, other members of internal affairs, and all high-profile corruption cases. They report directly to the top brass at One Police Plaza. Marsh was an overweight man with a far receded hairline and a gray mustache. He wore his bi-focal lensed glasses low on his nose and had the habit of a chain smoker. His smoking, Castillo believed, was a reaction to the pressures of his position, especially nowadays, with the department being so closely scrutinized. Still, Marsh was pleasant enough to work for and appreciated when his men worked hard for him.

"What can I do for you, Louie?"

"Well, Inspector, it's about that case I was working on Keegan. I think I'm onto something pretty big."

Marsh responded with a hint of skepticism in his voice.

"Alright Louie, let me hear it."

"I followed Keegan into this bar in Midtown last night. The bartender at the bar is named Daniel O'Brien."

He handed over O'Brien's photo to Marsh. "I did some research on O'Brien; he came over from Northern Ireland in 1978 and gained citizenship a few years later. His father was killed in the violence by British troops in 1972 and his brother is currently in a prison in Northern Ireland for a car bomb that killed an informant against the I.R.A. Both O'Brien's father and brother were active members of the I.R.A. If I were a betting man, I'd bet that O'Brien is as well."

Marsh pushed his chair back from his desk. Castillo had his full attention.

"And where, exactly, does Keegan come in to play?"

Castillo handed Marsh the second photo for inspection.

Castillo could hardly contain his excitement as he explained, "here is Keegan accepting an envelope from O'Brien. It's got to be some sort of a payoff for information Keegan has been supplying the I.R.A. with."

"Whoa! Hold it right there, Louie," Marsh interrupted. "All you have is the passing of an envelope in a bar. For all you know, O'Brien may have handed him directions to his house for a Sunday dinner. This guy doesn't even have a criminal record."

Castillo pleaded his case. "Boss, just hear me out. It makes perfect sense. Keegan works for the Joint Terrorist Task Force. He has as much information at his hands as anybody over at the FBI. He's associating with a likely member of the I.R.A. and I see him accepting a payoff."

"First of all, Louie, you have absolutely no proof that O'Brien is associated with the I.R.A. Maybe he came to America to get away from the violence that killed his father and imprisoned his brother. Have you ever considered that? You also don't know for sure what was in that envelope. Even if you did, it doesn't prove anything. You have nothing concrete. Besides, don't forget James Keegan is a national hero. He saved countless lives by breaking that case before any bombs were detonated. I told you once and I will tell you again. Tread lightly on this one. Dot your i's and cross your t's. Make sure you are one hundred percent sure of anything before you come to me."

That was when everything came together in Castillo's mind. He realized what it was all about; the department didn't want any more bad press. They couldn't face another black eye for the department. It seemed to Castillo that every time someone in his office caught a big case they were about to break, it got squashed by the department's hierarchy and handled behind closed doors rather than in the public forum where it should be. They were afraid of the bad press, and instead of letting anyone arrest corrupt cops, they would take care of it in their own way—either with a transfer to a non-enforcement detail or place the guy on modified assignment, with no guns and no shield for an undetermined amount of time.

"You're right, Inspector. The man is a real hero," Castillo said sarcastically, as he both shook his head and let out a barely audible laugh.

"Louie, I'm not telling you that if the guy is dirty, we're not going to go after him. I'm simply telling you we need a whole lot more than the passing of an envelope in an Irish bar in Midtown to declare he is associated with an Irish terrorist organization."

Castillo rendered a cynical salute to Marsh and walked out of the office.

"Yes, sir."

This had been the case Castillo had been waiting for. This was the case where he could be a cop again, where he would feel proud to be a Detective and do a Detective's job. He would finally find redemption from the department that turned its back on him. But then the reality set in that the job would not only disallow him to work the case but may try to prevent him from doing it.

He had a gut feeling that Keegan was involved. He knew he was. It was the same feeling he used to experience on the streets of Brooklyn. A feeling, that was never wrong. When the hairs on the back of your neck tell you something is not right, you've got to trust them. Castillo decided neither Marsh nor anybody else could discourage him. If he was right, and Keegan was involved with the I.R.A., he was going to nail him.

CHAPTER 5

Sunday was a family day for the Keegan's. They always spent it together. The day would begin with nine o'clock mass and often follow with breakfast at the pancake house. They would then return home, change out of their church clothes, and around half past noon head over to the home of James Keegan's mother. This tradition seemed to have begun shortly after his father had passed away a few years back.

Kate studied her husband as he drove the Ford Explorer in complete silence. She knew something was on his mind. She hated when her husband got like this. He would never tell her what was bothering him, and she had learned not to ask anymore. It had to do with his job, she figured; it usually did. Not even the children's arguing in the back seat seemed to break his concentration.

"All right, what in the world are you kids fighting about now?" demanded Kate.

She turned around to face them, seeing Kevin and Timmy elbowing each other while Kerry was huddled in the corner steering clear of the confrontation. "Jim, tell the kids to knock it off."

This broke her husband from his daydream.

"You heard your mother. Cut it out," Keegan commanded.

"Daddy, I didn't do anything, I'm a good girl." Kerry was four years old and the apple of her father's eye. She adored her father; he was her hero.

"I know you are, angel."

Keegan looked out the window at a funeral procession making its way down the right lane of the Long Island Expressway. "Daddy, why do all those cars have their lights on? It's not nighttime."

Kerry was curious. Keegan paused for a moment before answering. She had been too young to remember her grandfather's funeral. He loved his daughter's innocence and hoped she wouldn't grow up too soon. "Well, angel, all those cars are following each other. They are driving with their lights on, so nobody gets lost."

It wasn't so far from the truth. Keegan didn't like to lie to his children if it wasn't necessary.

Kevin, sensing an opportunity to torment his younger sister, interjected. "No. That's not it. There's a dead…"

"Enough, Kevin," barked Keegan, cutting off his son, mid-sentence.

Keegan's thoughts had momentarily been derailed, but he soon started to think again of the task he had in front of him. It had been one thing before the kids came along but now… Keegan wondered what would happen to his family if anything ever happened to him. The radio was tuned to Fordham

University's radio station. Every Sunday afternoon, the station aired a program of all Irish music. The station was playing a playful Irish tune called <u>The Unicorn Song.</u> It was a cheerful song explaining how the extinction of unicorns had come about.

"Angel, your favorite song is on."

Kerry sat in the back seat singing the words to the chorus as best she knew. Kate was happy to see her husband snap out of his own little world. Kerry and her father sang along with the radio as the boys sat in the back seat mocking their sister. The scene brought a smile to Kate's face.

When the song ended, Kate applauded. "Very good, sweetie. You sing that song so well."

"Dad, can't we listen to something else?" Timmy crossed his arms in the back seat defiantly as he spoke. "We listen to this junk every week."

"This is not junk, Timothy. Just by listening to this program once a week, you can learn so much about your heritage and Ireland's history and culture."

Timmy refused to be deterred. "I don't want to learn about my heritage. I want to listen to good music."

"This is good music, and we are going to listen to it. When you get your own car, you can listen to whatever music you want." Keegan couldn't even understand the music of his children's generation, let alone enjoy it. This must be exactly how Timmy felt about the Irish music, he reasoned. Keegan pulled the Explorer into the driveway of his mother's New Hyde Park home where he had grown up. The children barely waited for the car to come to a complete stop before they jumped out. Kerry was the first to announce their presence as she ran up to the front door. "Grandma, we're here!"

The house was a modest, red-bricked, three-bedroom cape with a dark gray roof. It was easy to spot the house as soon as you turned onto the block because of the large oak tree in the front yard. Keegan noted that the shrubbery in front was well manicured. As a teenager, it had been his job to mow the lawn and trim the hedges. The irony is that he still feels responsible for the upkeep since he is the one who pays the landscaper fifteen dollars a week to maintain it, once the spring arrives. It is the least he can do to help his mother. Of course, the landscapers know that they are not to touch her rose garden. That is for her hands only.

Eileen Keegan came to the front door wearing a wool sweater, and slacks. She was a slight woman with silver-blue hair and hazel eyes. Although in her mid-sixties, there had hardly been a wrinkle on her until her husband had passed a few years ago. After his passing, it seemed her age had caught up to her in a hurry. The only thing that still kept her young at heart was her grandchildren. She would look forward to Sunday every week, just to spend time with them. Kerry grabbed her grandmother around the waist. "Hi, grandma. I missed you." Kevin and Timmy kissed their grandmother hello.

After the formalities, Kevin and Timmy went

into the basement to play the video games which they kept at their grandmother's house just for Sundays. "Kerry, dear, would you like to help grandma cook dinner?"

Kerry bit her lower lip and her eyes lit up. She nodded her head, indicating she would. "Okay, then, go wash your hands," her grandmother instructed.

Kate put on a pot of coffee. The kitchen was much smaller than her kitchen at home. The yellow and white floral wallpaper was way out of date. Kate remembered that style being popular when she was a teenager. The dull yellow cabinets and counters hadn't been touched in over twenty years, Kate figured. There were two cabinets with missing handles. She hoped her husband remembered to bring the replacements. It seemed like every week for a month now he had been promising his mother he would replace them. There was a small wooden table and four chairs in the corner where Kerry helped her grandmother prepare a pot roast. Quartered red potatoes, sliced carrots, and chopped onions sat in separate glass bowls. Under her grandmother's supervision, Kerry used the electric can opener to open a can of beef broth.

Over the course of the next hour, they caught up on the week's events. Kerry was seated at the dining room table with the adults and the boys had gone to the backyard to play football. Keegan glanced out the window at his boys. *They grew so big, so quickly*. He decided to go outside to join them in the game.

He removed his pager from his belt so it wouldn't fall during the game and set it down on the kitchen table. He exited the sliding glass doors into the backyard, where he had played so much football as a boy. It was an average size backyard for the neighborhood. The patio furniture was stacked and covered in the corner for the winter, leaving that much more room in the yard for the football game. The end zones were marked by a small tree on one end of the yard and the edge of the patio at the other. The same boundaries Keegan had used when he played as a child. "It looks like you guys need an official quarterback."

"Are you gonna play with us, Dad?" Timmy was excited. He loved when his dad played football with him.

"Alright, now I'm gonna really beat your butt in!" Kevin was quick to proclaim. "You're dog meat!"

Keegan played ball with the boys for almost an hour, while Kerry continued to help her grandmother prepare dinner. Kate walked over to the window and watched the boys play ball. Her sons were good at football, she boasted to herself. She gave the credit to Jim, who was always there to teach them. She knew he was a genuinely good man. He devoted so much time to his children and she loved him so much for that. He was a wonderful husband and father.

"Alright, men, it's a tie game; next touchdown wins. It's Timmy's ball."

Keegan hiked the ball to himself and pitched it

back to Timmy. Timmy threw the ball as far as he could back to his father who had run out for a pass. Keegan caught the ball with one hand and scored the game-winning touchdown for his younger son. He waited for Timmy to come to the endzone, handing the ball to him. Timmy excitedly took the ball and spiked it in celebration.

"I won! I won!" Timmy was announcing to anyone who would listen. Now it was his turn to tease his big brother. "Who's going to beat whose butt?"

"No fair, Dad. You can't do that! That's cheating," Kevin protested.

The boys stayed outside playing ball on their own and Keegan went back inside. Kate met her husband at the back door, kissing him as he entered. "You're wonderful," she informed him.

"You're not so bad yourself. I'm going upstairs to wash up before dinner is ready."

He walked up the stairs. There were thirteen. He remembered so many times as a child counting them as he climbed. He entered the first bedroom on the left. He looked around the room, which jarred many memories. After a few moments, he exited what was once his bedroom. Walking into the master bedroom, he quietly closed the door behind him. He picked up the telephone and dialed a number. After hearing the familiar tone of a pager, he entered the second number and hung up the receiver. He opened the door and went into the bathroom to make it seem as if he were washing up before dinner.

Kate heard her husband's pager go off, as it lay on the table. She hoped she was wrong, but it was almost always his job when that damned thing went off. She picked the pager up and read the number. It was just as she had feared; his office number. They didn't bother him very often at home, but when they did bother him; it always seemed to be on a Sunday when the family was together. Maybe he wouldn't have to go in, she hoped. Maybe they just wanted to ask him something or tell him something. She knew better, though. As Keegan emerged from the top of the stairs, Kate looked at him and in a disappointed voice informed him that his job had paged him.

"Really? Not today." He feigned disappointment. "Let me give them a call and see what this is about."

Keegan carefully punched in the numbers to his office. He listened as it began to ring. "How ya doin', Cap, it's Jimmy. You paged me?"

Kate, who was only able to hear one end of the conversation, listened attentively. After a brief pause, he continued. "Right. Yeah, I'm familiar with it." He rolled his eyes for effect. "Where are they now?"

He looked at his wife as he shook his head and shrugged his shoulders. "Okay, it'll probably take about forty-five minutes or more until I can get there though."

Keegan hung up the receiver which had still been ringing at the other end. "I'm sorry. It's one of those times I can't say no. A couple of guys in my team are staking out a place they think those Middle-Eastern radicals are storing explosives and they need me there right away."

Kate understood how important her husband was and how important the job he does was, but nevertheless, she was greatly disappointed. "What time will you be back?"

"I have no idea. Why don't you and the kids just sleep here, either way? I'm sure Mom will enjoy the company."

"I love you, Jim. Be careful."

If there was one thing that he could count on tonight is that he would certainly be careful. "I love you too. I'll see you later."

Keegan made a left-hand turn and got on the entrance ramp of the Long Island Expressway eastbound. He put the radio on to enjoy the last half-hour of the radio program. He could feel the nervousness in the pit of his stomach. Just like every other time he had done his part. He had to draw the line somewhere, put an end to his involvement before it backfired on him.

He got off the expressway at exit forty-nine and drove south on Route 110. He pulled his Ford Explorer into the parking lot of one of Long Island's many gun stores. He sat in the car, reached into his inside jacket pocket, and reopened the envelope Dan O'Brien had given him the previous Thursday night. Keegan counted out the money, all in one-hundred-dollar bills, and placed them in his wallet behind his police department identification card. He then read the list that had accompanied the money.

It had been a rather small order this time around. He put the list back in his pocket and put the single key which had also been in the envelope on his key ring before he entered the store. It was a long and narrow store. There were hundreds of guns in glass display cases on one side of the store and an assortment of hunting and fishing gear on the other side. Against the wall, behind the glass display cases were rifles and shotguns of every size and caliber standing upright. The man behind the counter was in his mid-thirties; he had a medium build and stood just under six feet tall. Keegan noticed right away the Browning nine-millimeter handgun strapped to the storekeeper's right side. "Can I help you?"

"You certainly can," Keegan replied as he took the list out of his pocket. "I'd like to buy three Beretta model 92Fs, one Intratec-nine machine pistol, and five hundred rounds of ammo."

"That's a big order. I assume you have the proper identification."

"Of course, I do."

Keegan reached into his back pocket to retrieve his wallet.

The store clerk handed a clipboard with several forms that he intended Keegan to fill out. "I assume you have a collector's license. You'll have to fill out these forms for the background check, then by next week, assuming all goes well, you can come back and pick up the guns."

"No. I don't have a collector's license." Keegan handed the clerk his NYPD identification card. "I'm a Police Officer in New York City."

The man examined Keegan's credentials. "I'm sorry, Mr. Keegan," the man began as he handed Keegan back his identification card. "It's just that most guys who come in here and want to buy so many guns at one time are either dealers or collectors. Dealers usually get the guns at wholesale, so I assumed you were a collector. As a matter of fact, I can't ever remember a Police Officer coming in here and buying so many guns at one time. Would you like to go downstairs to the range and test fire the guns to make sure you like them before you buy them?"

"No thank you and no need for apologies."

Keegan felt he should explain. "Things are getting pretty bad out there. A few guys in my office decided they should carry a second more powerful gun on patrol with them as a backup to the standard issue, .38 caliber revolvers. I mentioned I was going to pick up a Tec-9 this weekend and they asked if I would mind picking them each up a Beretta since I was coming here anyway. The paperwork involved with selling guns between cops is minor, so we will take care of that first thing Monday morning."

The man never seemed to doubt his story for a second. Keegan had used it many times before, and never once was there a question. "Let me just go to the stock room and get you those guns, and I'll be right back to ring you up."

As the clerk went into the back of the store, Keegan reflected on how the new laws have made it so hard to legally purchase a gun for the common citizen. There were half a dozen forms that had to be filled out. An extensive background investigation had to be done by the FBI and by the local police. Even in the southern states, you couldn't buy a gun with only a driver's license anymore. Keegan hoped that the new laws would slow down the number of illegal guns on the street. All of the laws, new or old didn't apply to Police Officers, however. All a Police Officer had to do was walk into a gun store, show his identification card and walk out with whatever firearm he desired, from a pellet gun to an assault rifle.

"Here you go, Mr. Keegan. I have everything you wanted. Do you need any gun cleaning kits or holsters?" asked the man, trying to improve on what was already the day's biggest sale.

"No. That will be it. Thank you."

Keegan paid the merchant in cash and put his identification card back in his wallet. He wished the man a good day and left the store. Keegan made one more stop on the way back to his house. He stopped at a sporting goods store and picked up two identical duffel bags.

As he approached his home, he activated the automatic garage door opener and drove the Explorer inside the garage. He closed the garage door behind him. After removing his coat, he walked over to his workbench. He picked up his drill and inserted a medium-sized bit. He plugged the drill in and pulled the trigger. The drill jumped to life. He put on a pair of plastic gloves so he was sure he wouldn't leave his fingerprints on the guns, as he removed them from their boxes. He examined each one, making sure they hadn't somehow been loaded. One by one, he took the guns and drilled out their serial numbers, permanently defacing them. He drilled down about an eighth of an inch, making sure even acid could not possibly raise the serial numbers.

It took about a half-hour until all four of the guns were completely defaced and he was confident they were untraceable. He held the Tec-9 in his hand thinking about what a destructive weapon the machine pistol was. He laid the weapons out along his workbench, picked up a couple of unused t-shirts that had been cut up to use as rags, and wrapped the guns in them. After wrapping each gun, he placed them inside one of the duffel bags, along with the ammunition. He then placed a ratchet and sockets in the other duffel bag. He zippered the second duffel bag closed folded it up and placed it inside the bag with the guns. He ripped the boxes, which the guns had originally come in, into small pieces and threw them into the garbage along with the plastic gloves. Keegan got back into the Explorer with the duffel bag. The garage door opened. He was surprised to see that it was now dark outside. He hadn't realized how much time he had spent in the garage.

He backed the car out of his driveway and hit the remote control, closing the garage door. He sifted through the assortment of music he had in the car and selected a collection of Irish rebel songs to listen to as he drove into Manhattan. The traffic was unusually light. Going into the city after nightfall on a Sunday was about the best time to go if you wanted to avoid traffic.

As he drove down the West Side Highway on Manhattan's Lower East Side, he saw a Toyota Camry parked in the spot where he had seen so many other cars before. The Camry was parked just off the highway near one of Manhattan's many piers. He parked his Explorer down the block and walked back to the Camry with the duffel bag in his left hand. He examined the key which had been in the envelope and sure enough, it was a Toyota key.

Keegan stopped next to the car, looking around to make sure he was not being watched. Not seeing anybody, he opened the car door using the supplied key. Reaching in, he tugged at the hood release and then picked up the copies of today's New York Times which had been left on the front passenger seat. He opened the duffel bag and removed the second duffel bag which he had earlier stuffed inside. He unzipped the bag, removed the ratchet and socket set, and placed the folded-up newspapers inside the now empty bag. He compared the two identical duffel bags. They were both rather bulky now and nobody would be able to tell the difference. He placed the duffel bag containing the newspapers on the passenger seat and carrying the other bag, he got out of the car. He opened the hood of the Camry and once again looked around. There was nobody on the street anywhere near him.

Across the highway, he could see a couple of prostitutes on the prowl and a couple of parked cars on the side streets. More than likely, the cars were johns getting blowjobs from the whores, he decided. He couldn't understand how anybody could go to a prostitute in today's day and age with all the diseases out there. Keegan quickly looked at the Vehicle Identification Number in the windshield of the car. *It looked pretty good.* This was definitely one of the better VIN jobs, as cops called it. He thought about how much money criminals made off VIN jobs. First, someone steals a car and buys another car which is the same year, style, color, and make from a junkyard. They usually pay a very minimal amount for the wrecked car. Then they remove the V.I.N. plate from the stolen car and replace it with the one from the junked car. Now if anybody were to run the V.I.N., it would come back to the correct car and nobody would be the wiser. It took a highly trained cop to recognize a good V.I.N. job. Most street cops could not spot a *tagged* car, so a few of the shrewder criminals in the city were driving around in a car they spent only a couple of hundred dollars for, even though the car could be worth in excess of tens of thousands of dollars.

Keegan put the duffel bag down on the ground

next to him and took out the ratchet set from his pocket. He started to loosen a few bolts on the firewall which didn't belong there, to begin with. As Keegan removed the bolts one at a time, the firewall became loose exposing a hidden compartment behind it. It was about one foot deep, one foot high, and two feet wide. He pulled the false firewall forward until he had enough room to stuff the duffel bag inside.

He only played a small part in the transport of the guns. There were probably very few who knew exactly how it was done, but Keegan had a theory of his own which he knew was probably very close, if not right on the money. The way he saw it, someone on the other side put the order in and contacted Dan. Dan would contact someone to steal the car and alter its V.I.N., undoubtedly someone familiar with cars. That person would park the car in the designated spot and leave it there. Keegan would be supplied with a key for the car and the money to buy the guns. He would then buy the guns, deface them, stash them in the false wall, drive the car to the next designated location and leave it there. He would lock the key in the trunk. The next guy would pick up the car have it shipped to Ireland, where a member of the I.R.A. would be awaiting its arrival.

Castillo was unable to tell exactly what Keegan was doing under the hood of the Toyota, as he watched him from across the West Side Highway through his binoculars. He knew for sure Keegan hadn't realized that he was being followed since he left his home on Long Island. There had been a couple of times during the ride that Castillo was afraid Keegan realized he had grown a tail. Castillo thought for sure he had blown it when Keegan exited the highway near the Toyota. With such little traffic in the area, Castillo couldn't just stop, so he kept going and made his way around to the other side of the highway.

It was almost by pure luck that he found Keegan again. Castillo knew if he had stopped in the same vicinity as Keegan, the entire last few hours of sitting on Keegan's house and tailing him to Manhattan would have been a waste. It may have even blown the entire operation. If Keegan knew he was being watched, he surely would not continue doing whatever it was that he was involved with.

Castillo desperately wanted to get closer and see what he was doing but he knew if Keegan recognized him from the bar the other night, it could jeopardize the entire investigation. *What was in that duffel bag and what was he doing here on a Sunday night?* Castillo couldn't see the duffel bag anymore, nor could he see what Keegan was doing under the hood of the car. Castillo picked up his department-issued cell phone and dialed 911.

The radio run was picked up by sector Ida. The call was for a male white stripping a blue Toyota Camry on the service road of the West Side Highway near Pier 26. The call further said the male had a black gym bag containing a gun. The sector pulled up quietly behind Keegan with their headlights off. He was just finished tightening the last bolt and had never heard the cops approaching him from behind. The female officer saw the gym bag on the front seat of the auto and alerted her partner. Police Officer Kenneth Williams approached Keegan from behind. "Police. Don't move! Keep your hands where I can see them," Williams commanded as he held Keegan at gunpoint. P.O. Laura Reed opened the door to the blue Toyota and looked in the bag, only to find today's edition of the New York Times.

"I'm on the job," Keegan announced to the officers. "My shield and I.D. card are in my wallet in my back pocket and my gun is on my right-side hip," Keegan further explained, as he kept his hands on the Toyota's fender.

Officer Williams challenged Keegan's claim. "What house do you work in?"

"I'm the Executive Officer of the Joint Terrorist Task Force. My name is James Keegan. I'm a Lieutenant."

Police Officer Reed moved in and took Keegan's service weapon from its holster, exactly where Keegan said it would be. The officers then asked Keegan for his I.D. card. He turned slowly towards the officers and removed his wallet, handing Reed his NYPD identification card. After examining his identification, the officers returned his I.D. and firearm and apologized, telling him the nature of the radio run. "No need to apologize." Keegan was very humble about the confrontation. "You're just doing your job and I like the way you both handled yourselves."

"Thanks, Lieu," Williams replied, in a slightly relieved tone. Confrontations with off-duty members of the service, especially those who outrank you, can be unpleasant sometimes. "What's the matter with your car, anyway? I used to be a mechanic before I came on the job. Maybe I can help you out."

"Oh, it turned out to be just a loose wire on the alternator. Let me see if it starts now."

Keegan got in the car, turned the key and the engine immediately started up. "Problem solved," Keegan was quick to announce. He was greatly relieved and thanked the radio team partners for offering their help and the professional way in which they handled the job. Keegan bid them farewell before driving away. "Stay safe, guys."

Keegan could not wait to get out of there. This was the closest he had ever come to being caught. A few minutes earlier...he didn't even want to think of the implications.

As Keegan watched the radio car pull away, he couldn't help but wonder what would have happened if they got this call when the car was being dropped off? If the guy who dropped it off was a member of the I.R.A., he might have had a gun and tried to shoot it out with these unknowing cops. *At least they'd handled themselves well and used good tactics. What if some more laid-back cops picked up the job and the guy dropping off the car wanted to shoot it out?* He would never forgive himself if he was even indirectly involved with a cop getting hurt or God forbid, killed. He had been to too many Inspectors' funerals over the years.

Time and time again, Keegan was haunted by the thought of how many lives in Northern Ireland he may have helped ruin. It wasn't so much the soldier's lives that bothered him, though he understood that they had families, too. The I.R.A. had declared war a long time ago and soldiers, unfortunately, get killed during a war. Every time he would read that a cop in Northern Ireland had been murdered by the I.R.A., he would cringe. He always felt they should leave the cops out of it. They weren't really political figures; they were just cops.

Then he began to wonder who could have possibly called 911. Was it a pure coincidence that they said there was a gun in the duffel bag, or had somebody been watching him? He looked around again, not seeing anything unusual; he decided whoever called had no idea that he actually did have guns or that he was a cop. It was very common for a person to call 911 and say there was a gun involved to get a quicker response from the police. After a brief debate, Keegan decided. *That must be what happened.* At least he hoped it was. He drove the car a couple of blocks away to the predetermined drop-off point and exited the auto, his duffel bag in hand. He opened the car's trunk; put the key inside and walked back to his own car. Keegan started the car up and began his journey back to his mother's house.

Castillo watched intently how the radio team handled the job. He noticed the female officer had looked inside the gym bag before Keegan had the chance to identify himself. At least there was someone who knew exactly what was in the bag. Castillo jotted down the radio car's number next to the license plate of the Camry on his notepad. Castillo was confused as to what Keegan was up to. His first impression was that the bag contained some sort of contraband that he had secreted in the auto; he doubted that now seeing Keegan carrying the bag back to his private auto. Or could it be that Keegan was taking something from the car which he would then deliver to O'Brien? If so, he would surely be on his way back to McBride's to pass it off to O'Brien.

Castillo followed Keegan's Explorer from a safe distance realizing that Keegan would be more alert than ever after the confrontation with the officers. Castillo was surprised to see Keegan go through the Midtown Tunnel. He had been sure that Keegan would be heading back to the bar to meet up with O'Brien. Castillo decided he must be on his way home for the night. There would be no sense in taking the chance of being spotted by Keegan if he was headed back home.

Castillo pulled off his surveillance of Keegan and decided to go back to the pier. His best play now was to find out more about the Toyota that Keegan had left behind. Who did it belong to? What was Keegan doing with it? Castillo wrestled with the option of sitting on the car to see who came for it next or calling department tow to bring it to a police facility so it could be more closely scrutinized. Castillo decided he would sit on the car himself for a couple of hours and if Keegan, or anyone else, did not come back for the car he would have it towed.

It was less than fifteen minutes since Castillo had begun following Keegan until he returned to the spot where the Toyota had been parked. It was gone. Castillo shook his head in disbelief. He immediately second-guessed himself. He should have stayed with the car, he now realized. The car was the bigger piece of the puzzle than where Keegan was headed. He couldn't believe how it took only a few minutes for someone to pick the car up and drive away. He knew the car was long gone, but that there was nothing he could do about that now. He was very frustrated; still, he felt that he was inching ever so close to finding out exactly what Lieutenant James Keegan was up to.

Officer Reed picked up her portable radio from its holder on her gun belt, "Sector Ida to central."

The radio dispatcher at the other end of the radio promptly acknowledged. "Go, Ida."

"You can mark the gun run a 10-91, proper I.D; off-duty member of the service with car troubles."

"10-4, Ida."

Williams gave his partner a sideways glance. "Did you recognize him, Laura?" Williams inquired of his partner.

"No. But he did look familiar."

"He's the cop who broke the attempted federal courthouse bombing. He was in all the papers. He even went to the White House and met the President."

"Holy shit! Ya know, you're absolutely right, Kenny. I knew I recognized the face, but I didn't know where I knew him from. Well, that makes him an even bigger asshole than I thought," Reed instantly proclaimed.

Williams was clearly confused by her comment. "Asshole? Why does that make him an asshole?"

She began to defend her assessment. "Well, if I remember the picture on the cover of *Spring 3100* correctly, he was shaking the President's hand while his wife and three children looked on."

Williams still wasn't seeing the connection. "Okay...so what does his picture with the President in the department's trade magazine have to do with him being an asshole because his car broke down?" Williams was eager to defend Keegan.

"You just don't get it. You men are all alike. He's married, Kenny."

"I still don't get what that has to do with anything?"

She had a disgusted look on her face as she explained. "Think about it, Kenny. It's a Sunday night. He's in the Joint Terrorist Task Force. In a detail like that, there is no way in hell he works weekends. And if he was called in for something big and was on duty, he would be driving a department car. Not his private vehicle. So why in the world would he be around here except for the prostitutes. He's got a wife and kids at home, and he's here fucking some whore!"

Williams wasn't buying her argument. "Relax, Laura, just because you caught your boyfriend cheating on you, doesn't mean all men cheat. He could have some perfectly legitimate reason for being here."

"C'mon Kenny, around here, there's no legitimate reason for him to have parked his car. There are no stores, no apartments, nothing…except the working girls."

"Well, I'm still giving the benefit of a doubt to a hero cop." Williams shook his head at Reed. "Did you ever think maybe he actually did break down?"

Keegan pulled his Explorer into his mother's driveway at about ten-thirty. He was extremely alert on the way home. He had gotten off and on the expressway several times, constantly checking his rearview mirror making sure he wasn't being followed. He had a bad feeling in his gut. Being stopped and questioned by the sector car had made him a bit paranoid. Over his years of gun-running for the I.R.A., this was as close as he had ever come to being caught, and he didn't like the feeling.

The plan worked like it was designed to; this obviously was the reason they wanted him, a Police Officer, to buy the guns and to conceal them in the car. If anybody were to stop him, he would just identify himself as a Police Officer and there would be no reason anyone would question him any further. If any other civilian was stopped in the same scenario, however, they would certainly be scrutinized a lot more closely and the entire plan would likely unravel.

He parked his car and as he exited, taking a deep breath. He was relieved the long night was behind him. He used his key, which he had never given up, to open the front door of his mother's home. Kate and his mother were seated at the kitchen table, drinking coffee. Kate was the first to speak. "How did everything go tonight, hon?"

"We staked the place out for a few hours before we got a search warrant. When we hit the place, we came up empty. I guess either our confidential informant gave us bad information, or somebody told the mutts we were watching. Either way, we came up empty; very frustrating, a giant waste of time." Keegan sounded legitimately annoyed. He didn't like that he became so comfortable lying to his wife, but he knew there was no other option. "Where are the kids?"

"They're all fast asleep upstairs. Would you like to get them, or should I?"

"You're not going to wake up my grandchildren this late, are you, Kate? Why don't you sleep here tonight? Tomorrow is a holiday. The kids don't have school."

Eileen Keegan had been terribly lonely since the passing of her husband and welcomed company anytime day or night.

"Alright, Mom, we'll stay here as long as Kate doesn't mind," offered Keegan.

"Of course, I don't mind," Kate agreed, as if her husband had left her a choice.

"Oh, good, then it's settled. I'll warm up your dinner for you, you didn't eat, did you, Jimmy?" Eileen Keegan inquired of her son.

He had in fact stopped on the way home for a burger since he hadn't eaten all day. "Now, why would I eat when I know my mother has a home-cooked meal waiting for me?"

After eating, he and his wife went upstairs to go to bed while Grandma Keegan stayed downstairs washing the dishes. Keegan checked in on his sleeping children, giving them each a kiss goodnight on their forehead. He climbed into bed with his wife and gave her a kiss on the cheek. "Good night, Kate. I love you."

"I love you too, Jim." She took his hand in her own and held it gingerly.

Keegan held his wife for most of the night. He was having a hard time sleeping. He couldn't help but wonder what would happen to Kate and the kids if he ever got caught. He would be sent to prison. There would be no pension or even a paycheck coming in for that matter. He prayed he would never find out.

CHAPTER 6

Keegan sat with his cup of coffee on his desk, reading through the morning paper. There was an article on how far the conflict over religion had come in Northern Ireland. The article had stated, with peace talks currently being held between the British government and the I.R.A., that there was hope that peace would come to the region before the end of this century.

Martin Devine, the man who will in less than two months become the first Protestant Grand Marshall of the Saint Patrick's Day parade, said that barriers between Catholics and Protestants had been broken with his selection as the Grand Marshall. The paper quoted him as saying, "I'm honored by being selected to take part in the world's largest Saint Patrick's Day Parade. My selection, in itself, is a symbol of how close the end of the strife which has plagued Northern Ireland actually is. Eight hundred years of troubles will soon be behind the Irish people, so all can live in peace and harmony."

Keegan resented the fact that a Protestant had been selected and thought this guy was sending a political smokescreen to get into the public eye. *He must be getting ready to run for office.* The media really seemed to like him, as he appeared more and more in the news as the parade approached. Yet there was something about him Keegan and many other Catholic-Americans did not trust.

Keegan thumbed through the rest of the paper as he took a sip of his coffee. He briefly read the sports section, scanning the highlights of the Islanders' victory the previous evening over the Red Wings. Articles started to appear concerning the Yankees and Mets as spring training was only a few weeks away.

After closing the paper, Keegan opened his desk drawer and examined a printout of the radio run. It had been over two weeks since the radio car team pulled up on him as he secreted the guns in the car. He carefully read every word, as he had done every day for the past two weeks, looking for some kind of clue. He wanted to believe it had been a coincidence, but his instincts told him he had better be careful. Who could've called and what did they know?

The only other person who knew what he was doing was Dan and there would be no reason for Dan to *drop a dime* on him. Reading the printout, he could see the person was close enough to have gotten his description and the license plate to the car. He remembers constantly looking around so how had he missed them? There had not been anybody watching from that close, he would have noticed. He was sure of that. Unless it had been a passing motorist who called from a cell phone, he thought.

If they left a call-back number, he could have traced the number and find out whom it belonged to, but they did not.

A knock at the door interrupted Keegan's thoughts. He quickly put the computer printout back in his desk drawer and invited the person on the other side of the door to enter. "Jimmy, here's a copy of the *fives* that you asked for," said one of the Detectives in Keegan's squad, as he handed Keegan a stack of pink papers.

"Thanks a lot, Pete."

Detective Pete Smyth walked out of the door, closing it behind him. Keegan read through the DD-5's, which was the name of the form used by the department to document anything done in an ongoing case after the initial report had already been filed. Most of the time, a five would have an interview with a witness, a canvass of an area, or something else of value to an investigation. The *fives* that Keegan had asked for were concerning the murder of Judge Boden. An outsider to the police department would assume after an arrest is made in a case, the case is over but that is not necessarily true, especially, in high profile cases. The arrest can sometimes be made at the beginning of a case.

Over the last few weeks, Keegan's men had been working on finding out as much as they could about Judge Boden's assassin. They conducted an in-depth profile on his family, and any known associates both in this country and abroad. It was imperative to find out if he acted alone or had co-conspirators still at large. Especially, if they were still here on American soil. Keegan read through the fives, one by one, and signed his name in the space captioned, Supervisory Officer. Most of them didn't reveal any new information. They were mostly interviews with neighbors who claimed not to have known the assassin too well. They mostly said he kept to himself, had few visitors, and no family they were aware of.

There had been only one lead a couple of weeks ago which had unveiled a co-conspirator in the Boden homicide. That subject was nowhere to be found. Keegan believed he must have fled the country before the assassination was even carried out. After signing off on the paperwork with nothing of interest jumping out at him, Keegan put them in a basket so they could be filed away in the case folder.

He once again opened his desk drawer, trying to figure out if it was time for him to walk away from his secret life or should he just be a little more careful. The more he thought about it, the more concerned he was for the welfare of his family. Maybe sometime soon he would tell Dan O'Brien that his days of running guns are over. Although he knew Dan would be greatly disappointed, he figured Dan would thank him for his many years of service and to keep in touch. Or, maybe, he wouldn't even have to quit, if peace was truly so close.

After contemplating a few minutes, Keegan decided he was being paranoid. If anyone had any information about gun-running to the I.R.A., that information would eventually come across his desk.

Being the second in command at the Terrorist Task Force, he would be made aware of any investigations involving the transportation of arms to any terrorist group. Keegan had once again convinced himself his secret was safe.

Louis Castillo sat at his desk at the Internal Affairs Bureau. He was reading the case folder he had been working on about James Keegan. Castillo wondered why anyone would get involved with a war in which they really had no personal involvement. He wondered how long Keegan had ties with the I.R.A. and what exactly he did for them.

He checked Keegan's personal access code for the department's *Finest* computer system. Castillo learned that Keegan hadn't used his code to get information on anything in months except for the radio run he had called in on Keegan a couple of weeks ago. It didn't make sense that Keegan was selling information to the I.R.A. The I.R.A. had never operated outside of the British Isles, so he wouldn't have any valuable information for them. So, what was he doing? There was no doubt in Castillo's mind that Keegan was somehow involved with them, but what exactly was he doing, and for how long had it been going on? Castillo had discretely followed Keegan every night for the last two weeks as he left his office, and every single night, Keegan went straight home.

Castillo thought for sure that by now he would have made another contact with the bartender at

McBride's. Castillo stared at O'Brien's photo wondering how deeply O'Brien was involved with the I.R.A. He then stared at Keegan's photo. Looking down at his personnel folder, he could see Keegan was the department's dream cop. He had received over fifty citations for excellence and heroism in the line of duty. He was a standout cop and Detective in every unit that he ever worked. He had broken dozens of high-profile cases and made over six hundred career arrests. He only had three unsubstantiated civilian complaints lodged against him and had never been sued or ever had charges and specifications filed against him. Castillo knew he had better have Keegan dead to right before telling his supervisors too many details.

Castillo filled out a notice to appear for Police Officers Laura Reed and Kenneth Williams. It was easy enough for Castillo to track down which officers handled the job he had called in that night in Manhattan. All department autos had numbers and there always had to be a record of which officers were assigned to each vehicle on every tour. He decided to make the appearance for February 27. This way he could make sure he did a day tour on the final payday of the month. Plus, since his regular days off were Friday and Saturday he would make a longer *swing* for himself. He hoped that Officer Reed would be able to fill in some of the missing pieces for him by telling him what had been in the gym bag. Castillo knew that one cop would not be willing to tell on another cop, so he had to come up with a plan that would make Reed tell him what she saw. At least he had some time to come up with a plausible story.

At roll call that afternoon, before the four pm to midnight shift, the roll call Sergeant handed Reed and Williams their notifications to appear at the Internal Affairs Bureau on February 27. The notification instructed them to appear at ten hundred hours on that day and to report to Detective Castillo. The notification also ordered them to bring their memo books for January 15 and to wear the uniform of the day. Both officers, upon receiving their notifications, flipped through the pages of their memo books. They wanted to see if anything eventful happened that night. All Police Officers were required to keep a memo book. It was a log consisting of the jobs they responded to, people they stopped and questions, summonses they issued, any arrests they made, and any other police-related services they may have rendered.

After looking over their memo books for the day in question, they decided they were being called in on what must've been an allegation made by the lawyer they had arrested at the end of their tour for driving while intoxicated. The lawyer had told them they would be sorry if they arrested him.

"I can't wait to see the allegation this asshole made against us," said Williams to his partner.

"He probably said we tried to shake him down or some horseshit like that. This job is something else.

We're out there doing our job and yet they'll entertain an allegation made by a drunk."

"Relax Kenny, we don't even know for sure he made an allegation; besides, we didn't do anything wrong. We'll just have to wait until next week to see what this is all about," trying to put her partner at ease.

The date on the personnel orders was February 19. Keegan read the orders carefully; making sure none of the members of his team had been omitted. Receiving medals wasn't the thrill they once were to Keegan, but he still did feel a sense of accomplishment when they were posted in the orders. The medal which came down today would be his fourth Commendation. A Commendation is a pretty high medal and Keegan thought how many Police Officers go through their entire career without receiving a medal that high. He went over to the copy machine and ran off a copy of the personnel orders and put it in his jacket pocket. It was almost six o'clock and time for Keegan to sign out. Keegan spent over an hour and a half in traffic on the way home that night and he never noticed the nondescript department auto that was following him most of the way home.

Kate had warmed up his dinner as she and the kids had eaten almost two hours earlier. The kids were upstairs tending to their homework and Keegan thought this would be a good time for him to take out his scrapbook. Keegan never allowed his children to see his scrapbook. It was a conscious decision. Maybe someday he would when they were a little bit older. He wanted to shield them from the brutality of the real world or maybe he thought they just wouldn't understand how much it meant to him. He always said one day when he felt it was appropriate, he would show them his many accomplishments over his career.

Keegan went into the living room and retrieved the scrapbook from the bottom cabinet of the chestnut-colored entertainment center. He sat down on the ivory sectional, grabbed the remote, and turned on the hockey game. He took a quick glance to the top of the staircase to make sure the children were not coming downstairs. He set the book down on the glass-topped coffee table, setting aside an assortment of Dr. Seuss books, and opened it up. He noticed a reddish stain on the beige and light green area rug that he was pretty certain was not there this morning. *No doubt, a spill from Kerry.* She always sat in that spot watching her television shows while drinking her juice and having a snack.

Keegan took the copy of the personnel orders from his pocket, wrote the date of the order and the words Commendation # 4 on the top of the page. Looking through the book, he reminisced about all the times he had been in the newspapers, reading the articles which he had clipped out. It seemed every time Keegan took the scrapbook out, he read every article he had in there. He also had a copy of the personnel orders for every medal he had received. He had photos of the many *Cop of the Month* awards he'd earned, as well as numerous *Certificates of Excellence,* he'd been awarded from different Police Commissioners.

His crowning jewel to date, however, would undoubtedly be the photo of him shaking hands with the President of the United States which appeared in hundreds of newspapers across the country. After breaking the case of the attempted courthouse bombing, Keegan and his family were invited to the White House to meet the President of the United States. The photo was published everywhere. Not just newspapers but also periodicals like TIME magazine and it was also the cover of the department's trade magazine which was mailed out to over thirty-five thousand Police Officers in New York City. Keegan had the original photograph, which was signed by the President, hanging in his office.

Kate watched as her husband read through his scrapbook. She remembered how, when they were first married, she used to be so interested in her husband's war stories about which bad guy he had locked up that night. In more recent years, however, she saw his job as a threat to their marriage and only feigned interest when he would tell her anything related to his work. "Were you in the newspaper again today or something?"

Kate was trying to figure out what her husband was putting in the book.

"No, that medal finally came down today from the terrorist cell we locked up."

"I'm so proud of you, Jim."

It was the truth. Not many women could honestly say that their husband is a real hero.

"I know you are, sweetheart."

He put the scrapbook away and embraced his wife.

CHAPTER 7

Northern Ireland

The Toyota was driving through Ireland's hills and valleys in a suburb north of Belfast. There was too much anger and hatred in the driver's eyes to take in the countryside's overwhelming beauty. There were so many rich shades of green to be seen through the hills, separated by the winding and twisting roads. There were ancient castles, charming, thatched cottages, and small mountain ranges in the distance. It is said there are fifty shades of green to be seen in Ireland. The man saw none of this. He had shoulder-length dirty blond hair and a medium build. His boyish face was offset by the coldness in his slate-gray eyes. He had seen and caused more bloodshed in his twenty-one years than most people see in a lifetime. He wore a pair of blue jeans and a t-shirt under a black field jacket which concealed the Russian-made, nine-millimeter handgun tucked in his waistband.

He was having a hard time getting used to shifting the vehicle's gears with his right hand. *God-damned yanks*, he thought to himself, *why do they have to do everything backward*? He had driven to an abandoned barn house outside the town of Balleymena, twenty miles north of the Northern Irish capital of Belfast. Twenty miles away seemed to be another world from all the violence in Belfast. As the Toyota approached, the three men inside the barn opened the barn and the vehicle was driven inside. The doors were quickly closed behind him.

The barn was constructed of grey, brown, and tan stones. The roof was crude at best and in need of repair. The structure itself was easily over a hundred years old. There was nothing warm or inviting about it. On the inside were a couple of desks and a workbench. A ladder used to climb up to the loft where materials were stored, lay on the floor.

Eamon Quinn was the first to greet him. Quinn was a field general for the I.R.A. There were very few who actually got to meet him. He was a brilliant strategist who had devoted over thirty years of his life to the cause of freedom in Northern Ireland. Quinn was a man in his mid-fifties whose full head of gray hair looked awkward against his dark eyebrows. He was of medium height and weight and was clean-shaven. "It is good to see ya looking so well, Gerald Flynn."

Gerald Flynn had practically been born into the I.R.A. His uncle was one of thirteen people shot and killed by the British during a peaceful civil rights march in Derry in the early 1970s, before Gerald had been born. His father had been arrested when Gerald was a young boy under the prevention of terrorism act, which enabled the British troops to arrest anyone and hold them for up to a week without ever charging them with a crime. Gerald's father died in a prison riot during his week of internment and was never charged with any sort of crime. He, himself, had been arrested at the age of nineteen and spent a year in the H-blocks of Long Kesh prison where his only brother was still serving out a five-year sentence for possession of explosives. Gerald Flynn brushed his long hair back with his hand as he exited the auto.

"Ello, Eamon, I see you're doing a lot better than Owen."

Flynn's remark referred to his comrade. Flynn stared at the cast on Owen's leg, which extended from his lower leg to his upper thigh.

Owen Dunn sarcastically responded, "It's good to see you too, ya fucker, ya."

"Did we identify the bastard who kneecapped him yet?" Flynn wanted to know. "I'll take care of him me self, if you just give the order, Eamon."

Declan McKee quickly interjected. "You can't always be so hot-headed Gerald."

McKee was Quinn's right-hand man and second in command. He was in his early forties and stood about five and a half feet tall. He had dark hair and a dark beard. There was a large scar above his left eye; a reminder of the prison time he served in his youth. McKee was the most knowledgeable man the I.R.A. had in the field of explosives. He had been building bombs and training others to do so for close to twenty-five years. This would not be the first time he would lecture Flynn. Most likely not the last either, he realized. "Sometimes it makes more sense to think before we react. You do understand that lad, do you not?"

"When we find out who kneecapped Owen, we should deal with him swiftly and justly," argued Flynn.

Gerald Flynn wanted nothing more than to avenge the assault on his childhood friend. Owen Dunn had gotten into his car one night last week, unaware a Unionist guerrilla was hiding in his backseat. He was kidnapped and brought down by the shipyards in Belfast. Once there, he had been tied up, tortured, and beaten by two masked gunmen over a two-hour period. They believed Owen was an active member of the I.R.A. If they had known for sure, they would've killed him on the spot. After two hours of him denying any involvement, they had told him they were going to kneecap him anyway, just in case he was an I.R.A. soldier.

Kneecapping was used often enough by the I.R.A. to send out a message. It was usually reserved for someone who talked too much or for someone who tried to leave the organization. The motto *once in, never out* was often told to someone before the gun was put to the back of their kneecap. When shooting someone in the back of the knee it would cause the person excruciating pain as it would shatter the kneecap, often beyond repair.

Eamon Quinn put an assuring hand on Flynn's shoulder. "Don't worry Gerald; those who are responsible will be dealt with accordingly. In the meantime, you have some training to do for your trip across the Atlantic."

The barn house was used by the I.R.A. for many reasons. It was used as a safe house for those on the run. It was also used as a training camp of sorts, equipped with a target range, and a storage facility for arms, ammunition, and hundreds of pounds of explosives. Declan McKee had put together many bombs in that very barn house over the years.

Declan and Eamon carried out stanchions to place the targets on. They placed them about fifty feet downfield and fifteen feet apart. Flynn took of his field jacket and placed it on the car before joining the other two men outside. Flynn walked out and without saying a word pulled the gun from his waistband firing first at the target on the left then at the target on the right. Flynn fired at three-round intervals as he had been taught. After firing the initial three-rounds at each target, he dropped to one knee continuing to fire three-round bursts, alternating targets.

In all of Eamon Quinn's years in the I.R.A., he had never seen a more deadly accurate shot than Flynn. He figured Flynn's accuracy was certainly one of the factors that had made him the I.R.A.'s top assassin. He didn't have to get as close to his target as the others did. Flynn could hit a target fifty feet away with a handgun with the same accuracy as someone firing from the same distance with a rifle.

"He's a remarkable shot, is he not Dec?"

"Aye. He is at that, Eamon. He is at that. I just fear he might take matters into his own hands. Especially if he knew that we already know who capped Owen."

"No need to worry about that. He is as good a soldier as he is a marksman. He won't do anything until he's given the order to do so. I may even let him go ahead with the hit before we send him to the States." Quinn let this idea slip, testing his comrade's reaction.

"Eamon, he's leaving tomorrow. He's too important for the plan overseas to chance him getting caught over here."

"He won't get caught and, besides, he is the best we have, ya know."

That was a point McKee couldn't argue. As much as he did not want Flynn to be involved in the retaliation, it was ultimately Quinn's decision and he knew that. "Well, it's your call, now isn't it Eamon." He reluctantly gave his support.

"Nice shooting Gerald."

Quinn examined the targets whose centers had been blown out. "However, you're not going to be able to use a Russian-made gun in the United States. Why don't ya give this gun a try?"

He handed Flynn a Beretta, model 92F. He also handed him an extra magazine. While Flynn was occupied loading the nine-millimeter rounds into the magazine, McKee and Quinn replaced the targets with fresh ones. They also added about a dozen or so stanchions around the original two and marked only one of the targets with a big letter X.

The field outside the barn was an ideal place to practice. There was only one unpaved, dead-end road that leads to the barn and there wasn't anybody around for miles to hear the gunshots. The only real danger of getting caught was by a helicopter that could fly overhead. "How does it feel?"

Flynn weighed the gun in his hand and felt the grips. "I like me own gun better, but I'll give er a go."

Flynn put his field jacket back on and slipped the extra magazine in the left-hand pocket. Flynn had his back to the targets and couldn't see what was being done. He slipped the Beretta in his waistband and waited for an order.

"Whenever you're ready Gerald, walk away," was Eamon Quinn's initial command. As Flynn was walking in the opposite direction of the target, he heard Quinn's next order. "Identify your target and eliminate them."

Flynn pulled the Beretta from his waistband and turned towards the targets in one fluent motion. Without hesitating, he identified the target and let four three-round bursts go into the center of the target from a range of over seventy feet. He had seen no other marked target and therefore only fired at the one target marked by the X, out of the fifteen in the distance. All twelve rounds he fired hit their mark in the dead center, but the drill wasn't yet over.

"Make your getaway. Run towards the barn, head around back and get into the car."

Flynn followed his orders knowing his drill had

been a success. He ran as hard as he could to the barn which was about fifty feet away. When he got to the far side of the barn, he made the right as instructed. His heart almost stopped when he saw two British troops around the corner. Instinctively, he brought the Beretta up to eye level and emptied the gun on the first soldier on the left. Without missing a beat, his thumb hit the magazine release, while his left hand inserted the fresh magazine into the gun. He released the slide and continued his onslaught in three-round bursts. After the first series of bursts, he threw himself into a somersault, came up on his right knee, and continued to alternate targets with three-round bursts. In less than ten seconds, Flynn had emptied his gun, reloaded, and hit his targets without missing a shot.

Had they been actual soldiers instead of dummies Quinn had made, they would've had no chance of survival against this killing machine. This was, however, a new lesson to Flynn to never assume you're home free. You must always expect the unexpected. He also realized he should have reloaded his gun right away. Had he been facing live adversaries with only three-rounds in his gun, he could have had serious problems.

Flynn knelt over as he caught his breath. McKee and Quinn looked on, pleased at what they had witnessed. "Let's go back inside and go over the details of your trip, Gerald."

The men collected the targets and the dummies and brought them inside just in case a chopper would happen to fly over. It was better to be safe than having attention brought unnecessarily to the barn house. Owen Dunn had remained inside while Gerald had been training. Owen was seated at a desk, putting together a rather large gelignite bomb. McKee had taught Dunn how to make a bomb a few years ago and Dunn had become quite skilled at it. The men gathered around a table off to the side of the barn. Quinn picked up the manila envelope that had been lying in the middle of the table. He opened the envelope and counted out five thousand American dollars and handed it to Flynn. "This should be more than enough to last you a few weeks in New York."

"I'll make sure it does Eamon," Flynn assured him.

Quinn took out numerous documents from the envelope and examined them. He had a United States passport and a New York State driver's license baring Flynn's image, in the name of Sean Murphy from Woodside, Queens. There were also various other documents such as bogus credit cards, a social security card, and a college identification card all in the name of Sean Murphy. If anyone were to stop Flynn in New York, there would be no question as to his identity.

"Study these good now lad, you must know the information backward and forwards. For the next few weeks, you are Sean Murphy. Know your address, your phone number, your ma's maiden name. Every bit of information in that packet you best learn. Know it like the back of your hand. Do ya understand, Gerald?"

Flynn nodded in agreement. "Aye, I do. Sean Murphy it is."

Eamon Quinn handed the assassin a piece of paper. "Once in New York, you will go to a bar in Manhattan. Here's the address. You'll see the bartender; his name is Dan O'Brien. He's good people; he's been running many things from that end for years. He'll fill you in on anything else you might need to know. And Gerald, make sure you get to know the area of the job inside and out. Your escape is essential. You're much too valuable to us to rot your life away in a Yank prison."

"That's one thing you don't have to worry about, Eamon. There is no way I'm going to prison over there, I'd sooner die, I would."

Eamon Quinn knew Flynn was not exaggerating; he was being genuine. Quinn had mixed emotions about sending Flynn to the United States. Flynn had become a legend in his own time within the I.R.A. Though few had ever actually met him, Flynn's legend was well known throughout their ranks. He had over a dozen hits under his young belt and the Brits had no idea of his involvement other than an arrest a couple of years back for rioting and assault. Quinn knew it was a great risk sending his top assassin to another country to carry out a hit in unfamiliar surroundings. He also knew, unfortunately, that Flynn was probably the only one in the I.R.A. who could possibly pull it off and still manage to escape capture.

"Do you think you're up to one more mission to-night before you leave?" Quinn asked of his soldier, although he was sure of the answer before asking.

"Aye and I'd never refuse an assignment, Eamon Quinn. You should know that by now." Flynn was eager to hear what the assignment entailed.

"Good. I want you to come outside and try your hand at this weapon. It's a Tec-9 machine pistol."

Flynn studied the gun for a moment. It looked like it could do a lot of damage. Flynn liked that idea. "It's been altered so it can fire as fully automatic, but you have to be careful, you only have thirty-two rounds in the magazine. You don't want to empty the entire magazine too quickly," Quinn cautioned him.

Flynn familiarized himself with the weapon, studying the location of the safety and magazine re-lease. Once he was satisfied, he loaded the magazine full of nine-millimeter ammunition. "I think I'm going to like it; I do."

Declan McKee grabbed a target and the men walked outside. McKee set the target about twenty-five feet away. "Have you no faith in me Declan, I could shoot the center out of that target blindfolded from here."

"Gerald, tonight's assignment doesn't require your marksmanship. This is why we're giving you such a destructive weapon. We will be sending out a message tonight. A show of raw force if you will, and there will be no innocent people around, no matter how many there are. Our informants have identified Owen's assailants. We have information that they will both be in a loyalist bar in Belfast tonight."

A smile came across Flynn's face as he squeezed the trigger on the machine pistol in one-second bursts. After blowing out the middle of the target, he sprayed the top and then the bottom with prolonged sweeps until the weapon ran out of ammunition. "I appreciate the assignment Eamon. Who are the targets?"

Flynn's tone was in a very eerie, yet businesslike manner. "Both, we believe, are members of the Ulster Volunteer Force. Both are in their early twenties and neither is married," Quinn would explain, although he knew Flynn considered them to be legitimate targets and therefore was uninterested in their marital status.

"Our informant tells us they will be at a pub on Shankill Road during the early evening tonight. I'm sure I don't have to remind you to be extremely careful, you'll be in their neck of the woods."

Quinn handed the hitman two photos. "This is Noel Hughes, and this is Martin Lynch."

Quinn held the photos tightly as Flynn tried to take them, delaying the exchange momentarily to get Flynn's full attention. Their eyes met. "And remember, Gerald, our goal is to only eliminate the two of them unless it becomes absolutely necessary. If your safety is threatened, your escape is jeopardized, or someone tries to interfere then you do what you have to. If all goes well, just Hughes and Lynch. Is that understood?"

Quinn wanted to drive this point home as Flynn could sometimes take matters into his own hands.

Flynn looked back down at the pictures and studied them without blinking an eye. The photos were of two men with the faces of young boys. They were clean-shaven with almost a hint of innocence to them. Flynn did not see this. All he saw were two soldiers from the enemy who had wounded one of his own. The look in Flynn's eyes as he stared at his potential victims would instill fear in the hearts of anyone who would look in his direction. "Gerald, Gerald...Gerald, are you listening?" barked Quinn.

"Aye, I'm listening; just Hughes and Lynch."

"Good. You need to listen to everything I'm telling you very carefully or may not make it back. You are too important to us to get yourself killed or caught because you let your emotions get in the way of your job. Declan will be waiting for you in the get-away car along with Owen. They'll be waiting on the far side of the alleyway in the back of the bar. You take care of your end and Owen will take care of his end."

Flynn considered this for a moment. Since Owen was in a cast up to his thigh, he was obviously a liability, but if Eamon wanted him to go along there would certainly be a bombing as well, deducted the assassin. Flynn decided not to let his mind wander. His job was the hit and that's all he was going to be concerned with.

He loaded the machine-gun and then the extra magazine. He put the extra clip in the left-hand pocket of his field jacket. He then checked to make sure his nine-millimeter backup was fully loaded. After assuring himself it was, he tucked it back into his waistband where over the years it was practically a fixture. He then took an old shoelace from a boot that was lying around the barn. He tied one end to the front of the Tech- 9 and the other to the back making a makeshift sling.

It was shortly after seven-thirty that evening when the carefully laid plan began to unfold. Flynn and Owen Dunn were in the Toyota while Declan McKee followed behind in the getaway auto. They drove through the heart of Protestant Belfast in the town of Shankill. Less than ten percent of the population in this area was Catholic and the I.R.A. men knew if they were to be caught by the wrong people they would be killed on the scene.

Flynn parked the Toyota in front of the bar, while McKee drove to the end of the block making a right turn. Flynn adjusted the zipper on his jacket, making sure the machine pistol which hung from his shoulder was undetectable. Dunn remained inside the auto while Flynn entered the bar.

Flynn walked straight to the bar and ordered a pint of Guinness. He studied the bar. It was smaller than most he'd been in. There was a vestibule in the front of the bar used as a coatroom. There were only about a dozen or so stools at the bar which was fully enclosed. The back room had eight square tables and a dartboard hanging on the wall. The bar was dimly lit with about thirty patrons. It took Flynn less than a minute to identify two men at the end of the bar as his targets. As he drank his Guinness, he had even overheard them boasting about the job they had done. Flynn's blood began to boil but he cautioned himself to remain calm. The anger in his eyes was again visible as he stared coldly at his targets. The bartender studied Flynn. "Is everything all right, lad?"

The query broke Flynn's trance.

"Everything is just wonderful, it is," Flynn replied in a very chilling manner. "And getting better by the minute, I might add."

Noel Hughes and Martin Lynch hadn't even noticed the man who was about to end their lives walk in the bar. The men had been in the bar for over two hours now and had been drinking rather heavily. They were talking about the way that Owen Dunn had squealed like a pig when they blew his kneecap apart. They reflected on how he was begging for them not to kneecap him. The laughter grew louder as they picked up their beers in a mock toast. "Here's to the I.R.A."

Lynch raised his glass above his head. "You know what I.R.A. stands for don't ya, Noel? It stands for I Ran Away."

In his inebriated state, he almost fell off his barstool laughing. "That fucker from the other night won't be running for a long time, now will he?"

It was at this time that Lynch first felt Flynn's cold eyes meet his. He elbowed Hughes and motioned to Flynn. "Hey mate, can I help ya with something?" asked Lynch arrogantly.

Flynn calmly shook his head and raised his hands submissively. "No. No problems pal." He put his unfinished stout down on the bar and made his way out the door.

"Who the fuck was that?" Hughes wondered out loud.

Shrugging his shoulders, Lynch replied, "I don't know. I've never seen him before." The two men watched Gerald Flynn walk out of the bar and got back to their conversation never giving him another thought.

Owen Dunn was still seated in the passenger seat of the Toyota when he saw Flynn emerge from the pub. He watched as Flynn gave him the thumbs-up signal before disappearing back into the pub. Dunn reached into the backseat of the auto and grabbed the black suitcase. It took both of his hands to lift the heavy suitcase into the front seat. He looked around before opening it and exposing the fifty-pound gelignite bomb he had put together this afternoon. Dunn set the timer to eight forty-seven, which was exactly a half-hour from now. Dunn then zippered the suitcase closed and placed it on the driver's side floor of the vehicle. Dunn exited the vehicle and walked to the rendezvous point where De-

MR. GEORGE P. NORRIS

clan would be waiting.

The fifty pounds of gelignite would be plenty to totally disintegrate any clue that the Toyota had ever existed, figured Dunn. Even the best Detectives wouldn't be able to piece it back together and find out the vehicle had been stolen from New York City, especially since every VIN plate had been removed already. Dunn figured that his end of the assignment was complete, as he got into the getaway car. He only prayed Flynn's part would go as smoothly.

Flynn walked back into the bar's vestibule, giving Owen Dunn about five minutes to complete his task and walk back to the car. Flynn took out a ski mask from the right pocket of his field jacket and placed it on his head making sure to tuck his long hair under the mask. He unzipped his jacket, exposing the Tec-9 machine pistol. He took the gun in his hand and walked into the doorway of the pub. His entrance went unnoticed by the crowd until he let go a short burst of machine-gun fire into the pub's ceiling. Then another into the mirror behind the bar sending shards of glass from the mirror and assorted liquor bottles, flying throughout the bar.

There was an instant outburst of panicked screams as the patrons in the bar scattered for cover. The bartender immediately hit the floor, avoiding any confrontation with the masked gunman. Flynn fixed his eyes in on Noel Hughes and Martin Lynch. The men sat frozen in their barstools.

"Noel Hughes, Martin Lynch, I assassinate you in

the name of the Irish Republican Army!" announced Flynn as he leveled the machine pistol in their direction.

The spray of bullets ripped through Noel Hughes' upper torso striking him four times. He had been killed instantly, tumbling backward to the ground. Martin Lynch ran from the bar area, dropping the pint of beer he had been drinking. Lynch frantically reached for the nine-millimeter handgun which was in his waistband when the first shots hit him. He had been struck numerous times in the legs. The pain was too much for him, as his attention was drawn from the gun in his waistband. Lynch lay incapacitated on the floor, looking up at the masked gunman.

The wounded man shook his head vehemently and put his hands out in front of his face. "Please. No. I'll do anything you want." Flynn walked menacingly toward the helpless man, being careful to step over Hughes' motionless body.

"So, who's the squealing pig now Martin? Stop beggin' and die like a soldier."

Flynn quickly scanned the bar making sure there were no heroes among the crowd. Then he squeezed off another short burst of machine-gun fire right into Lynch's head, blowing off part of his skull. Flynn enjoyed killing but this particular assignment had been uncommonly enjoyable for him. Hearing the men laugh and mock Owen and the rest of the I.R.A., as a whole, had incensed him.

Flynn knew he should have killed him straight

away instead of wasting time by torturing him first. The truth is, he didn't care. He savored every moment of watching Lynch suffer and plead for his life. Flynn knew there was no way Eamon would find out. And even if he did, the look on Lynch's face as he was pleading for his life would be well worth the chastising Eamon would give him.

Flynn dropped to one knee and surveyed the rest of the pub. Not seeing any problems, he let one last long burst of fire into the ceiling, deterring anyone from following him. Flynn quickly got to his feet and made a right hand-turn as he left the pub. He ran to the end of the block and around to the alleyway behind the pub. He ran across the alley to the other end where McKee had started the getaway car as soon as he heard the gunfire erupt. Flynn got in the backseat of the car and removed the ski mask from his face. They headed toward Westlink Road, driving at an even pace; making sure not to draw any attention to themselves.

"How'd it go, Gerald?" a concerned Declan McKee inquired.

"No problems Dec."

Owen Dunn, who had suffered a great deal of pain at the men's hands needed to be sure. "So, you got them both, then, did you, Gerry? Dead that is?"

Flynn shot his friend a smile. "Aye, Owen. I did."

It took less than fifteen minutes for the Northern Irish police to arrive on the scene, evacuate the occupants of the bar to the parking lot where they could be interviewed, and set up the bar as a crime scene. The two dead bodies remained undisturbed where they fell. The handgun lying next to Lynch's body was covered in blood.

Inspector Ian Walsh examined the scene. Walsh was a thirty-one-year veteran of the police department and was no stranger to crime scenes in Northern Ireland. He was careful not to step on what appeared to be dozens of shell casings. He could see brain matter and parts of a skull sprayed about. It was one of the more brutal scenes he had witnessed in a while. He ordered everyone, including his own men to stay out of the bar. He wanted the scene to remain intact until the forensic team could conduct their investigation.

He exited the bar into the parking lot where dozens of witnesses were being detained. Most of whom were young men and women in their twenties and thirties who had been patrons of the bar. Some were being treated by medical units on the scene for minor injuries sustained from flying glass or hitting their heads as they ducked for cover. *Thankfully, nobody else had been struck by gunfire*, thought Walsh. Others were from the restaurant next store or another bar up the block.

Witness accounts varied as to the height and weight of the killer. They all agreed, he wore a mask and announced the shooting was on behalf of the I.R.A. before murdering the two men. None of them had mentioned the long-haired young man who had left the bar just moments before until a uniformed officer called out to the Inspector.

Inspector Walsh walked over to the officer who introduced him to Brendan Crawford. "This is Mr. Crawford. He was bartending at the time of the shooting," the officer had explained to Walsh. "He said there was a guy in there just before the shooting that didn't seem right to him."

Walsh studied the bartender for a moment, noticing the trickle of blood from his forehead. "Would you be able to describe him for me?" asked Walsh of the bartender.

"Sure, I would." Crawford began giving his description when Walsh interrupted him.

"Pardon me for one second."

Walsh turned to the uniformed officer. He directed the officer to take down the license plate of every vehicle parked in the parking lot where they stood. It would be the last order Ian Walsh would ever give.

Declan McKee drove from the scene slowly and inconspicuously. They were about five minutes away from the safe house when they heard the explosion. If Eamon's plans had been as precise as they usually were, all of the patrons of the pub would be standing outside being interviewed by the local authorities when the bomb detonated. There was an excellent chance the bomb would kill many at the scene, but they would have to wait and watch the news to find out for sure.

Eamon Quinn was able to hear the explosion in the distance from somewhere in Derry City. The bomb had certainly been a powerful one, he thought. Quinn picked up the receiver of the payphone and dialed a number. When a voice answered at the other end of the line, Eamon spoke. "I call to claim responsibility for the assassination of two Unionist soldiers as well as the bombing outside the Shankill Pub earlier this evening in the name of the Irish Republican Army. Britain and her subjects should remain ill at ease until our country is no longer occupied by hostile forces."

Quinn hung up the receiver and took a pack of cigarettes out of his coat pocket. He opened the pack, pulling a cigarette out with his teeth. He lit the cigarette and took a long satisfying drag, enjoying the night's accomplishments.

Eamon Quinn drove his soldier to the airport early the next morning. They listened to the radio's accounts of the incident. The radio reported the bomb had killed an additional five people to the two men slain inside the bar including two Police Officers: one, a thirty-one-year veteran. Another dozen were injured. Flynn was disappointed. "How could a bomb of that magnitude only kill five people?"

"It's not all about killing, Gerald. It's about sending a message and believe me a message was sent. It was a complete success," Quinn explained.

Flynn closed his eyes and reclined while Quinn

drove. Almost out of habit, Flynn's hand reached down to his waistband to check on his gun before he realized it wasn't there. "I feel weird without me gun."

"Don't worry Gerald. Once you make your contact in the states with Dan O'Brien, he'll help you get a gun. Dan is a good man. He is very loyal to the cause. He was our best bomb man years ago, even better than Declan. Unfortunately, the Brits started to suspect Dan and we felt it would be best to send him away for a little while. Once he got to the other side, his services became too valuable to bring him back. Gerald, if there is anything you need when you're over there, Dan can get it for you."

"The only thing I'll be wantin' is to complete the bloody assignment and come home."

Eamon Quinn wished Flynn the best of luck as they arrived at the airport. Gerald Flynn opened his wallet and examined its contents. All of the counterfeit identification looked in order. He double-checked to make sure he hadn't taken any of his real identification with him by accident. *Sean Murphy...* he could live with that name for a few weeks or so if that's what was necessary.

Flynn looked forward to the long flight to JFK Airport in New York. He hoped he could catch up on the sleep he had not gotten the night before. He was a little bit nervous and excited about his mission in New York. If there was one thing Gerald Flynn could count on, it is that this trip was going to be exciting, no matter how it turned out.

CHAPTER 8

February 27 was a relatively mild day compared to the last few weeks. The warm sun was melting the last traces of snow that had fallen earlier in the week. It was about twenty minutes before ten am when Police Officers Laura Reed and Kenneth Williams arrived at the department's Internal Affairs Bureau. They had stopped on the way over to pick up their morning coffee and a couple of newspapers.

Cops would always bring the newspaper or a book when they had to go to a departmental hearing or a court case. It would help them kill time while they waited for their case to be called. They walked into the office of Internal Affairs and saw the Police Administrative Aide, which was the department's official title for a secretary or clerical person, seated next to the sign-in log.

They signed in the log at 0945 hours and informed the P.A.A. they had an appointment with Detective Castillo, at ten hundred hours. The P.A.A. instructed them to have a seat and wait to be called. The officers went into the waiting area where nearly a dozen other cops were already seated. It was a typical type of waiting room by police department standards. A couple of dozen blue cloth chairs against the walls, many of which were littered with discarded newspapers. There were a couple of small end tables and a water cooler in the corner. In the middle of the room was a coffee table that had been collecting newspapers for weeks it seemed. After seeing there were so many other cops there ahead of them, Laura Reed commented, "I hope we're not down here all day."

Williams explained to her that most, if not all of the people there, were probably there for other investigators and had nothing to do with their case. "Most of the time it only takes a couple of hours and it's back to the precinct. You'll see."

Williams looked around the room for any familiar faces to catch up on old times with. Most of the cops in the room sat patiently reading their newspapers, books or doing a crossword puzzle. There was one young cop, however, that caught William's attention. He was obviously a rookie, Williams thought. He was biting his fingernails while nervously pacing the floor. Williams wondered why he was down here but then figured it couldn't have been anything too serious.

Over his ten years on the job, it was Williams' experience that if you did anything real serious, I.A.B. wouldn't call you in for a hearing. They would come to your precinct; have you brought in off patrol and arrest you. Williams had been to I.A.B. about a half dozen times over his career and every time it was because of nonsense. Usually, allegations someone had made against him after an arrest, or a traffic summons was issued. Other times a simple misunderstanding, such as an arrestee would accuse the officer of having stolen his money only to find out that the officer had *vouchered* it for safekeeping. He wondered what the allegation was this time.

Laura Reed studied her environment. She told her partner she had to use the ladies' room as an excuse to more closely investigate her surroundings. She got up and walked down the hall turning left at the end of the hall. She saw several Internal Affairs investigators walking the hall with their identification cards clipped to their shirt pockets. She wondered if any of them were Detective Castillo.

She felt slightly uneasy about having been called down to I.A.B. In her five years as a Police Officer, this was the first time. She knew she hadn't done anything wrong, but until this was all over, she figured to be a little nervous. Reed peeked into an interview room as an interview was being conducted. She saw two investigators questioning a cop who was sitting with his union-appointed lawyer. Police Officers always had their union supply them with legal representation whenever an allegation of any kind was made against them and an official department investigation was being conducted. Reed thought it was kind of unnecessary to have a lawyer if there was no allegation of criminal wrongdoing, but it was for her own best interests, she realized.

She continued to walk down the hall peering

into interview rooms where she saw many cops discussing the allegations made against them with their lawyer. She decided to go back to her partner in case their lawyer had shown up, at least then she could find out why they were there. Reed immediately recognized the look of annoyance on her partner's face. "What's wrong Ken?"

"I asked the P.A.A. if our representation had arrived yet and she told me that she had been informed by Detective Castillo that we didn't need a lawyer and the prick called the union to cancel him. I'll tell you right now, Laura, I'm not answering any questions regarding any allegation, no matter how minor, without a lawyer present. He's going to either wait for our lawyer to get here or reschedule this for another day."

Reed felt even more nervous now, but she relied on the instincts of her partner. She had always looked up to him and decided that he is very knowledgeable about the inner workings of the department. She would let his time on the job and experiences make the call and she would follow his lead.

"Whatever you think is best Ken, I'm with you."

Williams gave his partner a wink and a smile. "All right kid, let's just see what the hell all of this is about when he calls us in, but I am telling you right now, we should grab a lawyer when he comes out of another interview to represent us."

The P.A.A. called out to them at half-past ten. "Officers Reed and Williams, Detective Castillo will see you now in interview room three."

Reed and Williams walked down the hall, along with the union lawyer they had secured when he was finished representing an officer on a different case. They found interview room three and knocked on the door. The voice on the other side of the door invited them in.

Louis Castillo was seated behind a desk, wearing a powder blue shirt with a floral print tie. He was very annoyed to see the officers show up with representation. He wanted to keep this interview as low-key as possible. He quickly assessed these officers were not going to be easily fooled and he needed to proceed with caution.

William's attention was immediately caught by the tape recorder on the desk next to Castillo. He knew every interview room in I.A.B. had tape recorders since all official investigations were recorded, but he wanted to make sure the one next to Castillo was not on. Kenneth Williams was very suspicious of his surroundings.

He had a strange feeling this was not going to be a typical I.A.B. investigation. He observed that the tape recorder was not on and he wondered if anybody else was going to sit in on the interview. A Police Officer was required to answer any question narrowly related to his duties that a supervisory officer asked him. A Detective, however, was not a supervisory officer. Williams read Castillo's I.D. card which was clipped to his pocket to make sure he was in fact a Detective and not a ranking officer. Castillo got up from behind his desk and extended his right hand. "Hi, I'm Louie Castillo."

Williams apprehensively took his hand followed by Reed.

"Have a seat," directed Castillo, as the officers pulled up chairs to his desk. "Ms. Thompson, my P.A.A. told me you were upset I took the liberty to cancel your lawyer...who you brought anyway," acknowledging the lawyer with a grin.

"Let me just fill you in on why I brought you guys down here. You are not the subject of any allegation of any kind so a lawyer wasn't necessary," Castillo explained, hoping they would believe him.

"Although I am assigned to Internal Affairs, I actually work for a detail within I.A.B. that investigates robberies in which the perpetrator identifies themself as a cop to gain his victim's trust. It's called the Police Impersonation Unit. So, you see, you have no reason to be apprehensive to talk to me. I don't work on anything other than robberies."

Reed felt relieved, she knew that anytime someone impersonated a Police Officer, the Internal Affairs Bureau had to be notified. Castillo was obviously one of the Detectives who caught such cases. It made sense to her.

Williams was still a bit skeptical. "So, what does that have to do with us?"

"I was just getting to that. There is a case I've been working on for a few weeks now. It's a robbery pattern involving one male white, perp in his forties, identifying himself as a cop and forcing his way into homes. He handcuffs the victims and ransacks the house. In one of the robberies, the perp was seen fleeing in a blue Toyota Camry with New York plates. I ran a check on the plate through the *Finest* computer system to see if it had been used in any other crimes and I saw you two handled a job with the same vehicle. I think it came over as an auto stripping and the guy had a gun in a gym bag. In my robbery pattern, the guy carries the handcuffs he uses during the robberies in a gym bag. I was wondering if you guys saw a gym bag or remember anything that can help me with my case. I'd really appreciate it and believe me if I break the case from any information you supply me with, I'll write a letter of appreciation to your commanding officer."

Laura Reed, who was eager to help, jumped in. "I remember the job and he did have a gym bag but all he had in there was a newspaper. I looked through it pretty well because that's where the gun was supposed to be. We stopped looking because he identified himself as a cop. He had a real enough looking shield and I.D. card too."

Williams gave his partner a slight kick under the table telling her to shut her mouth. She turned red almost instantly and could feel her face go flush. She wondered why Ken had shut her up and if she said something she shouldn't have. Castillo sensed Reed's embarrassment and tried to put her at ease.

"There's no reason to be embarrassed. This guy, from what I gather, has a stolen Lieutenant's shield and a real-looking I.D. card as well. He could've fooled anybody. What else can you tell me about this guy?"

Castillo studied the officer's facial expressions for a clue as to whether or not they believed his story. He was confident Reed did but a bit skeptical on Williams.

Williams slapped his knee. "Oh, man!" He pointed at Castillo. "You know what. Now that you mention it, Laura and I handled a robbery on Vestry Street a couple of weeks ago where the guy impersonated a cop. The perp was a male white in that robbery. Was that robbery part of your pattern?"

Castillo tried not to look too excited. It was his good fortune that the radio car team had handled a similar robbery to the pattern he had fabricated. "Yes. That was the first one he did," replied Castillo. "It's extremely important if you can remember anything about him. What name did he give you or where did he say he worked? Anything at all?"

Williams jumped in before his partner could answer and hoped she would follow his lead. "I can't for the life of me remember the name he gave us. Can you Laura?" He gave her a gentle nudge under the table.

"No, I really can't."

"Do either of you remember where he said he

worked? It could be very important in the case." Castillo grew frustrated.

Reed shook her head. "I can't remember."

"Neither can I, sorry," Williams added.

"Well, I'm sure you must've put the information in your memo books. Can you see if you have anything that may help my case in there?"

Both officers perused their memo books even though they knew they didn't have any information about the job other than the job itself and the disposition. Williams looked over at his partner's memo book and again down at his own. He looked up at Castillo. "Sorry, we only have the job in there, not any of the details."

Castillo's frustration became visible. His face began to redden. "Don't you know you're supposed to put details of all of the jobs that you handle in your memo books?"

Williams, indifferent to Castillo's anger shot back. "'Whoa, you're starting to sound more like a member of the rat squad all of the sudden. So, what are you going to do, write me up for improper memo book entries? You better get a boss in here for that, *Detective*."

Castillo realized he did exactly what he was trying to avoid; sound like an I.A.B. cop instead of a robbery Detective. He was, however, upset because if they would've made memo book entries in their books or been able to remember his name, they would have been able to corroborate his story when he finally nailed Keegan. Even if they didn't want to testify or said on the stand, they couldn't recall any details, their memo books are legal documents and could be used as such, in a court of law.

Castillo had to think of something quick to cover his tracks. "I'm sorry for snapping. It's just that I know you're supposed to do a *Stop Question and Frisk* report when you stop someone on the street and if you had done it, it could have helped me to nail this scumbag before he hurts somebody."

Williams wasn't convinced by Castillo's story and continued to stonewall him. "I'm really sorry. I thought he was a cop, so I didn't bother to make the report out. Is there anything else we can help you with?"

"There is just one other thing I wanted to ask you. What was he doing under the hood of the car when you guys first pulled up?"

"He was tightening a loose alternator belt as far as I could tell."

"Officer Reed is there anything you can add?"

Reed was a bit confused but followed along. "No. I'm afraid not."

Castillo handed them each a business card and asked them to give him a call if they remembered anything else. He watched the two officers as they left his office. He was very upset the officers were unable to assist in his investigation. At least they bought his story, thought Castillo, in case he had to talk to them again. If nothing else, they would corroborate that someone, who they identified as a cop, was at the location on the night in question.

Castillo looked down at his watch, it was almost noon. He would go to meal for an hour, wait for his paycheck to arrive at three, and go home. Tonight would be the first time in almost a month that he wouldn't be following Keegan home. Keegan hadn't been to the bar for almost a month now and it seemed unlikely he'd go tonight since he was only working until four.

Being in Internal Affairs, it was very easy to obtain Keegan's work schedule. Every Detective Squad in the department had to fax over a copy of their personnel's schedule a week in advance. He looked down at it and saw Keegan was working a four to twelve tomorrow. It seemed much more likely for Keegan to go to the bar after a four to midnight shift than it would be after a day tour. Castillo would do a six pm until two am tomorrow night and follow Keegan home to see if he stops off somewhere along the way.

The officers thanked their lawyer, who, as it turned out was not necessary, and headed back to their command. "Would you mind filling me in on what was going on in there? I don't remember handling any robbery where the perp identified himself as a cop."

Williams nodded his head, slightly annoyed. "That's because we didn't handle anything like that. I made it up to see if Castillo was legit or if he was a rat. Guess what...he's a rat!"

"How can you be so sure?"

"C'mon, Laura, use common sense. He fell for my trap about the fake job saying it was part of his pattern. When we get back to the command let's look at the current robbery patterns. If there is a police impersonation one that matches that Lieutenant's description, lunch is on me. He asked us what he was doing under the hood of the car. How would he know that when we arrived on the scene, the guy was under the hood of the car unless he had been watching the guy...and us? And finally, that guy is no mutt. We both recognized him as that Lieutenant from the Terrorist Task Force."

"Holy shit, you're right Ken. I had forgotten about that."

"Castillo, the rat bastard, must be working some sort of a case on the Lieutenant and he thought we might be able to unwittingly help him. He seemed very concerned about the gym bag. What was really in it?"

"I told Castillo the truth, a newspaper. What was the Lieutenant's name anyway, I can't seem to remember?"

"Offhand, I can't remember either, but I'll find out. What should we get for lunch? I'm starving."

Williams and Reed got back to their precinct after one o'clock. After checking in with the Desk Sergeant, they went into the Anti-Crime office where the Stop and Frisk log is maintained. Williams browsed through the reports until he got to the one, he had filled out on January 15th. It was on the West Side Highway and Hubert Street. The name of the person who was stopped was James Keegan. "I thought you told Castillo you didn't do a *Stop, Question, and Frisk* report on him?"

Williams looked up at his partner. He was smug. "Gee, did I forget to tell that rat that I made the *UF250* out? I feel horrible."

Williams picked up the telephone and dialed the number for the interdepartmental telephone directory. "Good afternoon, could I please have the number to the Joint Terrorist Task Force?"

He jotted the number down on a piece of paper and hung up the phone.

Reed seemed suspicious of her partner's actions. "What are you doing now?"

"I'm giving Keegan a head's up. He should know he's being watched."

"Maybe you shouldn't do that. If they have a case on him, he could be involved with something bad."

"Laura, I can't believe you're talking like this. That man is not just a hero to the department. He is a hero to the nation. Castillo is just some *cheese eater*, trying to make a name for himself. And what better way to do it than by digging up dirt on a member of the service who is that well known and highly regarded. He probably envisions himself as a modern-day Serpico or some shit like that. Fuck Castillo! He probably thinks Keegan is messing with the prostitutes like you originally said or something equally ridiculous."

Laura Reed considered her partner's theory. "I guess you're right."

The telephone rang in Keegan's office. He was hoping it was Kate so he could tell her he wasn't going to be home right away tonight. Keegan answered the phone. "Joint Terrorist Task Force, Lieutenant Keegan speaking, can I help you?"

"Lieutenant Keegan, this is a friend," began the voice. "'I just want you to know there's a rat named Castillo watching you. He is a Detective in I.A.B. He was watching you over by pier twenty-six last month. Watch your back, Lieu."

The line then went dead.

"Thank you," Keegan mumbled under his breath as he hung up the receiver.

He felt a sudden queasiness come over his stomach. *Who was this Castillo and how much could he possibly know?* If Castillo was watching him down by the pier what could he have seen? The only way Castillo could have him is if he impounded the car. Keegan broke out in a cold sweat when contemplating the thought that Castillo could possibly have the car. Then he reasoned to himself that if Castillo did have the car, Dan would have let him know that something went wrong. For the first time since his involvement with the Irish Republican Army, Keegan had a genuine fear that he could lose his job, his freedom, and his family. For the rest of the day, Keegan was unable to concentrate on work.

He flipped through the pages of the newspaper not reading any of the articles until one article caught his attention.

I.R.A. Bomb Kills Five; Gunman
Kills Two Others in Belfast Bar

The story, which was reported by the Associated Press, went on to detail how a masked gunman walked into a bar in a Protestant section of Belfast and opened fire with a machine-gun killing two Protestant men. The men were said to have ties with the outlawed Ulster Volunteer Force. After the bar had been evacuated and police arrived on the scene to conduct their investigation, a powerful car bomb was detonated killing an additional five people and injuring thirteen others. Two of those killed, reported the story, were Police Officers. Reading about fellow Police Officers dying struck a nerve with Keegan. He wondered if there would ever be peace in the land of his ancestors. He also wondered for the first time, if what he was doing was in any way helping to attain peace or just adding fuel to an already out of control fire.

Either way, tonight was the last Thursday in February. He wasn't too concerned by this fact. Throughout the many years that he had gone to McBride's, O'Brien had never asked him to do anything two months in a row. Keegan figured his work was done until about April or May at the earliest. Maybe they wouldn't even call on him again for six or seven months. He found some comfort in the thought that he wouldn't have to do anything for a while. This way, if Castillo was watching him, he wouldn't be doing anything wrong, and by the time his services were needed again, Castillo will have lost all interest in James Keegan.

"Hello," Kate Keegan answered as she picked up the telephone on the third ring.

"Hi sweetie it's me," Keegan began; knowing what he had to tell her was going to upset her.

"Oh, hi Jim. What time will you be home?"

"Well, that's why I'm calling, hon."

"Jim, please don't tell me you're stuck with overtime. I told you our friends were coming over to play cards tonight. We've had these plans for weeks."

"I know Kate, I'm sorry. We just got a lead on a big case and we have to stake out a warehouse in Queens," Keegan lied. "I'll make it up to you, I promise. We'll go out to dinner Saturday night, just the two of us. I'll ask my mother to watch the kids."

"Jim, can't you get out of the stakeout tonight? I don't want to go to dinner Saturday, I want you home tonight. I thought I was done making excuses for why you have to break plans with our family and friends all of the time."

"Please Kate; don't give me a hard time. If it was my choice, I'd be on my way home right now. You know that."

That was the truth. After the recent events, the last thing Keegan wanted to do was to associate with Dan O'Brien and the I.R.A. He would be extra careful tonight to make sure he is not being followed.

"Okay, hon. Just be careful. I love you."

"I love you too Kate." He hung up the telephone.

After staying back at his command for a few hours to catch up on paperwork, he left for the night. Keegan walked down Third Avenue towards McBride's remembering how cold it had been the last time he was there. The upper thirties were a welcomed relief as far as he was concerned. He walked about halfway down the block from Forty-Third Street when he stopped and leaned against a storefront. He was watching the corner of Forty-Third Street to see if anyone would turn the corner that might have been following him. He stood patiently in the doorway of a store for over ten minutes until he was satisfied, he wasn't being followed. He then continued on his way to McBride's.

Once inside, he made his way across the bar to sit in his usual seat on the far end of the bar. He studied every patron to walk in the door trying to figure out if any of them could be Castillo. He sized up most of the crowd. It was made up of quite a few couples, some older gentlemen, many of the regulars he had come to know, and a couple of younger guys and girls. There was nobody there alone and nobody that fit the mold of an internal affairs cop. Still, he did not want to let his guard down. He would try to keep his interactions with Dan to a minimum tonight.

Dan O'Brien put a pint of Guinness down in front of Keegan and walked away. Keegan shouted across the bar. "Thank ya, Daniel."

Tonight's crowd was much livelier than the last time he was here. In the half-hour since entering the bar, the crowd filled in nicely. It was a much larger crowd than he had seen in there all winter. Tommy McDermott was singing his heart out as many clapped along. Keegan was looking around the crowd trying to spot Nora. After he was unable to find her, he decided she was either on a break or she didn't work there anymore. He hoped she was only on a break.

Keegan started on his second Guinness of the night when O'Brien finally engaged him. "How goes it, Jim?"

"Dan, were there any problems on the other side with the last delivery?"

"No. Everything went just right. Perfectly I might even say. I heard you had a little problem with your own people, but you handled it just fine."

"You know Dan; I'm not sure how much longer I can keep this up."

Keegan decided this was as good a time as any to feel the bartender out. "I got an anonymous phone call this afternoon to warn me Internal Affairs was watching me. I can't get too deeply involved where I'm going to put my family at risk. If I ever lost my job or went to prison, how would my family survive?"

O'Brien became slightly annoyed. "There are too many of our men in the H-blocks of Long Kesh back home who also have families Jim. We are fighting a war, and sometimes people have to make sacrifices for the cause of freedom."

O'Brien actually felt for Keegan. This wasn't his war, but he was too valuable to the cause, especially tonight, to let him just walk away.

O'Brien's words hung there, and Keegan thought about them. *'To make sacrifices for the cause.'* He had heard O'Brien's speech before. It was over fifteen years ago when he first became involved. He had been a beat cop in the precinct, and he would come into the bar a couple of times a week after a four to midnight shift. He had become friendly with a young Dan O'Brien and loved to listen to his stories of the I.R.A., unaware that O'Brien's stories were a firsthand account. It had become a routine for Keegan to close the bar at least once a week with O'Brien. Keegan was infuriated by the stories of the English domination of his people.

It had been one night after four am when Keegan was voicing his opinion on the English occupation of Northern Ireland. O'Brien, sensing that Keegan had a little more to drink than he should have, seized the moment. "We can all do our part for the cause, ya know Jim," said O'Brien leading Keegan on.

"The cause?"

"Yes, the cause of a free and united Ireland. And you can do your part to help win Ireland her freedom."

Keegan seemed to sober up almost instantly. He was intrigued to see where O'Brien was going with the conversation. The idea of being involved with fighting for Ireland's freedom was a romantic notion to Keegan. "What could I possibly do to help?"

"Well, you are a policeman, are you not Jim? Therefore, you can easily buy guns without anybody questioning you. Leave the rest up to me to get them over to our men."

Keegan realized for the first time that not only was O'Brien dead serious, but he was also an active member of the I.R.A. "Yes Dan, I am a Police Officer, but that's even more of a reason I could never do anything like that. I'm sworn to uphold the law and you're asking me to break it by running guns to terrorists."

"Terrorists, is it Jim?   Terrorists?" O'Brien snapped at Keegan. "Being dragged out of your bed at three am, by armed soldiers and thrown in a prison cell for a week without just cause, that's terrorism. Having soldiers in tanks patrolling the streets of your city and beating you up as you walk home, that's terrorism. Having the soldiers fire plastic bullets into a crowd at a civil rights march, that's terrorism. The I.R.A. are not terrorists, they are freedom fighters. They are an army who by anyone's standards, is well outgunned and outmanned by the occupying forces. They are forced to fight an underground war because that's the only type of war they stand a chance of winning.

I'm sorry I even brought it up. I should've known you were just another goddamned pretend patriot. You'll come into a bar, sing the rebel songs and talk about the troubles as long as there's no risk to you. You've never seen your own ma or pa thrown in jail or brutalized for no reason. You've never had a loved one gunned down in front of ya. Me own da was gunned down in front of me when I was a lad. That is everyday life over there in occupied Ireland...to you, it's a storybook." O'Brien paused momentarily for effect.

"It doesn't matter to you how many Irishmen are beaten and thrown in prison each year for no reason. It doesn't matter that the Irish Catholics are treated like second-class citizens and can't even get an honest job in their own country. As long as you're here in America with a job and freedom, it doesn't matter what plight your people suffer."

He shot Keegan a look of disgust. O' Brien was a powerful and influential orator and had made Keegan almost feel ashamed. The set of circumstances after that wasn't so clear to Keegan anymore but it was shortly after that night, that he had begun to run guns for the I.R.A. He remembers how he had decided to quit after marrying Kate and then again when the kids were born but for some reason he never did.

"Don't get so upset Dan, all I'm saying is that maybe you can slowly cut me out and replace me with somebody else. I'll still be around if you need me for something really important and you can't get anybody else to do it. You have my beeper number to get in touch with me if you need me any time day or night. You know how loyal I have always been."

He hoped O'Brien would agree. There was no reason to think he wouldn't.

O'Brien decided to test him. "If it's important enough, you don't mind though?"

Keegan felt as if maybe he was swaying O'Brien to see his point of view and agreed. "No. Of course not. If something comes up that is that important, I'd be glad to do my part."

He realized this was his chance. It had not been as bad as he thought. O'Brien seemed to agree with him, and this could be his way out. He knew it would take time but just having O'Brien agree to back him out slowly, was a step in the right direction.

Dan O'Brien placed a hand on Keegan's left shoulder. "Good, I'm glad to hear that lad."

He pulled an envelope out of his pocket and slid it across the bar to Keegan.

Keegan's heart skipped a beat when he saw O'Brien retrieve the envelope. He hadn't expected it and was apprehensive to do anything after the phone call he received earlier in the day. This was unprecedented. He had never in all of the years running guns for the I.R.A, been asked to do so two months in a row.

They were generally very careful. They wanted to make sure if something went wrong, they would know about it, so they would not use the same personnel or methods again. Keegan immediately looked around the bar. His mouth went dry. He stared down at the envelope and downed his Guinness before picking it up. Once he was satisfied that he wasn't being watched, he quickly put the envelope in his pocket. "Haven't you listened to a word I've said, Dan?"

"And sure, I have, lad. You said if it was important enough you didn't mind, now didn't ya? Well let me assure ya now Jim, this is the most important assignment we've ever given ya. As a matter of fact, it's so important we need you back in here tomorrow night to personally deliver the property."

The importance of the mission was no conciliation to Keegan. He thought he had an opening to back out and now realized O'Brien had been setting him up the entire time; just as he had done to him in this very bar over fifteen years ago. Keegan felt trapped. "Deliver it in here? To whom?" demanded Keegan as he drained the last of his Guinness.

O'Brien gave Keegan a reassuring wink and a nod. "Everything you need to know is in the envelope, Jim. I will see you here tomorrow night." O'Brien placed another pint of Guinness down in front of Keegan."

"Make it a Jameson on the rocks." Keegan turned a little pale.

Dan O'Brien smiled ever so slightly as he poured out the Guinness, reached under the bar and grabbed the bottle of Jameson, and poured Keegan his drink. "You're not losing some of your nerve, are ya Jim?"

Keegan never answered and instead put the glass to his lips. After taking a sip, he opened the envelope and was careful not to let any of the money be seen. The order was for one Beretta nine-millimeter handgun and fifty rounds of ammunition. He looked up at O'Brien with a hint of suspicion in his eyes. "You said you want me to deliver this to somebody in here tomorrow?" He looked around, pulled O'Brien close, and whispered. "Why would somebody need a gun in the United States?"

"To further the cause lad, to further the cause. Why else?"

"To further the cause?" questioned Keegan. "This is America. What in the world could the I.R.A. need a gun here for? Dan, I've never questioned your judgment or instructions before, but I want to make absolutely certain it doesn't wind up in the wrong hands."

"Well, I assure you, James Keegan, this isn't the time to start questioning me," lectured O'Brien. "As a matter of fact, maybe if all goes well, we won't be in need of your services much longer."

O'Brien decided telling Keegan exactly what he wanted to hear would make this easier to swallow. Even if there was no truth to it whatsoever, this might stop him from asking too many questions.

"Really, Dan? That would be great. You understand it's not that I no longer want to help, I'm just afraid for my family's well-being."

It was true, he was worried about his family, but he was also afraid of losing his job. Keegan loved being a cop. It meant a great deal to him. The only thing he loved more than being a cop was in fact, his family.

"I understand. Let's see how things go first but

we may be able to cut you out shortly."

Keegan felt liberated. He stared down at the order as if it would tell him something. He then put it back in the envelope and put the envelope back in his pocket. Would this really be the last time he was needed? He believed it would be. If he could just get by tomorrow, he was home free. He would no longer have to worry about losing the job he loved so much or losing his family. He was extremely excited, although he knew he would have to be especially careful tomorrow. If he were to be caught giving somebody a gun his whole career would be over. It wouldn't matter if this was his last job for the I.R.A. or not. Keegan reached into his wallet and put twenty dollars on the bar. "Good night Dan. I'll be seeing ya tomorrow."

Keegan nodded goodbye to Tommy McDermott as he sang on stage and he confidently walked out the door.

He had mixed emotions as he walked out of the bar. He was elated that he would finally be done with his secret double life. The toll it had taken on his marriage was not yet beyond repair, but it was getting worse as time went by. But then there was the fear and apprehension. He knew he was being watched. The stakes, for him, were higher now than ever. But still, one more night. One more night of being careful and going undetected was all he needed. He prayed it would go off without a hitch.

O 'Brien felt bad about not being completely honest with Keegan, but it seemed like the best strategy at the time. Besides, he hadn't planned on using Keegan again for about six months or so anyway. Keegan would believe he was done until O'Brien would have to break the news to him that he was needed again. O'Brien felt this was the best course of action.

Keegan made his way through the Queens-Midtown Tunnel leaving Manhattan. His mind began to wonder about who Castillo was and who had made the phone call to warn him. Castillo had to be from Internal Affairs, but Keegan didn't have any friends there so who could have warned him. He was passing College Point Boulevard when he first noticed the headlights of the Grand Fury behind him. He became worried as he continually looked back in the rear-view mirror. He switched lanes waiting to see who was in the car.

He figured Castillo to be a Hispanic male from the surname and would see if the man in the car matched what he thought Castillo would look like. After changing lanes, he waited for the Grand Fury to pass but it did not. He slowed down but the car still wouldn't pass. He switched over to the right lane and exited the expressway at the Kissena Boulevard exit, waiting to see if the Grand Fury would follow. It did not. He waited in front of Queens College, but the Grand Fury never exited the expressway. He breathed a sigh of relief as he realized he was just being paranoid again. Keegan drove on the service road for miles before he got back on the Long Island Expressway at the Queens-Nassau border and headed home.

Arriving home shortly before eleven, the kids were fast asleep. He checked in on his children. Kevin and Timothy were sleeping comfortably in their bunk beds. Kerry was tossing and turning in her bed. He decided she must've been having a bad dream. He wondered what kind of bad dream a four-year-old could possibly have. He sat with her for a few moments and rubbed her back. "It's all right, sweetheart."

Keegan put his daughter's teddy bear on the bed next to her, Kerry hugged the stuffed animal and it seemed to comfort the child and she fell back into a sound sleep. He then undressed and got into bed next to Kate. Kate was deeply involved in a novel. She always read before going to sleep if time would allow. She looked up from her book long enough to acknowledge her husband and ask how his night went.

Keegan felt rejuvenated in the thoughts of putting his days of gun-running behind him. After tomorrow night, things would get back to normal forever. He would no longer have to lie to his wife. He'd done his part and putting it all behind him made him feel great. He lay next to Kate and stared at her, as she read. He reached his hand under Kate's nightshirt and began to gently caress her breasts. He kissed the nape of her neck until his touch broke her from her novel. She turned over and looked her husband in the eyes.

There was something there she hadn't seen in quite some time. There was a youthful sparkle in his eyes. Once their eyes met, he pressed his lips against hers and they kissed passionately. Kate ignored the beer on his breath. She knew he occasionally went out after work with the guys for a quick beer and she was okay with that. The kisses grew deeper and more passionate. After making love, Keegan rolled off his wife. She looked deeply into her husband's eyes as she played with the hair on his chest.

She looked up at him with a playful smile. "That was wonderful, Jim, you must've had a good night at work?"

"No, it was a pretty boring night, actually. I just love you so much and I appreciate you more than you will ever know. That's all."

Keegan could feel his eyes begin to well up.

Kate knew something had to summon up all the passion she had experienced tonight and whatever it was didn't seem to matter to her. Jim hadn't paid this much attention to her in some time, and she missed it. She missed the romance they once shared. She knew it was normal for the spark to go out of a relationship, but she also knew his job played a big part in it as well. It seemed for a time, he was never home and always at work instead. He would miss holidays, family functions, barbeques, the kid's birthdays and so much more. She knew he planned on retiring in the next few years and that is something she felt they could both look forward to.

"I love you too, Jim."

CHAPTER 9

Kate returned home from walking the kids to the bus stop shortly after nine am Jim had been sleeping soundly when she left. Hearing the upstairs shower running, she knew this was no longer the case. Kate went into the kitchen and decided to prepare an omelet for him. She listened carefully for the shower to stop. When it did, she figured to have about ten more minutes before Jim would come downstairs.

She knew his routine probably even better than he did. After his shower, he would always shave and get dressed immediately, even if he had no place to go. Kate put on the pot of coffee and figured if she timed it just right everything would be ready just as Jim walked down the stairs. It's a gorgeous day, thought Kate. She felt very energetic and was eager to surprise Jim, even if it was only by making him breakfast. Kate finished the omelet with a side of *Irish bangers* and put it in front of his seat at the walnut finished dining room table. She retrieved his mug, which bore the shield of an NYPD Lieutenant, and filled it with coffee. She set the morning newspaper down next to his breakfast and almost girlishly waited for him to come downstairs. Keegan walked down the stairs smelling the sausages. He looked over to his smiling wife. "To what do I owe this pleasure? A king's breakfast and it's not even my birthday."

"Let's just say I wanted to show you how much I love you."

She greeted him at the bottom of the stairs with a peck on the lips. Keegan enjoyed his breakfast as much as Kate had enjoyed making it for him. After breakfast, he called his mother up on the telephone and arranged for her to watch the kids the following night. "It's all settled." Keegan hung up the phone. "My mother is going to watch the kids and you, and I will go out for a nice romantic dinner. How would you like to go to that new French restaurant? I hear the food is fantastic."

"That sounds great. You know I've been dying to go there, what's the occasion?"

"Does there have to be a special occasion every time we go out to a nice restaurant?"

This would be a celebration of his liberation from his secret life, but he obviously couldn't share his enthusiasm with Kate. He would be extremely careful tonight to ensure that tomorrow was in fact a reason to celebrate. Since it was Friday, Kate would be off to the supermarket to do the grocery shopping. Keegan hoped this would give him enough time to go to the gun store, buy the gun and deface it before she got back home. He patiently pretended to read through the newspaper until Kate finally went to the store. He gave her a five-minute head start before he, himself left the house.

Keegan had just finished drilling out the serial numbers on the Beretta when the garage door began to open. He quickly hid the drill under the workbench and put the handgun in his waistband. Kate pulled the Explorer into the garage. Jim had a startled look on his face, and he stuffed a gun into his waist.

"I'm sorry hon, did I startle you?" She continued before he could answer, "What were you doing anyway?"

"Nothing love, you just took me by surprise, that's all."

This was as close as Kate had ever come to catching him. *Two close calls in one week.*

"What were you doing with the gun?"

He was hoping Kate hadn't noticed the gun, but it was now apparent that she had. "Oh, I was just cleaning it when you opened the garage door; I tucked it away until I saw that it was you."

He had no idea if his wife had bought his story but what else would she possibly think.

Kate never thought twice about his story and accepted it as truth. "Well do you think you can come and give me a hand with the groceries?"

He helped her carry in with the groceries and breathed a sigh of relief when she didn't bring up the gun anymore. He explained to her that he was going to be out in the field tonight on the same stakeout that he was on last night. This way, she wouldn't try to call him in the office. He also assured her he would be home on time and that no matter what happens tonight during the stakeout, he would be off tomorrow night so they can go and enjoy the romantic night out as they had planned. The thought of the night out without the children pleased Kate. She gave her husband a kiss goodbye as he left for work.

Keegan was scheduled to work a four to midnight shift that night, but once at work, he cleared it with Captain Anderson to take three hours vacation time off from the end of his shift. It was really just a formality; he knew ahead of time he would be able to take off, but it still had to be cleared by his Commanding Officer. Keegan left work around nine o'clock and left the familiar instructions. If anyone called for him, especially his wife, he was out in the field on an assignment. He signed out and left the office carrying a small canvass duffel bag. He got into the department's Crown Victoria and looked around to see if there were any unfamiliar cars there. He started the car up and drove to McBride's. He couldn't believe his great fortune when he arrived to have actually gotten a parking spot right in front of the bar. That was a rare thing, especially on a Friday night. This was a good sign, he convinced himself.

Keegan opened the door to the bar. It was even more crowded than it was last night. Probably more crowded than he has seen it in many years. His usual night is Thursday, not Friday. People were standing four-deep at the bar. His usual barstool was not even a remote possibility tonight.

Keegan hadn't been to McBride's on a Friday night in many years, and this was probably an average Friday night crowd, he guessed. He slowly made his way through the crowd, tightly holding the duffel bag. It took about two full minutes to go from one side of the bar to the other. There were no barstools available for him to sit on. He stood patiently at the end of the bar, waiting for O'Brien to notice him. He examined the crowd to see if there was any danger to him. He would be damned if he was going to get caught the last time that he did anything for the I.R.A. after getting away with it for well over a decade.

Studying his environment, Keegan decided everybody there fit the scene. The only person who was there by himself was a young man with long dirty blond hair sitting in a rear booth. He had a three-day growth on his face which didn't mask the fact he was barely out of his teens. Keegan guessed he was about twenty years old or so. There was something about him that gave Keegan the chills. There was that feeling of the hairs on the back of his neck standing up again. After studying him for a few moments, he decided that he was overreacting. The man was much too young to possibly be an undercover for I.A.B., aside from that he looked Irish, and the last name Castillo definitely did not fit him.

"Jim."

Keegan heard his name called out and looked over at Dan O'Brien, who was motioning for him to come over. And so, he did. O'Brien pulled a stool out from behind the bar. He put it down at the edge of the bar and invited Keegan to have a seat. "Thanks, Dan."

"I've been savin' that stool all night for ya Jim. Now, what would ya be havin' tonight, a Guinness or something harder?"

Keegan smiled at the bartender. "My nerves are much calmer than last night Dan. I'll have my usual Guinness."

O'Brien poured a Guinness, as Keegan's attention now returned to the man with the long hair. He was now talking with Nora. She looked good tonight as usual. She was wearing a black skirt and a loosely fitting white blouse with the top three buttons open exposing just enough cleavage to capture a man's attention. The man was flirting with Nora and she seemed to be having a good time with it. Keegan figured if the man played his cards right, he wouldn't be alone much longer. O'Brien returned with Keegan's Guinness. O'Brien nodded toward the duffle bag Keegan had carried in with him. "'I assume everything went well today. No problems on such short notice?"

"No problems Dan. I have exactly what you asked for right here."

He set the duffle bag down behind the bar.

"Good, I'm glad to hear that Jim. Why don't you go have a seat over in the booth with that young fella over there?"

It was more of a direction than a suggestion and Keegan realized that. "Take the bag with ya."

Keegan looked at the man again. "Him?"

Keegan was surprised, although there was something eerie about the man, Keegan did not make him for an I.R.A. operative. Keegan wasn't sure what he had expected but he figured whoever he was going to meet would be a grown man; maybe someone closer to his or Dan O'Brien's age. This was a kid. He couldn't be much more than twenty, Keegan estimated. He certainly had a cold look in his eyes but nevertheless, he was barely out of high school. Upon reflection, Keegan felt stupid. What had he really expected, a white-haired man wearing a brown overcoat? He realized that his stereotypical expectations had been ridiculous. The I.R.A. is fighting a guerilla war and the overwhelming majority of their soldiers are probably not much older than the man sitting before him; *a boy growing up in a world where he never had a chance to be a kid.*

"Aye, that's him. His name is Sean Murphy. He's good people Jim," O'Brien vouched.

Keegan got up from the bar, Guinness in hand, and walked over to the booth where the assassin waited for him. Sean Murphy, as Keegan now knew him, watched as Keegan approached. "Nora me love, would you excuse us while me old friend and I have a word?"

Old friends? Keegan thought. He was old enough to be his father. Keegan sat down across from his *old friend*

"No problem Sean, are we still on for tonight after I get off of work?"

"I wouldn't miss it for the world, love." Flynn winked and he blew her a kiss.

Louis Castillo was working a six pm until two am shift so he would be able to follow Keegan when he got off work around midnight. At ten-thirty, Castillo decided to go and stake out Keegan's department auto, just in case he left early. When Castillo arrived at Federal Plaza, he observed that Keegan's parking spot was empty. He was sure Keegan had been scheduled to work a four to twelve tonight.

Castillo parked in Keegan's spot and entered Federal Plaza. He went to the office of the Joint Terrorist Task Force. He had been directed by one of the Detectives in the squad room to the office of Captain Anderson. He took out a phony identification card that he was authorized to carry for such investigations as this one. He clipped the I.D. card to his shirt pocket and knocked on Captain Anderson's door. "How are you doing Captain, I'm Lieutenant Monet from Quality Assurance Division. I'm here to do a spot check of clerical records."

Captain Anderson always kept good records and didn't have anything to fear whenever any internal department units came to inspect his logs.

"You have my full cooperation Lieutenant. What

would you like to see?"

"Just your sign-in log to make sure everyone that is supposed to be here is accounted for."

Anderson handed Castillo the log and he quickly scanned it, noting James Keegan's signature signing him out for the night at 2045 hours. *Three hours L/T*, the department's shorthand for lost time scribbled next to his name. At least Castillo knew that Keegan had left for the night and was not in the field. Now he didn't have to waste his time waiting for Keegan to return to the office. Castillo handed the log back to Captain Anderson. "Thank you, Captain, everything seems to be in order."

Anderson thought it was weird that the Lieutenant conducted such a short inspection but the shorter the better he figured. After Castillo walked out of the office, Anderson looked over the log himself to make sure there was nothing inappropriate that could have been spotted. Anderson was satisfied that everything was in order and never gave it a second thought.

Castillo went back to his nondescript department auto and started it up. He didn't know where Keegan had gone but his only shot would be to see if he was at McBride's. Castillo drove to McBride's wondering if he would find him there or if he had possibly left work early to go home. Castillo had the feeling he would find Keegan at the bar. As Castillo drove along Third Avenue, he observed Keegan's unmarked department auto parked directly in front of

McBride's.

A smile came across Castillo's face as he looked for a parking spot of his own. Once he found one, he made sure to take his camera book with him, hoping to catch Keegan on film doing something incriminating. Castillo was excited. He felt this would be the night he could make his case against Keegan. Keegan hadn't been here in about a month so there had to be a reason he was back tonight.

Castillo entered the bar scanning the patrons for Keegan. He wasn't at the bar where he had been last time. It took about five minutes or so for Castillo to locate him. How ironic, Castillo thought to himself. Keegan was seated in the same booth Castillo had been in last time they were here. He was sitting there with a much younger man. Keegan looked uncomfortable; a look unfamiliar to him. Castillo saw the two men were talking and wished he could hear what they were saying. There was no way he'd be able to hear them over the music, even if he was sitting at the table right next to them. Castillo tried not to stare at the men as he was waiting for the hostess to seat him.

Castillo was seated three tables away. He sat in a way that he could keep both men under discreet observation. Castillo held the camera up to eye level and snapped a couple of pictures of each man individually and an additional few of them both in the same photo. When Nora came over to his table, he politely diverted his attention to her and ordered a beer, offering a smile in the process.

As soon as she walked away, he returned his attention to Keegan and this mystery man. Castillo saw the man was shifting uncomfortably under the table and Castillo couldn't tell what was going on. Castillo couldn't see the man's hands and wondered what he was doing. It was odd to be seated at a table yet keeping your hands under the table the majority of the time. Nora returned with Castillo's beer and put it down on top of a napkin.

After a few moments of idle conversation, the man who had been introduced as Sean Murphy got to the heart of the matter. Flynn looked down at the floor where Keegan had set the duffle bag. "So now Mr. Keegan, I understand you brought something for me. Would you mind handin' it over?"

"Yes, I have, but first I need to know what you plan on doing here in the United States of America that would require the need for a gun?"

Keegan had a right to know what exactly he was getting himself involved in. Could it be the man simply needed to protect himself while he was stateside? Keegan had no idea who this man was. It was possible that he has been in America before and has made some enemies. Keegan could live with the idea that he needed to protect himself.

"Mr. Keegan, I don't believe that's your concern. That's me own business. Your business is to get the gun for me. It's not that hard, is it?"

Keegan was growing agitated. He was used to getting answers to the questions he asked as soon as he asked them. He recognized the hard look in the man's eyes, but he had successfully interrogated men much harder than the man seated in front of him. "Sean, do you know what my job is here? Do you?"

Keegan decided a soft approach would be the best way to start. If he needed to get tough, he would but he didn't think that would be the case. After all, they were on the same side and once he realized that Keegan was a well-respected and influential police Lieutenant, he wouldn't want any problems from him.

"No Mr. Keegan, I don't. But I also don't give a rat's arse. I have a job to do, and I plan on doing it. With or without your help, see."

Keegan wasn't making much progress, but he didn't let up. "Listen, I'm a Police Officer in charge of anti–terrorism here in New York City. I have no intentions of interfering with you, but I still must insist on knowing what you plan on doing before I put a gun in your hands."

Flynn pulled a cigarette from the pack with his lips. He looked Keegan in the eyes as he lit up. He took in a deliberately slow and deep drag and blew the smoke in Keegan's face. He was not intimidated by Keegan in the slightest. As Gerald Flynn, he had numerous encounters with the police and never backed down from them. As Sean Murphy, it would be no different.

"Mr. Keegan, all I plan on telling you is that it's a legitimate target. That is all that you need to know."

"A legitimate target!?"

Keegan shook his head. He could feel the angst building up inside him. Keegan began to lecture him. "You plan on killing someone...here in America? Listen, Sean, I demand you tell me who and what you are talking about! I could lose my job if I was connected in any way to a murder. Do you understand that?"

"I don't give a damn about your job, your country, or you. Do *you* understand *that?* Me only concern is to further the cause of freedom for Ireland. I have a job to do and, rest assured, it will be done with or without your help. If you plan on helping me, give me what you came here to give me. If you don't, then be on your way. But Mr. Keegan, or should I say, Officer Keegan, don't get in me way. Dan seems to think highly of ya. I'd hate for him to have one less mate."

Flynn was not intimidated in the slightest by Keegan. He was almost bored by him. He was thinking more of his chances of bedding the waitress tonight than his current encounter with the Police Officer.

Keegan could sense the man's arrogance and indifference towards him. There was a feeling of fear that came over Keegan. He wasn't used to being afraid of anyone or anything for that matter. There was just something about the man. Maybe the hardness in his eyes, or maybe his demeanor, but whatever it was, he was intimidated for the first time in a very long time.

Keegan was used to dealing with street punks throughout his career. This guy was no ordinary street punk, however. After taking another drag of the cigarette, he once again discarded the smoke into Keegan's face. "Well, what's it going to be Mr. Keegan? I haven't all night to waste me time with you."

Keegan waved his hand, dissipating the smoke, and softly coughed. He pushed the duffel bag over, not sure why he was doing it. "Here, this is what you wanted."

Flynn accepted the duffel bag and its contents. He brought the bag down to the seat next to him, unzipped the bag, and looked inside. He removed the gun from the bag, careful to keep it under the table so nobody else in the bar would see it. He pressed the magazine release, dropping the magazine into his hand. With his thumb, he felt the familiar feel of a copper jacketed round in the magazine. Now he knew the gun was already loaded. He inserted the magazine back into the pistol.

Keegan wondered what Murphy was doing. Why was he keeping his hands under the table? Then Keegan recognized the familiar sound of an automatic handgun chambering a round. What the hell is he thinking? The guy was not only dangerous, but he was also reckless, Keegan determined. He had nerves of steel, but it certainly was not the smartest thing to do. The bar was packed. There are people everywhere.

Keegan's mind was racing in different directions. Why would he feel the need to load it right here, right now? *Is his target here in the bar with us? What if someone noticed and called the police on him? What if Castillo had followed him here and was watching their every move?* Keegan became extremely nervous and looked around to see if anybody had been watching. The Irishman shifted his body. Keegan figured him to be putting the gun in his waistband. At least he was not about to shoot someone right here, Keegan assured himself.

Nora caught Keegan's eye as he was scanning the crowd. She was bent over a table, serving a patron his beer. Keegan recognized the man instantly. It was the same man he had seen last month that he thought had been watching him. The man was once again reading a book, just like he had been doing last month. Keegan figured he could be a regular at the bar that he had never come to notice. The man seemed to be staring in their direction a moment ago, but he wasn't sure. Keegan became anxious. The man would fit the mold he figured Castillo to be. He wasn't Irish, or at least he didn't appear to be. He was about thirty years old and was sitting alone in a bar on a Friday night. If he was just a regular guy trying to meet women he'd be hanging out at the bar, not at a table in the back.

Keegan excused himself and got up making his way back to the bar. Once he got to the bar, he again got Dan O'Brien's attention. "Dan, do you see that man sitting at the table by himself, the one wearing glasses and reading a book?"

'Yeah Jim, I see 'em."

"Do you know him? Is he a regular in here?"

Keegan hoping the answer was yes.

It wasn't. "No Jim, I've never seen him in here before."

Keegan felt his heart pound heavily against his chest. Was he Castillo or was Keegan being paranoid yet again? Keegan now studied the man as he read his book. The man never looked up from the book, but Keegan had an uneasy feeling about him. "Dan, I think he might be the one I was warned about. Would you help me with something?"

"Of course, I would, Jim. If he's a problem for you, he is also a problem for me."

"Can you call the waitress over here? I'm going to need her for this."

Keegan wrote a message on a cocktail napkin at the bar.

"No problem Jim."

O'Brien signaled for Nora to come over to the bar area.

Nora walked over to the bar to see what O'Brien wanted. After making sure the man was not watching him, Keegan handed Nora the napkin and explained what he wanted her to do. Keegan thanked both O'Brien and the waitress and made his way back to the table where Flynn was still seated. Keegan sat back down opposite him.

"Miss me?" His initial fear of the Irishman had given way. He was no longer Keegan's main concern.

If the man with the book was in fact an internal affairs cop watching him, then that danger is more imminent to Keegan than whatever the hitman had planned. Flynn didn't even bother to respond. He emptied the remaining nine-millimeter rounds from the box and put them into his inside jacket pocket. He passed the now empty duffel bag back to Keegan. Keegan accepted the bag, but his attention was fully on the man he suspected to be Castillo.

The man had been looking but then quickly looked away. He didn't know if his plan would tell him for sure that the man was Castillo, but it might. At worst, the bookworm wouldn't understand what was going on. There was nothing Keegan could do now except wait and watch.

Castillo hoped Keegan didn't notice him staring in his direction a couple of times. Castillo rationalized to himself; there would be no reason for Keegan to expect anybody to be watching him. Castillo was very interested in what was going on at the bar when Keegan walked away but he felt Keegan's eyes burning on him, so he didn't dare to look up. Castillo kept his nose in the book pretending to read it. He would turn a page every so often to keep up appearances in case anyone was watching closely. He was cautious not to expose any of the mechanical devices in the book that would indicate to someone that he was really holding a camera.

When Keegan rejoined the young man at the table, Castillo looked up for a moment in time to see the man hand Keegan a duffel bag. Castillo desperately wanted a look inside the bag, thinking it could be the piece of evidence that he would need to nail Keegan once and for all. He studied the bag. It didn't appear to be heavy at all. Castillo wondered what could possibly be in it except maybe cash. The bag could contain a payoff of some sort.

Castillo's thoughts were interrupted when Nora walked over to him and began to put another beer down in front of him. Castillo was slightly confused. "I didn't order another beer. I'm not even done with this one yet."

"I know," said Nora as she set the beer down on the table in front of Castillo and walked away. Castillo hadn't noticed the waitress place the napkin on Tommy McDermott's keyboard. Castillo tried to figure out why the waitress would bring him a beer without asking for it. Was she being courteous and buying him a round back? That didn't make much sense. He was apprehensive and wasn't sure he really wanted to know the answer.

He glanced ever so slightly in Keegan's direction. Keegan was still seated in the booth with the other man, but he seemed to be looking in his direction. Castillo immediately looked back down to his book. He had to be careful. It had to be some sort of coincidence. There would be no way Keegan knew he was being watched. Even if he did, he had no way of knowing who was watching him.

Castillo decided not to panic, and he would assume there was a logical explanation for the beer, other than Keegan letting him know he was aware of his presence. Castillo put his book down on the table and took a big gulp of the beer. He turned away from Keegan and watched the Tommy McDermott Band as they entertained the crowd. He felt this was his best option to blend into the crowd.

After finishing the song, McDermott picked up the napkin set there by Nora. He silently read it to himself. Tommy McDermott introduced the next song. "I have a special request for the next song ladies and gentlemen. This song is one of my favorites. It's called, <u>the Streets of New York.</u>"

Keegan stared at the man he suspected of being a rat to see if there were any reactions to McDermott's words. Keegan could only see the man's profile and hoped that would be enough to tell.

McDermott continued, "As always, this song is dedicated to any members of the NYPD we might have in the audience tonight. A special dedication for this song goes out tonight to Castillo from Jim." McDermott began to belt the song out.

Keegan watched as Castillo's face turned red instantly. Their eyes met for a brief instant. There was no longer any doubt in Keegan's mind. The man was, in fact, Castillo. Whoever warned him was right on the money. He wished there was some way to repay the person. Keegan came to the realization that there was an open case against him. He was nervous but he figured I.A.B. couldn't have too much on him if they were still following him. Keegan said good night to the man he knew as Sean Murphy and got up from the table. He waved to Dan O'Brien and bid a good night to Tommy McDermott. Keegan walked past Castillo towards the exit, glancing down at him as he passed. "Enjoy your beer."

Castillo could feel his face go flush when he heard the singer dedicate the song to him. He prayed Keegan was only going on a hunch and didn't know who he was. He didn't want to look in Keegan's direction because he knew that would almost be like admitting guilt. Nevertheless, he couldn't stop himself. It was almost instinctual. Their eyes met briefly, and Castillo quickly looked away. He tried to remain calm and emotionless so he wouldn't confirm any suspicions Keegan may have. He could see Keegan getting up from the table and wishing a good night to various people. He picked up the duffel bag Castillo had been interested in and began to walk in his direction. Castillo didn't even peek up at Keegan as he passed. When Keegan passed the comment, there was no doubt in Castillo's mind. He had been made. *But how?*

He was now more determined than ever to nail Keegan. He remained in his seat and snapped a few more photos of the man who was still seated in the booth. He noticed a tattoo of a shamrock on the man's forearm and discretely took a photo of it. After about fifteen minutes, Castillo asked Nora for his check.

Castillo was dejected. How could he have blown

his cover and how many people in this bar knew who he was? He looked over at the man that Keegan had been seated with. He showed no signs of leaving or any interest in Castillo. Neither the bartender nor Nora seemed to take a particular interest in his departure either. Castillo paid his tab and left the bar wondering where he went wrong.

Keegan had already passed through the Midtown tunnel by the time Castillo exited the bar. He thought very carefully if he truly had something to worry about. He figured the investigation couldn't have been going on for too long. And that he hadn't done a job except for last month and tonight in over six months. What could Castillo have seen that night by the pier? The guns were in the duffel bag and he knew he didn't seize the car so there's no way he would know there were guns in the bag. Furthermore, if he ran the plate on the car it would have come back legitimate.

As far as tonight was concerned, everything was done under the table and Castillo couldn't have seen anything. Keegan assured himself he had nothing to worry about. He had just completed his last mission for the Irish Republican Army and Castillo couldn't have one ounce of solid evidence against him. Keegan was relieved to know that this was all behind him now.

CHAPTER 10

Flynn remained seated in the booth, smoking a cigarette and drinking a beer long after Castillo had left. As the crowd started to thin out, Nora O'Donnell sat down in the booth with the man she had only met a few hours earlier. The two of them flirted for a little through some light conversation until one of the remaining patrons bothered Nora for his check. When Nora got up, Flynn walked over to Dan O'Brien. He would take the opportunity to express his concerns. "I don't trust em, Dan. I don't think he's true to the cause."

"Gerald...I'm sorry, I mean. Sean," O'Brien began, covering up his slight of tongue. O'Brien wanted to defend his long-time friend. "He's been with me for years and I've never had a problem with him."

"That may be so but he's still a cop, and we're going to do a job in his own backyard. I want to make sure he won't be a problem. I want to know where his loyalty is going to lie."

O'Brien did his best to sound reassuring as he wiped down the bar. "I don't think you have anything to worry about. He won't do anything stupid. I promised him that if this operation was successful, we wouldn't need his services anymore. All he really wants to do is put this all behind him and be a family man. For cryin' out loud, that's the same ambition too many of our men back home have aspired for. Trust me, Sean, he won't be bothering you."

"I hope not...for his sake that is. If your friend tries to stick his nose in my business, I will kill him. Make no mistakes about that Dan."

O'Brien heeded the warning. "Understood and agreed. This is too important to have anyone get in your way. This will surely capture worldwide attention."

Flynn returned to the booth and waited for Nora to get off from work. There were less than a dozen patrons still in the bar and it was after two. Nora would be getting off work shortly and they could go out and get a cup of coffee. Nora checked with her boss and since there were no more customers in the dining area, her services were no longer needed. She walked out arm in arm with Flynn and they walked to a nearby, twenty-four-hour coffee shop. They sat down at a booth in the back. Flynn felt much more secure with the nine-millimeter handgun in his waist. At home, he always carried a gun and in the short time he didn't have one, he felt naked.

It was a narrow establishment, furnished with six booths on one side and less than a dozen blue cushioned barstools at the counter. There were only a handful of patrons. Two other couples seated at booths and three men sat separately at the counter. Two were most likely coming from bars, Flynn figured, and the third was a newspaper truck driver getting ready to deliver the morning editions to local stores. The waitress was in her early fifties and wore too much makeup. She took her pad from her pocket and took their order.

The coffee began to sober him up from the beer he had throughout the night. Nora had a diet soda along with a toasted corn muffin. She enjoyed Murphy's stories about her native country. She moved to the states with her parents from County Cork when she was a young teen and has yet to return. He charmed Nora over the course of the next hour or so and she agreed to go back to his hotel room with him in Queens.

The two of them left the coffee shop together and got into his rental car. He had a hard time getting used to getting in on the wrong side of the car to drive. He stepped on the clutch and turned the key starting the car up. He pulled away from the curb and drove along Third Avenue. He placed his hand on Nora's knee and caressed it as he enchanted her with the charm he could turn on at will.

Nora really liked the man and thought they had hit it off, unable to see through his guise. She couldn't tell when looking in his eyes that he was in fact a ruthless murderer and not the polite, adventurous young man she believed him to be. It was just after three am and Flynn didn't see any harm in making a right-hand turn through the red light. His hotel was still a twenty-minute drive from here and he was anxious to get there.

The Police Officers were reviewing the complaint report they had just prepared for a stolen vehicle when they noticed the rented Nissan make a turn through the red light. The officers sped up until they were directly behind the vehicle. They ran the license plate on the police car's mobile digital computer. After a few seconds passed, the computer beeped alerting them to the new message. The car was not stolen. It was a rental car.

The officer in the passenger side of the police car flipped on the toggle switch, activating the blue and white auto's turret lights. The driver of the radio car was an officer named Ed West. West was, by anyone's standards a collar man, as cops referred to a fellow officer who made a lot of arrests. His partner, Pete Lynch was more of a ladies' man than a collar man. He would make his collar a quarter just to keep the bosses off his back. He never had a problem with his partner taking most of the arrests the team affected.

The Nissan pulled over and the officers cautiously approached. Officer West would approach on the driver's side and take control of the car stop. Lynch would approach on the passenger side, keeping an eye on any passengers in the vehicle.

"Shut the engine off," West commanded, as he approached the driver's side of the auto with his flashlight in one hand, the other on his service revolver.

West observed the long-haired man and a rather attractive woman in the car. The most important thing in any stop was to make sure you saw the person's hands at all times. The man kept both hands on the steering wheel as the officers approached.

The man seemingly aware of the officer's concerns, especially at this time of night, was careful not to move them until the officer directed him to. The officers let their guard down ever so slightly. "Can I please see your license, registration, and insurance card?"

"No problem, Officer. What did I do?"

Flynn reached into his wallet and took out the forged driver's license Quinn had supplied him with. He then reached into the glove box and retrieved the rental papers as he looked up at Lynch, whose flashlight was concentrated on Nora's partially open blouse.

Flynn sized up the situation quickly, as he debated whether to kill the officers right here and now. If he had to, he would kill the officer on his side first. He was more businesslike and professional and therefore more dangerous. His hand was already on his gun. He stood behind the rear door, not in front of him at the window. Flynn realized the positioning would give the officer a tactical advantage over him, but he figured he could still overcome it.

The officer on Nora's side was too busy trying to steal a peek at Nora's chest to be concerned with him. The officer's own distraction would buy him

the extra time he would need to kill them both before either of them would be able to draw their
weapons. Flynn held out the documents at chest
level not reaching out of the window. He wanted to
test the officer and see if he could get him to reach
into the car to take them. If he did, killing him
would be that much easier.

"You ran the red light back there, coming off
Third Avenue. You can't make a right on red in the
city. I'm sure you know that. I'm still waiting for
your license."

"Sorry officer. Here you go."

Sharp copper, Flynn assessed. He knew enough
not to reach into the car. He then handed the officer
the documents and decided to let the officers decide
their own fate. He decided there would be no need to
kill them and attract unnecessary attention to himself unless they did something to endanger his operation. A manhunt for a double cop killing couldn't
be good for him. It could possibly doom the entire
assignment.

On the other hand, if these cops were like the
cops back home in Northern Ireland and decided
to pull him out of the car and search him, he
would be forced to kill them. He knew he couldn't
carry out his assignment from an American prison
cell for concealing an illegal weapon. He glanced
over at Nora momentarily, thinking how he would
have to kill her as well, to eliminate any potential
witnesses. She glanced at him and smiled unknow-
ingly. Flynn's right hand moved down to his waist-

band and touched the butt of the gun through his shirt, making sure he knew exactly where it was.

"Keep your hands where I can see them!" West saw the man drop his hand from the steering wheel after handing over his documents but did not think much of it. He didn't believe it to be any sort of threat. The man most likely began to relax. Of course, it was better to be safe than sorry and West always tried to employ good tactics. Car stops were the most dangerous part of police work. They never knew who they were pulling over. It could just as easily be a perp fleeing a double homicide as a person rushing because they are late for work.

His partner's loud command momentarily distracted Lynch from taking in Nora's beauty. Officer Lynch shined his flashlight on the driver's right hand, not noticing anything unusual. He watched as the man placed both hands back on the steering wheel. He glanced back down at Nora. "Tell your boyfriend not to make any sudden moves. My partner scares easy." Nora smiled at the officer's joke.

Flynn thought to himself how alert the one cop was and that he would definitely have to take him out first, quickly and cleanly before he could fall back on his training. Flynn decided, however, that the officer's training was nowhere as intense and certainly not superior to his own. He reminded himself they were both wearing bulletproof vests so headshots would be necessary.

West stared at the driver's license. There was something about it that bothered him, but he couldn't put his finger on what it was. He would compare it to his own license when they got back to the car to see if he could figure it out. "Stay in the car. I will be with you in a few minutes."

Flynn saw the way the officer was examining the license he had just handed to him and he wondered how good of a forgery Quinn had supplied him with. The officers then went back to their patrol car and took a seat. Flynn watched closely in his rear-view mirror and reached under his shirt, taking the safety off the automatic handgun in his waist. Nora seemed oblivious to what was going on and commented on what a pervert the one officer was.

West shook his head at his partner. "There's something about this guy I don't trust. I get a bad vibe from him. He's definitely been drinking. I can smell the booze as soon as he opened the window. What did you think of him?" Although Pete Lynch did not make a lot of collars, West respected his opinion. He was usually a pretty good judge of character.

"Honestly Ed, I was focusing my attention on his girlfriend. She was very perky if you know what I mean?"

"Lots of help you are." West handed his partner the driver's license the man had given him. "Take a look at his license. I don't think it's real. I can't see the state seal when I shine my flashlight on it like you're supposed to. The color looks a bit off too."

West offered his own license for comparison. "Here look at mine." After a brief moment, "What do you think of it?"

Lynch agreed. "Yeah, I'm with you. This license doesn't look legit."

Lynch punched the Client Identification Number into the computer to conduct a license check on the document provided. The computer once again beeped. Both officers read the screen. It read no hit. "I think you have yourself some overtime here Eddie. Let's check this guy out a little closer if you want. As long as you're taking the collar, that is."

West looked at the clock on the radio car's dashboard. He decided he could get a decent amount of over time for a forged document collar. "Don't worry about it, Pete, I wouldn't dream of sticking you with a collar."

"Hey, who knows, after we cuff him up maybe I will need to console his little Colleen there. I can't leave her all alone in the middle of the night, now can I?"

Lynch flashed his partner a quick smile and raised his eyebrows up and down. West just shook his head and laughed. The officers exited their marked department radio car and began to approach the Nissan.

Flynn watched through the Nissan's sideview mirror as the officers approached. He observed the officer on his side was approaching him once again with his hand on his gun. This signaled to Flynn, without any question in his mind, there was something wrong. Flynn reached down under his shirt and grasped the butt of the nine-millimeter. He calculated his plan in a matter of seconds. The moment the officer reached his window, he was going to pull out his gun, spin around and eliminate the first cop. He would fire three quick rounds squarely into his face. He would then get out of the car while firing upon the less aggressive cop. He figured he could kill them both in a period of about five seconds.

He would then, of course, drive to a different location before killing Nora. He was always taught never to waste any more time than necessary at the scene of a hit. He also knew if he left Nora's body at the scene with the dead Police Officers, he would inevitably be linked to the killings. Too many people had seen him with Nora, leaving the bar and then again at the diner. Flynn's heart began to pound against his chest as the officers got closer. He firmly held the gun in his right hand as they were only feet away.

"**10-13 Shots Fired**! Forty-Second and Second!" was frantically broadcast over the department's portable radio. "**Shots fired, central**! Get me some units here! Shots fired!" The sound of terror resonated in the cop's voice as he frantically called for backup. He was clearly fired upon and possibly engaged in a gun battle that could end his or his part-ner's life.

West threw the man's license and other paper-work towards the Nissan as he and Lynch scampered back to their department auto to respond to their fellow officer's call for help. West dropped the car into gear, and they sped off towards Forty Second Street and Second Avenue. Officers West and Lynch would go home that morning after their shift, not realizing how close they had come to losing their lives.

Gerald Flynn took his hand off the gun and watched his papers fall harmlessly to the ground. He got out of the rental car to retrieve them. He had no idea what had just happened, but he felt it was better off this way. If he had been forced to murder the cops, he would have had to lay low for the next couple of weeks. He wouldn't be able to conduct reconnaissance missions to prepare him for what needed to be done. He figured at very least, the police would release composite photos of the man wanted for murdering two of their own. Now he remained faceless in a city of millions and that was exactly what he wanted to do.

Flynn was pleased with how everything played out tonight. He reflected on it as he and Nora lay naked on the bed of his hotel room. The brush with the law had seemed to make his tryst with Nora even more stimulating. It acted almost like an aphrodisiac. It seemed to have the same effect on Nora as well. She had been all over him from the second they entered the hotel room. Flynn had lit a cigarette and glanced at Nora's naked body, deciding she had been quite a trophy. He had his share of women, but Nora was far prettier than most and had a fantastic body.

Nora had been taken back slightly when she saw Flynn remove the gun from his waistband, but she never questioned him about it. In fact, it had actually turned her on. She started to sense there was something dangerous about this man, but she didn't mind, it was exciting. She enjoyed the mystery. He could be a cop, a federal agent, or perhaps a gangster. She wondered but did not ask. Nora slipped under the covers, getting ready to sleep a good part of the day away and she rested her head on Flynn's chest.

"I wouldn't get too comfortable if I were you love." He took a long drag from the cigarette and the orange glow grew bright in the dimly lit room.

Nora was a bit confused. "And why is that?" She half thought he was kidding. "I thought we could spend the day together. Sleep until noon, then make love again."

She playfully scratched his chest with her fingernails and licked her lips seductively at him.

"That won't be happening. I've got things to do, and you best be on ya way."

He wasn't kidding. She could see it in his eyes. The warmness was gone. Nora began to feel a bit uneasy at the harsh manner in which he started to speak to her.

She began to reason with him. "But I don't understand. I thought we..."

Flynn cut her off mid-sentence. "There is no we, Nora me love, we had our fun but it's time for you to go." He didn't yell or even raise his tone of voice, but he made himself unmistakably clear. "I'm finished with ya."

He was very callous and matter-of-fact.

Nora felt used and in fact, she had been. She held the sheets around her body as she gathered her clothes and took them into the bathroom to get dressed. She fought back tears that began to well up in her eyes. She was mortified. She stayed in the bathroom for nearly fifteen minutes, trying to gain her composure. She became more furious than upset.

Flynn sat up in bed and watched as Nora stormed into the bathroom. He continued to draw from the cigarette while thinking about the days ahead. Nora emerged from the bathroom fully clothed with a hint of a tear in her eye.

"Will you at least be kind enough to drive me home? I live on the other side of town." She was distraught and hated herself for even asking.

He shook his head. "No. I don't think I will."

Flynn motioned to his wallet on the night table. "Why don't you take twenty dollars from me wallet and call a cab. Just wait for it in the lobby. I need me sleep, love."

Nora was enraged. She yelled at him. "I don't want your fucking money! I'm no whore Sean!"

"And so, you're not, now are ya Nora? Oh well, at least a whore gets paid for her services. Take the money or walk home. It's up to you."

Flynn exhaled a drag of smoke from his cigarette and stared at the television.

Nora O'Donnell had never been so ashamed of herself. She used anger to mask her hurt feelings as she left the hotel room. "Fuck you, Sean, you're a real bastard!"

Nora's words were meaningless to Flynn and he didn't think twice about them as he lay there.

Nearly a half-hour later, he began to get dressed. He tucked the handgun back into its familiar position in his waistband. He left his hotel room in the predawn hours and drove into Manhattan before the city came to life. The crisp morning air shook any signs of weariness from Flynn's body. He parked the rental in a parking garage, informing the attendant he would return in less than two hours.

He walked from along Fifth Avenue, studying the stores in the area. He examined every cross street to Fifth Avenue from Forty-Fourth Street until Eighty-Sixth Street. He was looking for the best place to make the hit and for the most opportune escape route. He had been told a clean escape would be nearly impossible, but he figured with all of the confusion on his side, he had a good shot at getting away. He was told countless times this would be a suicide mission, or he would end up in an American prison. He did not believe this to be the case. He decided if anyone could pull this off and get away, he could. Flynn had an almost arrogant confidence in himself. The city began to slowly awaken from the darkness as he continued to walk along Fifth Avenue. Flynn had walked up and down the Avenue for almost an hour and a half, studying its every building and intersection.

Flynn stopped in front of Saint Patrick's Cathedral on Fiftieth Street. He walked up the stairs leading to the Cathedral's entrance. He had heard of the Cathedral and even seen it in pictures, but he had never seen it in person until now. *It could possibly be the most famous Catholic cathedral in the world outside of the Vatican,* he thought. It took up an entire city block. He took in the elegance of its architecture from the outside while slowly ascending the stairs. The two steeples in front were breathtaking probably over three hundred feet tall. It looked as it had been sculpted from marble rather than built. The rising sun caught one of the stained-glass windows just right causing a myriad of colors to be reflected on the ground ahead of him. The church, although well over a century old, was in pristine condition.

When Flynn entered the Cathedral, he dipped his right hand into the holy water and blessed himself as he had done so many times in his life when entering a church. He was overwhelmed with the size of St. Patrick's. Dozens of brilliant chandeliers hung down from high above. There were too many stained-glass windows for him to count; each a work of art. It was much larger than any church he had ever seen in Ireland. It could easily hold a couple of thousand people. Flynn genuflected as he took a seat in the last pew in the church. He sat quietly thinking to himself and watching as the priest conducted seven am mass from in front of the exquisite white alter. Flynn remained in the church well after the mass ended. He thought long and hard. He figured this to be the most dangerous place of any to carry out the hit. It would also send the loudest message. *A murder for the cause, directly in front of St. Patrick's Cathedral, a location known and recognized throughout the world. Yes.* It was decided.

Flynn exited the church at the Fifth Avenue exit. The first thing that caught his eye was the statue across the street. A partially clothed man holding what appeared to be a globe over his head. Atlas, if he remembered his Greek mythology correctly. He stood on the top of the steps looking down onto the street. There were many more cars and pedestrians now than when he went inside. The crowd would be good for him. He could get lost in a crowd. He stared at the spot he knew would immortalize him in the ranks of the I.R.A. His name would one day be as well known as James Connolly or Michael Collins, he assured himself. *Maybe even Atlas*, he laughed to himself.

Walking back to the parking garage, he couldn't help but wonder what Eamon Quinn would think of his choice of location. He imagined Quinn would not approve, thinking it was too dangerous. The thought of seeing Quinn's face turn red with anger brought a smile and a chuckle to Flynn. *He did leave it up to me where I thought would be the best place to carry out the job, now didn't he?*

Flynn liked the pressure and the danger, he thrived on it. It was almost like a game to him. Could he possibly pull it off and get away with hundreds of Police Officers and cameras everywhere? Flynn felt his chances were good in spite of the odds being against him. He was eagerly awaiting his opportunity to prove wrong those who said he couldn't do it. He never even considered the possibility he would be caught. It really wasn't an option.

Flynn drove the rental back through the Midtown Tunnel into Queens. He couldn't believe how much traffic there was going in the other direction. He was sure people would be waiting upwards of a half-hour just to pay the toll at the tunnel's entrance. It certainly was a lot more congested than Belfast ever was. It was a quarter to nine when he parked in the hotel's parking lot. He was tired but he felt good otherwise. The night had been a total success. He conducted his first recon. He figured out exactly where the hit would go down and he even managed to get himself laid. He thought briefly how irate Nora had been with him. He was amused. He got undressed, placing the handgun on the dresser. He settled into bed and drifted off into a deep sleep.

CHAPTER 11

Keegan's heart was pounding as he slept. The tension was mounting until he abruptly sat up in bed, waking him from the nightmare. He had broken out in a cold sweat and was shaking ever so slightly. His uneasiness had also woken Kate from her sleep. She rubbed his back, comforting him. "What's wrong, hon?"

She was concerned. He used to have such terrible nightmares. It had been a long time since he had one, but Kate recognized the symptoms instantly. It had gotten to the point during the Federal courthouse trial, and all of the death threats that came with it, that her husband was taking medication to suppress his dreams.

"Nothing, love. I'm fine." He rested his head in his hands. "It was just a bad dream."

It wasn't uncommon for Police Officers to have such nightmares. He figured most cops experienced them every so often. He was off duty, on the way home, when he stopped to buy gasoline. He pulled into the gas station unaware that he drove in on a robbery in progress. He began to draw his off-duty weapon when one of the perps wheeled on him with a shotgun and pulled the trigger. He could almost hear the explosion as he saw the muzzle flash just as he woke up. Keegan was breathing heavier than normal until he finally settled down. He didn't want to think that the violent nightmares he used to face at night could be returning to him. This whole situation with Castillo and the Irish could be triggering them. He hoped this was not the case.

Kate kissed her husband on the cheek. "It's okay, Jim. Do you want to tell me about it?"

"I can't even remember what it was about sweetie."

Keegan never told his wife too much about his nightmares. Clearly, she knew that he had them, but he never wanted to share the details. He didn't want to scare her about his job any more than she already was.

"Come back to sleep Jim."

She patted his pillow with her hand and eased him down. She rubbed his back, hoping it would soothe him enough to fall back to sleep.

Keegan glanced at the alarm clock. It was just before six and he decided to stay awake. He realized he would not be able to fall back to sleep. He never could after the nightmares. He climbed out of bed, got undressed, and went into the bathroom to take a shower. The hot water felt good on his body, rinsing off the sweat. It had a soothing effect on him.

Kate shut off the alarm clock before it had a chance to ring. She put on her red terry cloth bathrobe and went downstairs to make breakfast for the family before waking the kids up for school. She first made herself a cup of instant coffee. Kate fried bacon and scrambled some eggs. Between the coffee and the smell of the bacon, it was enough to shake the sleepiness out of her system.

She continued to prepare the breakfast although her mind was elsewhere. Kate was preoccupied with the thoughts of Jim's nightmare. Jim's bad dreams were usually triggered by a real-life threat. They had become quite frequent during the aftermath of the federal courthouse arrests, but that was not when they first started. He used to get them when he was still a uniformed cop on patrol. They were never random, however. They were always precipitated by a traumatic event, often that Jim wouldn't even tell her about. It was always after something dangerous happened. Jim would always try to keep it from her, but she would often find out.

There was one time he had bad dreams for nearly a week straight. She had no idea why, until reading a locally published newspaper detailing how he had been dragged by a car and shot at during a car stop. He wasn't shot and the perp was apprehended but the harrowing experience was nonetheless terrifying, she imagined.

Kate was not aware of anything that happened to her husband recently at work. She wondered if maybe he was worried about the Middle-Eastern terrorists striking again. Or maybe, even though Jim had assured her this was not the case, he was in danger with the same extremists that killed Judge

Boden a couple of months back.

She didn't think that was it. In the past, when Jim received any credible death threats, he would always bring a department radio home with him. She wished he would tell her what was going on, but she knew he wouldn't. Kate was setting the table for breakfast when she heard the bathroom door open upstairs. She looked to the top of the stairs and watched as her husband began to descend. She noticed an uneasy look on his face that only she would be able to recognize. She had no idea for sure what his dream was about, but she said a silent prayer that he wasn't in some kind of danger.

Keegan went into his office, closing the door behind him. He took off his coat, hung it on the coat rack, and had a seat behind his desk. *Another Monday.* Mondays meant catching up on any work that may have been generated by the men in his office over the weekend. He opened up the cup of coffee he bought at the deli before scanning the paperwork. He sipped the coffee slowly and thought once again about the dream.

Then he thought how wonderful Kate was, as always. He was glad they went out for a nice romantic dinner on Saturday. If anyone deserved to be treated like a queen, it was Kate. She was always so understanding, especially when it came to his job. He realized being a cop's wife was not easy. She always seemed to support him through tough times, even if she was not happy with his job and the commitment that came with it.

Keegan emptied the stack of papers from his in-basket and sorted them into three piles. First were the Unusual Occurrence Reports. The next pile was the Complaint Follow-Ups, or DD'5s, his Detectives prepared regarding their ongoing investigations. Into the final pile, he stacked the Intelligence Reports. This was Keegan's Monday morning routine.

It would take him the better part of the morning, to read through them all and catch up on his necessary paperwork. Keegan made it a point to tackle the *Unusuals* first. They were the most informative and often garnered his interest. He read one report which detailed the Bomb Squad being called into a safe house in Brooklyn where they recovered nearly two pounds of explosives and a dozen live hand grenades. One arrest was affected.

Keegan figured his men must have definitely caught a case on that, as he took another drink from his cup, finishing the coffee. It took Keegan almost an hour to read through all the unusual occurrence reports. He got up from his desk to stretch his legs a bit. He walked out of his office, through the Detective's squad room, and into the kitchen. He saw a freshly brewed pot of coffee and refilled his cup. He added one sugar and a very little bit of milk. He took a sip to make sure it met his approval.

"Hey, Jim, did you read that unusual yet about the explosives they found in Brooklyn?" The Detectives assigned to the unit were all on a first-name basis with their Lieutenant.

Keegan acknowledged. "Yeah, I just finished reading it."

"Al and I caught the case. I think it's going to be a good one."

We pulled him out of Brooklyn Central Booking and brought him back here to debrief. He seemed to have a decent amount of info, so we notified the FBI and had his case flagged at arraignment. They're going to remand him without bail. He seems more of a domestic criminal than a terrorist. After he lawyers up, we are going to set up a *proffer* and have him tell us everything he knows on the record for a chance of a reduced prison sentence."

Keegan was happy to see how on top of things most of his men were. He was pleased with their motivation. He didn't have to assign the case to anyone; they picked it up on their own. They didn't need their hands held or to be told what to do. They just did what they were supposed to. "Be careful. Sounds like this guy must mean business with that kind of firepower. Let me know if you get any leads as to where he got the explosives from and what he was going to do with them. Also, touch base with the precinct Detectives involved. Let's keep them in the loop. You never know, maybe they come up with more information on their end. After all, this guy was working in their command, whatever he was up to."

Keegan was not only an excellent Police Officer; he was also a top-notch supervisor. He knew what had to be done and how to do it. He wasn't afraid to lead by example and it was this quality that earned him the undying respect of his men. "Sounds good boss. I'll give them a call right now."

Keegan was a strong believer in praising his men whenever appropriate. "Let me know how you make out Dave and keep up the good work."

Keegan returned to his office with his coffee and once again took a seat behind his desk. He looked at the remaining two piles of papers, debating which he should review next. He decided since there were far fewer intelligence reports, he would get them out of the way first. He read through the first couple without taking any particular interest in either of them. He then sipped his coffee as he began to read the next one. The words almost seemed to jump off the page at him and he started to gag on his coffee. He could feel his face go flush and felt a bit faint. He rubbed his eyes before he once again read the report...as if maybe the words would now be different.

The report had been forwarded from the department's Intelligence Bureau. It read very simple and to the point; Possible I.R.A. hitman in New York to assassinate the Grand Marshall of the Saint Patrick's Day Parade. That sentence alone brought anguish to James Keegan. He felt his mouth go dry and he slammed his fist down on his desk. "God damn it! How could I have been so fucking stupid?" Keegan said it out loud, even though he sat alone in his office.

He dropped his head and rested it on his desk trying to figure out what his next move should be.

He picked up the report again, staring at it. He got up, report in hand, and paced back and forth in his office, searching his mind for an answer.

I knew I should've insisted on knowing why he wanted the friggin' gun. If anything happens to Martin Devine, it'll all be my fault. He sat back down in his chair and picked up the telephone. He punched in the extension to Bob Wolf's office.

Robert Wolf answered the other end of the phone. "Bob. Jim Keegan, how are you doing?"

Keegan tried to sound as calm, even though he could hear his heart pounding against his own chest.

"Not too bad Jim, and you?"

He lied, "Never been better."

"Don't tell me, I think I know why you're calling."

This took Keegan by surprise. His anxiety level rose. He wondered how in the world his friend could possibly know why he was calling. "You do?"

Robert Wolf answered knowingly. "C'mon Jim give me some credit, huh. You want to know what we have on the safe house in Brooklyn with the explosives."

Keegan was relieved. "Right on target as usual Bob. You never cease to amaze me."

"Unfortunately, Jim, we really don't have too much to go on yet. The last person who rented the house hasn't been seen by the landlord in weeks and when I ran his name through the computer, we come up empty. The guy they locked up has only a few priors for drugs and guns. No known terrorist links. But don't worry, I promise as soon as we know anything else, I'll let you know. I spoke to one of your guys earlier. They said the perp was cooperating. Maybe we can have him introduce an *uncle* to whoever he bought the explosives from."

Introducing an undercover would be prudent, Keegan agreed, but he had more pressing matters on his mind. "Sounds like a great idea Bob. Thanks a bunch. Oh, there is one other thing. I wondered if you could run a name through the computer and see if you come up with anything for me."

Although Keegan worked for the Joint Terrorist Task Force, alongside of the FBI, the FBI agents had more information and resources at their disposal. It wasn't unusual for Keegan or one of his men to tap into these resources during an investigation.

"Sure, no problem. What's the name?"

"Sean Murphy. I'm looking for any connection with the Irish Republican Army."

"The I.R.A.? What's the NYPD getting involved with them for?"

The thought seemed to have piqued Wolf's interest. Keegan was hoping Wolf didn't ask too many questions that he wouldn't be able to answer. He paused for a moment before he responded by lying to his friend. "An intelligence report came across my desk that this guy may be in New York conning money from people for the I.R.A."

Keegan felt a sense of relief that Wolf seemed to buy the story. "Wow, that's something. The Irish Republican Army, here in America? Well, I'll run the name through the computer, and I'll give you a call back in a little bit."

"Thanks, Bob. I appreciate it."

Keegan hung up the receiver and wondered if Wolf bought his story. He figured his friend would have no reason to doubt what he told him and felt slightly relieved. Keegan sifted through the rest of the papers on his desk anxiously awaiting Wolf's return phone call. He skimmed over them without actually reading them. His mind was preoccupied and wondered what he was going to find out about Sean Murphy.

Keegan looked at the clock in his office. It had been less than fifteen minutes since he hung up the phone but to him, it seemed more like hours. He was staring at the intelligence report when the phone finally rang. Although he had been expecting the call, he was nevertheless, startled by the ringing. He felt the butterflies return to his stomach. He drew in a deep breath and lifted the receiver during the second ring. "Joint Terrorist Task Force, Lieutenant Keegan speaking."

"Jim, it's Bob. I got that information you asked for."

"Great. Thanks. What have you got?"

Wolf went on to explain, "Well, I have two Sean Murphys with ties to the I.R.A."

Keegan became slightly excited. He figured now maybe he would find out exactly who and what he was dealing with. One of them *must* be *his* Murphy. "The first guy is thirty-seven years old and served a ten-year sentence in Northern Ireland for a car bomb in Derry which the I.R.A. had claimed responsibility for."

Keegan was disappointed. "No. Thirty-seven is much too old for the subject I'm investigating."

"How old is your guy, Jim?"

"I believe he's in his early twenties."

"Okay, I think Sean Murphy number two might be your man then."

Keegan hoped it was. "What kind of background do you have on him?"

He spoke as calmly as he could, attempting to mask his enthusiasm.

Wolf read the description. "The file says he's a male white. Light brown hair and eyes; five feet, ten inches tall, weighing one hundred seventy-five pounds."

"That sounds like it could be my man."

Wolf could sense the excitement in Keegan's voice. "Not so fast," cautioned Wolf. "According to my file, this Sean Murphy is currently serving a five-year prison sentence in the Maze prison for an attempted armed bank robbery."

"Is there a way you could verify to make sure the information is accurate, Bob? See if he's still in. Maybe he was paroled or something and the computers haven't updated the case status yet."

Wolf assured his friend he would verify. "They usually are pretty accurate Jim. I can double-check with INTERPOL and my connections in Northern Ireland if you'd like."

"Would you mind Bob? I'd like to be sure. It would make this much easier if I knew who we were looking for," Keegan explained.

"No problem Jim, I'll check it out. But Jim, be careful, if this is the guy you're dealing with, he's really dangerous. Don't underestimate him; he's a real bad guy."

Keegan hung up the phone with his friend as the words stuck in his head, *a real bad guy*. He was used to dealing with bad guys, that didn't worry him. What made that guy more of a bad guy than the others, he had arrested over the years? He thought about the situation and realized it didn't matter if this was the Sean Murphy his friend warned him about or a different Sean Murphy or someone just using the name. No matter who he was, he was bound to be an extremely dangerous man. Keegan once again picked up the report and stared at it, almost expecting some kind of answer to jump out at him.

He read the report's brief contents over and over again. He decided to call the Intelligence Division to see what they knew. By the time Keegan hung up the phone, he learned the report had been initiated by INTERPOL. The interrogation of a suspected I.R.A. soldier netted the information. Although it was vague, they believed it credible. The snitch heard a rumor that a man who went by the name of "Gerry" would be the one to carry out the hit.

Of the numerous *Provos*, known to the Northern Irish Police, none had recently left Northern Ireland for the United States. A similar check was conducted in the Republic of Ireland which also met with negative results. The belief was, if the information was correct, the hitman must have traveled using an alias and false documentation.

Keegan realized that the I.R.A. wouldn't send any of their men who were anything less than *'real bad guys'*, to use Bob Wolf's words, to carry out such a major operation. He knew he must be more careful now than ever. For the first time, Keegan faced the fact that he had directly aided a terrorist. A terrorist, who intends on committing murder, right here on American soil. In New York City, no less. He weighed it in his mind and found irony that he would likely be in charge of preventing the attack. Not only would this fall under his jurisdiction within the Joint Terrorist Task Force, but he was also trained in dignitary protection.

He found himself in an impossible situation and sought a solution in his mind. He could either, ignore the facts of the matter and let the man he knew as Sean Murphy carry out the assassination, or he could do everything in his power to stop him. The risk of possibly losing his job and even going to prison himself for his involvement was also a factor. There would be no more hiding the skeletons in his closet. His long-term involvement with a known terrorist organization would certainly be brought to light.

The idea of being walked out in handcuffs in front of Kate was a horrible thought. She didn't deserve that. The press would hound her. Her world would be turned upside down. And his children... *what would they think of their father?* He couldn't bear thinking about that. There must be a solution, he reasoned with himself. He just had to figure out what it was. He had never had his back up against a wall quite like this before.

If he arrested the assassin before he could carry out the attack, he could be sure Murphy would detail his involvement with not only the assassination plot but also his years of running guns to the I.R.A. Everything would surely unravel.

On the other hand, if he let the man complete his mission and flee back to Ireland his job would be safe and he was in the perfect position to make sure the case was never solved. His mind was racing in many different directions. He determined the real decision was between the cause he for so long believed in or his loyalty to the job he loved, regardless of the consequences to himself.

It didn't take him long to come to his decision. It was really the only decision a man like Keegan could possibly make. He was ashamed of himself for even contemplating that he would allow an innocent man to be gunned down in cold blood. He needed to contact Martin Devine and warn him. His biggest problem now was how to stop the hitman without it costing him his job, his freedom, or his life.

Then the solution came to him. He could talk the assassin into aborting the mission and going home. He'd promise to squash the investigation so there was no chance of either of them getting into any trouble with the law. If the parade went off without a hitch, that would be easy. No crime would have been committed. It would look as if someone made up a story to try and stay out of prison. Nobody would think twice about it or have any need to further investigate the allegation. He convinced himself this was the road to take. *It's a win, win situation. Nobody has to die, and nobody goes to prison.* It wouldn't be a hard sell, Keegan figured...as long as he could find the hitman before the parade. He didn't even know his real name or where to find him, but he felt confident he knew who did.

Keegan was filling out a Request for Leave of Absence Report, or a *U.F.28*, as cops referred to them, when the phone rang. Keegan answered the phone. It was a short conversation. Bob Wolf had called back to confirm that Sean Murphy was still in a prison in Northern Ireland. No surprise there.

He completed the U.F.28, which granted him the rest of the afternoon off. He put his coat on and walked out of the office wondering if he would be able to find the hitman, whatever his real name was, in time. He prayed he would be able to talk the man out of the hit but then the words Bob Wolf had once said to him, echoed in his ears. "*A professional terrorist.*" A professional terrorist couldn't simply be talked out of an assignment, he guessed. But he also knew he wouldn't know for sure unless he tried. The plan made perfect sense to any reasonable person, which of course could be the plan's flaw, in itself.

It was a huge city, one in which the man had no ties that Keegan was aware of, except for maybe one or two. The only thing Keegan had on his side was a place to begin. It was in the early afternoon when Keegan entered McBride's. About a half dozen men were sitting at the bar and a couple of dozen patrons were seated in the rear, eating their lunch. He thought to himself, they had a pretty good lunch crowd. He searched the dining area, looking for Nora O'Donnell. He saw there were two waitresses waiting tables and neither one was Nora. He saw Dan O'Brien standing behind the bar engaged in conversation with one of the few men seated at the bar. He slipped into the dining area hoping that O'Brien hadn't seen him.

He waited for one of the waitresses to come over to him to seat him. After a couple of minutes, he caught the attention of a waitress. She picked up a menu and walked over to him. She was a brunette in her mid to late thirties with striking, greenish eyes. She was slightly overweight, but Keegan decided there was still something very attractive about her. "Will you be dining alone or are you waiting for someone?"

"Actually, I'm not here to eat," Keegan explained. "I'm looking for Nora. Is she working today?"

"Not right now, she'll be in later. Who should I tell her was looking for her?"

"She wouldn't know who I was by name if I told

you. We have a mutual friend I wanted to talk to her about. Can you tell me what time she'll be in?"

The waitress looked down at her watch before answering Keegan's question. "She usually comes in around two but I'm not sure if she's starting then today. If you want to make sure you can ask the bartender. He makes the schedule and knows what time everyone comes and goes around here. His name is Dan." She began to walk towards the bar. "Better yet, wait right here I'll go and ask him for you. I have to pick up some drinks for my customers anyway."

"No! Wait." Keegan panicked. The waitress apparently didn't hear him and continued on her way to the bar and Dan O'Brien. Keegan, who didn't want O'Brien to know he was there, walked as quickly and calmly as he could for the exit.

Once outside, Keegan ducked into a card store next door in case O'Brien went outside to look for the mystery man he would be told about. He felt cornered and hoped O'Brien wouldn't think of poking his head inside the store. The last thing Keegan wanted to do was to attract any unnecessary attention to himself inside the store, so he started to browse through the greeting cards.

He read over a dozen birthday cards until he decided to look for a card for Kate. When they first began dating, he would often buy greeting cards for her for no other reason than to say he loved her. He couldn't even remember the last time he bought a card for her, without it being a special occasion, like her birthday or anniversary. It would be a nice thing to do, he decided. He would get her a card just to let her know how much she meant to him.

For about the next twenty minutes, Keegan divided his attention between watching the front door for O'Brien and picking out just the right card for Kate. He selected a card that had a picture of a dozen long stem roses in a vase on the cover. He opened the card and the words on the inside were simple, but they spoke to him and how he felt about his wife.

I love you
You mean the world to me
I sleep at night dreaming of you
And wake up in the morning to fall
in love with you all over again

He felt good about himself for buying the card for Kate and knew she would appreciate it. He walked to the counter, still keeping an eye on the front door, and purchased the card. Keegan peeked out of the card store. There was still no sign of O'Brien, so he exited the store. He turned in the opposite direction from McBride's and quickly walked down the block. He looked down at his watch and saw it was a quarter before one. He decided to go to the bar almost directly across the street from McBride's.

Once inside, he asked the hostess for a table near the window facing the Avenue. He kept the doorway of McBride's under observation watching for Nora.

He hadn't even opened the menu when the waitress came over to take his order. He ordered a well-done cheeseburger and fries to go along with a diet cola. After placing his order, he looked back down at his watch noting only a few minutes had passed.

The waitress returned with his soda a few moments later. He took a sip as he continued monitoring the street for any signs of Nora. He was determined not to miss her when she reported to work. As much as Keegan had always liked and trusted Dan O'Brien, he would much rather contact the hitman through Nora if she would be able to help him. He didn't want O'Brien to know he was looking for the man unless he had no other choice. He wasn't sure if Dan would agree with him about calling off the hit and felt it best to take the matter up with the hitman directly. If he had to take an educated guess, he figured Dan would not be so easily dissuaded from aborting the plan. O'Brien did not have as much at stake as he or the hitman did, he reasoned. Keegan was nervously contemplating another meeting with the assassin when the waitress returned and broke his train of thought.

She placed his lunch down on the table in front of him. "Can I get you a refill?"

He looked down at his half-full glass before answering. "No thank you. What do you have on tap?"

After she took his order, she walked away and left Keegan alone with his thoughts. He had to figure the best way to broach the topic. He wasn't sure if he should try to reason with him or to use his position as a Police Officer to threaten the man. He spent the better part of the next hour wrestling with his dilemma and the possible outcome. It was almost time for Nora's shift to start and Keegan thought it would be best to settle the check. He got the waitress's attention and motioned for her to bring it over. Keegan had barely touched his food. Most of his burger and about half of his fries went neglected. He did; however, manage to polish off a couple of beers over the hour.

After paying his check, Keegan left the bar and crossed the street back to the same side of the street as McBride's. He waited in the doorway of a store a few doors away. Pedestrian and vehicular traffic filled the sidewalks and streets as was common in Manhattan. Everyone in the city always seemed to be in a rush to get somewhere, Keegan noted. There were people as far as the eye could see in every direction. Yellow cabs stopped at every intersection discharging and picking up fares. He hoped the other waitress was correct when she told him Nora usually starts her shift at two o'clock. He also hoped he wouldn't miss her in the masses of people when she did report to work.

Keegan was waiting patiently in the doorway when he saw the bus come to a stop across the street. He watched as it pulled away from the curb. Nora O'Donnell appeared from behind it, wearing a full-length leather jacket, which in his opinion was much too heavy for the mild March afternoon. She walked to the corner, along with about thirty other people, waiting for the light to change so she could safely walk across the busy Avenue. Keegan made his way to the corner to greet her when she crossed. When the light changed, Nora crossed the street and hadn't noticed Keegan. "Nora, can I speak with you for a moment?"

Keegan caught Nora off guard. She stopped briefly to speak with him. "What about?"

"Let me first explain who I am."

Nora interrupted. "I know who you are. I wouldn't have stopped if I didn't know you." She gave a knowing smile. "You're the cop that comes into the bar every few weeks or so; Dan's friend, right?"

Nora's response brought a smile to Keegan's face. He was curious. "How did you know that I'm a Police Officer?"

"Just because I'm a waitress in a bar, doesn't mean I'm stupid. I have eyes and ears just like you. You've been coming into the bar for as long as I've worked there and it's not really too hard to figure out. You're not the only Detective in town, ya know."

She was teasing Keegan.

His face turned slightly red. "I wasn't implying you were stupid; I was…"

Nora decided to let him off the hook. She shoved him playfully on the shoulder. 'Relax, I'm only kidding. What can I help you with?"

Keegan smiled back at her. "Do you remember

the last time I was there? I was sitting at a table in the back room. You were my waitress that night. I was with a young guy you seemed to be pretty friendly with."

The smile quickly disappeared from her face. "Yeah. What about him?"

Keegan sensed something amiss. The smile quickly disappeared from Nora's face and now she was the one turning red. But it was more from anger than embarrassment. "I was wondering if you knew where I could find him. It's important that I speak with him."

"How should I know?" said Nora curtly. "I thought you cops always knew where to find one and other."

The mention of Sean Murphy seemed to have struck a nerve with the waitress.

Keegan was confused. "Cops? Did he tell you he was a cop?"

"No, but he did have a gun, so I figured...maybe... listen, I'm going to be late for work. She began to abruptly walk away from Keegan without having finished her thought.

Keegan took after her. "Please, Nora. It really is urgent I find him."

Keegan knew from experience, that quite often when a Police Officer was asking for someone's whereabouts, it was assumed they were in trouble with the law. He would do his best to reassure her, this was not the case. "He's not in any kind of trouble. I just need to speak with him."

He thought about how many times he used that line to convince a family member or friend to betray someone they cared about and then he would arrest the person anyway. It was a common ploy used by investigators to track a wanted person down. The irony was not missed on him that this time, he was telling the truth. He had no desire to arrest anyone. He just needed to talk to him and convince him to call off the hit.

She stopped in her tracks, turned around, and looked Keegan in the eyes. "Look, I don't know where your friend is, and to be honest, I don't give a shit."

Keegan's eyes met hers and he studied them as she spoke. He had become adept at knowing when someone was lying to him or telling the truth. He was disappointed in the realization that Nora spoke the truth. He was sure of it. The eyes never lie.

She continued. "I can't help you. If you really want to find him, ask Dan. They seemed to be pretty tight."

Her eyes dropped. Keegan recognized that Nora had somehow been betrayed by the man. He thanked her for her time. She then, once again, turned her back on him and entered the bar without uttering another word.

Keegan remained motionless on Third Avenue watching Nora disappear inside the bar. He debated in his mind as to what his next course of action should be. Nora was clearly unable or unwilling to help him. It looked like he would have to fall back to his last resort, after all. He would have to solicit the help of Dan O'Brien if he had any chance at all of locating the hitman. Keegan paced the sidewalk, deliberating if he should go in right now and talk to O'Brien or wait and see if the hitman shows up at the bar later tonight. He thought back to what Nora had said, *'that they were tight'*, and wondered if she was trying to tell him that the man had been frequenting the bar. Keegan decided O'Brien would find out about his impending showdown, either way, so he would take the direct approach. *Maybe not totally direct, though.*

He took a deep breath before entering the bar. The crowd had thinned out over the last couple of hours. He saw Dan O'Brien standing behind the bar with only a handful of patrons to concern himself with. He surveyed the bar. He was hoping, although it would be a longshot that the man he sought might be in there right now. It would have been nice to find him without involving O'Brien. As he expected, the man wasn't there, and he was left with no alternative than to speak with the bartender.

He didn't notice Nora walking up from behind him. She grabbed him gently by the upper arm and he turned around to face her. She felt the need to explain herself to the Police Officer. "Listen, I just wanted to apologize for coming off so rudely before. I had a bad experience with the guy you're looking for and I assumed you were a friend of his because I saw you sitting with him." She paused before continuing, "So, you're not a friend of his then?"

He shook his head. "No. I'm not."

Nora pondered the implications. "Well, in that case, he's been in here on a semi-regular basis after ten until about one or two."

"Thank you, Nora. I really appreciate it."

Keegan looked up at O'Brien. He was pretty sure O'Brien hadn't noticed him and he wanted to slip out before he did. "I owe you one. I'll be back later. Please don't mention I was asking about him."

Keegan started to head toward the door when he heard a familiar voice call out to him.

"James Keegan, you weren't going to come into this bar twice in one day and not say hello to me either time, now were ya?"

Keegan turned to see Dan O'Brien pouring a draft from the tap. *Why couldn't Nora have told me this outside the bar, so I could've avoided this?*

There was no way to avoid him at this point. "Of course, not Dan, I was just going to hang my coat up on the coat rack in the front."

It was a horrible excuse. One he was pretty sure O'Brien would not believe. In all the years he's been coming here, he had always put his coat on the back of the barstool, never on the coat rack. He then reasoned to himself, that a bad answer is better than no answer at all. Keegan took off his coat, hung it on the rack, and returned to his usual barstool. There was a pint of Guinness waiting for him on the bar.

"So, Jim, was I wrong about you? Do you have a little something going on the side with Nora after all?"

The barman was trying the feel Keegan out and studied his face for a reaction. Keegan glanced in Nora's direction and watched her wait on a table. He hadn't noticed the black mini skirt she was wearing until now. Keegan decided she looked as good as ever today. He then looked back at O'Brien with a devilish smirk on his face.

"I wish I could say I did, but unfortunately I don't."

"Well, if not Nora, then do what do I owe this unexpected surprise to?" probed O'Brien.

Keegan thought carefully before answering. There was no reason to deny the truth and he was sure O'Brien must have figured things out anyway. "I need to talk to Murphy."

O'Brien became concerned even though he had expected as much. "Murphy, is it? Now, what might you need to speak to him for? He's a busy fella, you know."

"I don't want to seem rude Dan, but it's really something I want to discuss with him."

Keegan swallowed about half of his drink in one swift motion.

"I see, Jim. I don't have any way of reaching out to him, ya know. He does come in here at night a wee bit but there's no guarantee when and if he comes in."

"Dan, it's of the utmost importance that I speak with him as soon as possible. If he comes in here tonight or tomorrow or whenever page me right away. Please."

Keegan sounded very businesslike. O'Brien figured there was no harm in trying one more time. "Are you sure there's nothing that I can help you with, Jim?"

"I'm sure. Just do me the favor and make sure you get in contact with me as soon as you see him, okay Dan?"

O'Brien agreed. "Will do, Jim. Will do."

Keegan got up from the barstool, picked up the rest of his Guinness, and drank it down. "Thanks, Dan."

He walked to the front of the bar to retrieve his coat, waving goodbye to Nora as he passed. Keegan put his coat on and left the bar. He felt relieved to at least get this far but he knew he was a long way off from accomplishing what he ultimately had to. Ironically, he left McBride's at about the same time he would've left work. Since he would get home around the same time, he wouldn't have to tell Kate any more lies, at least for the time being.

The traffic on the Long Island Expressway was uncommonly heavy. Keegan fought traffic for the better part of two hours before he finally arrived at his exit. As heavy as the traffic had been, it didn't bother him. He lost track of time on the ride home. His mind was preoccupied with stopping the assassination. When he got off the exit ramp, he realized the time and how long it had taken to get home. He then saw the card he bought for Kate earlier in the day on the passenger seat of the Crown Victoria. He put it there when he first got into the car, but he would've probably forgotten it if he hadn't just seen it.

Keegan decided to stop off on the way home and pick up some flowers to go along with the card. He bought a mix of mini carnations, lilacs, and roses which he was sure would be greatly appreciated by Kate. He sat in the flower shop's parking lot to fill out the card. He opened it up and stared at it for about two minutes, before finally writing inside of it. He simply addressed it to 'the love of my life' and wrote how much she meant to him. He then sealed the envelope and headed home.

Kate was preparing pepper steak with rice for dinner when she heard Jim's car pull into the driveway. The kids were upstairs in their bedrooms, doing their homework. Kate saw the bouquet of flowers in her husband's hands out of the corner of her eye. She stopped what she was doing, washed her hands, and walked over to him. Keegan presented the flowers and the card to her without uttering a word.

"What's the occasion?" she asked as she accepted the flowers and opened the card.

Kate read the words that her husband had written to her and a warm feeling came over her. It was nice to be appreciated and loved. She had a loving smile on her face and their eyes met. "I love you too, Jim."

The two of them tightly embraced and shared a kiss until the sound of the kids scampering down the stairs broke them from each other. She noticed that Jim held the embrace even after hearing the kids and did not seem to want to let go.

Returning to the kitchen, she got a vase from the bottom cabinet. She filled it halfway up with water and removed the flowers from their cellophane wrapper and placed them in the vase. She carefully arranged them until she felt they were just right. Satisfied they were, she could now get back to preparing dinner. She could hear Jim in the living room roughhousing with the boys. Kate always got nervous when Jim played so rough with the boys but then she decided boys will be boys, no matter how old they are. Concerned Kerry would get caught in the middle of the boys wrestling; Kate called her into the kitchen.

Kerry skipped her way into the kitchen as Kate was taking down the dishes from a cabinet above the sink. "Yes, mommy."

"Can you be a good girl and set the table for mommy?"

Kate knew how much Kerry enjoyed helping her. She was a typical little girl.

"Yes mommy, I can help."

Kerry took the dishes from her mother and began to walk out of the kitchen when she saw the flowers on the counter. "Oooh, mommy, where did you get the flowers? They're so pretty!"

"Daddy bought them for me, sweetheart. Aren't they gorgeous?"

Kerry put the dishes down on the nook in the kitchen and went over to smell the flowers. "You're so lucky, mommy. I love flowers."

There was a hint of jealousy in her voice.

"We can share them. C'mon, you promised to help me set the table."

Kate's redirection of her daughter was successful. Kerry walked away from the flowers and once again picked up the dishes to go and set the table. As she left the kitchen, her mother called out to her. "Kerry, tell daddy to come in the kitchen for me."

Once Kerry left the kitchen, Kate retrieved a small piece of cellophane from the trash and carefully selected one of each type of flower Jim had bought her as well as some greens and made a mini bouquet out of them. When Jim entered the kitchen and saw what Kate was up to, he immediately understood. He accepted the new arrangement from Kate and called his daughter into the kitchen.

Kerry returned to the kitchen and informed her mother that the table was set. She again focused her attention on the flowers. "Daddy, those are so pretty."

"Angel," began Keegan. "I have a surprise for you," concealing his left hand behind his back.

"What is it, daddy?" Kerry loved a surprise as much as any four-year-old would.

Keegan took his hand out from behind his back and presented his daughter with her very own flowers. Her eyes lit up and she bit her lower lip. She looked at both of her parents as if asking permission to take them. She gave her father a big hug and kiss. "Thank you, daddy, you're the best!"

Kerry sat through dinner with her flowers right next to her and even put them in a glass of water in her room before going to sleep that night.

Keegan grew slightly anxious as the night went on, waiting for his beeper to go off but it never did. It was almost eleven when all of the kids had finally fallen asleep. The Keegans checked on their children making sure they were all sleeping before settling into their own bedroom to renew the passion they had sparked earlier in the night. Jim Keegan edged closer to his wife and gently pressed his lips against hers. His thoughts entirely belonged to Kate right now. Thoughts of the I.R.A., Dan O'Brien, Sean Murphy, Castillo, Internal Affairs all seemed to be forgotten, if only temporarily. He thought of nothing more than how much he wanted to be with his wife.

CHAPTER 12

Castillo sat at his desk at the office of Internal Affairs. He opened the bottom right draw on the metal desk, sat back in his chair, and rested his right foot atop the open drawer. He ran his hand through his hair while contemplating what to do next. After a brief moment, he drew himself closer to his desk and laid the photos from the bar across his desk. With his right elbow on the table, he rested his chin on his fist, scanning the photos below.

He focused on the photos he had taken of the man in the bar with Keegan. He was particularly interested in the tattoo on his forearm and decided to play a hunch. Based on his own observations of the man, he figured he was not from the United States, but instead from Ireland, more specifically, Northern Ireland. He also decided if he was right about Keegan, this guy must have some sort of ties to the I.R.A. Castillo was outraged at the blatant disrespect Keegan had shown him last week. He wanted to take down Keegan more now than ever. He realized he had to be careful and not let it become personal. Making a case personal leads to shortcuts and that is when mistakes are inevitably made.

More than Keegan however, he was upset at himself for having blown his cover. He thought how if he were out in the field in an organized crime detail or narcotics instead of I.A.B., blowing his cover could have cost him his life. He had to be more careful in the future. In the meantime, he hoped he hadn't completely screwed up the case on Keegan. He also reminded himself that when he finally placed handcuffs on the rouge Lieutenant, he would have the last laugh.

Castillo needed to regroup. He needed to gather his thoughts and come up with a new plan of action. His mind kept on drifting back to how his cover was blown. He decided it couldn't have been anything he, himself had done. The only bad move he made as far as he could see was to sit in the bar alone and keep Keegan under observation. He should have blended in better with the crowd. He should've brought a female Detective with him to make it look like just another couple out for a night on the town. Even that one minor mistake didn't account for how Keegan knew his name, however.

This ate away at Castillo. He must have been tipped off, determined Castillo. Who would do such a thing? Who would even know about his investigation? Castillo was racking his brain. He was the only one working on the case; it started as nothing more than a hunch. It's pretty clear right now that his hunch was correct, but he hadn't told a soul about it for fear of looking stupid; except for one person.

The only person in the world that he could remember telling about his hunch, was his boss, Deputy Inspector Marsh. *Of course*! Castillo pounded his fist against his desk. From the moment Castillo had brought the investigation up to Marsh, he was against it. Castillo theorized Keegan and Marsh must know each other from somewhere on the job. Maybe they worked together in precinct house years ago or maybe they had a friend in common. Marsh must have been the one to tip him off.

God damn it! Castillo was livid at this notion and decided not even his commanding officer would stand in the way of his investigation on Keegan. Castillo now realized he was truly on his own. He had no partner to confide in and clearly, he could not even count on his boss. He wondered if Marsh had run this up the chain of command and the top brass would also be watching and impeding his investigation. He decided Keegan would be locked up no matter what the repercussions. He didn't care if he, himself, was brought up on charges for disobeying an order or for not keeping his supervisors informed of his investigation. It didn't matter; he was determined to see justice served. Castillo felt himself, once again, becoming personally involved. He would salvage this case, no matter what the cost.

Castillo knew what he had to do. He decided when he had a substantial amount of evidence on Keegan, instead of reporting it to Marsh, as was the proper protocol; he would directly present his case to the District Attorney's office for a Grand Jury hearing. It would make the department look bad and they would come after him for doing it, but he didn't care. The repercussions could be severe. He would cross that bridge when he came to it.

On the other hand, he figured breaking a case like this one, would be front-page news and the department would not dare chastise the Detective who broke the case. If he played his cards just right and got a couple of well-timed breaks in the case, he could have the department by the balls and maybe even get a promotion to Detective Second Grade. A smirk came across his face contemplating this scenario as a possible outcome of the investigation.

He stood up from behind his desk. His leg was aching something awful. The inclement March weather was no help. Castillo wondered if he would carry this ailment with him until he goes to his grave. It was incredible the amount of pain a bullet wound could cause even so many years later. The pain always seemed most severe on rainy days such as this one. All Castillo could do was to grin and bear it.

He limped over to the metallic green file cabinet and opened the top drawer. He had to give a hard pull as the top drawer always sticks due to some dents near the top. *God forbid the department springs for some new file cabinets. These friggin things are at least twenty years old.* He flipped through then case folders which were filed alphabetically by the case Detective's last name. Once he found his case folders, he pulled the file on Lieutenant James Keegan. He knew he could no longer leave the file lying around the office or even in the file cabinet if Marsh was going to tip Keegan off. He put the file in his briefcase to take home with him every night.

As Castillo locked his briefcase, he could see Frank Balentine walk into the squad room out of the corner of his eye. Castillo got up to greet his long-time friend and the two of them shook hands. Balentine wore a gray, pin-striped suit, which flattered his six-foot-plus frame. He was a handsome man whose cleft chin added charisma to his already charming demeanor. Balentine wore his dark hair parted to the left never having a hair out of place. Castillo was always quick to tease his friend that he would make the perfect politician. He was a good speaker, a good looker, and a good liar. Balentine was amused by his friend's taunts, especially because he knew he was guilty on all counts.

Balentine handed Castillo a manila envelope with the word CLASSIFIED printed across the flap. In the upper corner of the envelope, Castillo read the words PHOTOS DO NOT BEND. Castillo was excited with the hopes that the contents of the envelope may help in his investigation. Castillo briefly glanced at the envelope without opening it. He could feel by its weight, there was a substantial amount of information in it. "Aren't you going to open it?" inquired Balentine.

Castillo looked around for Inspector Marsh before responding to his friend's question. "Yeah, I'm going to open it but not here. Let's go out to lunch like we planned on, I'll open it later."

Castillo didn't want to seem too excited, but the truth is that he was extremely impatient. He also didn't want Marsh to walk in on him as he examined the envelope's contents, fearing he might again clue Keegan into what was happening. Castillo hoped to deflect the conversation away from the photos and his investigation. "So where are we going to go for lunch anyway?"

"I've wanted to try this new Italian restaurant downtown. I've heard it's really good. Best veal in the city, I'm told."

"Then Italian it is."

The men left the office of the New York City Police Department's Internal Affairs Bureau. They got into the brand new, 1995 Ford Crown Victoria that Balentine was assigned to by the FBI. "Nice car," Castillo commented. "It must be nice to work for the Feds. The best car in I.A.'s fleet, not assigned to a boss, is a 92 Caprice with almost seventy thousand miles on it."

"Well, you should've listened to me back in college when I tried to get you to join the Bureau instead of the Police Department," lectured Balentine, as he drove the Crown Victoria over the Brooklyn Bridge into Manhattan.

Castillo stared at Police Headquarters at the foot of the bridge. He chuckled to himself as he thought of the building's comical nickname of the *puzzle palace*. A nickname no doubt, some wisecracking cop came up with and it just stuck. The traffic was mild for Manhattan and only ten minutes later they had parked the car and entered the restaurant. Castillo made sure he brought the envelope in with him, not wanting to take a chance of anything happening to them.

The restaurant was in the Little Italy section of Manhattan. It was a quaint little restaurant that offered sidewalk seating in the summer months. Castillo had never been here before. He observed the back wall to be completely mirrored, giving the impression it was bigger than it actually was. The other walls were beige, a couple of shades lighter than the table clothes and linens. Castillo recognized a weatherman from a local news station seated at the table closest to the bar in the far-left corner. The wall lamps were on the dim side. Not too dim though, Castillo decided. He hated going to restaurants that had the lighting so dim that you struggled to read the menu.

Once they were seated, they each ordered a cocktail to start with. They reminisced about old times and their days together in high school and college. Castillo asked about Balentine's wife. They had been together since college. Castillo felt momentarily depressed in the fact that he did not have anyone significant in his life. The waiter, who was dressed in a white buttoned-down shirt with black slacks and bow tie, returned to the table and set their drinks down in front of them. After placing their orders for lunch, Balentine got to the heart of the meeting.

"So, tell me, Louie, how in the world have you

gotten yourself involved with the I.R.A.?"

Castillo had grimaced at the question. Although he knew it would be impossible, he was hoping to skirt the issue altogether. Castillo at least had the luxury of knowing that he could trust Balentine, unequivocally. Balentine was not only Castillo's oldest friend but he was also the only one who had stuck by his side through thick and thin. While others chastised Castillo for going to I.A.B., Balentine supported him. Balentine was true to Castillo but he still somehow felt uncomfortable sharing the details of this case with him. He took a deep breath before answering. "I really can't say too much because right now I'm only playing a hunch."

He took a sip from his drink to quench the dryness in his mouth before continuing. "If it turns out I'm right, this will be on the headlines of every paper in the city...guaranteed."

"So...since your internal affairs...it's a safe assumption to say you've got a New York City cop involved with the I.R.A.?"

Balentine's interest was piqued. Castillo dropped his eyes and stared down at his drink. There was a slightly uncomfortable pause as Castillo weighed whether or not to tell his friend. Balentine sensed the reluctance but continued to probe him anyway. "Can you tell me a little bit without getting into great detail?"

Castillo raised his head and nodded to his friend in agreement. "All right Frank. Just please promise me that you make sure you keep it under your hat.

I've been burned already and don't even have the job's backing on this case. I can't afford them finding out that I'm still working it off the queue."

Balentine shook his head knowingly. He empathized with his friend's predicament. "You have my word, Louie."

Castillo brought his glass to his lips and this time took more of a gulp than a sip. He began to explain. "I think I'm on to a well-known and ranking member of the department, deeply involved with the Irish Republican Army. I can't say any more than that Frank, unfortunately, he's already made me, but I still think I can make the case against him."

"Wow. All right, I won't put any more pressure on you."

Balentine digested the information. "Do you want to take a look at the pictures? I had a friend of mine in the Anti-Terrorist Unit run a check through the computer for anyone with an arrest record in Northern Ireland who had a tattoo of a shamrock on his right arm. He also reached out to the anti-terrorist unit in Northern Ireland. We came up with eight possibles. I pulled a few strings and was able to come up with arrest photos of every one of them as well as a picture of their tattoos."

"It sounds like you had to call in a whole lot of favors for me." Castillo was humbled. "I really didn't want you to knock yourself out over this," Castillo lied.

He knew since he was basically on his own, he could use all of the help he could get.

"No problem Louie. You would have done the same for me. After all, what are friends for?"

Castillo knew his friend was right. He would bend over backward for Frank Balentine if he asked him to. Nevertheless, he still felt awkward for inconveniencing him. "Frank, I want you to know how much I appreciate this."

"Why don't you open up the envelope and see if the information you're looking for is inside?"

Castillo agreed. He picked up the envelope from the seat next to him. Just as he unsealed it, the waiter came to the table with their lunch. "Right after we eat, that is. Perfect timing."

Both men shared a laugh. Castillo was torn between wanting to tear the envelope open to see what was inside, and being afraid to, in case there was nothing inside to help further his investigation. If the latter were true, Castillo may have come to a dead end. It was quite apparent that he could no longer tail Keegan since his cover was blown. He couldn't even ask Inspector Marsh for assistance, believing Marsh was responsible for tipping Keegan off. Castillo was less than pleased that his entire case could hinge on what the contents of this one envelope held.

Balentine appeared to thoroughly enjoy his lunch while Castillo did very little more than sample his own. Castillo ordered another drink as the anticipation was eating away at him. Balentine noticed his friend's preoccupation with the envelope. "The food here is outrageous. Why don't you just open the envelope up now and then maybe you can enjoy your lunch instead of play with it?"

Balentine reached for the envelope and held it out, offering it to Castillo.

Castillo felt like a child being scolded by his parent. He took the envelope from Balentine. "I suppose you're right Frank. I'm just a little nervous that the whole case could go down the tubes if there's nothing in there to help me."

"Well Louie, there's only one way to find out."

Castillo was slightly uneasy as he peeled open the envelope. Along with the photographs, the envelope contained additional information such as the pedigree of each man as well as all of their arrest records. These Included sealed cases and juvenile arrests. All eight of the men had tattoos of a shamrock on their right arm. After each picture of their face, was a close-up photo of the tattoo itself. Castillo slowly examined each picture, one by one. He noticed they had been arranged in alphabetical order, according to the subject's last name. The tension grew in Castillo's stomach as he looked through the first four without any luck. When he pulled the fourth photo from the top of the pile, revealing the fifth, he felt like he hit the lottery. "I think that's him, Frank!" Castillo announced, almost out of breath. "His hair is much shorter in this picture and he had facial hair back then, but I'm pretty sure this is my man."

Castillo turned the photo over and read the name of Gerald Flynn, which had been written on the back. He compared the photo that he had taken with the photo of Flynn and decided this was probably his man. Just to be sure, he compared the two photos of the tattoos. The photo he took in the bar of the subject's tattoo depicted a small mole just below the shamrock. *Bingo!* There was no doubt, seeing the matching mole on Flynn's arm.

Castillo felt a great sense of accomplishment knowing that his case was now stronger than ever. It went from a hunch to now having tangible evidence that Lieutenant James Keegan, if nothing else, was associating with an Irish terrorist. And the case could only get stronger from here, he reasoned. He now had a name to go with the face. He decided he would continue to browse through the remaining photos to see what else was in there when the very next photo also caught his eye.

The next photo was of a man with an identical tattoo in the same place on the arm as Gerald Flynn's. The man's face also shared similar features to Gerald Flynn. Castillo turned the photo over. The second man's name was Patrick Flynn. A quick study of the close-up photo of the tattoo revealed no mole. Castillo was relieved. There was no doubt in Castillo's mind that these men had to be related, however.

"Can I ask you for one more favor, Frank?" Castillo imposed, knowing his friend wouldn't turn him down.

"You are lucky I'm in a giving mood. Sure, just name it."

"Can you check to see if there is any current information available on these two guys, including their current whereabouts, if known?"

"On one condition Louie."

Castillo was curious. "What's that?"

"On the condition that you forget all about the case for twenty minutes so you can enjoy your friggin' lunch."

Castillo chuckled at his friend's joke and agreed. "You got yourself a deal."

Balentine's recommendation had been right on the money. The food was excellent, and the service was great. Castillo figured this place would not be cheap, but it was worth every cent. Not only for the food but for the priceless information he acquired. After deciding to pass on dessert, the waiter brought the check. Both men reached for it but Castillo's hands were quicker. "This is my treat Frank; it's the least I can do."

Balentine shook his head with a smile on his face. He snatched the check from Castillo's hand, reached into his back pocket, and retrieved his wallet. He showed his friend a credit card. "Don't be silly Louie, this is on the Bureau. This was official business after all. You've got all those pictures to prove it."

"Oh yeah, I almost forgot about the fringe benefits of working for the feds." Castillo smiled and put his wallet away.

"I told you to go with the Bureau instead of the police department." Once again, Balentine teased.

Castillo returned to the office shortly before two o'clock. He walked directly to his desk, opened his briefcase, and removed the file on Keegan. He opened the file and stared at the pictures he had taken of James Keegan and Gerald Flynn. What the two of them could possibly be up to, he wondered. While he didn't know, one thing he did know was that he was determined to find out. Castillo was so distracted by his own thoughts and photos that he never saw Inspector Marsh walk over to him. "Louie, have you got a minute?"

Marsh caught Castillo off guard and Castillo quickly and as nonchalantly as possible stuffed the photos back into the case folder. "Sure boss," nervously responded Castillo.

Marsh then invited Castillo to join him in his office. Castillo followed his supervisor into the office.

"Louie, close the door behind you please," Marsh requested of him.

Once the door was closed, Marsh motioned with an open arm, inviting Castillo to have a seat on one of the blue fabric chairs in front of his desk. Castillo could feel his palms begin to sweat. He took a seat opposite Inspector Marsh's desk waiting to see what he wanted. Marsh stared out of the window momentarily before taking the seat as his desk. "Louie, I haven't seen too much paper on the case you've been working on. I was curious to know how it's progressing."

Castillo thought for a moment, trying to decide how to respond. He feigned confusion and crinkled his eyebrows. "Which case is that Inspector?" He was trying to buy precious seconds to think of the answers he knew he would still have to come up with.

Marsh grew slightly annoyed, and it showed in his tone of voice. "How many cases have you been working on lately, Louie?" inquired Marsh as he sensed the apprehensiveness in Castillo.

"Oh, you mean the case on Keegan."

"Yes, I mean the case on Keegan."

"Well, I haven't really made too much progress at all."

Castillo lied in an attempt to protect the integrity of the investigation. "In fact, I was thinking I might've been mistaking about him after all. I'm going to just close the case out I think."

Now it was Marsh who crinkled his eyebrows. "Really?" Marsh was clearly surprised by this revelation. "I thought you were so high on this case and sure Keegan was dirty only a few weeks ago."

Castillo felt backed in a corner. "I did. I guess we all make mistakes, don't we boss?"

"Louie, do me a favor. Get the case folder for me; I want to look through it. You haven't submitted a single *five* for me to review in nearly two weeks now."

"No problem, boss. I've fallen a bit behind on the paperwork, but I can bang out a couple of *fives* and bring the folder up to date."

Castillo got up from the chair and left Marsh's office. He closed the door behind him and walked back to his desk. He removed the file from his briefcase, opened it up, and as quickly and smoothly as he could, he removed the photos that he had just received along with as many of the more incriminating documents that he had yet to tell his supervisor about. He put these items in his desk drawer and locked it.

He inserted a pink DD5 into his typewriter and detailed a fictitious surveillance that he conducted of Lieutenant Keegan. He then did the same regarding Dan O'Brien. He signed the bottom of the forms and now added them to his case folder. The case was now up to date...at least as far as the paperwork was concerned.

He returned to Marsh's office and presented the file to Marsh for review. Castillo stood in front of the Inspector's desk patiently as Marsh skeptically read through the file. The five minutes it took for Marsh to examine the file were painstaking to Castillo. Marsh put the file down on top of his desk. Looking up at Castillo, he removed his eyeglasses and put them down on top of the file. "So, you think your chasing shadows on this one now Louie?"

Castillo could sense the doubt in his voice. "Yes, I do, Inspector. I was going to ask you if I could close it out as unfounded."

"Well, if you feel there's nothing going on, then close it out. But Louie, if you dig up anything else, I want you to report it to me immediately. I want to be kept abreast of anything you find out in this case. No surprises. Got it?" Marsh handed Castillo back the file.

"Got it, boss. No surprises. You have my word."

As Castillo left the office, he felt a sense of relief. *If Marsh could lie, so could I.* He knew Marsh would be happy to see this investigation closed out. He felt in spite of his apprehension that Marsh had bought his story about closing it. He thought about Marsh telling him to report any new findings to him immediately. He now felt for sure Marsh was the one who had tipped Keegan off. It made perfect sense. He thought again how infuriated Marsh was going to be when he finally took Keegan down. Castillo closed the door behind him and went back to his desk.

He took a new case folder, inserting the newly attained documents into it. He made photocopies of the original file making them also part of this new case folder. He then returned the original folder to its place in the file cabinet in case Marsh decided to look for it. He decided to carry the new folder with all the vital evidence in it, inside of his briefcase. This way he could be assured no one would see the true file on Lieutenant James Keegan until he presented his findings to the District Attorney's office and the Grand Jury.

Shortly after their meeting, Marsh emerged from his office and signed out for the day. Castillo wondered if Marsh was going to meet with Keegan to let him know the investigation had come to a close. Castillo was tied up in this thought when one of the other Detectives informed him, he had a phone call. Castillo thanked the Detective and picked up the line. "Detective Castillo."

"Louie, it's Frank. I have that information on the Flynn boys you wanted."

"Wow, that was quick."

"What's the fax number over there, I'll fax it over to you."

Castillo gave him the number and hung up the phone. He hoped Marsh wouldn't walk back into the office and catch him receiving the fax. He would've had a hell of a time explaining the information he was getting to his commanding officer. Castillo went over to the fax machine, anticipating it coming to life. It did. Castillo received the information when it came through. There were six pages in all. Castillo put them directly into his secret file on Keegan, rather than take the chance of reading them in the office. It was almost three-thirty and time for Castillo to sign out. He decided he could wait until he left the office to find out what valuable information the fax held.

After signing out, Castillo left the building; briefcase in hand, and got into his private auto. Castillo started his car and pulled away from the office of Internal Affairs. He had originally decided to wait until he got home to read the information, but the anticipation was too great. He got only a few miles from his office when he decided to pull over and examine the contents.

Castillo parked his car on Gold Street in between Flatbush Avenue and the Brooklyn-Queens Express- way. He parked his vehicle at an angle where he could watch the traffic back up on the B.Q.E. Castillo knew he would be sitting in traffic for quite a while, at this time of day, so the extra time he killed reading the report wouldn't make much of a difference. Cas- tillo reached over to his briefcase in the passenger seat of the auto and retrieved the file. He opened it up and soaked in the new information. He read the information on Patrick Flynn first, almost as if leav- ing the best for last to build up the anticipation.

The report documented Patrick Flynn's criminal record and his three arrests in Northern Ireland. He was on a list of suspected terrorists to be watched by the police and government in Northern Ireland. Patrick Flynn was currently serving time in prison for an I.R.A.-related bombing. A phone call had been made to the warden of the prison by the Northern Irish Police (at the request of the FBI), to verify if he was still incarcerated. He was.

Balentine was very thorough and a good re- source to have on his side, figured Castillo. Cas- tillo was impressed at how detailed the report was. These reports were much more detailed than the ones he had previously received. It listed all of his past addresses, his educational background, the fact that he had once used the alias of Paddy Taylor, and probably most importantly, all his known acquaint- ances and ties in the I.R.A., including his brother Gerald.

Four of the six pages of information Balentine had faxed over to Castillo were dedicated to Patrick Flynn. Castillo was slightly disappointed by this because that meant that only two pages of information would be on the man that was directly involved in his investigation into James Keegan. Castillo was almost afraid to turn the last page on Patrick Flynn fearing the information on Gerald Flynn wouldn't be what he hoped. Castillo scanned the pages on Gerald Flynn before reading in detail what they had to say. The information was basically the same as the information on the previous man except Gerald Flynn's record wasn't nearly as intense as his brother's. Gerald Flynn only had one arrest on his record but much to Castillo's delight, he was on parole. One of the conditions of Flynn's parole was that he not leaves Northern Ireland.

Castillo had a warm feeling of satisfaction. He finally had something semi-solid to go on. Flynn was in clear violation of his parole and Keegan was apparently aiding in his willful neglect of the conditions of his parole. Furthermore, Castillo now had real solid proof Keegan was associating with a member of the Irish Republican Army. This alone, was a substantial violation of department policy and enough to bring Keegan up on charges. It was not; however, enough to bring him up on criminal charges and send him to prison.

Castillo would wait and build the case against Keegan criminally, before taking any action at all. Castillo continued reading the information and learned Flynn's last meeting with his parole officer was in February and he had shown up on schedule. His next scheduled appointment is on March 30, so Castillo figured he was only here in America for a short time. Castillo wondered exactly what Keegan and he were up to.

Castillo's thoughts captivated him as he explored the possibilities. He figured maybe Keegan was involved in collecting money for the I.R.A. but how could he do something as public as collecting money without anyone in the department noticing. Castillo realized Keegan worked in the Joint Terrorist Task Force and wondered if maybe he was getting information from the FBI and passing it on to the I.R.A. That made more sense. The more Castillo threw this notion around in his head, the more he liked it.

It makes sense, thought Castillo. The passing of the envelope from Dan O'Brien to Keegan which he had on film was probably the payoff and the meeting with Flynn must have been the transaction of the information. Castillo decided the information was both too valuable and too dangerous for Keegan to send it through the mail or even through email so someone from the other side would have to come to New York to receive it in person. Whatever the scenario was, Castillo was sure Keegan was dirty and he was slowly getting closer and closer to finding out the truth as the investigation progressed.

Knowing that Keegan had made him, Castillo realized he could no longer follow him. Flynn on the other hand, might not know who he was. If he could find Flynn and keep an eye on him from a distance, he might get the hardcore evidence he needed to hang Keegan. It was a way to backdoor the investigation. He would have to run a parallel investigation and surveillance on Flynn until he crossed paths with Keegan again. Finding Flynn would be hard enough, conceded Castillo. Even if he did find him, Castillo knew he would have to be careful to avoid Keegan. That would be disastrous to the investigation, possibly blowing any chance at all of bringing the case home.

Castillo put the papers back into his briefcase and closed it up. He placed the briefcase back on the passenger side of his car and looked up at the clock on the dashboard. Castillo was surprised to learn he had been there over an hour, examining the information. He glanced over at the B.Q.E. and saw the traffic was as heavy as, or even heavier than it was before. For some reason, the fact that he was going to fight traffic for the better part of the next hour didn't seem to matter that much at all to Castillo. The only thing that mattered right now was the fact that the case on James Keegan—the case of his career —was beginning to pan out.

CHAPTER 13

Nora O'Donnell watched Gerald Flynn enter the bar. It had been almost a week since she had seen him, and she wondered if Keegan had ever been able to track him down. She had gotten the impression from him the other day that the two of them were not friends like she originally thought and that maybe the man she still knew as Sean Murphy was in some kind of trouble with the law. She prayed he was. It would serve him right. She genuinely hated the man. It hadn't been the first time a man had taken advantage of her for sex. It was the way he was so mean and obnoxious about it afterward, that really got under Nora's skin.

She wished she had taken Keegan's phone number so she could call him, and he could come in here tonight and maybe arrest the man for something. She reflected that Keegan didn't seem to be surprised when she told him that Sean was carrying a gun. Maybe that was why he was looking for him, to arrest him for the gun. No matter what the circumstances, she was greatly disappointed she had no way to contact Keegan.

Gerald Flynn walked into McBride's wearing a

pair of blue jeans, a black sweatshirt, and a blue denim jacket. His nine-millimeter handgun was in its usual place tucked into his waistband. Flynn walked directly into the back room of the bar and sat at an open table in Nora's section of the room. Every time he came into the bar, he sat in Nora's section just to watch her squirm and ask one of the other waitresses to serve him. He got a perverted kind of satisfaction out of the fact that Nora couldn't even look at him.

Flynn ordered a beer and sat alone at the table listening to the music of Tommy McDermott and his band. When the waitress returned with his beer, he reached into the inside pocket of his denim jacket and removed a pack of cigarettes. He wrapped the unopened box against the table, packing the tobacco to one end. He then opened the pack and removed one of the cigarettes from the pack by holding it up to his mouth and closing his lips around it. At the same time, with his free hand, he removed a lighter from his pocket and lit the cigarette. He set the cigarette down in an ashtray and took the first sip of his beer.

Flynn was halfway done with his first beer when Dan O'Brien finally got his attention. Flynn looked up at O'Brien as he motioned for him to join him over to the bar. Flynn's instructions, given to him by Eamon Quinn, were quite clear. While Flynn was over in the United States, O'Brien was his boss. Although Flynn always ultimately did follow their orders, he often gave his superiors a hard time before carrying them out. Flynn was not only a rebel of sorts, but he was also extremely arrogant. He knew he was good, and he also knew especially in an operation such as this one he, and only he, would be able to successfully execute it.

Flynn lifted his beer at O'Brien to acknowledge and chugged the remaining beer down testing O'Brien's patience. O'Brien continued to wave Flynn over but instead of immediately going over to see what the bartender wanted, he slowly finished his cigarette first. Once done, Flynn put it out in the ashtray and stood up. He took off his denim jacket, put it down on one of the chairs at his table, and walked to the front of the bar to speak with Dan O'Brien.

This was the third night in a row Louis Castillo had come to McBride's on his own time to see if Gerald Flynn would appear. Castillo had begun to lose hope and had figured that maybe Flynn had already returned to Ireland. He finally showed up tonight. Castillo was relieved and hoped Flynn would lead him to his ultimate goal; incriminating evidence he could use against Keegan. He took note that Flynn was wearing his long hair in a ponytail tonight and that he was here alone. He wondered if maybe Keegan would be in later to meet him. He hoped he would not. Castillo decided Flynn seemed to be rather smug as he walked up to the bar to meet Dan O'Brien.

Castillo was a sharp cop and wouldn't be burned

twice by the same mistake. He had enlisted an old friend of his from his Police Academy days to help him out. Sharon Winters was a shapely brunette with deep, light brown eyes. Her pouty lips a soft shade of red. She was thirty years old and like Castillo had never been married. In fact, she and Louis Castillo had been an item from their days in the Police Academy until some years later when they went in their own directions, parting on the best of terms.

Castillo had decided to call Sharon so he wouldn't return to the bar by himself and once again attract attention he didn't need. Sitting in the bar with a woman, helped him blend into the crowd a little better. He no longer looked out of place. He couldn't ask for help from his office without Marsh finding out. Even if someone would be willing to do him the favor, he couldn't be sure they would be loyal to him and not tell Marsh. He definitely wanted another cop's help in case something went down, so going off the grid made sense to him. Sharon was perfect for the job, he concluded. She was a seasoned cop and a Detective in the Special Victims Squad in the Bronx.

She trusted Castillo and went with him even though he didn't inform her of any of the details of the case he was working on. They had been in the bar for over two hours catching up on old times and sharing stories of the job like they had done the two previous nights when Flynn walked in. "That's the man I was hoping would show up," Castillo announced to his fellow Detective, pointing Flynn out.

"He doesn't look like a cop," noted Winters. His hair is too long, and he has a very rough look to him.

Castillo shook his head from side to side. "I never said he was a cop, Sharon."

"I assumed since you work for Internal Affairs you were investigating a crooked cop," explained a confused, Sharon Winters.

Before Castillo had time to dodge the question on his own, Nora O'Donnell rescued him almost on cue. "Excuse me," began Nora. "Is your cop friend going to be in here tonight?"

Castillo was cautious when answering the waitress. "Which cop friend is that?"

"I can't remember his name...I think it might be Jimmy. Don't you remember, he bought you a drink and I brought it over to you last time you were in here?"

Castillo would never forget that night. It was one of the low points of his career. "Of course, I remember. And yes, his name is Jim. Why do you ask?" baited Castillo.

"Do you see that man who just walked up to the bar wearing a black sweatshirt?"

Castillo was very interested to see where this was going. "Yeah, I see him."

"Well, your friend was in here looking for him earlier in the week and said it was extremely important that he find him. I forgot to take his phone number in case he came in here and now that he's here, I feel terrible that I have no way to get in contact with your friend. I think he is going to arrest him," further explaining her dilemma.

Castillo smiled and motioned for Nora to inch closer. He whispered, "Can I let you in on a secret?"

Nora leaned in and shrugged her shoulders. "I guess so, sure."

"Good." He could sense from the way Nora was speaking to him she did not like Gerald Flynn and Castillo decided to use this to his advantage.

"The man you're talking about is the subject of an investigation. The other Detective and I are working on a case against him. We've been staking this place out for the last few nights waiting to see if he would show up."

"Good, I hope you nail the bastard and hang him high." Nora O'Donnell was clearly angry with the man for whatever reason.

"Please, just do me one huge favor. Don't mention this to anyone. If my partner does come in here later, don't mention to him that I'm here. He'll just be relieving me, and I don't want that guy to realize that we are together. And please, make sure you don't even say anything to my partner about any of this. If that guy even overheard you telling my partner you saw me in here, the entire case would be compromised."

Castillo had told Nora exactly what she wanted to hear, and she wouldn't dare do anything that would jeopardize the arrest and prosecution of Sean Murphy. "You have my word," Nora promised as she walked away from the table.

"Well, well, well," began Sharon. "You've either

told that cocktail waitress more about this case in five minutes than you've told me over the past three nights that I've spent working on it, as a favor to you, or you were lying through your teeth. Which one is it?"

It was a fair question. Castillo laughed at the insinuation and responded by shaking his head. "What kind of Detective are you if you don't know when someone is flat out lying?" He wouldn't miss the opportunity to challenge his friend's Detective skills.

"Don't be obnoxious," she warned him. "I figured you were probably lying but I just wanted to be sure."

Castillo kept an eye on the bar area and watched as Flynn and O'Brien seemed to be getting involved in a rather heated conversation. He wished there was a way he could hear what they were saying but that was impossible, especially with the band blasting its music. Castillo had strategically selected the table he and Sharon were seated at. They were sitting almost directly behind the band so the chance of anyone seeing them was greatly diminished. Castillo liked his vantage point. He was able to keep an unobstructed view of what was going on at the bar.

Nora O'Donnell returned to the table with another round of drinks. " This one's on me." She placed the drinks down on the table in front of the couple.

They responded in harmony. "Thank you."

"You are very welcome. And the name is Nora if

you should need anything else."

Castillo raised his glass in her direction. "Okay, then. Thank you very much, Nora."

Nora O'Donnell flashed Castillo a smile and walked away from the table to tend to other customers at her station.

"Well Louie, you sure have her sold on that story."

Winters decided to push for a little more information. "Would she be disappointed if she knew the truth?"

Castillo ignored the question. "I can use all the help I can get on this one Sharon."

He once again focused his attention on the men at the bar and their rather intense conversation. "If I only knew what they were talking about."

Castillo was frustrated as he hopelessly tried to read their lips.

Neither Dan O'Brien nor Gerald Flynn had noticed Louis Castillo sitting in the bar. The fact that he brought a female companion this time, seemed to help him blend into the crowd. When Flynn arrived at the bar, he noticed O'Brien's face was red, either in anger that Flynn had been ignoring him or in frustration because he realized it was actually Flynn, who was running the show. Either way, Flynn rather enjoyed upsetting the bartender. "So, what is so important that you nearly jumped over the bar to get me attention?"

O'Brien poured Flynn a pint of beer before answering and tried not to let on to the fact that he was genuinely annoyed at him. No sooner did O'Brien put the beer down in front of Flynn than did he guzzle the entire beer down in one long gulp. Flynn wiped his mouth with his sleeve and set the empty glass back down on the bar. "It's Keegan. He asked me to get in contact with you to set up a meeting."

"I have no reason to meet with the man. As far as I'm concerned, he did his part and now he should mind his own business."

O'Brien became insistent. "Maybe he has some kind of vital information you should know about, Gerald."

Flynn's eyes grew narrow as he stared at O'Brien. He snapped at the bartender. "That's Sean to you. Or have ya forgotten me name?" Flynn didn't seem too eager to forgive O'Brien's error this time, as Eamon had told him any slip-ups could cost him dearly.

O'Brien shook his head apologetically. "I forgot. I'm sorry, Sean." His patience was starting to wear thin with the hitman. "He asked me to beep him the next time you were in here so he could come in and talk to you."

Flynn ignored O'Brien's comment. "How about another beer, barkeep? I'm mighty parched, I am."

He could see the frustration slowly mount in O'Brien. His face began to turn a shade darker.

O'Brien could feel his blood pressure rising at Flynn's constant indifference. O'Brien calmly picked up the empty glass Flynn had set down in front of him, walked over to the tap, and filled it up. With each passing second O'Brien could feel his blood pressure rise. After all, they were on the same side, trying to achieve the same thing. So why did Flynn have to keep acting so indignant? He couldn't figure the assassin out. Maybe it was the age difference between the two. Maybe Flynn didn't respect him since it was so many years since he left Ireland and was living in America, away from the troubles. O'Brien couldn't see Eamon Quinn tolerating such arrogance and disrespect. Nevertheless, he was trying to avoid pulling rank on the man or a confrontation of any kind, for that matter. With that in mind, O'Brien set the beer back down in front of Flynn and once again asked for Flynn's permission to call Keegan. "So is it okay with ya if I give 'em a call then, Sean?"

Flynn took a sip of beer and looked O'Brien dead in the eyes before answering. "No. It's not okay. I don't trust the man and I don't like the man."

Flynn picked up his beer and began to walk away from the bar and Dan O'Brien.

That was the final straw for O'Brien. "Sean!" yelled an obviously incensed Dan O'Brien. Flynn, however, ignored O'Brien and continued to walk away. Flynn walked up to the stage and while Tommy McDermott was in the middle of a break and made a request of him to play a song. McDermott, although he had only known the man a short time, had taken a liking to his fellow Irishman and usually played his requests.

Dan O'Brien came from around the bar and followed Flynn up to the stage, his blood beginning to boil. O'Brien wrapped his hand around Flynn's elbow and spun him around to face him. Some of the beer jumped from Flynn's mug, splashing on the floor. Flynn had a fierce look on his face, but it was child's play compared to the look on O'Brien's. O'Brien decided it was time to put his foot down and let Flynn know who was in charge. "You don't walk away from me when I'm talking to ya! Is that understood?"

O'Brien's anger and boldness had taken Flynn off guard.

He didn't figure O'Brien for the type of man to have enough nerve to stand up to him. He had severely underestimated O'Brien and momentarily forgotten that O'Brien was probably fighting for the cause before he had been born. O'Brien's actions had instantly won the respect of Gerald Flynn and he figured Eamon Quinn, himself, would have acted similarly if he had stepped over the line back at home. He always respected Quinn and now O'Brien as well. A solemn Gerald Flynn answered O'Brien in a barely audible voice. "Aye, Dan." I'm sorry."

O'Brien saw he had finally caught the man's attention and he started to settle down. He toned his voice back down. "Good, now I'm going to call Keegan up and ask him to come here right now."

Flynn began to protest. "But Dan…"

"But nothing!" O'Brien would have none of it and

cut him off before he could make his case. "Jimmy has been loyal to the cause for many years, probably since you were in grade school. He's a good man and he'll be heard."

"All right then, Dan. I'll meet with him. But I want you to know, I still don't trust 'em."

"What reason have you got not to trust him? He got you a gun to carry around and to use for the assignment, did he not? He probably has some intelligence information he wants to pass on to you so you can complete the mission safely and get back home in one piece. We have less than a week to go before the parade and any information at all could wind up saving your arse, so I think you had better listen to what he has to say. It's for your own good, lad. Don't ya get that?"

"I certainly hope so, but I still have a gut feeling about him...and it's not a good one."

Flynn's instincts were usually very accurate and no matter what Dan O'Brien thought. Flynn was certain Keegan was going to cause trouble. Dan O'Brien then ended the conversation with Flynn by walking back to his bar which he had abandoned only a few moments prior. As O'Brien walked away, Tommy McDermott began to play the song which Flynn had requested. Flynn then walked away from the front of the stage heading back to his table. In route back, he asked his waitress to bring him another beer.

It was almost midnight and Flynn wondered how long he would have to wait for Keegan to show up. He had the unmistakable feeling there was going to be trouble.

At first, Castillo's heart skipped a beat as the two men approached him. He thought he had been made again. He quickly motioned to Sharon, alerting her that the men were approaching. He buried his head in a menu. This was not the case.

Louis Castillo couldn't have asked for a better break. Not only did the two men have this conversation directly in front of the table where he was seated but the band was also in between songs. It was quiet enough in the bar, so Castillo didn't even have to stare at the two bickering men to try and read lips. Instead, he was able to stare down at the menu and still eavesdrop on their entire conversation. Neither of the men had any idea he was doing so.

Flynn had supplied him with his most incriminating evidence yet. He only wished he had captured the conversation on tape. From what he gathered out of the conversation, Keegan had been working for the I.R.A. for many years now and that Flynn was here to carry out some kind of mission. He was puzzled. *What in the world would the I.R.A. be doing in New York? And what significance did the parade hold, why did O'Brien mention it?* Most importantly, of course, was what Keegan's role in this conspiracy was?

Castillo then asked Sharon what she had made out of the conversation. She had told Castillo that as best as she could guess the two men and this Jimmy were partners in some kind of plan. Sharon's interpretation of the conversation delighted Castillo.

An independent account of the conversation to corroborate his account could be enough to indict Keegan for criminal conspiracy if he could only find out what the plan was. The fact that the independent witness was also a Police Officer would certainly make her a credible witness. Castillo then thought back to the conversation between O'Brien and Flynn. He was relatively sure he heard the mention of Keegan supplying Flynn with a gun. This alone was good enough to cause Keegan to lose his job and maybe do some jail time.

Castillo thought hard about his best course of action. He then came up with the idea to follow Flynn home and to get a search warrant for wherever he was staying. Then once he recovered the gun, he had Keegan dead to rights. Maybe he would also find some type of evidence detailing what they were planning. Even if no plans were found, if he could arrest Flynn and get him to roll over on Keegan in exchange for not going to prison, maybe Flynn would tell him what the mission was. His case against Keegan would be airtight.

If all went well, Castillo figured, he could be presenting the case to a Grand Jury by as early as next week. Castillo overheard O'Brien saying he was going to be calling Keegan to come to the bar. He was on such a good role that he didn't want to jeopardize it in any way. He determined it would be best if he left the bar so there was no chance in the world of Keegan once again seeing him there. He asked the waitress for his check.

Castillo looked at Winters and clumsily asked a favor of her. "Would you mind keeping me company on a stakeout?"

Sharon paused for a moment. Then she narrowed her eyes, tilted her head, and bit her lower lip. "I suppose I could lend you a hand. What's it worth to you?"

"I'm being serious Sharon. I'd really appreciate it."

Castillo decided maybe it was the alcohol causing his old flame to flirt with him but he was relieved when Sharon agreed to help him regardless. The waitress returned with the check and Castillo settled the tab as he had done the past few nights without asking Sharon for any money. It was the least he could do since she was the one doing him the favor.

They walked out of McBride's and headed to Forty-Third Street where Castillo's car was parked. He opened the passenger door for Sharon and held it open as she entered. Once she got inside, he closed the door behind her and walked around to the driver's side. He entered his car and turned the key. The car started instantly, and Castillo allowed it to idle momentarily, before putting it in gear. He drove around the block, positioning himself about a block and a half away from McBride's. He parked the car in the tail end of a bus stop and kept a sharp eye on

McBride's entrance.

He turned the ignition off, keeping on the auxiliary power so they would be able to listen to the radio. Sharon tuned the radio to a soft rock station as Castillo reached into his glove box to retrieve a pair of binoculars. He focused the binoculars in on the entrance to McBride's and wondered how long it would take for Keegan to show up. But even more important than that, he wondered how long it would take before Flynn would leave.

Gerald Flynn went back over to the bar where Dan O'Brien was still attempting to catch up on serving his customers from his five minutes of neglect that he had spent arguing with Flynn. After catching up, he walked over to the phone behind the bar. O'Brien carefully punched in the phone number which would page Keegan. After hearing the tone on the other end of the line, he punched in the bar's telephone number.

Turning around, he was met by a humbled Gerald Flynn standing at the bar. He was patiently waiting to speak with him. O'Brien almost felt bad at the way he had to pull rank on Flynn, but he was starting to act like a loose cannon. There was no place for that. Not when something so important was at stake. O'Brien sensed that he had the man back under his control. "What is it that you want, Sean?"

This time he was careful to remember to use the man's alias.

"'I just want you to know I'm not questioning

your judgment or anything like that Dan, but what if your buddy has other ideas? He is a Police Officer, after all. How can you know for sure his loyalty is to the cause and not to the police department?"

Dan O'Brien didn't want to let Flynn know that he shared his concerns. "Sean, think about it for a moment. Jim has been running guns for us for years. He's never asked any questions. He has always just simply done what I've asked of him."

"Aye, I understand that Dan. But you've also never asked him to get involved in anything on this side of the Atlantic Ocean, now have ya?"

O'Brien knew it was a fair question, to say the least. "No. I haven't. But that doesn't change anything. If he were to somehow try and interfere, he would be doing it at the risk of losing his job for what he has done over the years. I'm sure he knows all anyone would have to do is detail his role in the gun-running and not only would he lose his job and pension, but he would most likely go to prison for many years. I know James Keegan, Sean. He is a family man with three small children and a beautiful wife at home. He's not about to do anything that would jeopardize their future, or his own."

O'Brien was trying to convince himself just as much as he was Flynn.

"Dan, I don't mean to be rude, but you still haven't answered me question. What if he does try to stop the hit? I have me orders from Eamon and unless he personally tells me to call it off, I'm going to complete it, even if it means losin' me own life.

You know that Dan."

"I know you would Sean, and I agree. There is no way in the world I would call the hit off."

O'Brien once again saw the cold eyes of a murderer appear in Gerald Flynn as he spoke. The softness and humility had ebbed away in favor of his more familiar state. O'Brien knew Flynn was a loyal soldier and would not call off the hit unless he received an order directly from Eamon Quinn, himself. O'Brien agreed with him on this matter and felt it was much too important a mission to be aborted.

"So, what would we do about Keegan?"

The truth was that Dan O'Brien had no idea what to do if Keegan intended to try and stop the hit. He hoped that was not the case, but he had a strange feeling that it just might be. Why else would he demand to speak with Flynn alone instead of talking to O'Brien? "Let's not jump the gun, Sean. We'll give the man the benefit of a doubt. But if he does, I'll talk to him."

"You don't honestly think you can just talk the man out of trying to stop us if that is what he's fixed on doin', now do ya, Dan?"

"Well, I'll tell ya what I'm thinkin', Sean. If I sit Jimmy down and explain to him how important this is to the cause and what a powerful statement the hit would make around the world, maybe he'd just turn the other cheek and let ya carry out the hit. I'll explain to him that we don't have the authority to abort an operation of this magnitude on our own. If he doesn't go for it, well, then we'll have to deal with him by any means necessary if and when he tries to stop it."

A cold smile came across Gerald Flynn's face. "Ah Dan, now that's exactly what I wanted to hear."

Flynn had grown to genuinely dislike Keegan and despite O'Brien's vouching for the man's loyalty to the cause, Flynn felt he would be loyal to his job first.

Dan O'Brien wasn't pleased with the evil smirk he was watching appear on Flynn's face. It made him slightly uncomfortable. "Sean, I said *if* and *when* he tries to interfere and *not* any time before then. Is that clear?"

"And so it is. Crystal clear."

Gerald Flynn returned to his table where he sat alone. His beer was on the table waiting for him. He took a swig from the beer and lit up a cigarette. He thought it was kind of weird, but all of the sudden, he was actually looking forward to his meeting with Keegan. He pondered how he would like to terrorize him if he decided to do anything stupid. He would first terrorize him and then kill him without any hesitation if need be. Gerald Flynn, after all, was cold-blooded and actually enjoyed killing. Flynn reached down to his waist, feeling the butt of the gun through his clothes, just to make sure it was exactly in the right position. Flynn took another sip of the beer and listened to the music of Tommy McDermott as he waited for Keegan to arrive.

CHAPTER 14

The vibrating of the pager against the night table was enough to wake Keegan from his light sleep. He rolled over and looked at Kate, who was unbothered by the noise. He picked up the pager, hoping that it wasn't the office but rather Dan O'Brien calling to inform him that the hitman was at McBride's. The number was not familiar, but it did have a Manhattan exchange. Keegan quietly slipped out of bed with the pager in his hand and went downstairs into the living room. He picked up the receiver of his telephone and punched in the numbers into the telephone's keypad as he read them off the beeper. He was confident it would be Dan O'Brien who was paging him. He patiently waited for someone at the other end of the line to pick up the phone. In the middle of the seventh ring, the familiar brogue of Dan O'Brien answered. "McBride's. Can I help you?"

"Dan. It's me, Jim," explained Keegan in a voice just above a whisper, trying not to wake up anyone in the house, especially Kate.

"Our friend that you wanted to have a word with is here waiting for ya, Jim."

"Great. Do me a favor. Tell him to sit tight I'll be

there as soon as I can; probably about an hour or so."

O'Brien who wanted to discourage Keegan from speaking to Flynn if possible, suggested Keegan speak to him instead. "Jim, I don't know how long I can keep him here." He lied. "He's been wantin' to leave. Are ya sure you can't just talk to me? It would be so much easier."

"No Dan. This is something that's between me and him to settle, but thanks anyway. I'll be there as soon as I can."

He hung up the telephone. He was nervous. His meeting with Flynn was exactly what he had been waiting for the better part of the week, but he was also afraid the hitman might not care about his problems relating to the hit. Keegan walked as quietly as he could back up to his bedroom. He peeked in before entering and saw Kate was undisturbed. He went into the bedroom and picked up his pair of jeans from the floor as well as a sweatshirt from his dresser drawer. He carried his clothes out of the bedroom and got dressed in the hallway, fearing if he got dressed in the room, he might wake his wife.

After getting dressed, he went back into the room and opened his closet door. Kate began to stir. Keegan stood as still as he possibly could, watching his wife's movements until she seemed to settle back into a sound sleep. He then retrieved the Sig Sauer, nine-millimeter handgun he kept locked in a strongbox on the top shelf of his closet, well out of reach of the children. He closed the closet door and secured the gun in the holster strapped to the right side of his hip.

Keegan once again went downstairs and after putting on his shoes he went into the kitchen. He took a pen and a piece of paper from a pad in the kitchen's junk drawer. He wrote Kate a note in case she woke up during his absence, explaining that his job had called in the middle of the night and that he would be home as soon as he could. *Another lie.* The note would further explain that he didn't want to disturb her, so he let her sleep. Keegan ascended the stairs and entered his bedroom. He placed the note on Kate's night table with the corner of the note under her jewelry box.

He looked down at his sleeping wife and thought about how much he loved her and the kids. He thought that if all went well tonight, she would never know about his dealings with the I.R.A. He also knew that tonight could be a very important night regarding their future together. He wanted to give her a kiss before leaving but he didn't want to chance waking her up. The last thing in the world he needed right now was for Kate to wake up and start to question him. After debating for a minute, he decided to throw caution to the wind, and he leaned down and gently kissed her head. God forbid, something was to go wrong tonight at least, he would know he gave her a kiss goodbye. He knew he was dealing with a very dangerous man. "I love you, Kate." He whispered as he stroked her long hair. Keegan closed the bedroom door behind him and went into his children's rooms to check on them. After seeing they were soundly and comfortably sleeping, he gave each one of them a kiss on the head before leaving.

As he left his house, he realized it was a lot colder than he had expected it to be. The dark blue spring jacket he had grabbed on the way out was certainly not going to be warm enough for the current thirty degrees that it was outside. He unlocked his Crown Victoria and got inside. He turned the key and the car slowly cranked to life. The cold winter weather had apparently taken a toll on the car's battery. Keegan put the heat on full blast to take the chill out of his bones. He then allowed the car about a minute to warm up and glanced up at his bedroom window before throwing the car into gear. No lights had come on from within the house. *So far, so good.* He breathed a sigh of relief. He managed to sneak out of the house and start the car up without waking Kate. *Now, if only the rest of the night could go this well...*

The traffic on the Long Island Expressway had been rather light until he got to the Junction Boulevard Exit. He had been traveling at about seventy-five miles per hour the entire thirty-five minutes and he knew he jinxed himself when he thought how he was making such good time. The traffic started backing up, he became frustrated. He saw the turret lights of a marked Highway unit up ahead, but he wasn't sure if it was an accident or construction that was holding the traffic up.

After impatiently waiting in traffic for about ten minutes, Keegan put his dome light in his windshield and tapped his siren for cars to get out of his way. He didn't want to bring any unnecessary attention to himself but if he didn't get to McBride's soon, he might not have another chance to meet with the hitman before the parade. Staying in the far-left lane, he tapped the siren and the cars pulled slightly over to the right allowing him to pass. As he got closer, he could see two Highway units on the scene handling a serious accident involving a small truck and a Honda. Flares were blocking the two right lanes and a tow truck parked on the shoulder of the expressway.

As he approached, one of the uniformed highway patrol officers directed traffic out of Keegan's way. He realized the officer had no idea who he was, but he knew the officer would assume him to be a boss of some kind. When Keegan got to the scene of the accident, he slowed down enough to roll down his window and thank the officer for his assistance.

After thanking the officer, Keegan continued on his way, but not before he drew his own assessment of the accident scene. He saw the Honda had front-end damage and the truck had a flat tire. A tire iron lay on the ground next to the flat tire. The driver of the truck looked like he was seriously injured, and the driver of the Honda was being placed in handcuffs. He seemed unsteady on his feet. Keegan figured the truck driver was changing a flat tire on the side of the road when the other car rear-ended the truck. He shook his head at the thought. *Damn drunk drivers.* While Keegan enjoyed a couple of beers, he never drank to the point where it was unsafe to drive. The truck driver was just lucky to be alive.

Keegan continued driving without any further delays to the Queens-Midtown Tunnel. After showing the toll collector the parking permit and announcing the vehicle's car number, he proceeded through the tunnel. About a quarter of the way in, his radio went to static, so he inserted a compact disc into the player and listened to soft rock and roll music for the rest of his short ride. The traffic was average for a Friday night in Manhattan, and it took him about ten minutes from the tunnel before pulling up in front of McBride's.

Keegan saw an opening near a fire hydrant right in front of the bar. He might not have parked there if he had his private vehicle because it was a gray area whether he was far enough away from the hydrant to avoid a parking summons. But with the department car and parking permit, he thought he was okay. Especially since he would not be directly blocking the hydrant. In all his years of going to McBride's, he had never parked at the hydrant. But tonight, was different; he had wasted enough time fighting traffic on the way over here and he wasn't about to go searching for a parking spot. He reached above the sun visor and retrieved the restricted parking permit for department vehicle 8567 and placed it so it was clearly visible on the dashboard of the vehicle. He got out of the car, took a deep breath, and made his way towards the bar. He hoped Dan was able to convince the man to wait there for him.

Louis Castillo watched as Keegan parked the un-marked department auto at the fire hydrant. He was excited and felt it all might come together tonight. "That's him Sharon; he's the subject of my investiga-tion."

Castillo prayed Keegan wouldn't somehow see him again. He knew he was over a block away, but he was still afraid of getting caught a second time.

Sharon, although she didn't know what all the details were, was able to share in Castillo's enthusi-asm. "That's great Louie, maybe something big will happen."

Sharon was trying to be supportive of her friend even though he was keeping her in the dark with many of the facts.

"Yeah, you're probably right. Something *real* big. My big break in the case will go down in there to-night and I'll be sitting right here, unable to see it go down."

Castillo began to feel angry at himself. It was al-most a habit of his now. Every time he thought back to how Keegan had made him and then belittled and embarrassed him, he got enraged all over again.

Sensing his frustration, Sharon Winters tried to ease his concern. "It's not that bad Louie."

Castillo was clearly frustrated. "It's not, huh?"

Sharon reached over and slapped Castillo on the knee, hoping to give him some encouragement he desperately needed. "I have an idea how to find out what's going on in there."

Castillo perked up instantly. He was excited and willing to listen to any idea that could help. "Go ahead, Sharon. I'm listening. You have my full attention."

She began to explain. "Well, that guy may know who you are."

She poked Castillo playfully in the chest as she continued. "But I haven't been made. He has no idea in the world who I am. I can just walk right in there and see what's going on."

Castillo loved the idea and didn't mind showing his excitement. "You've got a point. You wouldn't mind going in there and keeping an eye on them for me? I'd really appreciate it, Sharon. I'll owe you big time."

Sharon gave him a playful wink. "That's what I'm counting on, Louie."

Sharon opened the door of Castillo's Nissan and was ready to leave when he grabbed her gently by the upper arm. She turned to face him. "Sharon, don't you even want to know why you're watching him?"

Castillo started to feel a little ashamed of himself for not filling her in on the details of the case.

"Of course, I'm curious. But you said you couldn't tell me anything and I respect that."

She paused for a few seconds before continuing.

"There is only one thing I want to know for certain before I go undercover for Internal Affairs," she said mockingly. "This guy is up to something really big, right Louie? I mean, it's not some nonsense that I'm watching him for?"

"No Sharon. It's very serious. You have my word on that."

"Well Louie, that's good enough for me." She once again attempted to leave the auto.

"Wait a minute."

Castillo was doing something he hadn't done in quite some time. He started to trust someone. He hoped it wouldn't come back to haunt him. "I think maybe you should know what the investigation is about."

"You don't have to tell me, Louie."

"I know I don't have to but if you're getting this involved, I want you to have an idea of what you are getting yourself involved with."

Sharon closed the car door until it was ajar and waited for Castillo's explanation. "I'm not sure how deep or in what capacity but I'm rather certain the off-duty member of the service who just walked into the bar is involved with the Irish Republican Army. The young guy inside, I believe is I.R.A. I'm pretty certain of it."

"The I.R.A.?"

She was both shocked and excited at the same time to be on the ground floor of such a major investigation. "But what in the world are they doing in New York?"

Castillo shrugged his shoulders. "I'm afraid I have no idea. But I hope by the end of the night the all the pieces will fall into place and we will find out. If we can just grab his accomplice with the gun, I'm sure he'll roll on the cop and tell us what the plan was if we promise him leniency."

Sharon Winters thought the plan sounded great but plans usually did sound pretty good until they went into effect. That's when a myriad of things could go wrong, she knew. She hoped this one would go as smooth as it sounded in theory. "Louie. I have one question."

"What's that?"

"What exactly am I watching for when I'm in the bar?"

Castillo wished he had a better answer and shook his head at her. "To be perfectly honest Sharon, I have no idea what to look for. Just anything that seems odd or unusual."

"Odd or unusual," she reiterated as she nodded her head in agreement.

Castillo took her by the hand. "And please, Sharon, be careful. He held her hand slightly longer than he should have, he thought. Winters then pushed the door wide open and got out of the car, unmolested this time. She closed the door behind her and made her way across Third Avenue. Castillo raised his binoculars to eye level and wondered where the night would lead as he watched Sharon enter the bar.

It had taken James Keegan only a matter of seconds to locate the hitman in the crowded back room of the bar. He was seated at the same table as the last time they had spoken. He started to walk over to the man and glanced in the direction of the bartender. Dan O'Brien's eyes met his and Keegan quickly nodded and looked away. He nodded hello to Tommy McDermott as he walked past the stage. Upon arriving at the hitman's table, he took a seat next to the man and greeted him. "It's good to see you, Sean. How have you been?"

Flynn looked at Keegan and without returning his salutation, excused himself from the table and went to the restroom. Keegan figured this was most likely a ploy by the man to draw him into a confrontation of some sort and he wasn't going to fall into the man's trap. Keegan was relieved enough that the man was still here. At least he must be willing to hear what Keegan had to say. In Flynn's absence, Keegan got the attention of the waitress and ordered a Guinness. She was the same waitress he met the other day when he was looking for Nora. Her eyes didn't have the same gleam that they did when he first encountered her.

He kept a watchful eye on Nora as she would look in his direction every few minutes and immediately look away. It was peculiar behavior on her part. He was unsure what to make of it. She was probably just been curious as to why it was so important for Keegan to find the man. She probably thinks I'm here to arrest him. Nora wasn't the only one interested in the meeting. Dan O'Brien's eyes have been locked on him since he walked in. Keegan started to grow impatient waiting for the Flynn to return. *He's trying to piss me off. He's making me wait on purpose.* He reminded himself to keep his composure when talking with the man.

Sharon Winters entered McBride's only moments behind Keegan. She watched him walk over to the man she and Louie had been surveilling before they left the bar. As soon as Keegan sat down, it seemed to Sharon, the other man got up and walked away, almost as if he was annoyed at him. While Keegan sat alone at the table, she observed him looking around. She thought it would be best if she bought herself a drink, so she didn't look conspicuous. Sharon made her way through the crowd to the bar and waited to catch Dan O'Brien's attention.

O'Brien saw the pretty young lady walk up to the bar and stare in his direction. O'Brien made his way from the other side of the bar and greeted her. "And what might you be drinkin' lass?"

"I'll have a Sea Breeze. Thank you," a nervous Sharon Winters answered.

O'Brien brought Sharon her drink and after paying him for it, she returned to the spot she had been standing. It was a perfect location; she had an unobstructed view of Keegan's table. Sharon watched as the other man returned and practically seemed to sit on Keegan's lap. The Sea Breeze tasted good and it soothed Sharon's nerves a bit. She was about half-way finished with it and felt she was doing a good job blending into the crowd when she was greeted by an unfamiliar voice from behind. "Can I buy you another drink?"

Sharon turned around to greet the voice and she politely turned him down. "No thank you." The man was in his late twenties figured Sharon and he wasn't bad looking but he was the last thing she wanted right now.

"You look so familiar," the man continued. "Where do I know you from?"

Sharon Winters shook her head in disbelief. She knew she had never met him before. The last thing she needed right now, was some guy to be hitting on her.

The waitress returned with Keegan's drink before Flynn returned from the restroom. He was halfway done with the Guinness when Flynn finally rejoined him. Flynn sat down extremely close to him and this made Keegan uncomfortable. He was intentionally violating Keegan's personal space. "So, Mr. Keegan, Dan tells me you have some intelligence information you wanted to pass on to me to make me mission a little bit easier. Is that right?" He licked his lower lip and stared coldly into Keegan's eyes.

"Well, Sean," softly began Keegan, trying to gain the hitman's trust. "It's true. I did receive intelligence regarding a hit on the Grand Marshall of the

Saint Patrick's Day Parade."

Flynn was curious. "Now, Mr. Keegan, how would the New York City Police Department be gettin' such information?"

"Well Sean, it seems one of your buddies back home got caught in Derry with fifty pounds of explosives. When they interrogated him, he gave them the information about the hit in return for not going to the Maze for the next ten years. The good news is, he didn't point fingers at you directly. He said it would be done by a guy who went by the name Gerry...not Sean."

Keegan studied the man for a reaction.

"God damn traitor!" exclaimed Flynn. "Do ya know Mr. Keegan; the single most detrimental blow to the cause of freedom in Northern Ireland for hundreds of years has been traitors. The bastards should be publicly hanged, they should."

Keegan sensed this was exactly the right time to gain favor with the man. "Sean, you'll be very happy to know the man was found shot dead two days later in a back alley in the Bogside. Apparently, he took a hell of a beating too before they finally executed him."

Flynn was genuinely pleased with the outcome of the story. He couldn't wait to get home and speak to Eamon Quinn to see who the traitor had been. His money was on Mickey Clarke. He never did trust him. "Good. Then he got what he deserved, now didn't he?"

Feeling he may have gained the man's trust, Keegan took a deep breath and decided to get back to the heart of the matter. "As I started to tell you, Sean... here's the problem. I'm going to be the one in charge of security for Martin Devine."

Flynn started to see where the conversation was going, and he didn't like it. He was determined to infuriate Keegan. "Good, then, Mr. Keegan. You'll be able to make sure the security is loose enough for me to carry out the hit without any problems then, won't ya?" He gave him a gentle slap on the face. "I thank you for that. I owe ya one."

Flynn downed the rest of his beer and held his empty mug in the air to signal the waitress for another.

Keegan became slightly frustrated that Flynn didn't understand what he was insinuating and decided to clarify it. "Actually Sean, I was thinking it might be best if we called the entire operation off."

His heart raced slightly, anticipating the man's response.

"You do now, do ya?" snapped Flynn. "Now that's a good one. It is I tell ya."

Flynn lit a cigarette staring menacingly at Keegan.

Keegan started to become more annoyed at Flynn's tormenting. "Sean, I'm afraid you don't fully understand my predicament. I'm in charge of Devine's security. My job is on the line here," Keegan explained as if trying to garner some empathy from the man.

"Mr. Keegan, let me make this perfectly clear to

ya. I couldn't care any less about your job, nor do I care for you. I wouldn't call this hit off if me own life depended on it. I'm either going to carry out the hit or die trying."

Keegan finally lost his cool with the man and he decided a harsher approach was now necessary. Keegan pointed his index finger in the man's face and began to lecture him. "Sean, Gerry, or whatever your real fucking name is...I think you should *seriously* consider calling it off because your life may very well be in danger."

Now it was Flynn who became enraged. He wasn't about to stand for Keegan's disrespect. He had little tolerance for cops as it was. He had drawn Keegan into the confrontation that he had hoped to. Flynn raised his back up from the seat ever so slightly, extended his right leg and drew his gun from his waistband, and held it under the table. Keegan could feel the barrel of Flynn's gun against his own knee. He then heard the familiar sound of the cocking of a gun's hammer through all the noise and commotion in the bar.

Keegan's mouth went dry instantly as he looked Flynn dead in the eyes, witnessing the stone-cold eyes of a heartless murderer, staring into his own. Keegan had dealt with plenty of murderers in the past. This guy seemed different. Uncaring about anything, including his own well-being, Keegan assessed.

Keegan debated going for his service weapon.

After thinking about it for a few seconds, he opted not to. He decided the best course of action would be to wait it out and see what the man does. The man clearly had the tactical advantage over him. Keegan felt if he had gone for his gun, it would have given the man the excuse he may have been looking for to shoot him. He also realized even if he had gotten to his gun and shot it out with the hitman, there was the strong possibility of many innocent civilians getting seriously injured or even killed.

"Do you want to know me real name, Mr. Keegan?" It was a rhetorical question. "Well, I'll tell ya then. Me name is Gerald Flynn. And to be honest with ya, I've no qualms about blowin' your fuckin' kneecap to pieces right here and now. You do understand that don't ya, Mr. Keegan?"

Flynn then drew a drag from the cigarette and blew the smoke in Keegan's face. Keegan sat motionlessly and experienced a fear he had never before known. Flynn could sense the terror he brought to Keegan and he enjoyed every minute of it. I could shoot you right this second and calmly get up and walk out of here and nobody would dare look twice at me. I'm just one face in a city of millions. I'm a ghost Mr. Keegan, a ghost that can disappear and resurface at any time.

Flynn could hear Tommy McDermott had just finished a song and asked the audience if they had any requests. Flynn kept the gun flush against Keegan's kneecap as he called out to McDermott above the rest of the crowd. "Hey Tommy, play <u>The Patriot</u>

<u>Game</u> for me friend here. It's his favorite."

Keegan remained calm; the steel barrel of the gun still pressed firmly against his knee. He was familiar with the song Flynn had requested for him. He had heard it often enough over the years frequenting McBride's. It was about an idealistic young man who goes to join the I.R.A. because he wants to do his part to free Ireland. At the end of the song, he's killed at the hands of a traitor. The song was undoubtedly a message from Flynn that he had better not interfere.

He tried not to show how scared he really was. He thought back to all his years as a homicide Detective as well as back to his days on the streets as a patrol cop. He'd arrested over six hundred people during his career and had received numerous death threats. He had pushed that off as part of the job. He never took any one of them seriously. Any cop out on the street that makes a lot of arrests gets his life threatened every now and then. But this threat was different.

There was no doubt in his mind, that Flynn was not only dead serious but also quite capable of carrying out the threat. His heart was pounding heavily against his chest even after he heard Flynn uncock the gun's hammer. As loud as it was in the bar, Keegan had been tuned in to listen for that noise and was relieved to hear it. Flynn placed the gun nonchalantly back into his waistband. Keegan breathed a sigh of relief, listening carefully to the words of the last chorus.

Now as I lie here, my body all holes
I think of those traitors who bargained and sold
I wish that my rifle had given the same
To those quislings who sold out the Patriot Game

Keegan let the words sink in as Flynn got up from the table and threw his denim jacket over his right shoulder. "Well done Tommy."

Flynn applauded after the compliment.

He looked down at Keegan. "Great job he did on that song, didn't he? One of me favorite songs. Give Tommy a nice round of applause. That was just for you, ya know."

Flynn then picked up his beer as he stood over Keegan and chugged it down. To add to the insult, he picked up the remainder of Keegan's Guinness and drained that as well. Flynn pulled forty dollars out of his pocket and dropped it on the table. "That should about cover me bill...and yours too. No need to thank me."

He patted Keegan on the shoulder, bent down, and spoke softly into his ear. "Now, Mr. Keegan, I strongly suggest you consider our conversation. Think about your position. Dan tells me you've three youngins at home as well as a most beautiful bride. Think about them before you do anything foolish. They need ya, they do. I'm sure you'll make the right choice."

Flynn strode arrogantly to the door, never giving Keegan a second glance. He was pleased with himself. He enjoyed terrorizing people and Keegan; a big, tough, hero cop had been extremely enjoyable.

Flynn took in a deep breath of the night air as he walked down Third Avenue to the side street where he had parked his car. He felt confident Keegan would understand the nature of his threats.

Sharon had watched the entire exchange between the two men unsure what exactly was going on. She had almost stayed too long and when Flynn got up to leave the bar, she wasn't sure what to do. He was walking right towards her, so she turned her back to him and waited for him to leave. After Flynn exited the bar, Sharon placed her empty glass down and also left the bar.

She peeked outside and saw Flynn walking away without ever looking back. Once he was a safe distance away, she ran out of the bar's doorway, across the sparse traffic on Third Avenue to Louie Castillo's car. Castillo threw the passenger door open for her. She got in. He tried to catch up to Flynn. They watched as Flynn turned the corner onto Forty-Third Street and put his denim jacket on. "So, what happened in there?" Castillo couldn't wait to hear the details.

"I'm really not sure what to make of everything."

She went on to explain how the two men seemed to have gotten into a heated argument. At some point near the beginning, the younger guy took a gun from his waistband and appeared to hand it to the cop under the table. The cop looked genuinely frightened. Like maybe he was going to be caught or he was being watched. He was careful never to have taken possession of the gun, unless he did momentarily under the table. Then after a few minutes, the guy put the gun back in his waistband and left.

Castillo considered things for a moment. "That's great. That means we know for sure he has the gun on him, right? You are sure he took it back?"

Castillo couldn't chance a mistake this late in the game. Not now, when everything seemed to be coming together so nicely.

"Definitely. I'm one hundred percent sure he still has it on him."

Castillo made sure to keep a safe distance from Flynn's auto for fear of Flynn spotting the tail. "That's the best news you could've told me. Can I ask one more favor of you?"

"You're really pushing your luck." She offered a welcoming smile. "Of course, you can."

"I want to follow this guy back to whose ever house he's staying at. I'll call a uniformed sector from the precinct concerned and you can sit with them to secure the house and make sure he doesn't leave. I'll get an emergency search warrant for the location. When I get back, we'll search the house and when we recover the gun, we'll place this guy under arrest. With any luck, he'll give the subject of my investigation right up. If not, I'll trace the gun back to whoever bought it, which once again, I'm pretty confident will be the subject of my investigation.

Winters had another idea. "Why don't we just jump him right here and now and arrest him. He has the gun in his waistband. Why go through the trouble of obtaining a warrant?"

Castillo playfully tapped her on the knee before explaining. "The gun is only one piece to the puzzle. He's in America for a reason, and he and Keegan are plotting something. If we lock him up now, he may roll on Keegan or he may not. If he doesn't, we will never know what their plans were. A search warrant will give us a free peek into his life and there's a good chance we learn more about what they have planned and maybe who else is involved. I'm willing to bet we find more incriminating evidence if we wait on a warrant."

Castillo was very confident in his plan of action. *By the morning, I'll be drawing up the complaint with the District Attorney and by next week at this time, I'll be presenting the case to the Grand Jury.* Castillo was on cloud nine. He realized he was closer than ever to nailing Keegan.

Keegan remained motionless at the table for minutes after Flynn had left. He considered the threats the man had made against him and his family. He became angry at himself for allowing the punk to push him around the way Flynn had done. He glanced over at the bar and saw Dan O'Brien staring back at him. He turned away from O'Brien for a short period of time and asked the waitress to bring him another Guinness. When she returned with his stout, he gave her the forty dollars Flynn had left and added twenty dollars of his own to cover the bill and the tip. Keegan slowly drank a long swig of Guinness and got up to go over to the bar.

He put his Guinness down at the bar where Dan O'Brien was waiting. "So, what might the problem be Jim?"

Keegan had hoped to avoid this conversation with O'Brien, but he now realized it was necessary. His attempt to call things off with Flynn had blown up in his face. O'Brien was literally his last resort before he would have to take police action in the matter. "To be completely honest with you Dan, I think the hit on Devine is a mistake."

There was no point in denying the hit. O'Brien would hear him out. "How so?"

Keegan lifted his Guinness to his mouth and took a gulp. He was biding his time to choose his words carefully. "Well Dan, the NYPD has an intelligence report documenting the hit. I'm going to be in charge of the detail, most likely. And even if I weren't, someone else would. I think it's best if we called it off. The department is already aware of it. One of your boys from the other side gave up the whole operation. They even named Gerald Flynn as the shooter."

Keegan hoped his lies would help convince Dan O'Brien to abort the mission. "His photo was obtained through INTERPOL and every cop in the city was given a copy as they turned out for patrol. It's a suicide mission. He won't get anywhere near Devine on St. Patrick's Day. The parade security will be as tight as a Presidential motorcade."

Keegan continued to embellish as he saw the concern on Dan O'Brien's face, mount. "There is just no way in the world this gets done. Do you think you could talk Gerald out of it? Cut your losses before anyone winds up dead or in jail."

"Gerald, huh?"

"Yes, Gerald. He didn't deny his name, Dan. So, what do you think? Will you tell him not to go through with it?"

Dan O'Brien became extremely annoyed at Flynn. He had been given an alias for a reason and wasn't supposed to tell anyone his true identity no matter what. He should have denied it, even if Keegan did confront him with it. There was a reason he shaved his goatee and mustache off and grew his hair long. He currently looked significantly different than he did in his arrest photo. He could have even denied that it was him in the photo if he was stopped. To admit to Keegan that was in fact Flynn wasn't smart. If Flynn has jeopardized the operation with his arrogance, O'Brien made a promise to himself to inform Eamon Quinn back at home.

"No Jim. To be completely honest with ya, I don't have the authority to call it off even if I wanted to. Besides, this fella is really dangerous, and he enjoys killin'. I don't think he'd terminate the mission at this point no matter who gave the order."

O'Brien was telling the truth. While Keegan painted a grim picture that wouldn't matter to a man like Gerald Flynn. O'Brien had known many Gerald Flynn's in his day back home in occupied Ireland.

Keegan pleaded with the bartender. "Dan, don't you understand he has to be stopped, my job is on the line."

"Jim, there's a lot more on the line here than your job, ya know. Why can't you just turn the other cheek and after the hit goes down blame it on a flaw in security? If security is truly as tight as you say, maybe he will see he has no opportunity and opt out himself."

O'Brien didn't see this as a possible scenario but if it appeased Keegan, the lie would be worth it.

Keegan could see there was no reasoning with any of these men. His temper flared. "Goddamn it, Dan! I took an oath of office to uphold the law and protect the citizens of this city and you're asking me to turn my back and let one of those innocent citizens get murdered. Dan, I won't have blood on my hands for you, the I.R.A., or anyone else for that matter. I'm out! Don't ever call and ask me for anything again. Do you understand me? Have I made myself clear?"

Dan O'Brien let out a hardy laugh. He looked around and was careful not to raise his voice too loudly. "You're out, are ya? Now that's a good one. You're out!?" He let out a barely audible laugh.

O'Brien shook his head at Keegan as he mocked him. *"Once in, never out* Jim. Have you forgotten that? The only way out is when you're six feet under and there dropping dirt on ya. Now that's when you're out and not a goddamned minute before then."

Keegan didn't even want to think about the implications of what O'Brien had just insinuated. He had a sudden sinking feeling in the pit of his stomach. Keegan decided to backpedal. He quickly shifted the conversation in another direction. "What is so important to the I.R.A. about killing a lawyer in New York, thousands of miles away from Northern Ireland?"

O'Brien would bite. "Aye. What indeed is so important about this man? Nothing, that's what. The man himself is totally unimportant, Jim. What he stands for on the other hand is what we're after. By executing this Prot here in New York, it shows people all over the world, not just in Ireland, that the I.R.A. isn't going to put up with any more outlandish insults such as a Protestant Grand Marshall at a Catholic parade. This isn't the fuckin' Orangemen marching through Belfast in July. It's the *Saint* Patrick's Day parade in New York City. It's a *Catholic* holiday, not the fuckin' Prots. Not *this* time! Not ever.

We are not executing Martin Devine; we are simply executing what he stands for. He stands for the Protestants looking down upon us like where some pieces of shite to be scraped off the bottom of your shoe. We don't stand by idly during the Orangemen marches at home but that doesn't get the worldwide attention that this will."

James Keegan would not buy this explanation. "Dan, this is a human being who has never spoken out in words or in action against the cause. To execute him in the name of the I.R.A. just makes them seem like terrorists around the world. Don't you see that?"

Keegan was pleading for Devine's life on deaf ears. If he couldn't convince O'Brien the hit must be stopped, he would next have to go and personally visit Martin Devine.

"Jim, I think if you take a step back and look at it from our point of view instead of that of a Police Officer's, you'll see it our way. Why don't you go home and sleep on it? This is probably the single most important mission the I.R.A. has conducted to gain publicity since ten of our men starved themselves to death in the Maze in the early 1980s."

O'Brien paused momentarily and studied Keegan's face before continuing. "And don't forget Jim, you have a family to think of at home. I don't think the boys at home would appreciate it if someone who was supposed to be on their side turned coat on them and squashed their biggest plans in over a decade, do you?"

Another threat.

James Keegan got up from the barstool and wondered how he had gotten himself involved in such a mess. He walked to the door without saying a word to Dan O'Brien. He had to try and come up with a way out, where he wouldn't lose his freedom and his family and yet he is still able to prevent the murder. He had no idea how he was going to do it but he knew he had to try. Keegan walked out of McBride's well after three in the morning. After exiting the doorway, he looked back into the bar and vowed as long as he lived, he would never again step foot in that establishment.

Gerald Flynn parked his rented vehicle down the block from the hotel. On his journey back to the hotel from McBride's, Flynn had never noticed Louis Castillo's Nissan carefully following him. Flynn got out of the car, adjusted the gun in his waistband, and began to walk to his hotel. Louis Castillo and Sharon Winters watched from a short distance away. "I didn't count on him staying at a hotel."

Castillo thought about the implications. He was frustrated. "Now what am I going to do? I can't get a search warrant for the entire hotel, and I'm sure he didn't use his real name when he registered."

Castillo punched the dashboard in anger.

"I have an idea," she began to explain. "Why don't you call up the rental agency and find out what name he used to rent the vehicle under? I bet that's the same name he used to register in the hotel."

"Because Sharon, I wanted to do this tonight since I know for a fact that he has the gun on him. The rental agency is not open at this time of the night for someone to search through their paperwork and tell me who rented the car. It needs to get done tonight. There isn't a judge around who is going to give me a search warrant tomorrow because I saw a gun the previous night. It would be a different story if I saw him with the gun on numerous occasions, but I haven't. I can't even establish he is staying here for certain."

"Wait a minute, Louie. I have an even better idea. Why don't I follow him to his hotel room? Once we know what room he's in, I'll keep an eye on it to make sure he doesn't leave while you go to a judge and get the warrant."

Castillo shook his head deliberately in agreement. "You know Sharon...that could actually work."

After initially agreeing, Castillo started to have second thoughts about following the man. He was afraid to let his long-time friend and former lover follow an armed man by herself. No matter how badly he wanted to get Keegan, he didn't want to put Sharon in harm's way.

Sharon knew Castillo very well and sensed a change of heart. The look on his face went from excitement to a look of concern. "On second thought Sharon, maybe waiting until morning isn't such a horrible idea. We can just sit on his car until morning when the rental company opens and then just like you said check the hotel registry for the same name that rented the car."

Sharon immediately felt the need to stand up for herself. "I'm a big girl Louie; I can take care of myself."

Castillo hadn't meant to insult her. He shook his head. "It's too dangerous. He's armed. He's a fucking terrorist. I don't want you following him by yourself."

Sharon Winters felt the need to remind him, "Well I'm armed also. And I'm a trained Police Officer. Don't forget, I was an undercover in Bronx narcotics for over two years. I've been in some hairy situations and always came out without a scratch. I know what I'm doing and how to take care of myself."

"On your undercover operations, you always had a backup team and a *ghost* only seconds away if the shit hit the fan. It's not that I don't think you can take care of yourself it's just that…"

"Go ahead, Louie. I'm waiting. Just that what?"

Castillo felt awkward. This entire conversation had almost become a battle of the sexes which Castillo knew he was losing. He didn't have an answer for her and if she were a man, he probably wouldn't have thought twice about asking her to follow Flynn. After all, it was merely a surveillance operation. There would be no need in the world to confront the man.

As Sharon looked up the block, she saw Gerald Flynn enter the lobby of his hotel. She looked over at Louie Castillo. "Don't worry I'll be careful."

She got out of the car before Castillo could utter another word of protest. She ran towards the hotel's entrance trying feverishly to catch up with Flynn.

Castillo watched his former girlfriend running up the block with mixed emotions. He decided he was starting to have feelings for her again. If anything bad were to happen to her, it would be his fault and he could never forgive himself. On the other hand, once he found out what room Flynn was staying in, it would only be a matter of hours before Flynn, and eventually, Keegan, would be arrested and made accountable for their actions. Castillo was so close to winding the case up he could almost taste the fruits of his success.

Sharon Winters had caught up to Gerald Flynn in a matter of seconds. She kept an eye on him as he walked to the hotel's elevators. Flynn got on the elevator first and Winters followed. She glanced to see that the panel for the third floor was light up. She reached past the man and pushed the same button herself. She offered Flynn a casual smile as she did so, to see if he was amused by the apparent coincidence. Flynn barely even looked back at her and waited patiently for the elevator to reach his floor.

The elevator door opened on the third floor. As they stepped out, Sharon Winters intentionally dropped her handbag. She hoped that Flynn would not decide to be a gentleman and pick it up for her. Somehow, she was sure he would not. She bent down to retrieve her bag, Flynn continued on his way, creating some much-needed distance between them. She walked about ten to twenty feet behind him waiting to see which room was his. Flynn casually walked toward the end of the hall and as he did so, Sharon could see him reach into his pocket to get the key to the room. Sharon figured that his room must be one of the next few rooms if he bothered to retrieve his keys. Sharon was about twenty-five feet away now. She had slowed her pace to allow for more distance.

Her preoccupation watching Flynn kept her from noticing that when Flynn turned right at the end of the hall, it was into an open doorway. He never used his key. Sharon just blindly followed. As she got closer, she realized Flynn has disappeared into a stairwell. He had made her tail after all. Castillo would be so disappointed with her. She knew he probably ran down the stairs to flee the hotel, although she hadn't heard any footsteps running. It was weird, she conceded. She picked up her pace, realizing she needed to find him again.

As soon as she made the turn, uneasiness came over her. *Something's not right.* Strong hands grabbed her from behind the door and pulled her backward, slamming her into the wall. Her head bounced off the wall and she had the wind knocked out of her. She fought the blackness. "Don't you be falling out on me bitch!"

She fought through the daze and looked into the cold eyes of Gerald Flynn, experiencing a fear that she had never before known. Flynn immediately knocked her handbag to the ground and put one hand solidly around her throat. Without immediately saying another word to Winters, Flynn looked her up and down. With one hand firmly secured around her throat, he used his free hand to search her for any weapons.

Sharon went into a state of shock and froze. She

couldn't even fall back on her training which taught you to always fight back; never give up. Sharon came to the thought that her life was about to come to an end, right here in the stairwell of this hotel.

Flynn narrowed his eyes before interrogating her. He spoke in a quiet, yet stern voice. "Who are ya, and why might you be followin' me, lady?"
He saw the terror in her eyes and fed off of it.

Sharon Winters couldn't even muster up enough strength to answer. He watched as she turned red from the lack of oxygen. Her both hands trying to free herself from his grip was no match for his strength. He could feel her fight weaken. He released his grip and bent down to retrieve her pocketbook while keeping a sharp eye on her.

He opened her bag and saw a .38 caliber Smith & Wesson revolver. Flynn removed the gun without any protest from Winters and placed it in his jacket pocket. Sharon Winters bent over, hands on her knees trying to catch her breath as Flynn then went through her wallet. He removed an assortment of credit cards and papers. Flynn examined her NYPD identification card. "A Detective is it? A lady Detective at that, no less."

Flynn's sarcasm was not lost on Winters, but her only concern at this point was to survive the encounter. He hadn't killed her yet, so there was a chance she'd live, she assured herself.

"I'm so sorry. I am. Ya see…I'm from Belfast.

That's in Northern Ireland, you know? This is me first time in New York and I've heard how violent New York is. Even worse than home, they say. I thought you were followin' me to rob me." Flynn flashed her, an insincere smile. "I hope ya understand my confusion."

He then returned her identification card among other items and retrieved her gun from his pocket. He opened the cylinder, hit the ejector rod, and emptied the rounds into his hand. He pocketed the rounds before putting her gun back in her bag and closing it up. He went on to further explain. "Ya see, back at home, we don't have too many lady officers because it's too rough. Could ya imagine if they came up against a real bad guy? He'd no doubt, take her gun away from her and use it against her. Again, I apologize Detective Winters. Maybe I could stop by your flat sometime and buy you a drink as an apology."

He held her driver's license at eye level, showing her that he retained it. He read her address out loud, asking if it was a dangerous neighborhood. Flynn then reached up and gently caressed the face of a terrified Sharon Winters. "I hope I didn't hurt ya, lass. All a big misunderstanding, ya see."

Flynn continued to gently rub the back of his hand from her face all the way down to her right breast. He had caressed her breast ever so slightly to add humiliation to her already battered ego. "Ya coulda just bought me a drink at the bar...no need to come back to me hotel."

Sharon stood motionless as she watched Gerald Flynn disappear down the stairs. She wondered at what point he had made her tail, or did he recognize her from McBride's when she got on the elevator. She wasn't sure if she was more humiliated at his actions or her own neglect. She had always considered herself to be a good Detective so how could she have walked into such an obvious trap. This would be a valuable lesson to her in the future but nevertheless, it was a lesson that she almost paid for with her life.

She was too embarrassed and outraged at the whole incident to tell Castillo what really happened. She decided she would tell him that she lost track of him because he got into the elevator before she got into the lobby. At least that would be a plausible excuse. She would tell him that she waited around and walked floor to floor, hoping to find him. That should cover for the time she was missing. If Castillo found out that she had blown the entire case for him by getting made, she wasn't sure he would ever forgive her.

She went into the lobby restroom, studying the redness on her throat. She waited for a few moments to gain her composure and to catch her breath before leaving the hotel to rejoining Louie. She zippered her jacket as high as it could go to hide any evidence of a confrontation her neck would attest to. This would prove to be a night Sharon Winters would never forget.

Gerald Flynn jogged down the stairs to a rear

entrance of the hotel. He continued to run for six blocks without ever slowing down. He was barely even breathing hard when he finally stopped. Flynn was in remarkable shape and had been running and exercising every day in case his agility or stamina would come into play in either the hit itself or the escape afterward. Flynn laughed to himself at the thought of how the female Detective had been shaking. *Stupid bitch*, he thought to himself. *Did she really think she could follow me without me noticing?* Flynn wondered what Keegan was up to. Would there be a squad of undercover officers here to arrest me tonight to try and prevent the hit?

With less than a week to go before Saint Patrick's Day, Flynn decided he wasn't going to take any chances. He would abandon the few belongings that he had in America realizing it was not safe to return to the hotel to retrieve them. He opened up his wallet and saw that money would not be a problem. He had plenty of cash and his nine-millimeter. That would be all he would need to successfully complete his stay in New York.

By not checking out of the hotel, Flynn realized Keegan would be wasting manpower keeping it under surveillance. That could only help him. There was nothing of value in there so Flynn didn't care. They would also find and search the rental car he deducted, but once again there was nothing, they would find in there that could hurt him. Gerald Flynn was careful when it came to his plans. He'd have nothing written down on paper that could be used against him down the road.

Flynn concluded that at this point, he would have to stay off the grid and lay low. He would have no more contact with Dan O'Brien since Keegan would probably be watching him as well. Flynn liked the fact that it was the middle of the night. The streets were so desolate it would be easy to spot a tail. In the distance, he saw a police cruiser approaching.

He removed his gun from his waist and put it in his jacket pocket. He wondered if Keegan had the entire police force looking for him. The car drove right past him without as much as slowing down. The walk to the nearest subway station was well over a mile but Flynn knew exactly where it was. He prepared himself for a similar scenario and what his best options would be if he had to flee his Queens hotel. Flynn was unsure of his destination, but he knew it was going to be a small out of the way hotel where he could lay low until the day of the parade.

He entered the subway station on Astoria Boulevard, taking the N line to Manhattan. He shared a near-empty car with a homeless man, who stunk something awful. He wore a brown winter jacket torn at the right shoulder and side pocket. Flynn observed the man's once blue jeans were closer to black. Flynn was almost certain his unkempt white beard and hair were infested with lice. Flynn sat as far away from the man as he could but would not change cars. He liked the advantage of the empty train car. Knowing he was not being followed put his mind at ease.

At the Queensboro Plaza stop, a few more people got on. Most changing cars after getting one whiff of the rotten air the homeless man was creating. Two rather rough-looking young men remained in the car. They were young black men around the same age or younger than Flynn. One wore a Cincinnati Reds hat, the other a St. Louis Cardinals. Neither was necessarily a baseball fan, however. The red ball caps combined with the red bandana which they were *flagging* from their back pockets, suggested a gang affiliation. They surveyed Flynn, looking for an easy mark to rob. Flynn was no easy mark and they sensed it. Flynn met their cold stare with his own; almost daring them to make the first move. They exited at the very next stop without bothering Flynn.

He walked through Manhattan in the predawn hours looking for a place to lay his head. He found a rather less than desirable hotel, just outside of Times Square. It was the type of hotel that didn't have just nightly rates, but also had rates for blocks of four hours; the type of hotel frequented by prostitutes and their johns. Flynn could care less about the clientele, however.

He paid cash in advance, booking his room for several days after Saint Patrick's Day. He opened the door. The musty smell hit him at once. The walls were cracked in more than one place and the tan paint was so dingy that Flynn figured it hadn't been painted in many years. It was a very small room with a small television. Next to the remote control were directions on how to order porn. He set his gun down on the worn nightstand and got undressed. Flynn turned down the bed and sat down. The mattress was too soft and lumpy. He had, however, slept in worse he thought, as he lay back and closed his eyes.

James Keegan parked the Crown Victoria in the driveway of his home. He looked at the car's clock before shutting it off, seeing that it was after four o'clock. He locked the car and proceeded to quietly open the front door to his house. Once inside, he listened attentively trying to hear if there was any stirring from the bedrooms. Noting no noises, he quietly took off his shoes and left them in front of the door as usual. He made his way up the stairs and entered his bedroom.

His eyes hadn't yet adjusted to the darkness, so he felt his way over to the television and turned it on for some light to get undressed by. He kept the volume down, not wanting to disturb Kate. She didn't wake up but the light from the television must have bothered her because she turned over, trying to escape it. He unholstered his gun and put it away in its locked strongbox in the closet. Sitting on the edge of the bed, he finished getting undressed. He could see in the dimly lit room that the note he had left her remained untouched on the night table.

He walked over and took the note. If she hadn't

woken up and seen the note he might just as well get rid of it so she would never know he had ever left the house. He walked downstairs and buried the note deep in the garbage pail in the kitchen. He drank a small amount of antacid, to soothe his extremely upset stomach. Keegan never had an ulcer, not even with all the stress he had endured over his many years as a cop, but he thought he could feel one coming on after the last couple of weeks.

When he got to the top of the stairs, he sat in the children's rooms for a few minutes to watch each of them sleep so peacefully. He gave each of them a kiss on their head and felt a lump in his throat. He couldn't help wondering what would happen to his family if anything were to happen to him...or them.

Flynn's threat had been so real it terrorized him just to think of Flynn. Keegan closed the door to his daughter's bedroom on the way out and once again returned to his bedroom. Kate must've woken up momentarily at some point because the television was now off. When Keegan crawled into bed, the remote control was in his wife's hand. He gave her a gentle kiss on the face and rubbed her back. He then took the remote control and placed it in its proper place on the night table. Keegan got under the covers but couldn't fall asleep.

He kept reliving the night's events over in his head, especially Flynn's threats. He put his arm around his wife and pulled her close, but she continued to sleep and didn't reciprocate his affections. Keegan desperately needed to be held. He was frightened. He wanted in the worst way to wake Kate up and tell her about everything. He wanted to get his secret past off his chest and level with her. He would tell her how he'd been running guns to the I.R.A. for many years now and that he was going to get out. He would sometimes have this fantasy about being honest with Kate and telling her everything, but he knew he never could. Keegan tossed and turned in bed for the next couple of hours contemplating his fate before he finally fell to sleep at the crack of dawn.

CHAPTER 15

James Keegan got off the elevator on the fourth floor in the building where Martin Devine's law office was located. It was the Monday before the Saint Patrick's Day Parade and Keegan realized he had to act fast. He wished he had been able to get a hold of Devine over the weekend, but his attempts had been fruitless. Keegan read the sign on the door before opening it.

Martin Devine-Attorney at Law

He entered Devine's law office and was greeted by Devine's secretary. She was a petite blond with striking green eyes. She wore a beige skirt with a floral blouse buttoned to the collar. Keegan figured her to be in her mid-thirties. "Can I help you with something, sir?"

"Yes, I'd like to speak with Mr. Devine."

"Do you have an appointment?" not remembering having scheduled any for this time.

Keegan shook his head from side to side. "No, I don't. I'm a Police Officer and I'm here on official business."

Keegan showed her his Lieutenant's shield and identification card. He added, "It's extremely urgent that I speak to Mr. Devine as soon as possible."

"I see. Well, this is a bad time because he's in a meeting right now. If you want to wait, as soon as he's available, I'll tell him you're waiting to speak with him."

"I'd appreciate that. Yes, I'll wait for him."

"Have a seat then. Would you like a cup of coffee?" offered the secretary as she walked him to the waiting area.

Keegan politely refused the coffee and took a seat on the couch in the office's waiting room. The waiting area was very different from any law office Keegan had ever been in. His only points of reference would be the offices of the various District Attorneys and that of the New York City Corporation Counsel. Those offices were just a step or two cleaner than a police precinct. This office was in sharp contrast. It was immaculate and beautifully decorated. Keegan glanced at the artwork hanging on the walls. They were mostly prints from artists he was unfamiliar with, in addition to a couple of original pieces. The couch was the softest leather that he ever felt. He figured it was a fine Italian make. He thumbed through the magazines laid out neatly on the coffee table in front of him. The secretary returned to her station, the heels of her shoes echoing as she walked across the highly polished, granite floor.

After a few moments, he picked up the current edition of the Daily News from the coffee table in front of him. There was an article on page four of the paper about Martin Devine and the parade. The article went on to say that a rally protesting the protestant Grand Marshall of the parade was held yesterday without any incident. More protests were expected between now and the parade, but the police did not expect any problems.

Keegan shook his head; if they only knew the problems they might be in for. He stared at the picture of Martin Devine in the newspaper. He thought back to the first time he had ever heard of Devine and how he, along with every other cop in the city, hated him. It had been back in the late 1970s and Keegan was still just a patrol cop at the time. He didn't personally know the officer who was involved but every cop in the city was outraged at the story.

There had been a robbery of an elderly woman at knifepoint in the East New York section of Brooklyn. The women dialed 911 and gave the operator a description of the robber. The description was broadcast by central communications to the officers in the field. A seasoned and experienced officer in the precinct saw a male fitting the description. When the officer tried to stop the man, he turned on the officer with the knife in his hand. As he lunged at the officer, the officer sidestepped the stab and smashed the subject's hand with his nightstick, disarming the man. The man promptly punched the officer in the face and a violent fight ensued. The officer collapsed to the sidewalk, dazed. The perp stood over him kicking him repeatedly in and about the head and face. The officer's partner struck the perp about the head with his blackjack, but it did not seem to deter the man's assault of the officer. The man finally fell on top of the fallen officer, who was now semi-conscious. Even though he fell, the man still had his wits about him and had a plan of action, despite the one officer continually striking him.

As numerous backup officers arrived at the scene, they helplessly witnessed the man remove the fallen officer's service revolver from its holster. He turned and shot the cop's partner at point-blank range before they had the chance to join the melee. The man was subsequently placed in handcuffs and arrested but not before a second fierce struggle had ensued. The first officer had lost consciousness and suffered a concussion, as well as twenty stitches about the face. The second officer had been shot twice; his life saved by his bulletproof vest. The perpetrator had been on angel dust, a powerful hallucinogenic, and never felt any pain from the fractured arm, two cracked ribs, and broken eye socket he received during the life-or-death struggle with the officers.

When the case went to trial, a young and ambitious lawyer, looking to make a name for himself, took on the case. The lawyer's name was Martin Devine. Devine's defense strategy was that the cops were beating the man with their blackjacks and nightsticks although he did not resist arrest. He argued the officers were exacting street justice to a man *they* believed had robbed an elderly woman. This was deadly physical force; therefore, the man should be allowed to use whatever means necessary to protect his own life. Devine, theoretically, put the New York City Police department on trial.

The media, as well as the Police Department, watched the trial with bated breath. The thought of Devine using this as a defense for these crimes was unconscionable. This was an attempted murder and felony assaults on two uniformed Police Officers affecting a lawful arrest, in addition to an armed robbery. There was no way that could work. Not even in Brooklyn, most cops tried to convince themselves.

The acquittal of the man hit the front page of almost every newspaper in the country. The jury had been convinced by Martin Devine that the officers were using unnecessary deadly physical force and that the armed robber had a right to defend his own life against the over-aggressive officers. Devine had used photos and medical records to document the beating that his client had suffered at the hands of the police. He additionally convinced the jury, that the officer, who had suffered a concussion, was inadvertently struck by his partner rather than his client. Devine had done an excellent job of impeaching a police medical expert, who testified the defendant was suffering from psychosis due to the ingestion of the angel dust and therefore continued to fight the officers because he hadn't felt any of the blows the officers had landed on him. Rather, he convinced the jury, that the man fought so furiously because it was a life-or-death situation for him.

Devine had done a masterful job of turning the

trial from his client and placing the blame on the officers. The decision became a media sensation as well as a humiliation for the department. Every cop in the city at the time was outraged at the acquittal, but many officers today were too young to remember the incident. The perpetrator was acquitted on attempted murder, felony assault charges, weapons possession, and resisting arrest. The sole charge he was convicted on was the knifepoint robbery for which he was sentenced to six to twelve years in prison.

To add further humiliation to the Police Department and the city as a whole, Devine and his client sued the city for police brutality and civil rights violations. The last thing the city wanted to go through was another high-profile trial. Instead, they settled the case with 2.6 million dollars awarded to the man for damages, even as he sat in an upstate jail cell. The only justice the officers could find in the entire matter was that after serving five years in prison, and out on parole, he was shot and killed in a drive-by shooting in front of a Brownsville shooting gallery.

The trial had blemished the career of two officers and made an armed robber a millionaire for a short period of time, but most prominently, it made Martin Devine one of the best-known criminal and civil rights lawyers in the country.

James Keegan would be very careful in how and what he told Devine. He knew if things worked out the way he hoped they would, he could be in the clear. All he had to do was convince Devine that his life was in immediate danger and to relinquish the title of Grand Marshall. He should not march in the parade at all. If Keegan could accomplish this task not only would he be saving Devine's life, but he would also be saving his own neck.

Without Devine marching, the I.R.A. would have no target and therefore have no hit. It would even be a victory for them, he reasoned. No protestant Grand Marshall. That is what they wanted from the beginning. To Keegan, this meant neither his wife nor his job would have to ever find out about his connections with the I.R.A. Keegan was holding the paper in front of him, daydreaming about what was going to happen when Devine's secretary broke his concentration. "Mr. Devine will see you now."

He put the newspaper back down on the coffee table and got up from the couch. "Thank you."

Keegan smiled and nodded at her as she showed him into the office of Martin Devine. Devine was seated behind his desk, thumbing through some legal documents when Keegan entered. It was a generously sized office with tiled floors and light green walls with beige trim. Devine's desk was a dark brown wood, highly polished. It was littered with an assortment of case folders. On the wall behind Devine's desk hung various degrees and certificates issued to Devine. On the opposite wall were bookcases that contained more law books than Keegan thought possible to read. Devine stood up to greet his guest and extended his right hand. Keegan accepted his hand and introduced himself. "How are you, Mr. Devine? My name is Lieutenant James Keegan. I'm with the New York City Police Department's Joint Terrorist Task Force."

"Of course, I knew I recognized you. You're the Detective who broke that terrorist ring last year. That was some piece of Detective work; I'd have loved to have had a chance to cross-examine you on that."

Devine was showing his cockiness. He was a skilled cross-examiner and loved a challenge. Keegan examined the man behind the desk. He wore an expensive, custom-made suit and a large gold ring with the scales of justice embedded in it. Maybe a law school ring, figured Keegan. He had a far receded hairline and a neatly trimmed beard that was beginning to gray. *Clearly, he did not miss too many meals,* thought Keegan, noting his rather large frame.

Keegan decided to put his contempt for the man aside. As much as Keegan had once hated the man and did not respect him, especially after his comments about Keegan's collar, he still wouldn't let any harm come to him if he could prevent it. It would never be a personal matter with Keegan. He was a true professional Police Officer and took his oath of office very seriously. "Have a seat, Lieutenant."

Keegan accepted Devine's offer and pulled up a chair. "The name is Jim."

"Call me Martin. Now Jim, could you tell me why such an important man such as yourself is paying me a visit?"

Devine was genuinely curious.

Keegan sat on the forward edge of his chair before answering. "Well Martin, it seems that over in Ireland the Northern Irish Police arrested a man with a substantial amount of explosives. In return for not getting prolonged jail time, he told them of an assassination plot over in the United States."

"Fascinating, Jim. Please do tell more."

Keegan wasn't quite sure if the man was being genuine or if he was mocking him. "So, what does a snitch in Northern Ireland have to do with me?"

"The assassination the man was referring to was on the first-ever Protestant Grand Marshall of the Saint Patrick's Day Parade, during the parade itself. And Martin...you are the first protestant Grand Marshall. The I.R.A. plans on assassinating you as you march down Fifth Avenue."

Devine raised his eyebrows somewhat exaggeratedly and nodded his head. "Oh, I see," mocked Devine, in a skeptical yet dramatic voice. "So some I.R.A. bomber gets caught dirty, makes up a story to buy a get out of jail free card, and we all believe him? Why would the I.R.A. come and do something on American soil? They could lose the support of the Irish Americans they so badly covert. I'm not buying it."

Keegan was annoyed by Devine's skepticism. "Martin, I've checked this out myself from this end, and to tell you the truth if I didn't think it was a credible threat, I wouldn't be here in person telling you about it."

Devine waved his hands to calm down a visibly annoyed Keegan. "All right Lieutenant. Let's pretend this is all true. There's going to be an attempt on my life during the parade. So, what do you want me to do about it?"

"Well, I thought it might be a good idea for you to withdraw from the parade."

"Withdraw from the parade? Not a chance, Lieutenant."

"Martin, we are talking about your life here and I'm in charge of making sure no harm comes to you. I honestly feel the only safe choice is for you to withdraw from the parade. Don't march at all."

"As I said Lieutenant, not a chance. If you are in charge of my protection, I have all the faith in the world in your skills as a Police Officer. I've read enough in the papers to know you are a true hero and one of the most capable Police Officers in the entire department."

Keegan shook his head in disbelief. This man was either thick-headed or he didn't take the threat as seriously as he needed to. "Mr. Devine...Martin, why would you put your life on the line when you can just walk away from everything safe and sound?"

"Why indeed, Lieutenant? Do you remember many years ago I defended a man who almost killed a Police Officer with another officer's gun?"

Keegan started to feel the hatred for Devine resurfacing, at the almost boasting way he had brought the subject up. "Yes, as a matter of fact, I do."

"Good, I'm glad to see the man who is going to be protecting my life is as sharp as you," he prodded.

"Did you know that I received death threats for taking that man's case from your fellow Police Officers?"

Keegan for the first time in his life was slightly ashamed that he was a Police Officer. The thought of Police Officers threatening someone's life for simply doing their job was inexcusable, regardless of what their job was.

" No. I wasn't aware of that."

"Well, were you aware of the fact that every opportunity an officer had to stop my vehicle for a traffic infraction, he did so and issued me summonses?"

Once again, he admitted he hadn't been aware of these facts.

"What I'm getting at Lieutenant is this. Having a Protestant Grand Marshall for the parade is a giant step towards peace for the people living in chaos, in Northern Ireland. It's a step toward coexistence and harmony in the war-torn land. And I never have been, nor am I now, about to start being bullied by anybody. I made a commitment to be the Grand Marshall in the hopes it would be a step forward toward peace. There isn't a man, woman, or child alive who can either talk me out of marching or scare me from doing it."

Devine let the words sink in before he continued.

"Don't get me wrong, Lieutenant, I don't have a death wish and I do value my life. I'll be guided very carefully by your directions but under no circumstances will I step down as the Grand Marshall."

Keegan listened attentively and Devine made perfect sense to him. For the first time since Keegan had heard of the name of Martin Devine, he respected the man. He was truly a man of honor and conviction. "I understand you now Martin. You're a very brave and noble man."

"Thank you, Lieutenant, I might say the same for you."

Devine got up and extended his hand to Keegan which was a signal that the meeting had come to an end. As Keegan took his hand, Devine continued. "I hate to cut you short Lieutenant but if I'd have known you were coming, I would have allowed more time for you. Unfortunately, I have a press conference downtown to discuss the controversy that my selection as Grand Marshall has caused."

How ironic, thought Keegan. If the people really knew how many problems lie ahead, that would be a newsworthy story. Keegan was unsure what he would do next, but he knew whatever measures he would take to ensure Devine's safety, he would now have to go through the department. This was something even hero cop, James Keegan, couldn't handle on his own. "Martin, I'll be in touch with you once I figure out the best method of security for you on the day of the parade."

Martin Devine showed Keegan to the door but

before he left paused to ask him a question. "Lieutenant, in your honest and expert opinion, how serious of a threat do you think this is?"

"Let me put it to you this way Martin. I have never taken any threat so seriously before in my life."

Keegan wasn't trying to scare the man, but he had no intentions of lying and downplaying the situation either. "You know Martin, nobody would think any less of you if you did call it off. Hey, we could even fake an injury or ailment so people wouldn't know the truth."

Keegan figured he would try the one last angle even though he didn't believe Devine would go for it.

"Those aren't bad ideas Lieutenant; however, I will neither lie nor back down from anybody. I do appreciate your concern though."

Martin Devine closed the door after Keegan's departure. He hadn't been this scared in years. If the New York City Police Department was this concerned to send one of its finest Detectives out on the case, the threat must be legitimate. Devine walked back behind his desk and sat down. He pressed a button activating the intercom to his secretary and asked her to bring him in a glass of water. Devine then opened his top desk drawer and removed a bottle of prescription drugs. He removed one pill from the vial and returned the rest to their drawer. Devine waited nervously for his secretary to bring in the water. Devine was unconsciously tapping his ring against the desktop when his secretary entered.

"Is everything okay?" She noticed Devine's nervous habit and was a bit concerned.

"Everything is fine," Devine would reassure her, as he reached out for the glass of water. He knew it wasn't fine, however. Once the secretary handed Devine the water, she left the office and closed the door behind her. After putting the five-milligram tablet of Valium in his mouth, Devine drank a small amount of water to wash it down. He buried his face in his hands as his elbows rested on the desktop. Devine considered his options. He knew the easiest and safest thing to do would be to withdraw from the parade, but he had come too far to do that. If he backed down now from a threat of any kind, then standing up for what he believed in for his entire life would be meaningless. Devine drank the rest of the water and set the glass down on the desk.

Devine reached into his pocket and removed a set of keys. He fumbled through the key ring until he came across the appropriate one. He inserted the key into the bottom drawer in the desk and unlocked it. He opened the drawer and removed the .44 caliber revolver along with five rounds of ammunition. He blew the dust off the gun, realizing it had been some time since he had opened that drawer. Devine hadn't carried his licensed revolver since the last death threats that had been made against him many years ago. Looking at the gun, it was quite evident that he had been neglecting to clean it as he should. Devine opened the cylinder, making sure it was empty before cleaning it. Devine spent a good half-hour cleaning the gun and removing some rust that had oxidized on the frame.

He dry-fired it. After feeling secure that it was in good working order, Devine once again opened the cylinder and loaded the gun with five live rounds of .44 caliber ammunition. He then spun the barrel and snapped the cylinder closed. Devine hadn't carried a gun in so long he wondered if he was still as good a shot as he had once been. Devine reached back into the unlocked drawer and selected a shoulder holster from the assortment that lay in there. The gun was heavier than he remembered and would take some time to get used to carrying it again.

Devine looked up at the clock on the wall and saw it was almost time to go to the press conference. He felt bad about lying to Keegan and telling him he had to leave right away when he actually didn't. Devine decided that would be the last time he would lie to Keegan. After all, it might not be such a good idea to lie to the man who is going to be protecting your life. His suit jacket seemed to be a little bit tighter as he put it on over the shoulder holster. It felt a bit strange but before he knew it, he would get used to it. He wouldn't even notice it was there.

James Keegan had made it back to the office in time for the start of Martin Devine's press conference. Devine had called the press conference to answer any questions about his being the Grand

Marshall. He hoped the press conference would put an end to the controversy regarding his selection. Keegan had read in the morning newspaper that the press conference was going to be broadcast live and, in its entirety, on a local city news channel. Keegan turned on the television and tuned into the news station waiting for the press conference to begin. He wanted to see exactly what Devine would say.

Devine stepped up to the podium as the press conference was set to begin. He was wearing a dark gray suit with light blue pin stripping and an emerald-green tie against a white shirt. Devine looked very important and had several men standing around him. Keegan couldn't help but to wonder if Devine had taken his warning seriously and had gotten together some bodyguards in such a hurry. He noted Devine seemed apprehensive as he arrived at the podium and he seemed to scan the crowd suspiciously. He was glad to see Devine acting in this manner and prayed he would keep his guard up from this point on, until after the parade was over.

"Ladies and gentlemen of the press and of the viewing audience as a whole," Devine began his speech. "As all of you know, my selection as the Grand Marshall to this year's Saint Patrick's Day Parade has caused quite a conflict between some Irishmen. There have been protests demanding that I step down; others, who have suggested the same, behind closed doors. There are many people watching me at this very moment, who would prefer that I not march in the parade at all."

Keegan's attention hung on those words. He hadn't even told Captain Anderson about the death threats yet and he would have some real tough explaining to do if the Captain found out about them from a press conference. Keegan believed Devine was a smarter man than to mention anything about death threats on live television, yet he was anxious until Devine's next words.

"I assure everyone; however, there is no reason for me to step down. The reason I agreed to be the Grand Marshall was not to stir up any controversy, but on the contrary to bring us together as a whole. My selection should be a symbol to all Irishmen, Catholic as well as Protestant, that we are one, a united people, who can get along with one another. There should no longer be boundaries based on religion or anything else for that matter, which are built for the sole purpose of driving our people apart, instead of uniting them. Stepping down would be turning my back on the peace process in the land of my ancestors. That will not happen. It *cannot* happen."

Devine ended his opening statement with those words and then opened the floor up to questions. Keegan watched and most of the questions seemed to focus on Devine's bid for peace in his native Northern Ireland and how he had become almost an overnight spokesman on the topic. Keegan watched until the conclusion and was relieved that there were no questions regarding the possibility that Devine's safety could be in jeopardy. In Keegan's experience, he'd learned things routinely got leaked to the press, sometimes even before the officials who dealt with them knew all of the details. He was glad to see this was not the case here.

Gerald Flynn lifted his nine-millimeter semi-automatic handgun to eye level and lined up the sights perfectly on Martin Devine's forehead as he ended the news conference. Flynn pulled the hammer of the gun back until it remained in the cocked position. He then slowly and steadily squeezed the trigger until the hammer fell forward.

CLICK! Flynn laughed as he watched Devine step down from the podium. "Enjoy your last few days you bastard."

Flynn put his gun back down on the table of his seedy hotel room to finish cleaning it. He got up and shut off the television set. If he were to get as good a shot at Devine during the parade as he got over the television, it would take only one shot to kill him before anyone, except for maybe Keegan, would realize what happened.

Flynn had been laying low since the night he had the altercation with Keegan in case he was being sought. He didn't know for sure what Keegan was doing. Did he decide to let him go through with the hit without interfering or was he trying to hunt him down? He had to assume the latter, given his encounter with the female officer.

He desperately wanted to contact Dan O'Brien to find out if he knew anything, but he knew it was much too risky a chance to take...especially this close to the parade. Flynn knew the only thing he really could do was to remain in hiding until the day of the parade. He finished cleaning the semi-automatic handgun and made sure it was in perfect condition. He inserted a magazine and pulled the slide back to chamber a round. He then released the magazine and added the final round before easing the hammer down and putting the gun on safety. He placed the gun on the night table and laid back on the bed thinking about the hit and his escape afterward. He watched a couple of cockroaches run along the ceiling. He couldn't wait until he was back at home in Ireland.

Martin Devine stepped down from the podium, feeling the press conference had been a success. He had been nervous stepping up there at first and had cautiously looked over the crowd, wondering if an assassin was among the spectators just waiting for the opportunity to snuff out his life. As he started to speak, however, Devine put his fears aside and his words seem to take a life of their own. Devine had the feeling that the members of the press not only believed everything he was saying but also supported him.

During the questions he fielded from the press, Devine almost felt like he really could put an end to the problems in Northern Ireland. He knew it wouldn't simply go away overnight but maybe he would go down in history as the man who initiated the cause of a peaceful Northern Ireland. Only time would tell for sure, thought Devine. But at least for this moment Devine felt very good about himself and decided he wasn't going to worry too much about the possible hitman.

CHAPTER 16

"Come in," answered the voice on the other end of the door on which Keegan had just knocked. Keegan opened the door of his commanding officer and went inside. He realized he had exhausted all other means to prevent the hit on his own and now it was inevitable that he must bring the intelligence report to the attention of his supervisor. "Have a seat, Jim."

"Thank you, Cap.,"

Keegan pulled up a chair at the Captain's desk. He was nervous to tell Anderson about the impending hit but was even more scared of what could eventually happen on the day of the parade.

"So, what brings you into my office, Jim? You almost never come to me for anything."

Anderson respected him as the most competent investigator he had ever had the pleasure of supervising. He always seemed to know what to do and how to make sure it got done. He needed little or no supervision in whatever he did, and Anderson was surprised to see him. Anderson's first impression was that Keegan came to him to take the last few hours of the tour off since that was just about the only reason that he ever came in to see him. But then something disturbing caught Anderson's eye. Keegan had come into see him with a case folder under his arm. Anderson's suspicions were raised by that fact alone and then he noticed that Keegan was not his usual calm and composed self. He appeared to be nervous.

"Well Cap," Keegan handed Anderson a copy of the intelligence report as he began. He paused momentarily to give Anderson time to peruse it before he continued, "I get the feeling it's legit."

Anderson's face began to turn red, and he seemed to get annoyed. "Jim, this report is dated last week. Why did you wait until now to bring it across my desk?"

"I've been doing some investigating on the matter and wanted to make sure it was for real before I bothered you with it."

It was a feeble excuse, Keegan conceded. He had learned a long time ago on the job that one should always have an answer. Sometimes you'd have the right answer and sometimes you'd have a bad answer, but a bad answer was better than no answer at all.

"Jim, I'm surprised at you. This isn't the type of thing you can just keep under your hat and wait out. We have to reach out to Martin Devine forthwith and warn him."

"I've already done that, Cap. I just came from his office."

Anderson shook his head in disbelief. "Are you telling me you went and told a civilian about a death threat even before you told your commanding officer? We need to run this by the Threat Assessment Unit at Intel before you contact the person. You know that! Jim, you know I have the utmost respect and admiration for you, but this is an inexcusable error in judgment.

What would have happened if the hitman didn't wait for the parade and decided to take Devine out today, during a live televised press conference? Do you realize the potential embarrassment to the entire New York City Police Department you would've caused? What if the press found out we knew about it and did nothing to at least *attempt* to prevent it?"

"Cap, trust me, this guy isn't going to try anything before the parade." Keegan was doing his best to defend himself and his actions.

"How could you possibly be so sure of that, Jim?"

"I've been doing some research on the case and I'm pretty sure ..."

Anderson curtly cut him off. "Forget it, Jim. You really left me in a bind now. I have to act on this immediately before it's too late."

Keegan knew he was right and felt horrible to have put Anderson in the position he was in now. He knew downtown was going to have a fit once they heard about the delay in taking action. Captain Ronald Anderson picked up the telephone and dialed the number without having to look it up. Keegan sat patiently and listened.

"Hello, this is Captain Anderson from the JTTF, I need to speak to the Chief of Detectives immediately," Anderson explained. After waiting for a moment, Anderson then responded once again into the phone. "Tell him a priority has come up and it's extremely urgent he calls me back right away."

Anderson hung up the phone and paced the floor without uttering a word. Keegan remained seated and awkwardly looked up at Anderson unsure what he should do next. He knew he had his job cut out for him and his career was in jeopardy, but he wasn't about to come clean in case he could figure out a way around his dilemma. No matter how much he thought, however, he didn't see any way to do both; stop the assassination and save his job. If he were to stop Flynn, the easiest way for Flynn to get back at him would be to tell Internal Affairs about his years of gunrunning for the I.R.A. Still, until the ax was to fall, Keegan had to keep the faith no matter how bad things looked; if not for himself, then at least for the sake of his family. The silence was driving Keegan crazy, and he finally broke it by asking a question of his boss. "So, Cap, what do you want me to do?"

Anderson stopped in his tracks and looked down at Keegan. He answered in a soft voice. "Nothing right now. I'm a firm believer in the chain of command."

Keegan caught the sarcasm and knew better than to respond to it. "We are not going to make a move without the direction of the Chief of Detectives."

After his quick and rather sarcastic answer for Keegan, Anderson once again paced the floor of his office. The tension in the office was broken by the ringing of the telephone. Anderson practically leaped at the phone to lift the receiver. "Captain Anderson, Joint Terrorist Task Force."

Keegan listened attentively, trying to imagine what the Chief of Detectives had to say on the other end. Anderson explained the situation in detail. "I know it sounds strange that the Irish Republican Army would strike here in New York, but my men seem to think it's a very real threat."

He glanced at Keegan. "An I.R.A. member who got collared in Northern Ireland gave up the plan as a part of a plea bargain over there. The Northern Irish Police passed on the information to INTERPOL. We have verified as much information as we could."

Keegan watched as Anderson turned red. He could only imagine what was being said to Anderson over the phone. Anderson, who had remained standing for the first few minutes of the phone call, looked down at him. He shook his head in an annoyed manner and took his seat before he continued. "Well sir, we became aware of the threat a few days ago but I wanted to do as much research as possible before bothering you with it," he lied.

Keegan stared at Anderson, as he blatantly lied to the Chief of Detectives to cover Keegan's ass. He greatly appreciated that Anderson was willing to place his own neck on the chopping block in order to protect him. "Yes sir, all of the indications would lead us to believe that there will be an attempt on Devine's life at the parade. Yes, sir, I am aware that the parade is later this week. We are just awaiting your word to put the detail together. Lieutenant Keegan and I have been already working on it. We just need your approval before we officially map it out."

After a short pause, "I had Lieutenant Keegan personally go over to his law office and inform him today." More silence. "Yes sir, I'll let you know every detail as soon as I know them myself."

Once Anderson hung up the phone Keegan spoke. "You didn't have to lie for me Cap. I'll call him right back and tell him it was me who kept him, as well as you, in the dark. You shouldn't have to be accountable for my fuck up."

"Don't be foolish, Jim. You made a poor call in judgment. There's no reason to put your job on the line." Anderson had obviously cooled off at Keegan and once again displayed the admiration he held for his subordinate.

Keegan began to protest. "But what about your job and your career if something goes wrong? I can't let you be the fall guy for something I did...or in this case didn't do."

"Jim, you're a rising star on this job, and you're headed to the top in a hurry. What are you about twenty names away from getting promoted to Captain? Once you get promoted, you will be on the fast track. You will get the bump to Deputy Inspector in no time. I have over thirty years in the police department and I've already gone as far as I'm going to go. Nobody, not even the Chief of Department is going to give me a real hard time…and if they do…well Jim, I have my time in. I'll tell them to kiss my ass and I'll put my papers in and retire."

Keegan had always felt a special loyalty to Anderson, and it was incidents like this one that came to mind when he would think of him. "Thank you, Cap, I owe you."

"Yes, Jim you do. So, you had better get your ass in gear, preferably overdrive, and get this detail together before the Chief calls back."

For the favor Anderson had done for him, this wasn't a very big request at all. It was usually Keegan's job to put details together whenever the occasion arose. He was a great strategist and Anderson didn't mind using this attribute of his to ensure that the job gets done. "One more thing you can do for me, Jim." Keegan looked up at Anderson. "Make sure nothing happens to this guy, okay."

That was not as simple a task and Keegan knew it.

"I'll do my best, boss."

Keegan waited for the Chief of Department's office to fax him over a copy of the parade route as well as a copy of all the uniformed and plainclothes Anti-Crime details that were already in place. He received all of the documents he had requested from the Chief of Patrol's office in only a matter of minutes. He studied the detail rosters and the parade route.

He figured the hit would be attempted probably at the very beginning of the parade or towards the end. The middle of the parade would be where all the cameras, dignitaries, and the most uniformed Police Officers would be. Keegan figured the last thing any hitman, Flynn included, would want is to be caught on film. That would just magnify the chance of getting caught. Keegan tallied up all the figures and learned there would be well over three thousand Police Officers at the parade.

He thought that the assignment was an almost certain death wish for the man and he reflected on Flynn's own words. *"He would either carry out the hit or die trying to."* It seemed impossible for this man, no matter how good he is, to carry out the hit and believe he would have any chance in the world of escaping the area inundated with cops.

Keegan decided to play the odds as he mapped out his own detail. He had well over a hundred Detectives assigned to him, to cover the entire parade route. He strongly felt the hitman would almost certainly attempt the hit either at the beginning or toward the end of the parade. He would consider this when drawing up the detail. He assigned four men to every intersection for the first four blocks and the last eight blocks of the parade. In between those areas, would be where the parade was most heavily guarded with uniformed officers. In those areas, he would assign only two men per intersection. *To try anything in the middle of the parade was nothing less than suicidal.*

Keegan came to realize that there was one very strong bond he and Flynn shared. That was the loyalty to their job. As Flynn had said he would die before failing, Keegan also would risk his own life for the job he so strongly loved and believed in. Keegan decided he was going to walk right alongside Devine for the entire parade. If Devine objected, he would walk slightly off to the side but nevertheless, he wouldn't let Martin Devine out of his sight the entire afternoon. He was going to be Devine's personal bodyguard for the day, whether Devine liked it or not.

Keegan decided in no uncertain terms that if Martin Devine was going to lose his life on this Saint Patrick's Day, it would only be after Keegan did everything in his power to prevent it. He was one hundred percent dedicated to preventing the hit, no matter what the consequences to himself ultimately would be. He became so involved with planning the detail and where to deploy his personnel, that he had lost track of the time. Captain Anderson walked back into the office and broke him from his work.

"Jim, what are you still doing here? It's almost seven; you should've signed out nearly an hour ago."

Keegan looked up at the clock on the wall in the office. "Oh, shit! I gotta give Kate a call and tell her I won't be home for a while."

"There is nothing more to do tonight. I faxed over the preliminary details you drew up to the Chief of D's officer almost two hours ago. They were satisfied. I have the debriefing at headquarters at 2000 hours with the top brass. Any further concerns, they will let me know. You can count on that.

Then we could adjust the detail as need be to address their concerns in the morning. There is nothing more you can do here tonight."

Marsh appreciated Keegan's hard work despite his prior lack in judgment. "Jim, why don't you just go home? Tomorrow is another day."

"Cap, I feel terrible about everything. It was my fuck up that's causing all of these problems for you, so I'm going to stay right here with you until we sort this whole thing out."

Captain Anderson shook his head in agreement. He knew Keegan was a real stand-up type of cop and time and time again he proved this true of himself. "All right Jim, suit yourself. You might as well come with me to headquarters and sit in on the meeting in case they have questions."

Keegan thanked Captain Anderson for everything he has done to help him through this mess before calling his wife to tell her he wouldn't be home for quite some time. After hanging up the phone, he was relieved that Kate hadn't been as upset by the fact he wasn't going to be coming home for a while as he thought she would be. Every now and then Kate would take him by surprise and actually be understanding about his job.

There was less than an hour before the tactical meeting with all the top brass of the department to discuss what strategies should be employed at the parade. He wanted to have all the answers that it would be feasible for him to have. On the other hand, he didn't want to have too many answers where he couldn't supply them with his source of information. This way, if he got lucky enough to prevent the assassination, and Flynn didn't snitch on Keegan, nobody would be the wiser.

Keegan rang his friend, Bob Wolf's office, hoping he had not left for the day. He was surprised that Wolf was actually still there. The two men exchanged pleasantries before Keegan got to the heart of the phone call. "Do you remember a few weeks ago when I called you to look into a guy named Sean Murphy?"

"Of course, I do. You heard he was running a scam to raise money for the I.R.A. or something along those lines."

"You don't ever forget a thing, do you Bob?" Keegan continued, "As it turns out, I don't believe Murphy is his real name anymore and conning people out of money may be the last thing he is here for. I received another intelligence report recently that said an I.R.A. member was in New York to assassinate the Grand Marshall of the Saint Patrick's Day Parade. I think they might be somehow be related," Keegan baited his friend.

"I don't understand why the I.R.A. would want to murder the Grand Marshall of the parade, Jim. To what end?"

Rather than explain the history of Ireland to his friend, he kept the answer short and sweet. "I don't know, Bob; I guess they're looking to make some sort of point. I don't even know if it's true for sure, but I have to assume it is. I can't take a chance on Devine getting killed."

"Fair enough. So how can I help?"

"Could you just run it through the computers to see if there are any known I.R.A. members past or present who recently came into the United States? Use a time frame of within the last two months."

Keegan doubted the computer would come up with anyone and at worst case scenario they did come up with the name Gerald Flynn, he was sure Flynn would be laying low somewhere with only a few days to go before Saint Patrick's Day. "No problem, Jim. I'll call you back in a few minutes."

"Thanks, Bob. One of these days I'm going to pay you back for all these favors you're always doing for me."

After hanging up the phone, he looked back down at the detail rosters in front of him. It was almost seven-thirty and he was trying to figure the best way to present the details to the department's hierarchy. He went over all of the details about the possible assassination attempt that he should know. He wasn't about to tell the department's top brass, the Super Chiefs, as they were known to the rank and file, everything that he, in fact, did know from his dealings with the men of the I.R.A. He studied the details rosters and kept the number of cops he wanted on each block in mind.

Keegan needed a break from the paperwork in front of him and walked out of his office and into the squad room. He saw one of the Detectives had put on a fresh pot of coffee and decided to take advantage of the situation. He poured himself a cup of coffee when he heard the telephone start to ring in his office. He took the coffee with him and walked quickly back into his office. "Lieutenant Keegan, Joint Terrorist Task Force."

"Jim, have I ever told you how official sounding you are when you answer the phone?" Bob Wolf began to kid around with him.

Keegan didn't want to seem curt with his friend, but he just wasn't in the mood for the silliness of any kind. "Have you got anything for me?"

"No Jim. Sorry. I have no record of any known I.R.A. members at all entering the U.S. any time in the past six months."

Keegan, wanting to keep the conversation to a minimum, thanked his friend and hung up the telephone. He felt a lot better now. He would have more answers than anyone would expect him to. At twenty minutes before eight, Captain Anderson entered his office and announced it was time they leave for headquarters. The two men left the office of the Joint Terrorist Task Force and made their way to One Police Plaza.

CHAPTER 17

It was a typically windy March afternoon in New York. As he left the pharmacy, Gerald Flynn buttoned the bottom button on his denim jacket to prevent the wind from blowing it open. The temperature was in the middle fifties and spring wouldn't be far behind. Flynn was somewhat impressed with all of Manhattan's skyscrapers. He shielded his eyes from the bright sun as he looked up to examine an oddly shaped building in the heart of the city. Flynn had spent almost all of his time inside the hotel room since his confrontation with the female Detective. It was a relief to get some fresh air and exercise by taking a long, slow walk through the crowded streets of Manhattan.

Flynn figured with Saint Patrick's Day being tomorrow and nobody finding him yet, it was a rather safe bet the police had no idea where he was staying. He had been watching the news every evening at six and then again at eleven, as well as combing through the daily newspapers. He was relieved to see the police hadn't released his photo nor was there any mention of an Irishmen being sought for any reason in New York City. He was curious to go back to his original hotel to see if the police had impounded the rental car yet, but he knew the risk was too great in case Keegan had the car staked out.

On the way back to his hotel, Flynn took a momentary detour and stopped at a pizza parlor. He ordered one slice of pizza and gave the man behind the counter two dollar bills. After putting the little change that he got in return into his pocket, he picked up the slice in one hand, and walked out of the store. Flynn felt a bit awkward having no free hands. The slice of pizza was in one hand and the supplies he had bought earlier were in the other. He thought how if for any reason he had to go for his gun, he would drop the pizza. He doubted that would happen.

The pizza had curbed his appetite, for now anyway. It was quite good, he concluded. Flynn started to like New York City. There was good food, good nightlife, and it was a very exciting place, day or night. Although Flynn conceded to himself New York had a lot to offer him, he couldn't wait to be back home in Belfast. That was where he belonged.

The more thought Flynn gave to his eventual trip back to Northern Ireland, the more he realized what a tough task that could potentially be. If Keegan was really out to stop him, then after the hit he would undoubtedly have men at all of the airports in the area. His alias of Sean Murphy would also be useless. He was sure Keegan would put out an All-Points-Bulletin on that name as well as his real name of Gerald Flynn. *Maybe it wasn't such a good idea to have told Keegan me real name.* He realized that he wouldn't even be able to turn to Dan O'Brien for help since he was sure Keegan would have McBride's also staked out twenty-four hours a day. He was on his own to get back to his native country once his mission was accomplished.

It was a sobering thought but first things first. His main and only objective was to assassinate Martin Devine to further the cause of freedom for Northern Ireland. After the mission was complete, would be the appropriate time to start thinking about how he was going to get back home. He still had well over three thousand dollars left from the money Eamon Quinn had given him and that would surely be enough to live on the lam for a little while. He could pull off a stick-up or two if he had to, just to get enough money to get by if money eventually did become an issue for him.

Flynn figured after about two or three weeks, when the heat began to die down, he could call up Eamon and arrange for some way to get home. Eamon had his connections all over and Flynn figured at worst he would wind up stowing away on a ship bound for Ireland. Even if he had to take a ship to England first, it wouldn't be so bad. From there he could board a plane without the fear of being looked for. Whatever the future held for Flynn, he figured in twenty-four hours' time he would have a much better idea of what to do.

At shortly after three o'clock, Flynn returned to

his hotel room. He sat down on the bed and emptied the contents of the bag from the pharmacy on the bed next to him. He picked up the mirrored sunglasses and put them on. He walked into the bathroom, looking at himself in the mirror. He liked them. He thought they looked intimidating on him. He then took them off and returned to the other room.

Flynn examined the rest of the supplies he bought and then got undressed. He placed his nine-millimeter handgun on the night table next to the bed after bringing it up to eye level and setting the sights on a random target in the room. After stripping nude, Flynn went back into the bathroom and turned the hot water on in the shower. He watched as the faucet spat out brownish water. He allowed the water to run until all of the brownish color gave way to clear water. He turned on the cold water and adjusted the water to his liking. Flynn spent about fifteen minutes in the rather hot shower trying to relax. He carefully shampooed and conditioned his long dirty blond hair. When Flynn got out of the shower, he toweled himself off and wrapped the towel around his waist. Wiping the fog from the bathroom mirror, he studied his face. He had a three-day growth of stubble which needed to come off.

Once Flynn had finished shaving, he returned to the other room and retrieved some of the supplies from the bed, bringing them back into the bathroom. Flynn grabbed his slowly drying hair in one hand, crunching it into a ponytail. He then took the pair of newly purchased scissors in the other. The scissors fought their way through the wet hair. He cut it as short as he possibly could, discarding the excess on the bathroom floor. Flynn examined the hair as it lay on the floor. It had taken him a while to grow it that long and he was sad to see it go. *Well, we all have to make sacrifices*, reasoned Flynn to himself. He laughed to himself about his own joke and plugged in a pair of barber's clippers. He continued to cut his hair until it was as low as he could do by scissor and then he took to the hair with the buzzers. It was a crude job he admitted but nevertheless, it would change his appearance greatly. He had cut his once long hair, down to an inch-long crew cut.

He read the directions on the back of the box of hair dye before opening it. He had never dyed his hair before. He mixed the appropriate concoction and placed the mix in a dispenser supplied in the package. He stretched the smallish rubber gloves supplied by the kit over his large hands. These were probably made for a lady's hand, he reckoned. Flynn put another towel over his shoulders, not wanting to get the dye all over his entire upper body.

He carefully followed the instructions and combed in the dye exactly as instructed. During the process, which took less than an hour, Flynn wondered how long it would take him to get used to his new, short hair and how long it would eventually take to grow it long again as he preferred it. He never even considered another option like jail or even death. Flynn was quite confident he would succeed in his mission.

When his hair finally dried, it was now jet black. Quite the contrast from the dirty blond color it had been for his entire life, he observed. Flynn added a gel to his hair and styled it with short spikes. He once again put on his mirrored sunglasses to examine how his disguise was coming along. He liked the way it looked so far, but he wasn't quite finished yet. Flynn took off the sunglasses and tossed them on top of his bed. He took a seat on the bed and looked at the remaining items which he had bought at a costume store.

It was a set of false mustaches and the glue to attach them with. Flynn opened the pack and picked out one of the mustaches. He read the instructions and warnings on the tube of glue. The tube of glue stated that it was guaranteed to last for at least twelve hours. This was one guarantee Flynn wanted to be certain of. The mustache was going to be a vital part of his disguise and if it were to fall off, his entire ruse could be blown. Flynn stood in front of the mirror as he applied the adhesive to his upper lip. He waited about thirty seconds as the instructions had suggested and placed the mustache in place. The test for the glue would be to go to sleep tonight wearing the mustache, if it didn't fall off Flynn would have enough confidence to use it tomorrow when it really counted.

Flynn removed the towels from around his body and glanced at himself in the mirror. He liked what he saw. He decided to get dressed. After putting on a pair of jeans, Flynn picked up his gun and tucked it into his waistband. He put on a sweatshirt, careful to pull it over the butt of the gun. He put on his socks and shoes and walked back into the bathroom to take another look at himself in the mirror. Once the sunglasses were back in place there was only one more item to complete the disguise, a New York Yankees baseball cap. His image in the mirror stared back at him. He was satisfied by what he saw. There was no question in Flynn's mind that the disguise was brilliant. His hair was now not only a totally different color but also about a foot shorter. The mustache, baseball cap, and sunglasses added a lot to the disguise as well. Flynn was confident that even if Keegan were to look in his direction, he would never realize who he was.

Flynn grabbed the dark blue hooded sweatshirt which he recently bought. The windbreaker that he had taken with him from home had to be abandoned in his Queens hotel just in case it was being watched. He put the sweatshirt on as he exited the hotel room. It was almost five o'clock. He wasn't sure where he was going but he didn't feel like being confined on the night before the biggest day in his life. Tomorrow, he was certain to make history. There may even be rebel songs that would honor his accomplishments, he figured.

Flynn had been walking around the city rather aimlessly when a reckless thought came into his head. It really was a bad idea, he conceded but he considered it anyway. If he decided to go through with it, he would be chastised if anyone were to ever find out. Flynn didn't want to do anything that would possibly jeopardize his assignment, especially so close to the parade, but he really wanted to test his disguise to see if it was as good as he believed it to be. He wanted it to be a real test. He wanted to see if someone that had actually met him, would recognize him.

Flynn's idea was to go to McBride's Bar and Grill to see if he would be recognized. If he wasn't, then his disguise would undoubtedly be a success. Flynn had nerves of steel and even though he knew going to McBride's was probably the worst thing in the world he could do at this point, he didn't care. It would get his blood pumping and his adrenaline flowing. The rush would be quite welcomed after being so bored the past few days. It would be something to get him psyched up for tomorrow. He again wondered how Quinn or even O'Brien would react if they had only known what he was up to. *They'd be infuriated, for sure; more so than ever before.* This thought also gave Flynn's ego a boost. Flynn had always been a rebel and wanted to do things his own way. Getting under people's skin had become more of a game to him than anything else.

There was one more thing that needed to be done first. The curiosity was getting the better of him. He descended the stairs at the subway station located at Seventh Avenue and Forty-Ninth Street. He couldn't believe how crowded the subway was at this time of day. It was a sharp contrast from the last time he had taken the subway a few nights prior. He boarded the N train headed to Queens. He had to stand the entire ride, but it was still a more enjoyable ride than it was, smelling the homeless man last time. He enjoyed the brisk walk to get to the hotel where he had originally stayed. He walked down the block from the entrance to see that the Nissan was still parked in the exact spot where he had left it.

At first, he was surprised that it was still there. He had figured Keegan would have impounded it and dusted it for fingerprints. After a few moments, however, Flynn decided Keegan might have left the car right here and have it staked out watching for his return. Flynn got a sick satisfaction out of the thought that there were probably Detectives watching the car right at this very moment and here he was just walking past the car and they had no clue. He laughed to himself. "Stoopid fuckin coppers." He muttered under his breath. For a moment, he contemplated stopping at the car and leaning on it just to pique the Detective's interest. Flynn then thought that would really be pushing his luck, so he just walked right past the car, never slowing down or even glancing in its direction.

Later that evening, when Flynn arrived at McBride's, he glanced into the bar from the outside before entering. He could see that both Dan O'Brien and Nora O'Donnell were inside working. *Perfect!* He then looked at his reflection in a storefront's window, making sure every aspect of his disguise was in place. Flynn entered the bar with uncertainty. This would be the true test. He believed that he looked nothing like the old Gerald Flynn, but until he could get people who knew him to look at him and not recognize him, he wouldn't be confident.

It was nearly half-past seven o'clock and McBride's was far from crowded. Nora O'Donnell appeared to be the only waitress working at the time. Just to play it safe, Flynn sat at one of the tables in her section. He made sure, however, not to sit at the table he usually did. There was no reason to tip his hand should she suspect it might be him. Flynn patiently waited at the table for Nora to take his order. The sunglasses were probably rather conspicuous, Flynn conceded, but they were part of the disguise and they wouldn't be conspicuous tomorrow during the parade.

Flynn had been daydreaming about how he would carry out the assassination when Nora's voice broke his concentration. "We have two for one special on any draft beer until eight. Can I start you off with a drink or are you ready to order?"

Flynn looked up at Nora and quickly realized that she didn't have any notion of who he was. Flynn wanted to be very careful not to give him any clues to his identity. He answered her in a voice a couple of octaves lower than his normal voice and added his best impression of a New York accent. "I'll have a cheeseburga platta and a pint of Bud."

Nora O'Donnell never flinched or took a second

look at him. She answered in a gleeful manner. "Okay. I'll be right back with your beer."

Flynn studied her up and down. He liked what he saw. She was wearing a black skirt, a bit shorter than usual, and a white blouse. Flynn stared at her legs, thinking about how he parted them during the night they had spent together only a few weeks ago. She had no idea the man she had given herself to, just recently, sat right in front of her.

Flynn watched Nora as she walked up to the bar and asked Dan O'Brien for the beers. He watched for any unusual conversation between the two to see if Nora may have sensed something and asked for O'Brien's opinion. There was none. There was almost no conversation between them at all and Nora promptly returned with his beers. She set them down on a napkin in front of him. "Here you go, sir. Your dinner will be here shortly." She smiled.

Gerald Flynn returned the smile. "Thank you, dear."

He was very optimistic. It became crystal clear to him that Nora had no idea in the world she was just talking to the man she hated. Flynn took a long swig of the beer and set it back down on the table in front of him. He glanced over at Dan O'Brien. O'Brien was taking advantage of the extremely light crowd and watching the news on television.

Flynn knew before he left, he would somehow make sure O'Brien got a good look at him and see if O'Brien had any strange or suspicious reaction. Flynn downed the remainder of beer from the first mug and glanced around the bar to see if there was anyone, he thought might be an undercover cop watching the place. He decided there wasn't anyone in the bar who seemed to be out of place when Nora returned to his table with his cheeseburger deluxe. She set the food down in front of him and she noticed he had already drunk his first pint. She teased him. "Wow, you must have been thirsty. Let me know if there is anything else that I can get you."

Flynn looked down at his empty glass. "I was. How about some ketchup?"

"Coming right up."

Nora walked to the kitchen to get a bottle of ketchup. Flynn started to feel a little cocky and decided to push his luck when Nora returned by engaging her in conversation. He had just taken the first bite of his burger when she returned. "Excuse me miss, don't take this wrong. I'm not trying to hit on you or anything, but I just had to tell you that you have the most beautiful eyes I've ever seen."

Nora had been working in a bar long enough to know when she was being hit on. She usually tried to be as polite as possible yet cut the conversation short. There was no need to ruin her tip by insulting the guy. This time, however, she would see where the conversation would head. "Oh, thank you. I'm sorry I can't return the compliment, but I can't even see your eyes behind those shades."

Flynn cracked a smile at Nora's taunt. "Well, I would show them to you," Flynn began his lie, mindful not to let his natural brogue slip through his synthetic New York accent. "But right now, I'm afraid you wouldn't want to see them. I got jumped a couple of nights ago and the punks couldn't just take my money; they had to throw me to the ground and kick me in the face too. I have a real nasty black eye. There were three of them. There wasn't too much I could do.

"Oh, you poor thing."

Nora seemed to buy his lie and it made a good excuse for wearing sunglasses in the dimly lit bar. Flynn could see Nora was trying to steal a peek at the alleged bruise but all he had to do was look up at her and she immediately looked away. With nothing else to say she walked away, almost feeling ashamed she had been caught staring at him. "Let me know if there is anything else that I can get you."

Flynn felt a great sense of accomplishment and enjoyed his burger more than he had ever enjoyed a cheeseburger before. After finishing his meal, he signaled for Nora to bring him his check. He gave her a twenty-dollar bill to cover the bill plus the tip. Now would come the next step of the test, he thought. Dan O'Brien remained uninterested in anything in particular as he stood alone behind the bar.

O'Brien looked at the man as he approached. He thought there was something familiar about him but then he figured maybe he had just seen him in the bar before. He did think it was odd that the man was wearing sunglasses in the bar. New York was full of weirdoes, reasoned O'Brien, and this guy was probably one of them. "Excuse me pal, have you got the time?" he asked O'Brien, continuing to mask his voice.

The bartender looked down at his wristwatch and then up again at Flynn. "And so I have, lad. It's a quarter past eight."

Flynn thanked the man and was now one hundred percent comfortable that the disguise was a success. He made his way to the door and put his sweatshirt back on, zippering it up. There was something about Gerald Flynn's character however, that wouldn't let him leave things alone. His narcissism got the better of him. He felt the need to play with Nora's head before leaving. He had gotten all the way to the door and then turned back around to see Nora. Nora was quick to speak to Flynn before he had the chance to say anything to her. "Thank you again, sir. Come again. I hope your eye heals quickly."

He reached into his front pocket and removed a roll of cash. He peeled off a twenty-dollar bill from the top and handed it to Nora, which she accepted. She figured the guy to be a very big tipper, or he would be back to hit on her another day. His demeanor then changed, and a sadistic smile came across his face. "Ah Nora, you're very welcome, you are." Gerald Flynn now abandoned his adopted voice and spoke with his own. "That's for the cab fare you never took a few weeks ago, love."

Flynn watched as Nora turned beet red. He had

a feeling of satisfaction as he walked out the door. It was now raining steadily. The weather had changed dramatically in the hour or so he had spent in the bar. Not wanting to walk back to his hotel room, he hailed a cab. The most important day of his life was one night's sleep away.

James Keegan had just pulled into his driveway when the rain started to come down. Having worked a ten am to six pm shift today, he would now be off for the remainder of the night. He hoped he would be able to get a good night's sleep. If he did, it would be the first time in a week. He wished he could confide in Kate and tell her everything so he might feel a little better, but he knew this was something he couldn't do. He did decide, however, that he would tell her tonight after dinner about the possible hit at the parade tomorrow and that he was assigned to guard Devine. She wasn't going to be happy about this assignment, but at least she would know about it. From this point forward, he wasn't going to keep anything from his wife. Everything and anything that happened would be shared with her; *unless of course, it had to do with his past ties to the Irish Republican Army.*

He began to think about what Dan O'Brien had said to him. *"Once in, never out."* The more he thought about it, the more angered he became. *Who the hell did O'Brien think he was talking to? This wasn't Ireland or maybe O'Brien had forgotten that small fact.* Keegan walked in the front door of his suburban home and was promptly greeted by his family. Kate gave her husband a kiss hello as he took off his coat. "How was your day, hon?"

"Uneventful." He gave his kids a hug and kiss.

"Daddy, tomorrow is Saint Patrick's Day, right?" Keegan's oldest child said, leading his father on.

He grew suspicious but decided to play along. "Yes. That's right."

Kate then shook her head and jumped into the conversation. "Forget it, Kevin. You have a test in math tomorrow. You're not staying home from school."

He protested and wouldn't concede that easily. "But mom, Dad always says we should take our heritage more seriously and I think he's right."

"Forget it." Kate reinforced her decision.

"It's not fair."

He looked up disappointed in his mother's decision. He turned toward his father, continuing to plead his case. "None of the Jewish kids go to school on their holiday. So why should we have to go to school on ours?"

James Keegan looked down at his son and was forced to laugh. He patted him on the head, mussing his hair. "Nice try sport."

"I told ya it wouldn't work." Timothy would jump in at any opportunity to prove his older brother wrong.

Tonight was no different from any other night this week and Keegan's mind was preoccupied with the parade tomorrow. Kate called the family to dinner. Keegan couldn't help but wonder if tonight would be the last night he would spend with his family. Kate had prepared a pot roast for dinner. She promised corned beef and cabbage tomorrow as well as homemade Irish soda bread. Keegan sat at the table through dinner and hardly even touched his food. Kate had known something was bothering him all week but tonight was the clincher. Kate asked her husband to help her with the dishes while the children got ready for bed. Kate washed the dishes one by one and then handed them to her husband to be dried and put away. "What's the matter, Jim? You haven't been yourself all week."

He was relieved to finally get it off his chest. He placed the final dish in the cabinet and looked at his wife. After a deep breath, "Kate I'm scared. I've never been so afraid in my life. There's a death threat on Martin Devine at the parade tomorrow. I'm pretty sure it's a genuine threat."

Kate didn't understand what her husband was trying to tell her. "So, what does that have to do with you? Why are you afraid?"

"Kate, I'm in charge of guarding his life tomorrow."

"You mean you're in charge of the detail to protect his life, right?" She wanted to be clear.

He explained in greater detail. "Yes Kate, I'm in charge of the detail but I'm also going to be marching alongside him for the entire parade."

"Oh no you're not!" she insisted.

"I have to Kate, it's my job. You know that."

"I don't care about your job, Jim. I care about you. If you're so sure this threat is genuine why in the world would you want to be anywhere near the man."

It seemed to Keegan to be the same old story. No matter how many times he tried to explain what being a cop was all about, she wouldn't understand. Someone who wasn't a cop could never understand what it was all about. It was about never backing down. You'd go after a guy with a machine-gun when all you have is your six-shooter. You'd go after a six-foot- five-inch, three-hundred-pound guy, that you knew was going to fight you. You'd take on three guys at once if they challenged you. You NEVER back down. "Kate, it's my job. I can't run away when I know someone needs my help."

"Then call in sick. Do whatever you have to, but you can't go to work tomorrow. It's too dangerous."

The irony struck him just then that he had used a similar argument in an attempt to dissuade Devine from marching. "You know very well I can't call in sick. I'm running the detail. This guy's life is in peril."

Kate was angry now. "And what about your life, Jim. Who's worrying about that? Who's worrying about your children growing up without a father?"

"I don't want to argue Kate. You know I have to go to work, so don't bother trying to talk me out of it. I'll be careful."

Kate wasn't so willing to drop the conversation. "Jim, what about the kids? What about me? How could you risk your life for someone you don't even know and put your own family second?"

Keegan decided he wasn't getting anywhere with this and tried a new approach. "Kate, how could I face you and my children every day knowing I'm a coward and a failure. I'm proud of what I do, and I can look anybody dead in the eyes and tell them that I'm the best. How would I ever be able to look the kids in the eyes again if I were to run away from my responsibility?"

Kate left the conversation alone after that. She knew no matter what she said her husband's mind was made up and there would be no changing it. This was just one more example as far as she was concerned of the fact that her husband loved his job more than he did his family. The two of them didn't speak to each other again for the rest of the evening.

It was shortly before midnight when he decided to turn in for the night. He walked upstairs and checked in on his sleeping children. One by one, he awoke them from their sleep to give them a kiss and a hug and to tell them how much he loved them. The children returned their father's kiss but didn't think anything of it. He then joined his wife in bed. Kate wasn't yet asleep, but she pretended she was. He put his arm around her and held her tightly as he tried to go to sleep.

CHAPTER 18

The alarm clock sounded at 7:30 am waking James Keegan from his sleep. He sat up in bed after shutting it off. He looked to his right to see that Kate wasn't next to him. She must be getting the kids ready for school, he reasoned. He rubbed his eyes, which burned due to lack of sleep. He estimated that he didn't fall asleep until sometime after four am. He got up from his bed and looked out of the window to see a gloomy day. The rain danced in a puddle outside his window. It was a light rain accompanied by a gusty wind. *Terrific*, he thought to himself. He was going to be marching the entire parade in the rain. It almost seemed apropos to him. He hoped the gray skies weren't an omen for what the day would bring. He wondered if his luck could possibly be any worse.

At eight o'clock, Keegan was still in his bedroom when he heard a knock on the door. The Keegan children marched into his room all dressed in green to celebrate the Saint Patrick's Day holiday. They jumped on the bed with their father and in almost perfect synchronization spoke. "Happy Saint Patrick's Day, daddy!"

Keegan grabbed all three of them in one big hug and returned their wishes. He gave each of them a kiss and made sure to tell them he loved them. Keegan remained strong while his kids were in the room but after they left for school, he could feel his eyes well up with tears. He fought the tears back and wondered if the kids had just happened to come into the room on their own or if Kate had put them up to it. He determined it was probably Kate's doing, but either way he was happy they did.

Kate filed the children into the Ford Explorer to drive them to school. There was no need to make her kids wait at the bus stop on a rainy day like this one. As she drove her kids to school, Kate couldn't help but think about what the day would bring. She had laid next to her husband all night, watching him, as he tossed and turned. After he had finally fallen asleep, she had rubbed his back hoping to help him relax so he could get his rest. Kate, herself, didn't fall asleep all night.

She was both nervous about what was going to happen today as well as feeling guilty with herself for turning her back on her husband last night when he had come to bed. He needed her support and she refused to give it to him. Kate dropped the kids off at their school and wished them a good day. She watched them run through the rain to the school. She couldn't help but wonder as she watched them go what she would do if anything bad were to happen to Jim.

She looked at the clock in the car, noting it was a quarter before nine. She hoped she would get home before Jim had left for the parade so she could kiss goodbye and let him know she wasn't still upset with him. She was glad she had at least sent the kids to wish him a happy Saint Patrick's Day, just in case she didn't get a chance to.

Kate pulled into the driveway and saw the department Crown Victoria was still there. She was relieved and went inside to see her husband. She was just in time. Jim was about to leave the house and begin his drive into the city. He was scheduled to meet Martin Devine at ten-fifteen at his law office. Kate was pleased to see that Jim was wearing his dark blue suit. It was her favorite suit of his and he looked as handsome today as he was on the day they wed. Keegan finished adjusting his emerald-green tie and shut off the television, which had been tuned into the weather channel. He turned to face his wife and was unsure what to say. He decided to open the conversation with the oldest ice breaker there was—the weather. "They said the temperature is going to drop into the thirties today and it might even snow. I guess they don't know spring is next week, huh?"

Kate chose to ignore his comment about the weather. "Jim, I'm sorry I gave you such a hard time last night."

She had a tear in her eye. Keegan took his wife in his arms and squeezed her body tightly against his own. "I know you were upset, sweetheart. I understand."

"I'm just worried about you Jim." Kate fought back the tears she could feel building up. "Please, Jim, be careful."

"I will Kate. I will. I promise."

Keegan put on his overcoat to combat the inclement weather. He looked down at his watch. "I gotta get going."

Keegan looked his wife deeply in the eyes and gave her a kiss goodbye. "I love you."

"I love you too," as she watched her husband leave their home for what she prayed would not be the last time.

The rain had turned into a misty drizzle by the time Keegan arrived at Martin Devine's law office for a final summation of the detail. The three hundred Detectives assigned to the detail had met earlier in the day with Captain Anderson and were given their posts and instructions. The uniformed details were mustering up on various street corners throughout the parade route. Keegan agreed that Captain Anderson would oversee the Detectives detail while he would march next to Devine.

Keegan was immediately shown into Devine's office by his secretary when he arrived. Devine, Captain Anderson, and a few of the Detectives from the office were already there when Keegan walked in. Keegan watched as one of the Detectives was assisting Devine in adjusting the bulletproof vest he was requested to wear during the parade. Once the vest was properly fit on Devine, he took an open hand

and slammed it against the vest causing a loud thud. "Boy, this is uncomfortable," Devine announced. "I don't know how you guys wear this."

Keegan was glad to see that although Devine had been stubborn about some of his suggestions that he didn't balk at this one. "It can save our lives, Martin. That's why we wear it."

Martin Devine looked over in Keegan's direction and shook his head in agreement as he buttoned his shirt over the vest. "I guess you're right, Jim."

The starting time of the parade was drawing near so Keegan knew he too must get prepared. He opened the duffel bag he had brought from home and took out his own bulletproof vest to wear. He then took his Sig Sauer, nine-millimeter handgun from its holster on his right hip where he almost always wore it. He removed a shoulder holster from his duffel bag and put it on.

Keegan figured since he was wearing an overcoat, he would never be able to get to his gun in time, should he need it, if it remained on his hip. It didn't make any sense to even wear a gun if you can't get to it when you need it. Judge Boden could attest to that. Keegan placed the gun in the shoulder holster and put his overcoat back on. He placed his hand in the right front pocket of his overcoat, feeling his .38 caliber Smith & Wesson Chief. A second gun was a much quicker way to rearm himself if need be, rather than to try and reload his Sig Sauer. He loosely fastened the strap of the shoulder holster and reached into the jacket with his right hand to make sure his Sig Sauer was easily accessible. He had an eerie feeling he was going to need it today.

Gerald Flynn anxiously waited at the scene he had predetermined would be the sight of the assassination, in front of Saint Patrick's Cathedral. Flynn decided this would be the last place Keegan or anyone else for that matter would think he would attempt the hit. They would think it was too risky and escape impossible, figured Flynn.

Flynn, however, saw a different scene. He saw one of mass chaos; people running for cover at the densest part of the parade route. Flynn figured the more people, the more confusion and the more confusion, the better chance of a clean escape. But the most appetizing thing this particular site had to offer was the media. There would be hundreds of reporters and cameras there from all over the country to witness and hopefully capture the assassination on film. Flynn, aside from being the closest thing to pure evil most people would ever encounter, was also egocentric. He couldn't wait to see his work all over the news and read about it in the newspaper.

Flynn touched the butt of the gun as it sat in his waistband as he thought over his plan one more time. If Keegan was stupid enough to be there, he would go after Keegan first. He would simply walk up to him and shoot him at pointblank range right in the head, just in case he was wearing a bulletproof vest. Flynn was confident in his disguise after it had passed the challenges presented it. The one major drawback of the disguise was the weather. Since it was overcast and lightly raining, Flynn knew if he wore the sunglasses it would bring unnecessary attention to himself. Not willing to take that chance so late in the game, he left the sunglasses at his hotel, but he was still sure his disguise was flawless.

He thought it through, once again. After killing Keegan, he knew he'd have to act quickly and shoot Devine before the police had a chance to intervene. Once he was satisfied Devine was dead, he would make his escape. The escape itself would be the most difficult part of the operation. Flynn decided he was going to use the mass hysteria to his advantage and blend into the crowd and run for cover just like everybody else.

While in the middle of the crowd, he was going to drop the clip from the gun regardless of how many shots he fired during the hit and replace it with a fresh clip he had in his back pocket. That would be a precaution in case it was necessary to shoot it out with the police. Flynn then planned on ducking into a fast-food restaurant a block away, where he had been earlier in the day, and planted a change of clothes in a loose ceiling board above a stall in the men's room. The clothes he planted were a pair of green sweatpants, a green, white, and orange rugby shirt, and a baseball cap. These festive clothes were in sharp contrast to the dark clothes he was now wearing. He would put the clothes he wore to do the hit, along with the false mustache up in the ceiling tile where they wouldn't be found for years to come, he figured. Flynn knew if he made it this far, he would be home free. The police would be looking for a man with a mustache, wearing all dark clothing. He could then just walk among the crowds of people and nobody would ever look twice at him.

When Keegan, Devine, and Anderson arrived at the starting point of the parade, shortly before eleven am, Keegan got out of the car first to examine the crowd. There were thousands of people, all of whom seemed to be wearing green. They were lined up along the sidewalk, behind the blue police barricades, for as far as the eyes could see. Some teenagers or young adults were in the crowd that appeared drunk and slightly unruly but none of whom looked particularly threatening. Keegan saw numerous uniformed Police Officers as well as the plainclothes Detectives he had assigned at the parade's beginning.

Keegan, after assessing the situation and deeming it safe, looked back at the car where Devine remained along with Captain Anderson. He stuck his thumb out of his closed fist in an upward direction informing his Commanding Officer everything looked okay. Captain Anderson and Devine then emerged from the department auto. Anderson raised a portable radio to his mouth, inquiring if the detail was in place and if they saw anything unusual. Upon receiving acknowledgment from various checkpoints along the parade route, Anderson wished Keegan good luck. Devine stood and smiled at the parade-goers as the green, white, and orange sash, bearing the words **Grand Marshall** was adorned around him. "Everything is clear as far as our men can tell," Anderson announced. "You can begin whenever you're ready Jim. Be careful."

Keegan looked at Devine hoping for a sudden change of heart. In his heart, he knew there would be none, but he would try anyway. "Martin, you know even the mayor and a couple of councilmen pulled out of marching when we informed them of the threat. Nobody would think anything less of you if..."

Devine immediately interrupted. "I already told you, Jim, I'm not backing down for anybody."

Devine looked up at the crowd and gave a big thumbs up. He roared. "Let's march!"

Keegan was tuned into everything and everyone around him as they marched up Fifth Avenue. The sounds of marching bands and bagpipers playing assorted Irish tunes resonated off the buildings as they marched. After passing through the first four blocks of the parade without any incident, Keegan felt a bit more relaxed. He even began to wonder if Flynn had been all hot air and maybe he decided to call the hit off after all. He convinced himself he would remain alert through the entire parade, but he was sure nothing would happen until the last dozen blocks or so.

For Flynn to try anything between here and then would be a death wish, he reassured himself. Keegan continued examining the crowd looking for any signs of the Irish hitman. Instead, Keegan noticed the thousands of children waving and looking on along with their parents. *This was what it's all about,* he thought. *It was for the kids.* Parades always were and this one was no different. Seeing all the children enjoying themselves and boasting their heritage made him think of his own children.

He had never taken his kids to the parade because he usually marched with the Emerald Society of the New York City Police Department, but he vowed that next year he would take them to see the parade. Even if it meant they had to miss a day of school. *Kevin was right*, thought Keegan. *Saint Patrick's Day is a day to celebrate. A day every Irishman should be proud of their heritage.* Keegan had relaxed so much that he almost started enjoying himself. The bagpipers were playing the Garryowen and Keegan hummed along to the march. He did remain focused, however, considering the reality of the threat.

He scanned the spectators with every step he took, looking for the hitman. Instead, he observed people having a great time, waving both Irish and American flags. There were children dressed in kilts and Irish step dancing dresses. Some wore green wigs, others dressed as leprechauns. He had seen over a dozen different types of hats being worn by people of all ages. Keegan loved this parade, year after year, but often became frustrated by the politics that usually came along with it. He couldn't understand why anyone would overshadow such a festive holiday with politics.

He then glanced alongside himself and saw Martin Devine, a walking target, jubilantly waving to the spectators and seemingly having a great time. Keegan wondered if Devine really understood why a terrorist from Northern Ireland wanted to see him dead. Keegan, himself, no longer understood it. As the parade surged forward, Keegan looked ahead and could see Saint Patrick's Cathedral on the next block. He wondered if His Eminence, the Cardinal of New York, would be on the steps of the Cathedral waving as he usually did during this parade. Keegan had met the Cardinal on numerous occasions and was quite fond of him.

As they got almost directly in front of the Cathedral, Keegan had noticed the man in black crawl under the blue police barricade. He glanced over in the man's direction and noticed something familiar about him. He then looked back over at His Eminence who was waving hello to him. Something bothered Keegan and instead of returning the Cardinal's gesture, he turned back to the man in black, who was now inside the police line about twenty feet from them. He looked the man in the eyes and instantly recognized him. Flynn's stone-cold eyes were a dead giveaway to his identity.

The one thing Gerald Flynn hadn't counted on was the fact that Keegan was a top-notch investigator, who had seen through numerous disguises throughout his time on the job. Keegan, sensing the danger, shouted out to Devine. "Martin, get out of here!"

Instinctively, he reached down to his hip for his gun as he charged an off-guard Gerald Flynn. He quickly realized his gun was not on his hip but instead in his shoulder holster, but it was too late to go for it. He was almost right on top of Flynn.

Flynn hadn't expected Keegan to charge him and wasn't ready for him when he did. He frantically reached into his waistband for his gun and pulled it out. In his haste, Flynn was unable to get a proper grip on the gun and couldn't get his finger on the trigger by the time Keegan was upon him. Flynn took the gun and with all his might, smashed it into the face of a charging James Keegan.

The force of the blow landed squarely on Keegan's jaw and knocked a tooth out of his mouth while cracking two others. He tumbled backward banging his head on the pavement sending him into a state of semi-consciousness. He had twisted in the air awkwardly, as he fell backward and landed on his left side. The force of the fall momentarily evacuated the air from his lungs.

Keegan wanted to just remain on the floor and welcome the blackness, but he knew if he did, it would be permanent. Instead, he mustered everything he had in him to fight the dizziness, even though he almost passed out from the excruciating pain. Instinctively, he fell back on his training realizing if he didn't fight back...and win, he would never see his family again.

The force of the punch had dislodged the gun from Flynn's hand. Flynn watched Keegan fall to the ground and felt a great sense of satisfaction. Flynn quickly located the gun which had landed a couple of feet from Keegan's nearly lifeless body. Flynn knew he had to finish Keegan off without hesitation and go after Devine who was still standing nearby in a state of shock.

Flynn took a step toward the gun and bent down to pick it up when Keegan swept his feet out from under him with a picture-perfect leg sweep. Keegan's body went into autopilot; he no longer felt the pain. He followed the leg sweep by smashing his elbow as hard as he could right down on the bridge of Flynn's nose, causing a steady flow of blood. Flynn was unwilling to feel the pain and continued in his pursuit of the gun.

Keegan, who was lying on his left side as he fought, was unable to get to his own gun. As Flynn reached the gun, Keegan got partially up and jumped on Flynn's upper body, striking his head against the ground and causing Flynn to once again lose control of the gun. Keegan delivered a series of right-hand punches into the face of the hitman, who relentlessly tried to regain possession of the gun, ignoring the blows. Keegan's right hand took control over Flynn's hand as the two men fought over possession of the nine-millimeter.

Keegan realized he was much stronger than the assassin. He knew he could probably just take control over Flynn's body for a few seconds until the uniformed officers arrived to aid him in placing Flynn under arrest and recovering the gun. He saw them coming out of the corners of his eyes and realized they would be on top of the pair within seconds.

Time seemed to slow down to a crawl for Keegan. He saw it with a clarity he had not seen before. The fierce struggle that currently engaged him was his answer. He had found the solution to his near impossible dilemma.

Flynn was not about to give up the fight, Keegan knew. Keegan intentionally released Flynn's hand and made a play for the gun himself. He easily grabbed the gun before Flynn, who hadn't expected Keegan to release his grip. He held the gun firmly at his hand as Flynn, now attempted to disarm him.

POP! POP! POP! Three shots rang out. Keegan fired the gun three times at close range into Flynn's chest, killing him instantly. Keegan then fell on his back in the middle of Fifth Avenue with the gun still in hand. There was panic as far as the eye could see. Numerous uniformed and plainclothes Police Officers quickly whisked Devine to safety and escorted His Eminence back inside St. Patrick's Cathedral. There was chaos among the masses of people who had come to watch the parade.

The last thing he remembered seeing before he passed out was scores of uniformed Police Officers approaching him with their guns pointed squarely at him. He realized they didn't know who he was, and they were acting appropriately. It was nice to see good cops doing a fine job. That was what being a Police Officer was all about, not backing down. The officers had no idea who he was other than the fact that he had just shot and killed somebody and instead of hiding or running away, they came after him. *This is why these men and women are heroes.* Then everything faded to black.

Kate stayed at home all day afraid to tune in to the news or to watch the parade on television. She was a nervous wreck and couldn't wait to see her husband again. It was at one-thirty when the doorbell rang. She peeked out the window and saw Captain Anderson along with two uniformed officers. She had met Anderson at numerous functions and had almost expected the visit. At that moment, she was ready to face the fact that she had lost her husband. She opened the door and burst into tears before she could even invite them inside. "Is he dead, Ron? Is he dead?"

Anderson grabbed Kate by her upper arms to comfort her as he gave her the news. "No, Kate. He's quite alive. He's a little banged up but he will be fine. He had a few teeth knocked out; a cracked rib and he suffered a concussion. He's in Bellevue right now having x-rays taken to determine if his jaw has been fractured."

Kate composed herself after receiving the good

news. Kate couldn't believe the news wasn't worse. She was convinced Jim was dead when she saw what every cop's wife fears, uniformed Police Officers coming to the door when her husband should be at work. Kate was so happy she began to cry uncontrollably.

Anderson, who misinterpreted the reason for Kate's tears gave her a gentle hug and rubbed her back. "Would you like to go and see him, Kate?"

She answered through her tears. "Yes Ron, I would."

"Well then, what are we waiting for?"

Anderson held the door open for Kate and closed it behind her as they left. Anderson never bothered to explain how her husband was injured. She seemed to be expecting him, so he assumed she must have been watching the parade as it was broadcast live. "You know Kate; there are very few true heroes in today's world. You should be proud to know that you are married to one of them."

Kate didn't have any response for Anderson's comment, but the truth of the matter was that she would gladly trade in the title of a hero in a heartbeat, in return for Jim retiring from the police department and leading a less perilous life.

Kate walked into her husband's room at Bellevue Hospital and saw him sitting up in bed watching television. He wore a white and blue hospital gown with his legs under a white blanket. There was no beeping, no monitors; he was not hooked up to any machines. *Thank God.* She breathed a sigh of relief. Although Anderson had explained his injuries, she expected worse until she laid her own eyes upon her husband. She didn't notice that he was watching the news which aired the events as they unfolded earlier in the day in front of Saint Patrick's Cathedral.

He was relieved that the entire ordeal was now behind him and his ties to the I.R.A. were severed forever. Gerald Flynn was dead and could now never speak of their meetings. He was flipping from station to station, all of which were showing the entire sequence of events as each network's cameramen had captured it. Keegan decided he was impressed with his heroics as he watched them. Once the Police Department released his name as the officer involved in the confrontation, he was once again being praised as a hero by the media. He figured he would get a real high medal for this, an **Exceptional Merit**, perhaps.

Keegan didn't notice his wife enter the room until she ran over to him and threw her arms around him. Kate wept softly as she examined her husband's injuries. The left side of his face was swollen and discolored. He had a black eye and a few missing or cracked teeth but he was very much alive. "I love you, Jim."

Captain Anderson and the other officers excused themselves from the room and closed the door behind them.

"Did you thee what happened?" lisped a battered James Keegan.

"No, I couldn't bring myself to watch the parade today. But apparently, I'll be seeing you all over the news again, won't I?"

Keegan shook his head in agreement and gave his wife a sheepish smile, exposing his missing teeth. Kate grimaced, sympathizing with the pain her husband must be feeling. She caressed his head with her hand and as sorry as she felt for him, she couldn't pass up the opportunity to tease him. "Did you at least get the license plate of the bus that ran you over?"

Keegan once again smiled, appreciating his wife's humor and he gave her a playful slap on her shoulder. "Justh what I needed, a comedian."

A knock on the door interrupted the Keegans' conversation. The emergency room doctor treating him entered the room. He was about thirty-five years old with dark hair and glasses. He wore a white lab coat with a stethoscope hung around his neck. "I have good news for you, Mr. Keegan. The x-ray results were negative. You do, however, have a mild concussion. Usually, I would recommend you stay overnight but I respect your wishes and I will discharge you."

"Thanks, doc. I appreciate it."

The doctor handed him a prescription from his pad. "Get this prescription filled immediately," the doctor instructed. "It's a pretty strong pain killer that should let you rest comfortably. Get it filled before your current pain killers wear off or you will wish you had. Tomorrow or when you feel better, make an appointment with an oral surgeon. You need to get your mouth back in order. You are a brave man Mr. Keegan…it could have been a whole lot worse."

Keegan nodded in agreement and offered his hand. "Thanks again, doc."

The discharge nurse, who had accompanied the doctor, went over all of Keegan's discharge instructions. She handed Kate the prescription and the discharge papers. Captain Anderson arranged for one of the Detectives in JTTF to drive Keegan's department auto to his Long Island home for him. They would drive him home as well. He was in a fair amount of pain and winced as he got up to get dressed.

The pain was a small price to pay for everything he had won over the course of the afternoon. He stopped the assassination, severed his ties with the I.R.A., and kept his freedom, his job, and most importantly, his secret. His family would never find out about any of this. He took comfort that he would no longer have to lie to his wife or put anyone or anything before his family again. He looked at Kate and took her by the hand. He did his best not to lisp as he spoke through a swollen mouth. "Are you ready to get out of here, my love?"

"Jim, I can't wait to get home."

CHAPTER 19

Louis Castillo still couldn't believe the events of the previous day. He had watched the news over and over again on all of the major networks and saw James Keegan, once again, emerges as one of the great heroes of our country. Castillo couldn't believe his luck. It was less than a week ago when he was sure he was about to nail Keegan.

Since then, everything seemed to go awry. He lost track of Gerald Flynn, who had been the main link between Keegan and the I.R.A. Combining that fact with Keegan's own heroics yesterday, Castillo knew he couldn't present the case he had against Keegan to a Grand Jury without it being a rock-solid case. There wouldn't be a man, woman, or child that would dare indict Keegan unless the case was indisputable. Castillo stared at the newspaper that he had bought on the way to work. He read the headlines in frustration.

MASS-ACRE AT ST. PAT'S:
Hero cop injured in life-or-death battle
with gunman

Castillo stared at the headlines. He didn't even want to open the paper up, fearing its contents would only annoy him even more. He instead opened his briefcase where he kept the secret file on Keegan. *All of my hard work was for nothing.* He was so discouraged; he debated throwing the entire file in the garbage. He realized the only hope he might still have, is to find Flynn once again and bring him in for questioning. That would be very tricky, he conceded. He would have to do it behind his boss's back.

He thumbed through the now useless file and looked at all the photos he had covertly taken. Castillo then closed the file and returned his attention to the newspaper. He reluctantly opened the paper up to see there was a two-page pull-out of still photos of the confrontation.

Castillo skimmed the photos over as he thought to himself what a clean shooting it had been and that it was all captured on tape. The footage would be shown nationwide. There was no doubt of that. Castillo had barely glanced at the pictures when one of them jumped out off the page at him. It was a photo of the gunman as he lay dead on the asphalt. *Gerald Flynn!*

Castillo was almost sure of it. His hair was shorter and darker, and he wore a mustache, but Castillo was convinced it was him. Castillo excitedly reached into the file and removed one of the photos he had taken of Flynn. Castillo compared the photos, concentrating on the features of a face which can't be disguised, such as the shape of the eyes, nose, and chin line. The comparison was identical; the dead gunman was undoubtedly Gerald Flynn.

Castillo's world once again turned around. The case which he was ready to close out only five minutes earlier had now taken on new life. It was now a solid case, thought Castillo as he examined the numerous pictures he had taken of Flynn and Keegan together. The pieces all came together now for Castillo. Flynn must have come over from Ireland to assassinate someone, apparently Martin Devine at the parade, and Keegan was the one to supply the weapon.

The only unanswered question for Castillo was why he stopped the hit. That was one question that he didn't know the answer to, but still, the evidence was overwhelming. *It couldn't be denied.* Castillo then thought back to the night when he saw Keegan doing something under the hood of the Toyota down by the pier. He wondered if maybe he was running guns to the I.R.A. and the Irish bartender was his connection here.

It all made sense, and Castillo had plenty of evidence, as well as a couple of witnesses. Sharon would be able to tell what she saw and the two officers that stopped Keegan that night could corroborate the fact that he was there; in a car that Castillo was sure Keegan couldn't explain having.

Castillo looked at the clock hanging on the wall. It was twenty minutes past eight. He closed his file on Keegan after pulling the photos from the newspaper and stuffing them inside the file. Castillo got up and looked at the roll call to see what time Inspector Marsh was due in; a *four to twelve*. Feeling safe that he wouldn't get caught, Castillo picked up the file and entered Marsh's office. Castillo closed the door behind him; once he was satisfied none of the other Detectives in the office had seen him sneak in. Once inside, Castillo reopened the file and examined it closely. He again compared the photos in disbelief that his luck could have changed for the better so quickly.

Castillo figured his case against Keegan was enough to get him indicted but Castillo wanted more than just an indictment, he wanted to humiliate him and expose him for what he was, a gun runner to a terrorist organization. Imagine the irony, thought Castillo. The Executive Officer of the Joint Terrorist Task Force running guns to terrorists. Once the story got out to the press, Keegan would no longer be a hero but instead, he'd be exposed as a rogue; someone who abused his power and should be sent to prison for years to come. The press would finally vilify him instead of singing his praises.

Even after the indictment was handed down and Keegan was arrested, Castillo decided he would continue to build the case. He would order wiretaps on Dan O'Brien's house as well as the phone at the bar. If Castillo was correct, O'Brien would be in touch with the I.R.A. back in Northern Ireland after the hit was botched. Then he could ask his good friend, Frank Balentine, to run a check on whoever O'Brien gets in contact with.

Castillo realized that only he and Keegan knew the truth of the matter and Keegan certainly wasn't going to help in the investigation. He would rather just pretend he saw a guy with a gun on pure coincidence rather than tell anyone he knew about the hitman and the attempted hit. The case would be buried if Keegan had things his way, without the truth ever being told. Castillo shook his head smugly. He wasn't going to let that happen. He would blow the whistle regarding the entire conspiracy to assassinate a well-respected lawyer, in Martin Devine. He would build the case and eventually lock up Dan O'Brien as well as anybody else he found out to be involved in the conspiracy. Then he, Louis Castillo, not James Keegan, would be the hero.

Castillo spent the next hour going over all the photos and notes he had in the secret file he had been keeping. Castillo once again assured himself the case was airtight. He thumbed through the Rolodex on Marsh's desk. Upon finding the number he was looking for, he picked up the telephone's receiver and punched it in.

"District Attorney's office, can I help you?"

"Yes, this is Detective Castillo, from Internal Affairs. I'd like to speak with the Bureau Chief of the Integrity Bureau please," requested Castillo.

The integrity bureau always handled cases of police corruption and with a case of this magnitude; Castillo wasn't going to talk to anybody other than the person in charge of the bureau. He imagined the District Attorney of New York County would want to speak to him as well when Castillo explained there was a leak within his own department. The last thing he needed was another leak to get back to Keegan.

"I'm sorry; he's on vacation this week. He'll be back in on Monday. Can I take a message?"

Castillo was disappointed. "No thank you, I'll call back on Monday."

Castillo hung up the receiver. He thought about it briefly. He has waited this long, so a few more days wouldn't make a difference. He had Keegan dead to right and there was no place for him to run, and nothing that he could do about it.

Castillo wondered what the consequences were going to be since he was going over his superiors' heads and going right to the District Attorney's office. The hierarchy did not like to be made to look bad. There would likely be serious repercussions... unless he played his cards just right. Castillo figured when the case broke, his superiors would be mad at him, but they would jump on the bandwagon and say they were working on the case for a long time and Saint Patrick's Day was the break in the case they were waiting for.

This way, they too, would look like heroes. All he would have to do is go along with their lies. He could do that...if the price was right for him. Castillo figured this case could finally be his ticket out of Internal Affairs and into a Major Case Squad somewhere. He could once again be a real Detective, solving real cases. Maybe even get grade.

Castillo didn't want to take any unnecessary chances, so he got up from the chair and peeked out into the squad room. The other Detectives were busy typing and reviewing their cases. Castillo picked up his file on Keegan and walked out of Marsh's office undetected. He returned the file to his briefcase and was feeling good about himself. Castillo hadn't felt this good about his job since his days back in Anti-Crime in Brooklyn. Feeling really good about things, he decided to push his luck. He picked up the telephone on his desk and punched in a number. He sat back in his chair and put his feet up on the desk as it rang.

"Special Victims, Detective Winters."

It was nice to hear Sharon's voice. Castillo felt almost like a teenager calling a girl for the first time. Since his breakup with Sharon some years back, Castillo hadn't been in a serious relationship with anyone, and he felt a bit awkward. "Hi, Sharon. It's Louie."

"Hey, Louie, what's up?"

Castillo felt his palms begin to sweat. He couldn't believe he was actually nervous. "I was wondering if maybe you'd like to go out to dinner tonight. I know this great German restaurant in Maspeth."

She decided it might be fun to play a little hard to get. "Well, you know, it is a Friday night, Louie. You can't just call a girl last minute." She continued with a clearly playful tone in her voice. "What if I already have plans?"

Castillo sensed that his old flame was teasing him, and he would give it right back to her. "Well, then I guess you'll have to miss out on my celebration...unless of course, you break your previous plans to help me celebrate."

He seemed to flip the script on her. Now she was the one getting excited. "Celebrate! What are you celebrating?"

Castillo decided he wasn't going to tell Sharon any of the details. He was never one to count his chickens before they hatched. It didn't matter anyway. Within a few weeks, Sharon, along with the entire city, maybe even the entire country, would know the name of Louis Castillo as the greatest corruption fighter since the days of Frank Serpico.

"I'm celebrating the rebirth of my career and I'm hoping to also celebrate the rekindling of a romance with the only woman I've ever loved."

Castillo had surprised himself with his comment. He wasn't usually so cocky or so forward but there was something about this day that gave him all the confidence in the world. He was waiting patiently for a response from Sharon, who after a brief pause agreed to the date. "Great, I'll pick you up at seven."

Castillo was pleased with himself as he hung up the phone. He called the restaurant and made reservations for eight o'clock. Castillo got up from his desk and limped over to the coffee machine. The rainy weather had caused his leg to ache, but it didn't seem to bother him as badly as it usually did. He had just finished pouring himself the coffee when he heard the familiar voice of Inspector Marsh behind him. "Good morning Louie."

"Good morning, boss. What are you doing here so early?"

"I promised my kids I'd take them to the Rangers game tonight at the Garden, so I changed my tour. They are playing the Canucks at home for the first time since we beat them in game seven last year to win the Stanley Cup."

"Oh, it should be a good game Cap, they're on a tear. Maybe they can repeat and win back-to-back cups after all of these years without winning any."

He couldn't believe his good fortune. If Marsh had come in ten minutes earlier, he would have caught him not only in his office but also with the entire secret file on Keegan. Castillo was convinced his luck had changed for the better.

The couple returned to Sharon Winter's Forest Hills apartment after eleven. Castillo hadn't been in her apartment for quite a few years, and he was impressed by the remodeling she had done. Castillo had scanned the room as soon as he entered to see if she had received the flowers that he had sent her. It didn't take him very long to spot the dozen long stem roses in a pink vase, serving as a centerpiece for her coffee table. He was relieved to see that she had received them.

He decided she was still playing with him since she never mentioned receiving them over dinner or drinks. Sharon invited him to have a seat on the sofa as she went into the kitchen to get a bottle of wine and two glasses. Sharon joined him on the couch and handed him the wine along with a corkscrew. Castillo twisted the corkscrew into the cork and slowly pulled it out. There was a soft pop. Castillo poured the wine into one of the glasses until it was half full and handed the glass to Sharon. After pouring himself a glass, he raised it in the air and waited for Sharon to raise hers as well. Castillo softly touched his glass against Sharon's. He toasted. "To new beginnings."

Sharon echoed his sentiments and excused herself. As Castillo sat alone on the couch, he began to think about the fact that it was James Keegan who had somehow turned his life around. If it wasn't for Keegan, he would have never gotten back together with Sharon and he would have remained in the Internal Affairs Bureau for the rest of his career. Castillo decided he had wasted the last few years of his career and as soon as he got back from the District Attorney's office on Monday, he would put in a request for transfer to another Detective Squad. A Detective Squad where he would eventually show that he did in fact deserve the rank of Detective.

"Did I ever thank you for the flowers Louie?" asked Sharon Winters as she emerged from the bedroom behind Castillo.

He turned around to face her and saw she was wearing red lingerie, flowing apart at the hips to reveal the matching red panties underneath. The plunging neckline was made of a sheer material that clearly exposed her bare breasts; her nipples hardened. She modeled it for him and spun around giving him a good view of the g-string panties from behind.

Castillo stood up and slowly looked her up and down before responding. "No. I don't believe you did."

She looks like a model right out of a Victoria's Secret catalog, he thought. He got up, walked over to her, and pulled her tightly against his body. They slowly and deeply kissed, their tongues dancing in each other's mouth as they had done so many times, years ago. But this time it felt different, Castillo thought, as he felt himself becoming aroused. It all just felt so right.

CHAPTER 20

His aching jaw and fractured rib had prevented Keegan from getting a good night's rest as the doctor had suggested he do. He was taking the painkillers as prescribed, but it didn't seem like enough. He crawled out of bed on the Saturday after Saint Patrick's Day at twenty minutes before seven. He figured he only got about three hours of sleep at most. That was even less than the night before.

It was just his luck, he decided, that when he finally started to doze off at two-thirty in the morning, his neighbor's dog began to bark and woke him from his sleep. After that, he fell in and out of a light sleep for the remainder of the night. Kate held him all night. He wasn't sure if that was to comfort him or herself. When he got out of bed, it seemed every muscle in his body hurt. His head ached something awful and he was actually dizzy for a couple of moments when he stood up.

It had been a long time since he had been in a fight as fierce as the one that he had been in with Flynn. He'd be sore for at least a week to come, he estimated, and it would take much longer than that for his injuries to mend. Thinking back, he wished he had taken the advice of Captain Anderson, who suggested he go out line-of-duty-sick for a while. He already stayed home yesterday to try and rest but it wasn't James Keegan's style to let things hang in the wind. He wanted to make sure the case was closed out as soon as possible and put the entire episode behind him. After this was done, he would go out sick and give himself the time to heal that he needed.

It was his own suggestion that he meet with the Super Chiefs at nine o'clock this morning to explain in detail, his investigation as well as his version of the shooting. It was standard operating procedure of the police department that when any member of the service is involved in a shooting, he will be interviewed by his superior officers in the presence of legal representation, once the District Attorney's Office gave their permission. The District Attorney's investigation supersedes the department's internal investigation since they would criminally prosecute for any shooting deemed unjustified. In the case of someone dying as a result of a police shooting, however, the District Attorney routinely presents the case to a Grand Jury to determine if the police acted appropriately and within the guidelines of the law.

Keegan had nothing to fear though. This was as clean a shooting as there could be and it was captured by television cameras from around the country. The Police Commissioner and the mayor had already proclaimed him a hero and the Manhattan District Attorney closed their investigation out by nightfall, declining to even present the case to a

Grand Jury.

The only thing left for Keegan to do to put this all behind him was to give his statement and stick to his story. Something that he would no doubt be able to do. He had watched the incident numerous times on five different stations, making sure to watch from every available angle. He had been praised by every reporter for doing a heroic job. His role in thwarting the bombing of the federal courthouse was once again put front and center, as all of the news stations had made mention of it while reporting on this story. The media speculated the gunman, who remained unidentified, may have been attempting to shoot the Cardinal, thus making Keegan an even greater hero.

Keegan slowly eased himself down the stairs and went to the front door. He opened the door to retrieve the morning newspaper. The cold air immediately hit him and sent a shooting pain throughout the exposed nerves in his mouth. Grimacing from the pain, he bent down and picked up the paper. He brought it into his kitchen and set it down on the table as he got himself a glass of water to take his painkillers. He hoped the oral surgeon would be able to do something with his battered mouth. He had an appointment today at noon and figured he would go there directly from the meeting at Police Headquarters.

Keegan sat down at the table and for the first time looked at the front cover of the newspaper. Two days later and it was still front-page news. He had asked Kate to save yesterday's paper for him as well since he never read it, spending the majority of yesterday in bed. The painkillers had knocked him out and he slept most of the day. He decided to read yesterday's first. He looked at the rather graphic photo on the front page. Inside a green border, was a picture of him as he lay unconscious in the middle of Fifth Avenue with a gun in his hand next to the lifeless body of Gerald Flynn.

It was something most people wouldn't understand but he actually felt bad for having killed the Irish hitman. In all his eighteen years on the job, he had never before killed a man and he had only fired his gun one previous time. Many people believe that cops are in shootouts every day, but the fact of the matter is, most cops go through their entire career without ever being involved in a gunfight.

He began to think about Flynn. *Why couldn't he just back down*, then at least Keegan wouldn't have to carry the burden of killing another human being. Although he felt some remorse, he knew killing Flynn was to be the only way of keeping himself safe. The threat of losing his job or even going to jail was now all behind him.

He thought momentarily about Castillo and decided he couldn't have anything on him that would stand up. Even if he did have something, he would be laughed out of court unless it was airtight, especially after the endless praise the media has showered him with.

Keegan read through every article there was

about the incident in the paper and wondered if this was going to get even more press than the *Federal Courthouse Caper* did. The newspaper made a reference to Keegan's previous heroics in that case as well. The publicity from that case had just started to die down when Judge Boden was shot and killed. The Judge's assassination had put Keegan's name back in the papers, if only for a little while. Then on St. Patrick's Day, he was hurled right back into the center of a large media circus.

He wondered if he would be receiving another congratulatory phone call from the President of the United States. He then let his mind wander a little bit and wondered if maybe even the Pope might call to thank him for saving the life of New York's Cardinal. Keegan silently thumbed through the eight pages of coverage the confrontation had drawn. There were pages of photos alone, illustrating the encounter frame by frame. He took the time to carefully examine each and every photo.

Keegan got up from his chair and went into the living room where he retrieved his scrapbook. He brought it back into the kitchen and selected a pair of scissors. Seated at the kitchen table, Keegan started cutting out the articles from the newspaper to add to his collection when Kate walked in. "Hey, don't cut the paper up I haven't read about my hero yet."

"Good morning, love."

He greeted her with half a smile, conscious not to expose his broken teeth.

"How are you feeling?"

"Pretty good," he lied. "My mouth is a bit sore, and it hurts a bit when I take a deep breath, but I guess that's to be expected."

He wanted to play down the severe discomfort he was in so Kate didn't try to get him to stay home instead of going to work and closing the case out immediately. The sooner it was put to bed the better.

"So let me see what the papers have to say."

Keegan handed his wife the semi-mutilated paper as he pieced it back together. Kate's heart skipped a beat as she looked at the picture of her husband as he lay unconscious on the pavement. All she could think about the fact that he looked like he was dead and that he very nearly did lose his life. Kate was nonetheless proud of her husband. She knew his actions defined what a cop should be, not just yesterday, but always. He should be a role model for all young cops to emulate. Kate often hoped that their children wouldn't want to follow in their father's footsteps. Being married to a cop was bad enough and she didn't know if she would be able to handle being the mother of a cop in today's day and age.

Kate thumbed through the paper and looked at her husband, who had his head down, clearly fighting the discomfort he was experiencing. Kate examined her husband's battered face. The bruises were starting to come through on his cheek and around his mouth. She leaned over and gave him a kiss on the forehead without uttering a word. Kate glanced at all of the photos and wasn't sure she could read the articles. She still hadn't read a single article or watched the news since St. Patrick's Day. She did not need to be reminded how close her children came to having to grow up without their father.

She handed Jim back the paper so he could finish cutting out the articles and photos to put in his scrapbook. Maybe she would be able to look a little more in-depth at the articles and photos in a few weeks. The day after almost losing her husband was too soon for her own well-being to relive it.

Kerry was the first of the children to wake up on the Saturday morning. Kerry was always up before seven-thirty on Saturdays so she could watch her favorite cartoons. Keegan hadn't spoken to his children very much since coming home from the hospital. He went directly into his bedroom to try and get some rest and remained there for the overwhelming majority of the day yesterday. Kerry walked into the kitchen and studied her father's face, unsure what to make of the bruises and missing teeth.

She didn't know what to say and instead of immediately saying anything, she walked over to her father and gave him a tight hug. She then stepped back and again studied him. "Daddy, are you a hero?"

Keegan didn't know how to answer his daughter's question and he had even been embarrassed by it.

Kate saw her husband was having difficulty

fielding the question and she decided to answer for him. "Yes sweetheart, your father is a hero; a great hero."

Kerry seemed satisfied with the answer but offered no reply of her own. She simply looked at her mother as she answered and then at her father. She stared at him again for a couple of moments and then kissed his face. She left the kitchen and walked into the living room where she put on the television to watch her Saturday morning cartoons. As Kerry left the room, her parents looked at each other and shared a smile. Keegan returned his attention to cutting out the articles and photos from the paper and carefully putting them in the scrapbook.

"Don't you think it's about time you showed your book to the kids?"

Kate felt the boys were old enough to understand and she wanted them to know what kind of man their father was so they could be even more proud than they already were. "This way they can see first-hand all the medals you've earned and what a real hero you are."

"I don't know, Kate. They are still so young."

She reasoned with him. "Kerry might still be too young to understand but the boys are already eleven and eight. That's not too young."

Keegan did want to share his experiences with his children for a long time now, yet he wasn't sure if they would be ready for it. He debated it. "There's a lot of violence throughout my scrapbook, pictures of the guns I've taken off the street, pictures and articles about guys I've locked up for homicides, terrorist attacks, and now this extremely graphic encounter. I don't know if it's a good idea to expose them to such violence."

"You can't shelter them all their lives. They see the news when we watch it. They see what goes on in the world. All they could talk about yesterday was what a hero their father was. They had seen the footage on the news and are so proud of you. They started to call up their friends from school to brag and to tell them to watch the news."

Kate took pride in the fact that the children were so proud of their father.

Keegan had finished adding his new collections to the scrapbook by the time Kevin and Timothy had woken up. On the way back from headquarters, he would pick up the rest of the city's newspapers to read what they had to say. Keegan went upstairs to shower and get dressed but he knew he wasn't about to shave today. There was no way; his delicate face would tolerate being shaved. When he got to the foot of the stairs, Kevin and Timothy emerged from their bedroom. "Dad, you were great!" Kevin said enthusiastically.

His younger boy was quick to chime in. "Yeah dad, you really kicked his butt."

"Thanks, guys."

He didn't know how to react to their praise, and he didn't want them to think that killing someone was okay. He decided later today he would have a long talk with them about morals and what was right and wrong. Maybe Kate was right, the children should see his scrapbook, but only after he explained to them that he had killed the man in self-defense and if there was any other way for him to have arrested the man without shooting him, he would have done so.

Timothy wasn't quite finished yet. "Can you tell us all about it dad?"

Kevin clearly agreed. "Yeah, dad, please!"

"Not right now boys, I'm running late. When I get home later, I'll tell you guys all about it."

"You promise, dad?" They both added.

Keegan agreed. The boys were satisfied with their father's promise and went downstairs to eat breakfast and watch cartoons. He watched his kids scamper down the stairs and the look of excitement on their faces had been captured in his mind. He was looking forward to having this talk with the boys, but he still felt Kerry was too young for the harsh realities of the world.

As Keegan stepped out of the shower, he examined himself closely in the mirror. The left side of his face was swollen and had turned a deep shade of purple. He opened his mouth wide to see the eight stitches he had received in the hospital as well as the missing and shattered teeth. There was a small amount of dry blood in the corner of his mouth. He lifted his left arm and examined his rib cage. It was hurting him something awful whenever he took a deep breath. He saw a deep bruise in the middle of his rib cage and realized when he fell; he landed on his gun in the shoulder holster. That was what most likely caused the fracture. He stared into his own eyes to reassure himself that killing Flynn had been necessary.

He wasn't even going to attempt to put on a suit today. He was going to wear loose-fitting, comfortable clothing. He wore a pair of black Dockers and an Emerald Society golf shirt. He strapped his nine-millimeter back to its familiar position on his hip and thought about the fact that it wasn't even his gun that he had used to kill the hitman. *It was ironic that Flynn had died at the hands of his own gun.*

He thought back to the gun and was thankful that he had drilled the serial numbers out so there was no way the gun could ever come back to haunt him. He looked at the time on his wristwatch as he put it on. It was eight o'clock. Keegan knew he had to leave soon but he figured since it was a Saturday morning there wouldn't be too much traffic on the Expressway, and he could leave a little bit later than usual. Keegan went back downstairs and peeked in on his children as they watched the television together. He then went back into the kitchen where Kate was sitting at the table drinking a cup of coffee.

"Would you like me to get you a cup, hon?"

He shook his head adamantly at his wife. "No thank you, love. I'm afraid the hot coffee would get right into the nerves."

She grimaced at him. "Oh, I'm sorry, hon. How could I forget how much pain you're in?"

"That's all right, love. I hope this dentist can fix

me up today so you and I can go out for dinner by the end of the week; just the two of us. I'll have mom watch the kids again."

"That would be so nice, Jim, but only if you are feeling up to it. That reminds me, Jim, she called yesterday but you were trying to get some rest, so I told her you'd give her a call today."

Keegan walked right over to the telephone and dialed his mother's number. "Good, then I can kill two birds with one stone."

Kate listened to her husband's end of the conversation. After assuring his mother he was okay and going over the details of the parade with her, he secured her babysitting services for Friday night. Keegan looked over to Kate and gave a thumbs up. "Great, we'll drop them off at your house around six or seven. Thanks, ma, I'll see you tomorrow for Sunday dinner," he promised before hanging up the phone.

He looked over to his wife with a smile. "So, do we have a date for Friday night young lady? You pick the restaurant. Anywhere you want."

"We sure do. I just hope we don't have to bring a straw for you to eat with." Kate couldn't resist the opportunity to throw one more harmless taunt at her husband.

"Ha, ha, ha. What a comedian I married."

"I'm sorry Jim. I just couldn't resist."

Keegan took in all in good fun, as it was intended. He looked down at his watch and saw he had to get going. He was sure the Police Commissioner, himself, would be there as well as the Chiefs. The last thing anyone in the department would want to do is make the department's top echelon wait for you. Keegan was no exception, hero or not. The media saw him as a hero, but he couldn't let that go to his head and get cocky. Keegan put on his winter coat since it was colder than normal for this time of year. He went into the living room where his kids were still watching television. He gave each of them a hug and a kiss.

"What time will you be home, dad?" Timothy inquired.

Keegan considered the question before answering. He estimated he would be leaving the dentist's office somewhere after one o'clock. "I should be home around two or three."

He allotted an extra hour or so in case he needed to finish any paperwork to tighten the case up before he could leave his office. Keegan was greeted by Kate who came over to give him a kiss goodbye. "See you later, hon. I love you."

"I love you too, Kate."

He opened the front door and was met with a burst of cold air. He kept his mouth tightly closed to prevent any cold air from striking the exposed nerves in his mouth. He decided he would take the Explorer to work instead of the department auto. He remembered the Crown Victoria was low on gas and didn't want to waste time stopping at a precinct somewhere to fill it up. He informed his wife he'd be taking her car into Manhattan before closing the door behind him.

He unlocked the door of the Explorer and got inside. He couldn't wait for the car to warm up so the heat would come up. He inserted the key in the ignition and turned it, expecting the car to jump to life. Instead of turning over, the car didn't make a sound. The cold weather had evidently killed the car's battery. He looked at the clock on the dashboard of the Explorer and saw that the battery had died at thirty-eight minutes after two am. This was probably the coldest part of the night, Keegan estimated.

Not today, isn't that just my friggin luck.

He knew he couldn't be late but now he didn't want to chance getting stuck with the Explorer. He decided it wasn't worth jump-starting and taking the Explorer just in case it was something more serious than just a dead battery. He would worry about the Explorer later. His priority now was getting to the meeting and putting his secret life behind him. He had only about an hour to get to Police Headquarters. He hoped he had enough gas to make it to headquarters without having to stop off.

It was a chance he would have to take. Keegan got out of the Explorer and walked over to the department Crown Victoria. He unlocked the door of the car and got inside. If for some reason the battery was dead on this car also, he would be in a lot of trouble. He hoped the dead car battery would not be the indication of the beginning of a bad day. He inserted the key into the ignition and turned it, figuring it was not.

CHAPTER 21

The helicopter's rotors cut through the gusty March winds. The New York City Police Department's sharpshooters stood alertly on top of the rooftops to watch over the tens of thousands of Police Officers who had come to pay their final respects to their brother officer and fallen hero, James Keegan. The car bomb, which ended Keegan's life with the turn of a key, had rocked the quiet suburban town of East Northport. The explosion could be heard as far as the neighboring town of Commack.

The sharpshooters, some of whom were armed with sniper rifles and others of whom looked through binoculars, looked over the crowd on Northern Boulevard in Queens. They could see that there were not only thousands of fellow officers mourning his death, but also about three thousand civilians had shown up to pay their respects to a true hero. The thousands of officers were congregating with one another in an unorganized manner until a hush fell over the crowd. The men and women in their blue dress uniforms fell into ranks, standing as many as ten deep for as far as the eye could see. An additional three rows to the rear stood non-uniformed officers such as Detectives and retirees.

"ATTEN-TION!" was shouted through a mega-phone by the officer in charge of the funeral de-tail. Every officer in attendance stood motionless and in complete silence upon receiving the order. The motorcycle cops from throughout the city's highway patrol units led the procession. They drove along Northern Boulevard with their lights on trav-eling about five to ten miles per hour. Members of the police department's Emerald Society carried the color guard. The flag of Ireland was sandwiched be-tween the United States flag and the flag of the New York City Police Department. The men who made up the color guard marched slowly and evenly in per-fect choreography with each other. The somber beat of the Pipes and Drums Band drummers could be faintly heard in the distance as the black hearse grew closer.

The hearse was being escorted by the members of the Pipes and Drums Band, who were spread out evenly as they marched along each side of the slow-moving hearse. They continued to softly beat their drums while staring straight ahead. A black limou-sine, carrying the Keegan family, followed directly behind. Kate stared out of the window at all the offi-cers who had turned out to pay their respects to her husband. Kerry tightly clung around her neck while the boys sat emotionless in the back of the limou-sine, one on each side of their grandmother. Kate knew she had to be strong for her children. They were taking it very hard, as she would expect. They hadn't slept very much over the past few nights since Saturday. The hearse stopped and the limousine followed behind it right in front of the Roman Catholic Church.

"PRESENT ARMS!" was the next command. The mourning officers instantly rendered a sharp, white-gloved salute as the members of the Pipes and Drums Band began to play Amazing Grace. The pall-bearers removed the coffin of James Keegan from the back of the hearse and lifted it onto their shoulders. They then lowered their hands to their sides and carried the casket on their shoulders, into the church.

The thousands of officers remained completely motionless as the coffin was escorted inside. Kate carried Kerry out of the limousine. She refused to release the grip she held around her mother's neck. The boys exited, each holding one of their grandmother's hands. As Kate carried Kerry towards the church, Kerry started to cry uncontrollably. Kerry's wailing could be heard for what seemed like miles to anyone that had heard them. There was a lump in the throat and a tear in the eye of every officer in attendance, as they listened to the now fatherless girl mourn her loss. Kate rubbed her back assuring her everything was going to be okay, even though Kate, herself, was not sure it would.

Once the family, friends, and dignitaries had filed into the church the detail commander gave his next command. **"ORDER ARMS!"**

Thousands of white gloves broke the salute they

had been holding for some time now. It was an impressive sight the way the gloves, all in perfect harmony, snapped back down to the officer's sides. The mood remained gloomy as the officers slowly broke the formation while the funeral mass was taking place inside the church.

The cops began to once again look for old friends. The cops would walk around until they saw someone they knew, maybe someone they went to the Academy with or an old partner from a previous command. They would then stand around and catch up on old times as well as see what each other were doing now. Other officers would walk to the nearest coffee shop or fast-food restaurant to get themselves a cup of coffee; still others, to a nearby *watering hole*. The detail, which was over twenty thousand strong, was almost like a huge reunion of the men and women in blue.

Funerals brought cops together geographically as well as emotionally. There were cops from all over the country who had come to pay their last respects to James Keegan. There was an assemblage of cops from numerous jurisdictions in New Jersey, Boston, Miami, and numerous other cities on the east coast. There were cops from as far away as San Diego and Hawaii who had come to pay their respects.

It wasn't uncommon for cops to come from all over the country to bid farewell to a fallen colleague. What was uncommon was that all the Police Officers, who had come to New York City today to mourn the loss of a brother officer, had at least known who Keegan was. Most cop funerals were for cops, who until the time of their death were unsung heroes. After their death, they became a martyr of the times. Their names, usually forgotten soon after by all of those who hadn't personally know them.

This was not true of James Keegan. He was a hero time and time again. He had graced the front page of every newspaper in the country when he thwarted the attempted bombing of the Federal Courthouse in Brooklyn and again only a few days earlier with his courageous actions on Saint Patrick's Day. The fact that all of the mourners had known of Keegan's legend, made the funeral that much more devastating.

After about forty-five minutes of mingling with their friends and fellow officers, the rank-and-file Police Officers filed back into formation without being told to do so. It was an unwritten rule at these funerals that about forty-five minutes after the funeral begins inside the church the cops would reform the ranks and patiently wait for their next instructions. They talk quietly, barely above a whisper, until the order is barked out.

"ATTEN-TION!" A hush once again falls over the crowd. The focus of attention is on the doorway of the church which is slowly opened. The first to exit the church is the Mayor of New York with the Police Commissioner and the Cardinal on either side. Other dignitaries followed next, along with the top echelon of the police department. Kate, who had finally let out a good cry during the service, walked out next. She held Kerry in one arm and held a handkerchief to wipe her tears with the other. The red-eyed Keegan boys, along with their distraught grandmother followed.

"PRESENT ARMS!" The Emerald Society's Pipes and Drums Band began to play Taps. The flag-draped coffin of James Keegan was carried out of the church by the pallbearers made up of six sharply dressed officers from the department's ceremonial unit. Tears were rolling down the faces of many of the officers in attendance as the coffin was loaded into the hearse.

It was usually at this point of the funeral when fellow officers realized their own mortality. They watch as the casket disappears inside the hearse and think that it could've been them who died, only because they were doing their job. In a sense, it was them who lay there. Every time a Police Officer is slain in the line of duty, a part of every Police Officer dies inside. James Keegan had made the ultimate sacrifice, but sadly, each and every officer in attendance knew that Keegan would not be the last to do so.

The wind intensified momentarily as the sea of blue held its salute. Keegan's family got back into the limousine as the thousands looked on. Many thinking what will happen to their own family if God forbid, they were ever to be struck down. The starting of the engines is heard through the dead silence. Helicopters from the NYPD's Aviation unit fly overhead in a v-shaped formation with one heli-copter missing from the pattern. It's known as the *missing man formation*. Once the helicopters make their pass, the hearse and the limousine pull away. They are flanked on each side by highway officers on motorcycles. A dozen marked highway radio cars with their impressive lights trail the motorcade. The sound of the bagpipes could be heard in the dis-tance as the funeral comes to an end. The crowd of Police Officers remains in the formation for a mat-ter of minutes until the bagpipes could no longer be heard and the last of the motorcade had disappeared in the distance.

Many of the officers who had shown up on their own time will now catch up with old acquaintances they had met up with before the funeral began. Many will go to the bars along Northern Boulevard or nearby Bell Boulevard and have a drink in mem-ory of their colleague. Others, who are scheduled to work later in the day, will go to work this afternoon and put their own lives on the line for the good of the city in which they serve.

Once the funeral had broken up, numerous re-porters from all over the city had chased down the Mayor and the Police Commissioner and asked for a comment. This led to an impromptu press confer-ence given by the Police Commissioner on the steps of the Douglaston church, where Keegan's service had been held.

The Commissioner was an overpowering figure. He stood three inches better than six feet and had salt and pepper hair which gave him a certain amount of charm. He was a thirty-two-year veteran of the New York City Police Department and unlike many before him, had the respect of the rank and file. He was in his early fifties and extremely well-spoken.

"Our city, as well as our country as a whole, has suffered a great loss," the embattled Police Commissioner began. "When James Keegan was fallen to a bomb planted by a coward, not only did he lose his life but every citizen of the city he served suffered an insurmountable loss. The men and women of the New York City Police Department will not rest until Lieutenant Keegan's murderer is brought to justice."

A barrage of questions was directed towards him. He acknowledged a female reporter in the front row.

"Mr. Commissioner, do you have any leads?"

"We have a few leads we are following up on at this time," he lied before acknowledging the next reporter.

"When do you expect arrests to be made?"

He was stoic in his answer. "I wouldn't want to comment on anything that could jeopardize the investigation at this point."

He would do his best to skirt the issue even though he knew the questions would be asked and people wanted answers.

The last question came from a veteran police reporter for the Times. "Is there any connection between the assassination of Lieutenant Keegan and..."

The Police Commissioner promptly cut him off and ended the session as quickly as it had started. "You're going to have to excuse me. I didn't intend on giving a press conference right now. I'll have an official statement that will answer many of your questions later today at Police Headquarters. Have your questions ready then and I will do my best to answer them as long as they do not compromise the integrity of our investigation. "

The Commissioner swiftly walked down the steps along with the Mayor of the City of New York. They got into a Black 1995 Jeep Grand Cherokee, whose door was being held open for them by members of the Mayor's security detail, and quickly drove off.

The ride to the Long Island cemetery had taken only a little bit over a half-hour. Kate was impressed by the police escort of highway cars that the department had afforded. She reflected on how beautiful the ceremony was and what a shame such a well-organized and moving ceremony was only used on such a sad occasion as a funeral. She remembered how Jim would tell her the two things the department does really well, were promotion ceremonies and funerals.

Kate sat silently in the back of the limousine with Kerry's head nestled in her chest. She sat on her mother's lap. Kate knew that Kerry didn't quite understand why she would never see her father again. She looked over at the boys. Kevin seemed to be in a solemn mood, while Timothy kept looking out of the back window, impressed by the lights on the police cars that trailed behind them. Jim's mother was a strong woman; nevertheless, she had broken down into tears on the way to the gravesite. Kevin held his grandmother by the hand to assure her everything was okay. It was nice to see Kevin comfort his grandmother and it made Kate think how her eleven-year-old son would now be the man of the house.

The sun was shining brightly on the cemetery as the Keegan's got out of the limousine. The grass was well manicured and in the coming months would be a vibrant green, Kate was certain. Walking toward her husband's grave, she was wrought with emotion. She scanned some of the headstones as she passed. One of them was for a five-year-old boy. A teddy bear lay at the foot of the headstone. *Life can be so unfair.* There was complete silence in the air, broken only by the closing of car doors.

Kate looked around and saw people throughout the cemetery that had come to visit their respective loved ones. There were a few families that Kate guessed were there on an anniversary or maybe their deceased loved ones' birthday. Many had flowers or stuffed animals they set down at their graves. There was one man only a couple of rows from where her husband was about to be buried. He wore a black overcoat and a wool cap. Kate thought she would probably see the man here again sometime in the future since their loved ones would be buried so close to one another.

The friends and family of James Keegan gathered around the open ground where Keegan's body would be laid to rest. The gathering was much more intimate than the thousands that attended the funeral service outside the church. There were about two dozen who had joined the funeral procession and came to the cemetery. Father Palmero asked for the crowd's attention. Keegan had always spoken highly of the priest, who he had known since a child. Kate knew it would have meant so much to her husband for Father Palmero to preside over his funeral mass and gravesite prayer. The priest was in his early sixties with snow-white hair and a thin beard. Looking in his light brown eyes, anyone could tell he was a gentle man who lived the life in which he preached.

"My friends, we gather today to say goodbye to a man we all loved. But this goodbye is not for an eternity. We ask that God open his doors to James so that when we, ourselves, go to heaven, we can be reunited with him in Christ."

Kate had started to listen to the priest's words, but her mind began to wander. She looked around to see the many people that had shown up to say goodbye to her husband. He had so many friends and was respected by everyone in the police department. Captain Anderson stood off to the side with his wife, Judith. Kate had met her many times at different functions and hoped they would forgive her for not going over to them to thank them for coming. She figured they would understand.

Kate's daydreaming was broken when she realized that Father Palmero had stopped speaking. Two of the uniformed Police Officers in white shirts, who had served as pallbearers, removed the flag of the United States from Keegan's coffin. The sun's glare caught one of the highly polished buttons of the officer's dress uniform, causing Kate to monetarily squint, as he approached. The officers carefully folded the flag into thirds and presented it to Kate. She accepted the flag from them, and they rendered her a sharp salute.

James Keegan's coffin was slowly lowered beneath the ground as the Keegan children looked on in horror. Kevin and Timothy threw their arms around their mother's waist and began to cry. Kate felt totally helpless, as there was nothing that she could do to ease her children's suffering. After the coffin was below the ground, each of the mourners walked to the edge of the opening and dropped flowers down on top of it.

The mourners slowly left the gravesite, some of whom came over to Kate to extend their condolences once again. After the entire crowd had left, Kate escorted her grieving children into the limousine which was still waiting to drive her back to her home. She then returned to her husband's grave and said a silent prayer. She crossed herself once she was done praying and looked down at the flower-covered coffin. She spoke softly through her tears. "Goodbye, Jim. I love you."

She dabbed her tears away with her handkerchief. Kate got back into the limousine and it was now her turn to let it all out. She cried hysterically as her children hugged her tightly to comfort her. The limousine drove off from the cemetery with the Keegan family grieving inside. The body of Lieutenant James Patrick Keegan was now in its final resting place.

The man in the black overcoat watched as Kate Keegan said her goodbyes. He felt her pain as she climbed back into the limousine. He could hear her cries. He waited for the limousine to be a safe distance away from the cemetery before walking over to the recently opened grave.

He removed his wool cap and made the sign of the cross before silently saying a prayer. He reached under his overcoat and produced a small bouquet of flowers which he dropped into the open grave down onto Keegan's casket. He watched them float down, silently landing next to the other flowers. The man shook his head, wondering why things had to end up as they did.

There was a lump in Daniel O'Brien's throat as he watched the flowers land on the coffin of his longtime friend. O'Brien, like so many other men, had not only respected Keegan, but he also admired him. Losing a man like James Keegan wouldn't be easy for anybody.

O'Brien hated himself for what he had done, but he was nevertheless, a soldier in a war. It wasn't up to a soldier to question his superior; it was up to a soldier to carry out an order. Eamon Quinn's orders had been very specific. O'Brien, a former master bomb maker for the I.R.A., planted the twenty-pound car bomb under the hood of Keegan's Crown Victoria shortly after two-thirty in the morning a few nights ago. O'Brien shook his head again, this time with more purpose. *Why couldn't ya just mind yer own God damned business, Jim? Why?*

O'Brien knelt beside the grave of James Keegan and silently wept.

CHAPTER 22

Louis Castillo sat up in bed on the morning after James Keegan's funeral. He couldn't believe the turn of events that had taken place over the past few days. He looked at the clock on the night table and saw that it was six o'clock. Having set the alarm for six-fifteen, he decided to stay awake. He felt awkward being in unfamiliar surroundings. He had gotten a good night's sleep. The bed was more comfortable than his bed was. He glanced to his right where Sharon Winters was still sleeping.

Castillo gently caressed her hip through her panties which was the only clothing she was wearing. He leaned over and gave her a kiss before getting up to take a shower. The two of them had been spending a great deal of time together. They had spent both of their days off together and had only been separated for a short period of time when Castillo went back to his own apartment to grab a change of clothes. Staying at Sharon's apartment had its advantages. The travel to work was cut down by almost a half of an hour, which allowed Castillo to sleep that much longer.

As Castillo showered, he thought of what a dramatic change his world was going through. He and Sharon were getting along wonderfully, and he certainly didn't want this to end. As far as his career, he wasn't sure what exactly to do about Keegan. He figured he could keep an eye on Dan O'Brien and possibly arrest him for gun-running but without any corroboration from anyone else, it would be difficult to prove.

No matter what he decided, he was going to put in a request for transfer to another Detective Squad. Somewhere he could be a Detective without anybody prejudging him for his past. He hoped once he got transferred the label of a rat wouldn't follow. After all, it has been so many years, people were bound to have forgotten or even lost track of him. He wondered where he might go. If he did open a case on O'Brien and solved it maybe he could even get into the Joint Terrorist Task Force. *Wouldn't that be ironic?*

Castillo stepped out of the shower and toweled himself off. He wiped the mist from the mirror in a circular motion, creating a space large enough to see his reflection. He hadn't bothered to shave the last two days, so he knew he had to this morning. With no other option, he borrowed Sharon's toothbrush. Somehow, he was pretty sure she would not mind. When he left the bathroom, Sharon had woken up. She too had to do a day tour this morning. Castillo gave her a full kiss on the lips as they traded places in the bathroom. Castillo was happy to see the morning newspaper had been delivered so early. He looked at the front page of the paper.

Hero cop laid to rest

If the media only knew the truth, he thought. *Maybe they will, real soon.* Castillo looked at the photos which accompanied the story. He saw the thousands of fellow cops in dress uniform salute as Keegan's coffin was brought out from the church. The picture directly below this was a picture of a frightened little girl clinging to her obviously distraught mother. Castillo felt sudden compassion for the Keegan family. It wasn't unusual compassion, it was one that he would feel for any slain officer's family but nevertheless, it did bother him. They both got dressed and made plans to meet back at Sharon's apartment after work and go out for dinner.

The ride had gone quickly from Sharon's apartment to his office in Brooklyn. Castillo walked into the squad room and was told of the urgent message that Inspector Marsh had left for him. He was told Marsh had been trying to call him all last night and even had a sector car from his resident precinct go by his house. He walked over to his desk and picked up the note.

It was brief and right to the point. It ordered him to go immediately to headquarters and report to the office of the Chief of Detectives with the entire case file on James Keegan. Castillo realized he didn't have the entire file with him. The secret file he had been maintaining was still in his apartment. He had not expected to be staying at Sharon's all weekend. He would just bring the official file that he had been keeping.

Today would be the moment he had been waiting for. He could show not only Inspector Marsh his true career potential but also the department's top Detective, the Chief of Detective's, himself. He could both expose Keegan as well as break the case against him. He would undoubtedly be praised for both.

Castillo thought carefully about the options afforded him. He took a few moments before doing anything. He then took out a pink complaint-follow-up out from his desk drawer and inserted it into the typewriter still unsure what he was going to type. His fingers lay motionless on the keyboard for another minute before he reached a decision. Castillo punched away at the keys and proofread his work before making it a part of the Keegan file.

When Castillo arrived at Police Headquarters, he inserted his identification card into a scanner at the turnstile. His photo appeared on a screen in front of the officer assigned to guard the turnstile. Castillo crossed through the turnstile and waited patiently for the next available elevator. Castillo was daydreaming about how many times James Keegan had taken these very elevators when the sound of a bell broke his concentration. The elevator door opened, and Castillo pushed the button for the twelfth floor where the Chief of Detective's office was located. Castillo entered the office where Inspector Marsh and the Chief of Detectives were awaiting his arrival.

"Where have you been Louie? I've been trying to call you since yesterday. I left half a dozen messages on your answering machine."

"I'm sorry Cap, I was out all weekend and I uh, didn't sleep at home last night…" He raised his eyebrows before continuing, "…or the night before."

Under normal circumstances, Marsh would have at least cracked a smile at the inferences Castillo had made. This was not a normal circumstance, however. Marsh was less than pleased to have been summoned down to the Chief of Detective's office with one of his men that he couldn't find for two days before the meeting. The Chief of Detectives had ordered they both be in his office first thing in the morning. The fact that Marsh had been unable to get a hold of Castillo had been frustrating. If he had the chance to speak to Castillo before the meeting, he would at least have better insight as to what Castillo would say and he would not be blindsided by anything. Nobody in the Detective Bureau wanted to look bad in front of their boss. Marsh ignored Castillo's excuse and got to the heart of the meeting. "Louie, the Chief wants to know everything about the case you have on Lieutenant Keegan. Maybe it will lead to his murderer."

Castillo studied the Chief. He had never seen him in person before although he had seen him numerous times on television. He wasn't nearly as tall as Castillo had perceived him to be from television. He was only about five-feet, eight-inches tall and couldn't weigh more than one hundred and sixty-five pounds. He had a gray mustache and a receding hairline that wasn't far from baldness. His age of sixty was clearly shown through the wrinkles on his red face. Father time had not been all that kind to Chief Lawrence Courtney. The stress of almost forty years in the department showed.

Castillo offered up the Chief of Detectives the case folder without saying a word. Perhaps he was at a loss for words or perhaps he hoped the case folder would answer any questions his boss might have so he wouldn't have to. Chief Courtney took the folder from Castillo and opened it. He briefly scanned through it until he got to the final report.

It was the report, that unknown to the Chief had been typed less than an hour ago. The date on the report read March 15th, two days before Saint Patrick's Day. Courtney read this report slowly and carefully. It recommended the case be marked closed, unfounded, as there had been no substantial evidence to link James Keegan in any way to the Irish Republican Army or anyone associated with the same. Courtney was happy with the results of the investigation.

He silently wondered if Castillo overlooked the fact that Keegan may have been killed for interfering with an attempted hit by the I.R.A. It was too obvious for a seasoned Detective to miss...unless of course, he chose to miss it. Courtney really didn't want to know any more than he currently knew. "Thank you, Detective. We are trying to investigate every possible angle in this case. We have a press conference scheduled for noon and I want to have as many answers as I can," Chief Courtney explained, although any explanation on his part was unnecessary. "You don't mind if I keep this file, do you, Detective Castillo?"

The question was, of course, rhetorical. There wasn't a Detective alive who would refuse such a request. Castillo politely responded. "All yours, sir."

Chief Courtney once again thanked both of the men for their time and concern before dismissing them from his office. He got up from behind his desk and walked them to the door. He gave them ample time to have gotten on the elevator. Courtney then left his office with the case folder in hand.

Chief Courtney knocked on the door of the Police Commissioner. Having been waiting for the knock, the Commissioner answered immediately, inviting him in. Upon entering the office, he saw the Commissioner, the First Deputy Commissioner, the Chief of Internal Affairs, and the Chief of Department talking things over. He put the case folder down on top of the large, cherry wood desk that separated the men and pulled up a chair.

The Police Commissioner was anxious to know. "What did this Detective give you, Larry?"

"He closed the case out even before the parade and he seems confident that there was no connection between Keegan and the I.R.A.," the Chief of Detectives explained, even though he didn't totally believe Castillo had closed out the case.

Both the Commissioner and the Chief of Department shook their head in approval. "Good." The Commissioner looked around the room at his counsel. "Does anybody see any other angle that can come back to haunt us?"

The top echelon of the department looked blankly at one another and shook their head from side to side. Courtney was the only one to offer a verbal response. "I think that Detective was our only loose end."

The Commissioner nodded his head ever so slightly and had the smug look of a poker player who just drew to an inside straight. "Good. Then it is settled. We will go with our original plan."

Deputy Inspector Marsh had no objection to Castillo's request to take the rest of the afternoon off. Marsh had been somewhat surprised at the fact that Castillo had closed the case out. He had seemed so consumed by the case when he first opened it, that he was sure Castillo wouldn't let it go until he caught Keegan dirty. Marsh was greatly relieved when Castillo told his boss the investigation was closed out. It seemed to be exactly what the Chief wanted to hear. Marsh wondered momentarily if Castillo had really closed the case out, or did he just do what he figured to be the right thing to do. Either way, the results made them both look good.

Castillo had supplied Marsh with yet another surprise in the few short hours he had spent at work today. Before taking the rest of the day off, he handed him a *U.F. 57* or a request for transfer. Marsh had looked it over and asked Castillo if he was sure he knew what he was doing. Most cops don't want anything to do with a guy from Internal Affairs if they are transferred out to another command.

Castillo insisted he knew exactly what he was doing. He wasn't going to let something that happened years ago ruin his career. He had been buried in the Internal Affairs Bureau long enough and he was going to be a real Detective once again. Marsh had sensed the urgency in Castillo's explanation and signed the request for transfer with only one more question. "Where do you want to go? I think Chief Courtney would be happy to approve a transfer for you to any command you wanted."

Castillo was smug but had to be careful not to overplay his hand. "I think Chief Courtney knows a good Detective when he sees one; a good, hard-working...and *loyal* Detective."

Castillo was careful to emphasize loyal. He let the comment about loyalty hang there, making sure it sunk in. It was probably at least in the back of the Chief's mind that Castillo may know more than he let on and this would prove a fair way to thank him. "I was thinking maybe the Joint Bank Robbery Task Force. After all, any detail on this job that you get to work with the feds is a great detail."

"I don't think that should be a problem. The Task Force it is."

It was at that point that Marsh realized that Castillo knew more than he was letting on but if the department was satisfied, then so was Marsh. "I will personally call the Chief this afternoon and tell him of your request."

"Thanks, boss."

Castillo left for the day knowing his fortunes had changed for the better.

Louis Castillo had arrived at his apartment just before noon that day. His life had new meaning. His transfer was going to come through and he was going to make a name for himself, a good name, not the name of a rat. That was a promise he made to himself that he would keep. He opened his closet where his gun safe was. It was a large safe and weighed over two hundred pounds. It would certainly not be easy for a burglar to walk out with it should he ever get burglarized.

He carefully turned the combination and inserted the key. He removed his briefcase which he kept locked inside and opened it up. He took out his secret file on James Keegan and examined all the documents, photos, and other evidence he'd acquired. This would have easily been enough to get Keegan indicted, thought Castillo. He took the file out into the backyard of his apartment. Then he took one of the aluminum garbage cans from the side of the house and brought it too, into the backyard. The garbage can was completely empty.

Castillo took a lighter out of his pocket and held the file over the garbage can. He ignited the lighter and then set the flame to the corner of the file. He watched as the flame grew larger. When the flame became too intense for him to hold in his hand any longer, he dropped the entire file into the garbage can. He stared down into the can and watched as the flames consumed what was to have been his greatest case.

He decided Keegan had lived the life of a hero for most of his life and he shall remain one in death. There would be no sense in discrediting his memory. That wouldn't be fair to his family. They had nothing to do with his criminal acts and there was no reason they should suffer for his ill doings. Just like every other New Yorker, he had watched the news and saw little Kerry Keegan crying uncontrollably at her father's funeral. The picture on the front of all three local New York papers bared the image of a wailing little girl trying to be consoled by her mother.

Castillo had wanted Keegan brought to justice in the worst way. Yet, today, he would be the bad guy if he exposed the man for what he was doing. He would sully the man's name and legacy, as well as likely steal away the lucrative line of duty pension his family would now receive. Castillo's eyes glazed over as he watched until the flames died out. The case of his career had been consumed by the flames and reduced to a pile of ashes. Castillo hung his head. *Rest in peace James Keegan.*

CHAPTER 23

The press conference given by the Police Commissioner was set to begin at noon. It was no coincidence that it would start shortly after the midday news aired. Kate sat alone in front of the television in the living room. The children were being attended to by their grandmother who had decided to stay over for a few days to lend Kate a much-needed hand. Kate concentrated on every word spoken by the Commissioner in the hopes that her husband's killer would be caught.

The Police Commissioner of the City of New York, for the first time, gave an official account of the heartless assassination of one of the city's most celebrated heroes. It was held inside the second-floor press room at One Police Plaza. The Commissioner was flanked on either side by the Mayor of the City of New York and his Chief of Department. Other high-ranking members of the department could be seen standing stoically behind him. He stood an impressive figure at the podium, close to three dozen microphones mounted in front of him. There were journalists there from all over the country to cover what had become a national news event. There were even a handful of reporters from England, Ireland, and Northern Ireland on hand.

He began by stating that the perpetrator of the crime had cut the battery cable of the family car so Lieutenant Keegan would be forced to use the department auto. A large car bomb was placed under the hood of the car and wired to the starter. When Lieutenant Keegan turned the key to start the car, he had detonated the powerful explosive. The explosion had been so great it could be heard for miles. It blew out many windows in Lieutenant Keegan's home as well as the windows of numerous other houses on the block. The Commissioner continued, "At this time I would like to announce a break in the case. As many of you will remember, it was Lieutenant Keegan, who almost single-handedly broke the attempted bombing of the Federal Courthouse in Brooklyn. I'm also sure many of you are aware only a few months ago, Judge Samuel Boden, who had presided over the trial, was gunned down in the driveway of his home on the eve of the sentencing. It is with great despair, that I inform you that James Keegan was also a victim of retaliation by the Islamic radicals who are attempting to terrorize our city."

Tears started to roll down Kate's face as she listened. It wasn't fair that she had lost her husband to these men. *Why couldn't he have been more careful? He should've seen the writing on the walls when the Judge was murdered.* She had warned him to be careful, or at least she thought she did. She took a tissue from the box which sat next to her and blew her nose softly. She didn't know how much more torture she could take. Could the news get any worse? She hoped it wouldn't and she didn't want to see what else the Commissioner had to say but she seemed unable to turn the news off. She picked up the remote control, sincerely wanting to change the channel but she found herself unable to do so.

"We believe we have identified the man who planted the bomb. We are currently trying to track him down. He's apparently fled the country back to his homeland," the Commissioner willfully lied.

"At this time, I am not going to release his name or any pedigree information on him in fear of jeopardizing his capture." The Commissioner paused momentarily, intensifying the drama. "The arrest of this miscreant is imminent, and the men and women of the New York City Police Department will not rest until he is brought to justice," the Commissioner promised. A promise he knew he would never be able to keep.

Kate finally understood what Jim had always meant when he said that there was no justice in a murder case. When they caught the man responsible for taking Jim's life, he would undoubtedly be sentenced to twenty-five years to life in prison. Jim would still be dead in twenty-five years, so where was the justice? Her children would grow up from this day forward, fatherless. No justice in the world could change that. She buried her head in her arms and finally mustered up enough strength to shut the television off.

The Police Commissioner appeared visibly shaken as he spoke at the press conference. Most would assume it was due to the loss the department suffered. While this was certainly true, he was also shaken because he didn't like to lie and give false hope.

James Keegan was front-page news today but a few weeks from now, only the cops would remember his name. The press will have totally forgotten him and therefore they wouldn't be watching for the arrest, which of course, would never materialize. Although he did feel guilty for lying, he knew it was best like this.

Keegan dies a hero, and everybody is content. His family will get a sizable amount of money due to the death gamble attached to his pension, as it was deemed a line of duty death. The department has a hero, who lost his life to make the city a better place to live. There would probably be a community park or a street named after him sometime down the road. Everyone loves a hero, even the media. They loved a story like this. *If the media only knew what I know*, thought the Commissioner. Even if the allegations weren't true, they would have a field day with it. He could almost see the headlines.

Hero cop in the Irish Republican Army

It would be a black eye for the department and Keegan's family would forfeit all the benefits he worked over eighteen years for. There seemed to be enough evidence to support the theory that not only was Keegan mixed up with the I.R.A. but it was also them, who had him killed. It was much better, he assured himself, to let things be the way they were. Only the top echelon of the department had any idea of the truth and none of them would be willing to sell the department out. Only them, and Detective Louis Castillo, who was about to be transferred to the Joint Bank Robbery Task Force and promoted to Detective First Grade.

Kate sat a few more minutes silently weeping before regaining her composure. She knew she had to be strong for her children and self-pity would do her no good. Kate left the living room and went to see her children who were in the kitchen having lunch. She walked in and gave them each a kiss on the head. This had to be an equally horrifying experience for them, she imagined. They all sat at the kitchen table eating the sandwiches their grandmother had made for them.

"Are you all right Kate?" Eileen Keegan was a strong woman. She was more concerned with Kate and her grandchildren than she was about herself.

Kate nodded her head. "I'm fine."

"Why don't you go and lie down for a while, I'll take care of the kids for you."

Kate couldn't understand her mother-in-law's

strength. She too had suffered a great loss, her son. The woman had certain resilience about her. Kate figured maybe it was because she had already gone through the horror of losing a spouse when her husband passed on a few years back.

Kate declined the offer. "No. I'm fine, really."

She looked on top of the counter where today's newspaper was. Until now, she had been unable, or unwilling, to look at it. She walked over to the counter and picked it up. She looked at the photos of the funeral as well as a photo of her husband from his identification card. He was a handsome man; there was no denying that, she decided. She went on to read the articles written both about the funeral as well as about the hero cop, who gave up his life for the people of the city.

She wondered if she had told him often enough how proud she was of him. Kate took the newspaper into the other room and got her husband's scrapbook out. She looked through it like never before. She had gone through it dozens of times with Jim, but it was different this time. She looked at every photo and read every article in there. She read all the personal orders in which his medals were published. He truly was a hero.

Kate left the scrapbook and the newspaper in the living room while she returned to the kitchen. She saw that her children were just about finished with their lunch. She asked discretely if Eileen Keegan could keep Kerry entertained upstairs for a while so she could talk to the boys. Eileen Keegan agreed without protest and convinced Kerry to help her make the beds.

Kate escorted Kevin and Timothy into the living room and sat them down on the couch. The boys were old enough, she decided, to learn what a true hero their father had been. She did, however, respect Jim's wishes to not tell Kerry until she was a little older. Kate held the book without opening it. She explained to the boys that the book highlighted the many acts of bravery that their father had accomplished in his career. The boys were anxious to rip the book open and look through it, but Kate decided she would hold the book and look through it with them.

She went page by page, explaining what everything was and what exactly their father had done and why. They were especially impressed with the number of medals their father had earned. She knew the boys didn't fully understand everything, but they understood enough. It took well over an hour to go through the entire scrapbook and the boys had many questions which she did her best to answer.

Kate had a warm feeling in her heart after she finished showing them the book. She almost felt as if Jim was actually sitting next to her, turning the pages right along with her. She didn't know what it was, but she had a feeling of absolution. She didn't deny the fact that she would miss her husband of fifteen years terribly, but she now knew she would be able to go on.

Kerry came down the stairs ahead of her grand-mother. Kate figured she would keep the children home from school for the rest of the week and try to get their lives back on track next week. It was a picture-perfect spring day with a soft breeze compli-menting near sixty-degree temperatures.

"C'mon kids. Get your coats on," directed Grandma Keegan.

"Where are you going?"

"The fresh air will do them good, Kate. I figured I'd take them to the park for a while. Maybe you can join us. It was a good idea to get the kids out of the house, agreed Kate but she wasn't sure if she was ready yet.

"Why don't you go ahead, and I'll try to catch up with you."

After watching her children leave for the park with their grandmother, she got the pair of scissors from the kitchen. She then went back into the living room and sat down on the floor next to the news-paper. She cut out the articles from the newspaper very carefully. She opened the scrapbook to the first empty page. As she inserted the articles into the book, a deep sadness came over her. The reality of the situation set in. She had lost her husband for-ever. Her only consolation was that she knew she had lost him to something he truly loved, *the job*.

~#~#~#~#~#~#~#~#~#~#~#~#~#~#~

Epilogue

It had been a particularly uncomfortable night. The hot and muggy August air was bad enough but getting caught in the torrential downpour while waiting at the bus stop along Hillside Avenue, had soaked Nazeem al-Haq to the bone. The walk from the bus stop, along the Van Wyck Expressway service road to his South Ozone Park apartment had not been much better. The rain continued to pour down on him, causing his long hair to fall in front of his eyes. A hole in the bottom of his work boot allowed the water to soak into his sock, making his right foot wet and uncomfortable.

Al-Haq stepped out of the shower washing the night's sweat and rain from his body. He stared at himself in the mirror. There were hints of gray in his hair and beard that had been once been jet black; many years ago, before spending time in an American prison. He decided the twenty years he had spent in prison had aged him significantly. Al-Haq decided America was the only country in the world where you can be sentenced to life in prison, yet still walk free one day.

Once he toweled himself off, he slipped on a beige *chapan* which he had brought back to the states with him from his native Afghanistan. *It was so much more comfortable than American clothes.* He sat at the kitchen table of his small basement apartment. The apartment did not have a bedroom; a mattress lay on the floor in the corner of the room to allow for sleeping. The tan and brown carpet was stained with dog urine from the previous tenants. The walls, which were probably white, were cracking from years of neglect. There were times when al-Haq would turn on a light and the kitchen walls would seem to be moving. The cockroaches and the cramped quarters did not bother him. These conditions were better than the ones he had endured during the eight months he lived and trained in the Al-Qaeda training camp in Afghanistan; and certainly, better than the years he spent in prison.

Al-Haq opened the morning newspaper that he took from the gas station. He had gotten used to the midnight shift at the gas station. He wasn't even that tired most days when he got home from work. He would always make himself a light breakfast and read the paper before he would try to get some sleep. He stared at the date, August 16, 2013. *Where did time go?* Upon reflection, he knew where it went. The majority of it was spent inside an American prison cell. He had failed his brothers in Jihad, but they had forgiven him. They promised him redemption. He would have another chance to fulfill his destiny. There was no reason to doubt them. They promised they would be able to sneak him back into the United States, even though he had been deported, upon release from prison. They kept this promise. They supplied him with false identification, set him up with a job and an apartment. All he had to do was wait for them to contact him at the mosque to give him his orders. *The seventy-two virgins will still be waiting for me in the afterlife.*

Al-Haq was half daydreaming as he flipped through the newspaper. Then, when he got to page five, a photo jumped out at him, snapping him out of the trance. The picture was of someone from his past. A chill engulfed his body. There was no mistaking it. He would never forget the face of the man who caused him to lose so much. Not only did he spend so much time in prison, but he also never met his only son due to this man's actions. Al-Haq's son had been born only six weeks prior to his arrest and died at age seventeen at the hands of a U.S. drone strike, while Al-Haq was still in prison. His mouth went dry; his dark eyes narrowed. *Keegan!* He looked at the headline of the article.

Hero cop's son among 1,100 new recruits

Al-Haq scanned the article. It detailed the graduation ceremony at Madison Square Garden for the NYPD's Police Academy. Much of the article focused on the reduction of crime and how and where the Police Commissioner would deploy the new recruits. There was one paragraph however, that was dedicated to twenty-six-year-old Timothy Keegan. Keegan's father, **James Keegan,** was a hero cop who was assassinated by Middle-Eastern terrorists back in 1995. The assassination was in retaliation for breaking a case against them, in which they plotted to bomb the Brooklyn Federal Courthouse. The rage built up inside al-Haq. *I would have been a martyr and living with Allah and my son if Keegan had not* *interfered.* The article further went on to say that Timothy Keegan will be assigned to Brooklyn's, 67th Pct, the same precinct his father began his career. Timothy Keegan would also be wearing the same shield his father wore before being promoted to Detective.

Al-Haq had done a great deal of reading while in prison. He read about many different cultures and criminal enterprises. He was particularly fond of the way Columbian drug lords dealt with their enemies. Not only did they kill their enemy, but they also killed their enemy's children, for fear they could one day retaliate. He looked back at the photos in the paper. There was a photo of Timothy Keegan alongside the photo of his father. He stared deep into the eyes of the younger Keegan. He studied his face, memorizing his features.

As Nazeem al-Haq laid his head down the pillow of his roach-infested apartment, he had only one thing on his mind: REVENGE.

MR. GEORGE P. NORRIS

Acknowledgements

Exceptional Merit was a near twenty-year journey for me, almost as long as my career in the NYPD. This book never would have been written if not for the unconditional support from my wife of many years, Leah Rose. She encouraged me to write my own novel and I would have never thought of doing so on my own. She sat with me and read every chapter as I wrote it, offering constructive criticism, advice, and acting as my editor. She was not just the inspiration for me to write the novel, but she has also been a wonderful and supportive mother and wife.

I began writing this book in 1994. Once it was completed, I had no luck in having it published. I sent it to numerous agents and publishing companies who enjoyed the story but told me I needed to work on my writing skills. In hindsight, I can see they were correct and hope that twenty more years of life experience has paid off. In 1996, no closer to having it published, my first child was born. Exceptional Merit was put away in a closet somewhere and all but forgotten about.

Earlier this year, one of my oldest and closest friends, Mitch, asked me about the book and if I still had a copy. He told me about e-publishing. Had it not been for him reaching out to me and offering advice along the way, Exceptional Merit would still be locked away in a closet. Thanks, MF. I owe you!

Lastly, I would like to thank the men and women who go out every day and put on a uniform to protect and serve the rest of us. Especially, my brothers and sisters in blue, with the New York City Police Department. To all of you, I say please stay safe, do your twenty years and enjoy your families. You all deserve it!